Also by the Author

Awake in the Dark

The Listener

A Novel

‹‹‹‐›››

Shira Nayman

Scribner

New York London Toronto Sydney

Scribner
A Division of Simon & Schuster, Inc.
1230 Avenue of the Americas
New York, NY 10020

Copyright © 2010 by Shira Nayman

First Scribner hardcover edition January 2010

SCRIBNER and design are registered trademarks of The Gale Group, Inc., used under license by Simon & Schuster, Inc., the publisher of this work.

For information about special discounts for bulk purchases, please contact Simon & Schuster Special Sales at 1-866-506-1949 or business@simonandschuster.com.

The Simon & Schuster Speakers Bureau can bring authors to your live event. For more information or to book an event contact the Simon & Schuster Speakers Bureau at 1-866-248-3049 or visit our website at www.simonspeakers.com.

Designed by Carla Jayne Jones

Manufactured in the United States of America

1 3 5 7 9 10 8 6 4 2

Library of Congress Control Number: 2009027289

ISBN 978-0-7432-9282-5
ISBN 978-1-4391-8859-0 (eBook)

This project has been assisted by the Australian Government through the Australia Council for the Arts, its arts funding and advisory body.

To Louis A. Sass
And to my mother, Doreen Nayman

My subject is War, and the Pity of war.
The Poetry is in the pity.

—WILFRED OWEN (1893–1918)

Part I

Prologue

*B*ertram is gone.

The early morning light is struggling up from the flat, black lawn. My eyes are slits; my parched tongue sticks painfully to the roof of my mouth. All of me screams with a want that is like nothing else and that promises to be slaked by nothing.

But the day awaits: I must shower and change and prepare for morning rounds. I try to move my arms and legs but they will not obey me. I only watch as the light rises and fills the room; it is white and thin and uncompromising.

<{··}>

Chapter One

Early Fall 1947

Crossing the great lawn, I see that the Virginia creeper has turned red and gold, as it does for one week each year, making the old brick of the asylum appear to be alive with flames. I reach the pathway; in the Men's Garden, beyond the line of dwarf trees, several inmates are hard at work with hoes and rakes. Watching for a moment, I wonder if their troubles are at bay; perhaps the smell of fresh dirt really is a primal palliative that makes a mockery of our talking cure.

I pass through the grand foyer and head along the east corridor. The light streaming through the high windows hits everything in an oddly intense and precise way: the leather easy chair, the inlaid side table, the swan-necked reading lamp. I make my way down to Hall Two, where Bertram is waiting for me by the nurses' station.

During the War, I treated dozens of patients with battle fatigue. I remember one case in particular—a man named Hammersmith who made excellent progress, though there was always an undercurrent of tension between us. The day of his discharge—he was being sent back into battle—I visited his room to say good-bye. *I have you to thank,* he said, his stiff smile at odds with the glint of rage in his eye. He was the most memorable of my cases, until I met Bertram Reiner,

a young man whose graduate studies in biochemistry were interrupted by the War and who returned, when it was over, wounded and psychologically unbalanced. Despite enormous difficulties, he managed to complete his Ph.D. On graduation day, Bertram Reiner apparently cracked. Up at the podium, as the president of Columbia University handed him his diploma, Bertram accused him of a war crime.

Not long after this, Bertram committed himself voluntarily to Shadowbrook for long-term treatment. His insanity appears circumscribed—unusual in any psychosis, including "psychosis due to trauma," my preliminary diagnosis; for the most part, he remains lucid, showing some insight into his condition.

For the first time in more than twenty years, I find myself at a loss. In session with Bertram, I am aware that I experience him more like a colleague than like a patient; I feel as if I were suddenly in the body of a smaller, weaker man. This is troubling, and yet also oddly exciting. I can feel the hidden goings-on, like tiny poisonous fish scudding beneath the surface, shiny but deadly.

Throughout my evaluation, Bertram has given the impression of answering my questions, but once the session is over, I realize I understand little more about his condition; he is always slipping from my grasp. Early on, I noticed another peculiarity: Bertram's eyes seem to shift slightly in color with his changing mood.

We walk back to my office in silence. He sits in his usual chair across from my desk and begins speaking, as if we had been in the middle of a conversation.

"It's why I'm here," he says. "Why I came into the hospital."

"I'm not sure I follow you," I say carefully.

His eyes are impatient. "It's pretty obvious."

"Could you give me a little more to go on?"

"I'd have thought it was clear that I'm not really a psychiatric patient. That I've come here for reasons other than mental illness."

I've had many patients maintain they were as sane as I; only recently, an elderly woman insisted I was the one who should be locked up, not she. She claims to be "your very own Queen Victoria," and has taken to imitating my English accent with uncanny accuracy; she intends to try me for treason, for abandoning Mother England.

"I needed to find a place where there was little chance of being found," Bertram continues.

"Who is it you need to avoid?"

"My brother," Bertram says, looking a little surprised.

During the intake interview Bertram had struggled to explain why he'd voluntarily committed himself. What he finally said was, *The world seems strange. Nature, the light. People, sounds, food. I feel stranded. As if everything's becoming unmoored from itself.* He talked of a kind of elastic dread that made him jumpy and exhausted. But, there was no mention of a brother.

"I don't recall you mentioning a brother before today."

Bertram turns sideways in his chair. "I had my reasons for keeping quiet on the subject."

"What has changed?" I ask.

"You may think it a misuse of the hospital system. But the truth is, I fear for my life. I didn't know what else to do."

His gray eyes seem suddenly touched with green; I sense his fear.

"Go on," I say.

"I don't know where to begin."

"Just begin anywhere."

Bertram looks out of the window.

"We had a neighbor," he says. "Rosamund. We both loved her, though I loved her more. When I was twelve, and Rosamund was eleven, she and I decided that one day, we would be married. It wasn't a child's game; we were serious."

"What is your brother's name?" I ask.

"Emanuel. There was always something disturbing about him." Bertram pauses, seems to be searching for words. "As if he didn't live in the same world as everybody else but had learned to act as if he did."

He falls silent.

"You were talking about Rosamund," I prompt.

"Rosamund was killed in an accident." Bertram's voice catches on the words. "After Rosamund died, Emanuel started to seem crazy. I'd been afraid of him before, but now I felt like my brother might actually become dangerous. He blamed me for her death, I know he did. It wasn't rational. He also blamed me for the fact that she'd liked me more than she'd liked him."

"When did you last see Emanuel?"

"I haven't seen him since the divorce."

"The divorce?" I don't know what he's referring to.

"Soon after Rosamund died, my mother left my father. She took me with her; Emanuel stayed with my father."

"And you've had no contact with them, all these years? With your father and your brother?"

Bertram shakes his head. "We moved. We began a new life."

"How is this connected with your being in the hospital?"

"I needed to feel safe. I couldn't think of anyplace else to go." He is looking both at me and somewhere else.

"Safe from—?"

"I think Emanuel wants to kill me."

I feel a prickling sensation in the back of my neck.

"Why would he want to kill you?"

"It's complicated. I'm not sure I can explain it, not all at once."

Bertram's eyes dart around the room and then land back on me.

"I received a letter. It wasn't signed, but I know it's from him; he's tracked me down, after all. In the letter, he accuses me of terrible crimes, including the murder of a young girl. Craziest thing I've ever seen. Even the handwriting was weird. Long, skinny letters on one line, fat ones on the next. Like it had been written by different people. At the end, was a threat."

"Can you tell me what the threat was?"

"That I'd end up in the same kind of accident. That I'd die the way she did, if I didn't find a way to change things."

Bertram gives a helpless shrug. "I have no idea what he meant. Something about turning back the hands of time."

"Did you keep the letter?"

"No. I tore it up. I didn't want to have it around."

The next morning, on my way to the office, I pause to let the barbershop contingent pass: the Hall Two patients on their way to be shaved, many still in their pajamas, walking somberly in single file. They are led by

Nurse O'Halahan, a no-nonsense woman with a reputation for candor, whose spry step and air of professional cheer only emphasize the almost funereal mood of the men. My greeting is met with bleary replies; I watch as the group wait at the end of the corridor for their guardian to do a quick head count and then unlock the door and usher them through.

Two hours later, when I encounter those same men in the library on the ward, the mood is altogether different. Dressed and freshly shaved, they look relaxed, scattered about in armchairs, on leather couches, reading newspapers or magazines from the array on the long wooden table. Two orderlies in white coats attend to the men, lighting a cigarette, clearing away an ashtray, responding to a comment or query.

The sight of me functions as a signal; papers are folded and replaced, cigarettes snuffed out, conversations tapered, and the patients make their way to the dayroom for community meeting. Staff members file in and take their places in the circle of chairs. After I make a few announcements and Head Nurse Willoughby presents the weekly agenda, we open the floor to the patients. A prolonged silence follows, and then Frederick Collins speaks.

"I'm sorry to be difficult," he says quietly. "But I really must grow a beard."

In his nine months here, Collins has never spoken up in community meeting. He has been a benign fixture on the hall, cocooned in his own private distress.

"Allow me to clarify," Cuthbert volunteers. A long-term resident of Shadowbrook, Cuthbert is in many ways the polar opposite of Collins: gregarious, flamboyant, given to voluble pronouncements and manic flights.

Collins nods embarrassedly, and Cuthbert continues. "I believe this pertains to the matter of the barbershop. It's the long walk that bothers him—not the shaving per se. Today was particularly difficult; we took turns steering him away from walls and egging him on."

Collins stares at his feet. "I dread those hallways. Four days a week; it's too much."

"Sometimes, the poor man looks as if he were walking the Bridge of Sighs," Cuthbert continues. "Headed to his own execution."

"I should think a beard might suit you, Mr. Collins," I say carefully. "But perhaps we can also help you manage the unpleasantness."

Collins's face is hung with misery. "It's like purgatory. Like I'm going to be doing that forever—walking in a line of silent men. Down a long hallway. Going nowhere."

"Once we get there," Cuthbert adds, "we come to life—smoke cigarettes, read the papers and such. Eddie always has a fresh joke: a bit bawdy sometimes, and I daresay, that's all to the good! But Mr. Collins looks like he wished a hole would open in the floor and swallow him up. I know I'm speaking for us all when I say we feel bad for him—and support his request."

Some of the men call out "Hear, hear!"

"Perhaps what he's really concerned about are the haircuts," says Mr. Anderson, a professor of histology affectionately called the Professor, who occasionally claims he's a rooster and is known for his excellent tennis game. "I sometimes worry about that myself. What you might call the Samson effect."

Bertram remains aloof, regarding Collins in a curious way.

"Mr. Reiner, do you have something to add?" I ask.

"I was just thinking that I don't like the barbershop much myself."

"*Do* go on," Cuthbert chimes in. He is fond of employing the psychiatrist's stock phrases, which he does with pride rather than mockery.

"I'm more comfortable shaving myself," Bertram continues. "I know it's only Eddie, and he's the most good-natured bloke in the world, but submitting to the blade . . . It just doesn't seem right, not here—"

"Why—*not here*?" I ask.

There is something uncanny about the way Bertram is looking at me—as if he can tell what I am thinking.

"I see that as rather self-evident," he replies.

Toward evening, I head back to my office, stopping in first to see Cynthia.

"I've been waiting for you," she says pleasantly. "I need at least a dozen of your John Hancocks."

"I'm sorry. I seem to have been running late all day. I trust you had a good weekend," I say, as I flip through the papers she hands me and scribble my signature on each.

"Yes, very nice." Her lips smile, but there is loneliness in her eyes. "Quiet."

I always feel a little uncomfortable in Cynthia's office, with its carefully tended pot plants and shelves of alphabetized poetry: as if I'd stepped into a homily I was supposed to live up to. When I ask for Bertram's intake documents, Cynthia retrieves them from the locked filing cabinet.

"I'll be presenting this patient at the next case conference," I say. "So I'll need to keep these for a while."

In my office, I review Bertram's papers. The sections headed "Closest Relations" and "Emergency Contacts" are blank. No relatives, no friends. No brother. It's as if Bertram has excised his history—his arrival at Shadowbrook a strange act of both self-annihilation and rebirth. Although the blank spaces could simply reflect the truth: that Bertram is alone in the world—both parents gone, no siblings or enduring friendships. Perhaps he has split off the crazy, self-loathing part of himself and turned it into a phantom brother intent on killing him: a veiled confession of suicidality. I glance at the clock, startled to see the hour, then lock up the papers and rush home to change.

Reaching the white picket fence bordering the property of my house, I see Ursula's flower beds and shrubs arranged with forced perfection, like shiny-faced schoolchildren lined up and seeking approval. The soil bordering the pathway has been turned. And I think, for the thousandth time, how absurd it is that they put up just this kind of fence to separate the director's residence from the rest of the asylum.

Inside, the house holds the kind of silence that says something. Upstairs, Ursula is propped up in bed, the shades drawn. She looks at me apologetically.

"Migraine, my dear?" I ask.

She nods. "Wouldn't you know it? The night of the welcoming dinner. I spent an hour this morning ironing my dress."

"Not to worry," I say. "I will get along fine on my own."

I perch on the edge of the bed and pat her hand. In her eyes, longing flares for an instant.

"Busy day?" she asks.

"No more than usual. I see you made progress getting ready for the bulbs."

"I thought I'd plant jonquils this year. Do you think yellow might do, up against the red brick of the path?"

"I rather like jonquils," I say.

In the bathroom, I turn the shower to very hot, and soon there is nothing but thick white vapor. There is a fresh bar of soap: something different, luxurious, perhaps one of Ursula's occasional little extravagances. A familiar scent from the past—lavender or lilac, something Ursula once favored and has decided to reclaim. I see her as she was, long ago, lying on the bed, not in a flannel nightgown as now but naked beneath the sheet. I pass my eyes across the length of her and feel the rise of desire. Her cheeks are flushed; she smiles. I peel the sheet away to reveal her lovely body, awaiting my gaze: breasts spilling ripely, rounded belly sloping towards the soft triangle. Her eyes hover, and I can feel thrill rising from her.

The old feelings are there for an instant, then gone. Here, now, I hear her stirring in the other room. I turn off the faucet and wait until the steam thins. When I return to the bedroom to dress, Ursula has dozed off. I reach for my jacket and pants—what I still think of as my new tuxedo, though I've had it for ten years; it fits me as well now as it did when I bought it. Catching my reflection in the glass, I am surprised to see several marked lines in the forehead of the man looking back at me, whose dark hair is also, unexpectedly, frosted with gray.

Outside, the moon sits low, somehow casual, as if it wants to be part of things. The Men's Garden, empty now of patients, is washed with a half-light that makes it seem both more and less real. Passing by the main building, I am joined by several young doctors wearing crisp tuxedos.

"Good evening, Doctors," I say with playful formality. "I hardly recognize any of you!"

We make our way to Sturgiss Hall, which glitters up ahead, its leaded-glass windows shining brightly with the light of chandeliers. It is the first time since the War that we've had a goodly number of lightbulbs. The janitor has also managed to dig up some fairy lights; they drip from the eaves like jewels.

At the bar I sip a martini and survey the room. Under the vaulted

ceiling, everyone looks a little stunted, and the heavy shine of the parquet floor seems unnatural, as if this room were an enormous stage. Glancing around, I have the not entirely unpleasant feeling that all these people are not my colleagues and trainees but strangers—transformed magically, as if I'd fallen into another reality.

Approaching me is Percy Fenton, Chief of Medicine; usually sober-spirited, he now seems almost rakish, leaning against the bar, swirling ice in a highball glass.

"How's the handicap?" I ask.

"Lousy," he replies. "Can't seem to nudge it down. I'm dogged, though—out every Sunday, eight o'clock. When am I going to twist your arm to join me?"

"I never was any good with sticks," I say, offering my empty glass to the bartender, who fixes me another martini. "I'd only end up inadvertently clobbering you with the club." We've been through this routine dozens of times before.

Across the room is an elegant woman in green silk, talking with the chief resident and sipping from a champagne flute. When she catches my eye and smiles, I realize that, of course, I know her: Matilda Willoughby, head nurse of Hall Two, looking nothing like the pragmatic woman in the starched uniform at community meeting this morning. I smile back, startled by an unexpected feeling, as if for a moment we are joined by an invisible ripple of heat. Her smile fades, and something quizzical wavers in her face, as if she, too, has felt it. A woman in a violet gown appears beside her and takes her arm, diverting Matilda's attention; I have to squint to see that it is Nurse Vanessa O'Halahan. She says something, and Matilda laughs, gracefully arcing her neck; her hair, usually hidden by a nurse's cap and now stylishly swept up, is a warm shade of chestnut.

After dinner, the residents and younger staff members drift onto the dance floor. A chamber music quartet by the window plays a waltz; watching the couples move about, I become aware of the tightness of my collar and bow tie; the room feels uncomfortably hot. Then I am distracted by a mini-swarm of waiters, who appear from nowhere, clearing dishes and balancing trays of coffee and dessert. Not waiters, really, but the servants of the wealthier patients, whom we engage from time to time for events such as these.

Here at Shadowbrook, the servants seem to maintain the stock-in-trade of servants everywhere—to incubate for their masters an atmosphere of superiority and deserving privilege. To see this illusion scrupulously enacted here, where the objects of their attentions might be given to sudden shrieks or fits of hysterical paralysis, or the glazed demeanor of the melancholic, shows up the absurd side of the whole arrangement.

Sometimes I take a detour from my office to the ward by way of the servants' quarters, a warren of beautifully appointed rooms set under the eaves of the main building. The most interesting time to find oneself there is after lunch. Having served their masters in the main dining hall, the servants take an hour to themselves, bringing up their trays from downstairs. They pass down the long hallway: two dozen or more gentle-men in black suits, white shirts, and bow ties, balancing trays as they walk in and out of the afternoon sunlight that falls in bands, giving to their movements an eerily syncopated rhythm, as if their vividness itself were coming and going.

I catch sight of the dignified man I know to be the servant of Ber-tram Reiner; he is approaching my table with a tray full of dessert. I wonder where Bertram gets his money. His servant places a flaky pastry before me.

"Thank you," I say.

The man nods politely.

"I'm afraid I don't know your name," I continue.

The waiter-servant stands to a kind of attention.

"Mr. Thomas, sir," he says.

"Pleased to know you, Mr. Thomas. I trust you have settled nicely into your new lodgings."

"Our quarters are very comfortable, Dr. Harrison, thank you."

"And your master? I trust he is also comfortably settled."

Thomas stiffens. Staff are not supposed to discuss patients with the servants; it is a firm regulation, and to break it is something of a taboo.

"If you'll excuse me, sir," he says, giving a neat quarter bow.

By the time dessert is over, I realize I've had a drink or two too many. It is ten-fifteen; a half hour more, I think, and I'll be able to make my escape. From the corner of my eye, I see someone hastening toward me across the dance floor; it is Cynthia, looking distressed.

"Dr. Harrison," she says breathlessly. "I was in my office, catching up on some filing—your wife called. Her migraine has turned nasty."

We leave together; I give a quick farewell nod here and there to staff members who call out, "Good night." Cynthia fills me in on Ursula's condition: uncontrollable vomiting, the feeling that she has ice picks behind both eyes. Ursula and Cynthia have been fast friends since I became director and plucked Cynthia from the typing pool; they've come to depend on each other with the deep, familial connection of sisters. Now, I sense Cynthia's distress. We part at the fork, and when I glance back, she is still standing there, looking forlorn.

Ursula's headaches are becoming more frequent and more dire. Hurrying through the cool night, I feel a lurching sadness; the change of life seems especially cruel for Ursula, given she was never able to conceive. The migraines suddenly feel like something painful between us, horribly symbolic of an unborn child.

I find Ursula doubled up on the bathroom floor, her mouth slack, eyes inward with pain. Unable to speak, she whimpers responses to my questions as I prepare a syringe. After administering the injection, I wipe Ursula's face with a hot washcloth and then help her to her feet. She leans against me, and I guide her back to bed, where she sinks, with relief, into a drugged sleep.

In my study, I find myself thinking about Matilda Willoughby, disarming and unfamiliar in her green silk dress. Am I imagining it, or did something pass between us, back at Sturgiss Hall, under the blazing chandelier?

Standing by the window of my office, I watch lightning splice the late afternoon sky. Beyond the lawn, where the incline becomes steep, the royal oaks and sycamores shimmer through the driving rain. Beside the stone walkway edging the lawn, the hydrangeas nod heavily. Water pelts what's left of the summer roses, sending the worn petals fluttering to the ground.

I am counting in wait for the crash. Seven seconds later, the thunder hits, rattling the windows.

All day long, the dream images from last night have hung over

me, tugging at my attention. For so many years, I have been free
from the dreams that once plagued me; I feel blindsided by their
sudden reappearance, pained, caught unawares, and yet also secretly
enthralled.

At my desk, I lose myself in work. It is close to ten o'clock when I
realize the rain has stopped and night has fallen. A knock at the door
startles me.

Matilda—not resplendent, as she was the other night, but tense and
drawn. The hair showing beneath her nurse's cap looks wet.

"May I have a word with you, Dr. Harrison?" she asks.

"Of course. Come in."

Matilda sits on the sofa by the window, opposite my leather arm-
chair.

"I'm sorry to trouble you at this late hour . . ."

In the two years she has been head nurse, I have never seen Matilda
agitated. Though we've not discussed it, I know a little about what she
went through as an Army nurse in the Philippines from her discharge
file, which included newspaper articles from the tour she'd taken, after
her escape from Corregidor, to promote the sale of war bonds. Glancing
through the clippings, I was struck by the young nurse's poise. When I
met her, I saw that her beauty, evident in the newspaper photographs,
was muted; it was her intelligence that made the greatest impression. I
liked her immediately. How could anything here in this hospital, with
its gracious grounds and pavilions, its ample staff and plentiful sup-
plies and hallways laid with Persian rugs, seem difficult after what she
had experienced in the War? It is therefore arresting to see her in this
troubled state.

"We've had an incident on the hall," she says. "I was going to call you,
but one of the orderlies on the search team saw the light in your window,
so I thought I'd stop by instead. I hope it's not an inconvenience."

"Not at all," I say.

"A patient went missing. About an hour ago."

"Oh?"

"I instructed Janice to telephone you if we were gone more than
fifteen minutes, but it didn't take long to find him. We don't know how
he got past the nurses' station without being seen. I will look into that,
of course."

"Which patient are we talking about?" I ask.

"Oh! Yes, I'm sorry. It was Mr. Reiner. He was not in his room at the nine o'clock room check. After I sent out the search party, I realized I hadn't told them to cover the area beyond the formal gardens. I had a hunch he might be there, so I decided to go out myself."

Very abnormal indeed—to rush off into an onslaught of rain to help look for a patient. Matilda has a gauzy look in her eyes, as if she's so caught up in the drama of what has just happened that her professional distance has slipped.

"I thought he might have gone to the gardener's shed to take shelter under the eaves. That's where I found him, soaked to the bone. When he saw me, he said something perplexing: *I really shouldn't.* He said it four or five times. And there was something strange in his face."

Matilda looks past me to the door, as if she's expecting someone to appear.

"Is that so very surprising?" I ask gently.

"I'm sorry?"

"That there should be something strange in the patient's face?"

"No. I suppose it shouldn't be." She clasps her hands. "But it took me aback. Up until now he's seemed so . . . well, normal. I told him we should get in out of the rain. That's when he said he couldn't go back to the ward as long as there were scientists there."

Matilda bites her lower lip. "I think I was convinced that the poor man was just a bit shell-shocked and in need of a rest. It's just that . . ." A slow rise of crimson creeps up from the neckline of her uniform.

"Mr. Reiner seems different?" I interpose.

"Yes."

"Did you see a lot of soldiers with battle fatigue in the Philippines?"

The color spreads gently across Matilda's face, then dissipates. I glimpse again her subtle beauty: disquieting, the way it wavers in and out of one's awareness.

"Why, yes. I mean, no. We saw our fair share, I suppose. We couldn't really focus on that."

She looks away.

"I imagine it's not easy to talk about."

"I prefer to leave the past where it is."

"And where might that be?" I ask.

Matilda swings her gaze back to meet mine; I find myself looking into eyes that are steady and distressed at the same time.

"Not here," she says. "Certainly not here."

"What happened next?" I ask.

"I told him there were no scientists at the hospital, unless he considered psychiatrists to be scientists."

"You've dealt with more worrisome situations than this," I say. "And yet, what happened this evening with Mr. Reiner seems to have unsettled you greatly. Perhaps more than it might have with another patient."

Matilda reaches up and touches her white cap; her eyes flicker with anxiety.

"Could it be that Mr. Reiner reminds you of someone? That his behavior recalled an experience you had during the War?"

"I'm not sure what you're getting at."

"I know from personal experience—especially regarding war," I say. "It's not always so easy to leave the past behind."

At lunchtime, there's a baseball game in progress on the largest of the hospital's playing fields. It is a crisp day, and some of the patients, dressed in their exercise clothing, are hugging themselves for warmth. Bertram appears to be the umpire. The bases are loaded; the pitcher throws, the batter swings, and the shortstop catches the ball. All three men are already running before Bertram calls "Out." The batter throws down the bat and streaks toward first.

"Hey!" Bertram cries. "Come back here. You're out!"

There is freedom on the men's faces; they speed along and gain their bases but, instead of stopping, continue on. The patients waiting to bat catch the fun and leap to join them. They run wildly around the diamond; no one stops at home plate, each man runs on through. The diamond is a chaos of men tearing about, some whooping, some blank-faced, others touched with the joy of the unencumbered child.

Bertram stands and watches the mayhem, a look of consternation on his face. But then he sets his whistle down in the grass and joins them: not with abandon, but with poignant seriousness. As he skims across first, he catches my eye and offers a sheepish smile, as if to say,

This is apparently the thing to do. I think about Matilda and how surprised she was to see Bertram in that altered state out in the storm. It is true; Bertram is a changeling. Now, as he picks up speed, he looks like a staff member who has the decency and spontaneity to join the disturbed patients in their prank, not like a man who belongs among them.

"Hey, Dr. Harrison!" Cuthbert's face is lit with manic glee as he slides into home plate. "Pick up the bat!"

I am taken aback by a sudden urge to peel off my jacket and throw it to the ground. During the First War, we found ourselves fighting alongside American soldiers; on the occasional quiet evening, we'd set up a game. The Americans laughed at us British, though they had their comeuppance when we switched to cricket. At the memory, I am overcome by a pungent feeling: gaiety mingled with dread.

"Some other time," I say, giving a mock salute and continuing on, the sounds of the patients' cheers and hoots full in my ears.

I knew Frederick Collins only from the hall, as he was under the direct care of a colleague, but the idea that he might be a schemer never crossed my mind. Not surprising, I suppose; the suicidal patient is a rare breed. He may possess no malevolence toward others but is canny as a fox when it comes to doing harm to himself. Having convinced us all that he posed no danger in this regard, Collins was on the unlocked ward, where the windows have heavy metal screens instead of bars. I can hardly picture him being as focused as he must have been to loosen the large number of heavy screws—and with what?—that held the screen in place. And then managing to elude the evening collection of bathrobe belts and other ordinary items that can be turned into deadly devices. I try to imagine how he might have felt during that final room check, when the beam of the orderly's flashlight struck his face as he lay in bed. I see him creeping out of the window and then hurrying across the lawn, down to where the woods begin: finding a suitable tree and throwing the cord up over a sturdy branch. He displayed ingenuity, fashioning a noose from such an inadequate length, stringing himself up to dangle alone in the darkness with only the whispering leaves for company as he jerked out the last of his life.

Collins left a journal—a shabby wad of papers hidden in a picked-open seam of his mattress. I did not know the patients had a "Suicide Club." From his descriptions, I try to identify who the other members might be—surely not Bertram, who has never expressed overt suicidal thinking; besides, such mental-patient antics do not seem like Bertram's style. The "club's" chief goal was to achieve at least one "bump" per month—with three "rousing cheers" in celebration anytime one of their members managed to "go west." Perhaps, in his last moments, Frederick Collins pictured his friends on the hall slapping one another on the back and saluting his success. I close the file, which will be placed in the basement storage vault termed, appropriately enough, the Dead File Room.

We call a special community meeting to talk about Collins. The mood among the patients is sad, accepting and elegiac, in contrast to the palpable distress of the staff early this morning. I know from experience that the bewildered sense of collective failure will hang over us for weeks.

"It came as a surprise to some of the others," Bertram says later, in our session. "But not to me. I could see it in his face."

"See what?"

"That he'd had enough. Life wasn't worth it for him anymore; it was just too hard."

Bertram looks preoccupied; there is no sign of the ease that possessed him the other day at the baseball game.

"Life can feel that way sometimes," I say. "But then, the feeling passes."

"No, not passes," Bertram says thoughtfully. "Goes underground. Gets put away, locked up. I'm discovering here that distraction is a mighty force. Woodworking, the print shop, games. All the coming and going. It's pretty effective, some of the time, but at bottom, it isn't enough."

"Sometimes the *doing* is meaningful in and of itself—beyond serving to distract. I've seen the desk you're building; it's beautiful. And the vegetables from the patients' garden taste pretty real to me."

"Planting, reaping, sowing: that kind of thing," he says wearily, then sinks into a brooding silence.

After a time, I ask him what he is thinking.

He studies me, as if trying to decide whether or not to proceed. "I was thinking about Buchenwald."

I know Bertram was with the regiment that liberated the camp. "Tell me about it."

"I was thinking about how eerily empty it was when we got there. The inmates had been sent on death marches and the guards had fled. We'd been told to do a sweep of the place. I was with a young captain by the name of Jared. Building after building—nothing. It was like a ghost town. We went into the officers' mess. It was spookily quiet at first, but then I heard something—very faint, almost inaudible. I noticed fresh plasterwork in the corner."

A long pause. Bertram seems to be battling himself, as if he wants to forget but is unable to stop remembering.

"I don't recall kicking the wall in—but then there they were, crouched in the small space, looking up at me. Jared was pointing his gun at them: four SS, in full uniform. For some reason, I kept my eyes on the one; the others were a blur. A good-looking man: distinguished, maybe ten years older than me.

"I heard Jared cock his pistol; he whispered that they had weapons— that we had to kill them. I told him we were taking them alive. I don't know what happened after that. A moment later, Jared was dead on the other side of the mess hall. Blown clear across by a hand grenade. I must have jumped away quickly, in the right direction. No one else was killed. Maybe whoever threw it aimed directly at Jared."

Again, he falls silent.

"They were scientists," he says finally. "Dr. Harrison, do you know what they did with all those scientists?"

"No, Bertram, I don't."

"They're here. In the United States. Working for the CIA."

"How do you know that the one you took prisoner came to work for the CIA?"

"I was privy to a good deal of classified information."

Again, that eerie manner, as if Bertram knows something about me—something private and devastating.

"I don't mean to be ungrateful," he adds.

"Ungrateful for what?"

"For the charming bit about seeds, growing into vegetables. It's just that reality isn't like that, at least, not for me."

After he leaves, I unlock the cabinet behind my desk; my heart skips

with guilty pleasure at the sound of the click. I pour myself two fingers of vodka, then stand by the window and look onto the grounds and wait for the warm flow.

I don't know why the dreams have come back; it feels like the encroachment of an old self—someone else, not me.

They say that true love comes as a thunderbolt—and it did, for me, the moment I laid eyes on Delilah. I was chief resident; she was a patient, waiting for me on the admitting hall in the company of a nurse. Twenty-two years old, sitting erect in the chair, very still but taut, as if about to spring into action. She tracked me with her deep green eyes, assessing, alert, missing nothing, her face immobile. The pull of her gaze: it seemed as if she was not so much looking at me as sloughing away the external layers I had labored so hard to cultivate.

After Delilah's accident, I considered leaving psychiatry. I was only a few months from taking the boards; it would have been unusual to start a whole new residency, especially then. Many of us had lost time to the Great War and were eager to make it up. In the end, I stuck it out: finished the year as chief resident and passed my exams. I stayed on at Shadowbrook, where I have been ever since.

But for years after the accident, my nights were torture. I would lie awake, the ticking hours eating into me, and then finally slip into fraught dreams. Sleeping fitfully beside Ursula, I sometimes found myself crossing the room to where Delilah sat on the chaise longue in my small attic office, pausing briefly to look at her. Delilah would turn her pale face toward me, freed, finally, from her tremulous sorrow; I would raise my hand to her cheek, watch the slow spread of her smile, lean in for the kiss. She would open herself to me then, and I would feel intoxicated.

There was another dream. Delilah's paleness now a horror as the blood slowly spreads, staining her blue jacket to black. Still, I longed for sleep as one longs for a lover, for there was always the chance I would find myself in the other place: peeling away her soft cardigan, then her blouse, sliding my hand beneath.

To quench the insomnia I took to using laudanum. To my illicit delight, I discovered the drug improved my chances of dreaming myself into Delilah's arms. Very soon, the laudanum wasn't enough.

The first time I took the train into Chinatown, I felt like a fugitive from my own life. Walking the narrow streets, I was aware of a mysteri-

ous pulsing, both distant and near: the sense that my life was about to change. I passed an elaborately carved doorway, hung with red and gold silk; a man with a long ponytail motioned conspiratorially for me to enter. I followed through a series of dimly lit rooms to a parlor lined with wooden bunks and dense with sickly sweet smoke. The smell hit me the moment I entered; I recognized it at once, though I couldn't place why. It was only later, in a supervision session with Dr. Greely, that I realized I had smelled this odor on him: faint but perceptible beneath the ever-present reek of his pipe tobacco.

On almost every bunk in the parlor, people—Chinese and Western-ers, several of them women—reclined. Everyone moved languidly, as if underwater, leaning toward a pipe being offered, drawing in smoke, lowering back down to the bunk. Several heads turned slowly in my direction and then swiveled, disinterested, away. I followed my guide to an empty bunk and lay back against the silk-covered cushions. Fas-cinated, I watched as a young man prepared the opium. With the first inhalation, I was lost; the room became a wondrous vessel, and I sank into the exhilarating mix of helplessness and power that felt strangely akin to lust.

I returned to that parlor again, and again, until I'd learned to prepare the pipe myself; then, I brought the waxy, brown blocks of opium home, smoking late at night in my study while Ursula slept. She was a deep sleeper, so I didn't have to worry about her awakening; I was able to give myself over to the visions of Delilah: more lush than wakefulness and as heady as the sweet-smelling smoke.

The evening Ursula received news of her mother's stroke, I realized how estranged from each other we had become. She took the phone call in the hallway, and then returned to the dining room looking ashen. Her face crumpled as she relayed the news; I found myself looking at someone I hardly knew, someone standing there as if behind thick glass.

"I'm so sorry, my dear," I said, knowing I should embrace her, or at least take her hand. I felt suddenly ashamed, then realized to my hor-ror that I was cutting a piece of lamb with the intention of raising it to my lips. Ursula's eyes drifted to my plate; I froze, holding my knife and fork, unable to fight the undertow that had for so long been dragging me away.

Ursula hugged herself, struggling to stifle tears.

"You must go, of course," I said, and still I failed to rise, failed to take her into my arms.

Ursula nodded, then nodded again. She was looking at the floor with misery.

I hated myself then, but that didn't stop the upsurge of pleasure at the thought that, with Ursula gone, I would have the house to myself.

For a little over a year, Ursula made regular trips to Maine to care for her mother. I looked forward to her absences, though I was not unhappy when she returned. We settled into a new pattern, which in some ways was an improvement. Once her mother recovered sufficiently, Ursula's frequent absences stopped. That was when she told me she knew about my addiction. She told me that I appeared unwell, that my work was surely being affected. That I was putting everything at risk. With enormous conflict, I gave up the pipe; the dreams, the glorious as well as the ghastly, slammed to a halt. It was a terrible loss, though at some level, I suppose I was also relieved.

Now, looking out across the lawn, allowing my eyes to rest on the willow tree, I tell myself that I can bear it: that the memory of Delilah won't, after all, tear me apart.

"Actually, it's crazier than it sounds," Bertram says.

"What is?"

"The fact that Emanuel blamed me for Rosamund's death. I mean, he was the one driving the car."

Bertram looks at me accusingly—as if the death of his childhood sweetheart were my fault.

"What car, Bertram?"

"My uncle's car. The car that hit her. Emanuel was only fourteen, but he had a thing about cars. My uncle had a 1934 Ford Hi-boy that he only drove on weekends. Sometimes my brother cut school and took the car out. That afternoon, he was driving it down our street when he lost control. Rosamund was riding her bike and he hit her."

Bertram changes the subject before I have a chance to comment.

"I don't always have the easiest time with words," he says. "It's as if they have eyes."

Bertram is clearly not sleeping well; his face is beginning to look haggard. It has been two months since he came to the hospital; I'd hoped by now the barbiturates would have stabilized his sleep patterns and eased both the melancholia and the slightly paranoid edge.

"What do you mean by *eyes*?"

"They seem to mean one thing to other people and another thing to me."

"Can you give me an example?"

"You're fond of examples, aren't you."

"Yes, I am."

"*Victory*. That's a perfect example."

"What does *victory* mean to you?"

"What does it mean to *you*, Doctor? Maybe we could start there."

"Hitler dead in his bunker. The chance for the world to regain some measure of sanity."

Bertram gives a wan smile. "What better place than a psychiatric hospital for that?"

I return the smile. "Good a place as any."

Bertram's ironic expression fades. "That's another word that slips away from me," he says, directing his words to the window.

"Which word?"

"Sanity."

"That's a tricky one for the rest of us, too," I say. "But you were talking about victory."

He sweeps his eyes back across to me; I am startled by their dark glow.

"To me," he says, "it means only death."

Bertram places his hand in his jacket pocket; I see movement through the material, as if he's rubbing his fingers together in the pocket.

"I can see how you would think that," I say. "War is a terrible thing."

Bertram is suddenly on his feet. His hand flies up from his pocket, and I see he is holding a scrap of paper.

"Millions—and this one, horrible death—" He waves the piece of paper he is holding like it's a tiny little flag, then falls back into his chair and slumps forward, head in his hands.

I give him a moment, then quietly ask, "What is that?"

He speaks from his doubled-over position.

"What is what?" he says stonily.

"That piece of paper you have in your hand."

"It's not a piece of paper. It's a postcard." His voice sounds artificial.

"I see."

"No." His voice is barely audible. *You—do—not—see—*

"The postcard," I say. "Who is it from?"

"The postcard is from Rosamund."

"Rosamund," I repeat. "Your neighbor."

"Yes."

"When did she write you the postcard?" I ask.

"On the eve of her murder."

Murder: the sound of the word flutters for a moment in the room.

"She wrote you the postcard before the car accident?"

"It wasn't an accident," he says. "Just listen. 'Dearest Bertram.' "

He pauses for a very long time. I think he will not go on, but then, he does.

"You understand," he says, "I am translating. I assume you don't understand German."

I shake my head.

"Very well, then. 'We are allowed one postcard and only four hundred words. I am writing to you. I do not know if you will ever receive this. You are my true soul's love. God intended us to be man and wife, I am certain. I do not know how God's plan went astray. We are to report tomorrow for "work duty." Please remember me always. You are in my heart. Rosamund.' "

The postcard is worn with handling; from where I sit, the words Bertram is reading seem no longer legible—just a curl or line, here and there. He glances up, sees me craning to look at the postcard.

"It is true," Bertram says, his eyes shining with sadness. "The words are no longer visible. But they are here—" He points to his temple, then lets his hand drift down to his breastbone, where he holds his fist tightly against his chest.

How could his neighbor have been a German Jew, sent to her death by the Nazis?

"You know that I was wounded in the last days of the War." Bertram's hand now passes to his abdomen, which I know from his medical examination is where he sustained an injury. "When I was in the veterans' hospital, a pile of mail reached me. Things that had been sent to old

addresses and routed to the Army while I was away fighting. The date on the postcard was January eighteenth, 1943. It took more than two years to reach me . . ."

He holds up the card and taps the spot at the top; the paper looks as if it is on the verge of falling apart.

"This is what I came back to," he says in a thick voice. "This is what the word *victory* means to me."

"Bertram, you told me that Rosamund died when your brother struck her with your uncle's Ford," I say.

"My uncle had a Duesenberg. A large touring car, with running boards," he says.

"You said she died in an automobile accident," I persist.

"Yes," he says deliberately. "But that was not the truth."

"Why would you make up something like that?"

"Sometimes it's not possible to tell the truth."

"But why say that your brother killed her?"

Bertram's eyes go cloudy. "I'm surprised you would ask that. You spend half your life talking in metaphors."

"Then it was a metaphor. Your story about the car accident."

"I suppose so," he says offhandedly, glancing distractedly around the room.

"You seem to be looking for something," I say.

He brings his eyes back to rest on me. They are filled with a baffling expression: part contempt, part anguish, part dissimulation.

He sighs. "Sometimes, I don't see the point of all this."

"I'm simply trying to make sense of things," I say, deciding that now is not the time to ask about the fact that Bertram speaks German. If his neighbor was German, logic would demand that he is German, too. On the other hand, the story about the postcard could itself be a fabrication, everything he is saying about his brother, about Rosamund, a delusion.

"Have you ever considered, Doctor," Bertram says, "that perhaps there *is* no making sense of things?"

Mr. Cuthbert is waiting for me in the dayroom. He cannot bear to have sessions indoors—he says it makes him feel like "a bug under glass"—so

we talk while walking the grounds, no matter the weather. We head toward the tennis courts, where some Hall Two patients are going at it with gusto, watched by Gilmore, a wiry orderly well-liked by both patients and staff for his decency and sense of fun. Tracking the ball, he moves his head back and forth like a metronome. The sound of a rooster reaches our ears; it is the Professor, wildly waving his racquet and crowing in celebration of a good shot.

"He's quite the colorful poultry, isn't he," Cuthbert says indulgently. "Speaking of my fellow travelers, I've been meaning to talk to you about the new inmate. Mr. Thunderer. There's something not quite right about him."

I smile. "Do you mean Mr. Reiner?"

"He's less about Rain than about Thunder." Cuthbert squints into the sun and pulls down the brim of his fedora; his thin face is dominated by piercing eyes and full, red lips that seem somehow a mistake.

"Perhaps he's in the right place; we're hoping to help him."

"Yes, of course." Cuthbert tips his hat to the gardener crouched by the pathway pulling weeds. "But I'm not talking about mental illness. It's his existential condition I'm concerned about. Don't you feel it? The way he hauls the abyss with him wherever he goes. It's beginning to upset the other patients. You're going to have to stay away from the Ontic where he's concerned; it will only get him into trouble. A strict Ontological Therapy, that's what's called for. No time for *Being* where there's no time for *Time;* take the paradoxical course and you'll cure the oxymoron. Not that he's stupid, mind you; I'd venture his intelligence quotient tips the scale—a match for you and me put together, and that's saying something. Speak softly is my advice, and carry a big Heidegger."

Cuthbert smiles, pleased with himself. He waits, as if wanting his speech to sink in, then continues. "May I be perfectly frank with you?"

"By all means."

"He doesn't know what he's gotten himself into. I'm not sure he's up for it."

"Up for what?"

Cuthbert leans toward me, removes his hat, and holds it up to his

mouth as a shield. "For a journey to the dark side. I have a bad feeling. In the two years and four months that I've been in residence, I've never once been wrong on this score. This isn't the place for him, Doctor, if you don't mind my saying. He belongs elsewhere."

"Where do you think he belongs?"

Cuthbert slaps his hat back onto his head and looks momentarily confused. "Why—elsewhere."

"Such as?"

"Elsewhere doesn't have a *such as*. Elsewhere is by definition *somewhere else*. The unimagined, the unknown, the terra incognita, if you will."

"There's something about Mr. Reiner that troubles you," I say carefully.

Cuthbert looks impatient. "This isn't about me, Dr. Harrison. This is about Mr. Reiner. Look, I'll do my best to infiltrate; perhaps I can be of help. Leave it to me and I'll see what I can do."

"You've never mentioned what you did during the Great War," Bertram says after taking his seat.

"Is there a reason I should have discussed this with you?"

"Well, no. I suppose not."

He looks disgruntled.

"We're here to talk about you, Bertram."

"Yes, Doctor. But I'm curious. Were you in the British services, or had you already come to this country?"

I sometimes forget that I have an English accent. "Why is this important to you, do you think?"

"You could give me this one, considering."

"Considering what?"

"Considering everything I've divulged to you."

"I owe you, then."

"In a manner of speaking."

"Very well, then," I say. "I came of age toward the end of the War. I trained to be a medic and was posted for a time at a hospital outside

London. Then I was sent to the front—I was in France for almost a year."

"France."

"Yes."

"As I was."

I risk a smile. "It was a different war, you understand."

Bertram's face darkens.

"I didn't mean to be glib," I say. "I just mean that our experiences were certainly different."

"Did you do any hand-to-hand combat?"

"I spent a short time in the infantry, at the very end of the War. There was such a shortage of men . . ."

Something flashes in Bertram's eyes. "Did you ever shoot *Jews*?"

"I beg your pardon?"

"Executions. Point-blank. Dozens, even hundreds at once. Did you ever participate in an operation like that?"

"There were no operations like that in the First War," I say quietly. "Besides, I was in the British Army."

"You never shot a Jew, then," he says.

"Actually, I may well have shot a Jewish German. They fought in the war along with all other German men."

My answer seems to surprise Bertram. "I hadn't thought about that," he says mildly.

"May I ask you something?"

Bertram nods.

"Why do you ask if I ever executed Jews?"

"In *our* war, ordinary Germans did that—policemen, civilians. Roaming the Polish countryside—execution squads, killing thousands upon thousands of Jews: women, old people, babies. Everyone."

"Bertram," I say gently. "You were in France and Germany. France and Germany. Could you tell me what Poland has to do with it, for you?"

"Poland?"

"You were talking about Poland."

"Yes, I suppose I was."

He sighs and looks out the window. I follow his gaze, aware that I no longer keep track of the seasons as I once did. When I first came to work

here, I was acutely aware of the lavish seasonal changes on the grounds and in the surrounding woods. I made a study of the trees and plant life, and became familiar with the sounds of the little creatures I would encounter on my walks. How joyful I would feel at the eruptions of autumn color, or the bare branches and fields of white. Now the seasons simply glide by.

"We could talk about it—about Poland, about what happened to the Jews," I say.

"To what end?" he says. "What would that achieve?"

"Maybe nothing. But we psychiatrists believe in a leap of faith. That if you express what's on your mind, it is likely to take us someplace useful."

"Us."

"Yes. You and me."

"But you said this is about me. That we're here to talk about me. Why, then, do you say *us*?"

"I like to think we're in this together. That I'm here to help you."

"To help me what?"

"Make sense of your experience. Find a way toward some measure of peace."

His crackling look of hostility surprises me.

"But you never executed Jews. In the streets. Or into huge pits they were made to dig with their own hands."

"Neither, I daresay, did you."

Bertram sits back in his chair with a distasteful look of triumph.

"Perhaps, Doctor—and of course, you *know so much*. Such a learned man. But perhaps you are unaware of my origins?"

"I'm not sure what you mean."

"Did you not know that German is my mother tongue? I made a point early on of mastering English. It was not so difficult—I was only twelve when I came to this country."

"No, Bertram, I did not know you were from Germany."

"Precisely," he says.

"But that doesn't mean you massacred Jews."

He recoils, and then glances at the clock on the mantel.

"But what if my brother *did*?" he asks. "When my mother and I came to America, he stayed behind with my father. So of course, he

became a Nazi. Maybe that's why he's trying to find me. Maybe he wants
to *silence* me. So that I won't turn him in for what he's done."

I awaken to the sound of rain. I have an early morning meeting, so I
dress quietly, not wanting to awaken Ursula. Outside, the downpour is
heavier than I thought and the cold slaps at my face. I cross to the Pea-
body Storage Annex and duck into the tunnels that snake beneath the
hospital complex. Having fallen into disuse decades ago, they are dank
and eerily quiet. I've heard that incoming psychiatric residents are told
by their seniors that the tunnels are haunted by the ghosts of patients
past and that, before my time, a trainee hazing involved spending a night
alone there.

Belowground, the air is thick with mold and dust. The passageways
are dimly lit with low-wattage fluorescent bulbs that give off a resonant,
mechanical buzz. I feel as if I am trespassing on the past. I half-expect
to come across quaintly dressed doctors from another era, and patients
wearing crazed expressions, tied to the wall and reeking of bedlam. I
know that the passageways are used to store discarded furniture, but
here, they are empty.

The painted concrete walls are peeling in places, and elsewhere dark
with amoeboid spreads of damp. Here, a huge stain looms, uncannily
familiar. Hunched over a table: the outline of his head, his shoulders,
the hand holding a scalpel, unnaturally still. My mind fogs, I tumble
through time. It is Mac, my childhood friend: a faceless shape pressing
out through the concrete.

Mac McDermott—a tall, strong boy, a year older than I—was pas-
sionate about bugs. Nothing mattered to him more than finding a speci-
men and coming to understand what made the creature operate the way
it did. In his room, an array of jars, cotton wads soaked in ether, pins
large and small. I often sat with him as he made his preparations for a
mounting; every now and then, I would assist him, taking care to do
exactly as he said.

Though partial to the more glamorous butterflies and moths, Mac
also loved spiders, beetles, and giant red ants. He was bitten and stung
more times than I could count, though this did not seem to deter him.

Even as a child I suffered from insomnia. I was a night pacer, ago-
nizingly restless. One night, while I was pacing in our front yard, my
feet propelled me the three and a half blocks to Mac's house. Beneath
his bedroom window was a gauzy patch of light. I got the window with
the first stone. A corner of the curtain rose, and Mac's face appeared.
Moments later, he was at the front door. We crept together up the stairs
to his room, where I saw that Mac had a dissection under way. His
desk was laid out like a miniature operating table: instruments lined
up along one edge and pieces of insects—wings, beetle torsos, parts of
worm—carefully arrayed in sections. He got back to work, holding a
spider down with the sharpened tip of a pencil and then prying off the
legs one by one with a pair of tweezers.

I heard a sound coming from the corner of the room. There, nuz-
zling up against an old stuffed animal, was a small puppy, three or four
weeks old.

"I didn't know you had a puppy," I said excitedly.

"I found him yesterday in the gutter."

I walked to the puppy and picked him up. "Poor thing," I whispered.
"We'll take care of you."

Mac paused in his work, holding the tweezers in midair, and looked
at me coldly.

"Have you named him yet?" I asked.

Mac rose to join me where I crouched, cuddling the pup. He took the
dog brusquely by the scruff of its neck. The puppy startled and reached
his paws out to me.

"Don't pet him," he said, still eyeing me coldly, speaking with the tone
of finality that adults use when they will brook no disagreement. I had
the sudden feeling that something was terribly wrong. Mac went back to
his spider; after a few minutes, he seemed to forget that I was even there.

Before I knew what I was doing, I was back out in the street, running
blindly toward home.

My footsteps thud loudly through the tunnels; I am running, fran-
tic. My breath comes in wisps. I'd mistakenly supposed I would simply
head in the direction of the main building much as I would above-
ground, but the passageways wind this way and that, and I have no idea
where I am going. I scan the walls left and right; too much time seems
to be passing.

Finally, a door. I tug and tug some more, the panic rising. My arm wrenches, I pull with all my strength, and it gives; I almost fall back, then hurry up the stairs and thrust open the door at the top. I have emerged in the rear of the Rogers Gymnasium. Brushing off my trousers and coat, I take a moment to collect myself.

In the late afternoon, I find Matilda in the dayroom, involved in a game of contract rummy, Cuthbert, the Professor, and Bertram Reiner making up a foursome. This is a favorite time on the hall, when the patients, along with some staff, if there's nothing pressing to be done, have an hour to relax before dinner.

Friendly greetings are exchanged, and then I address Matilda. "The new patient is finished with the preliminaries and will be up shortly."

"The preliminaries!" Cuthbert gives a good-natured snort. "How I love the native gibberish. You just have to remember to reverse everything, and then the meaning doesn't go astray. In this case—the *finales;* out with the old life, in with the new. I hear the new fellow is a luminary. I've always liked writers. They make the likes of me look positively sane. Which is to say, negatively the same. Does he know about the staff? Confined to the cell every bit as much as we are—nunlike and monklike, too, I'd say; *who's kidding who, anyway?* A *seminary* for the *luminary.* Hah!"

Cuthbert throws down a sequence of four clubs. "Sixth contract, satisfied. Moving on!"

Bertram picks up a card from the pile with an indulgent smile. "The new man will love your tour of the hall, Cuthbert. Are you prepared?"

"I keep it primed." Cuthbert grins. "Like to tag along?"

"Five times is enough. Or has it been six?"

"Nurse Willoughby tells us the new man's a lush," Cuthbert says gravely.

"If we're going to use labels, we prefer the technical term," I say pleasantly.

"Oh yes, forgive me. *Acute alcoholism.* With or without neurasthenic features?"

"Why not leave the diagnostics to us?" I say with a smile. "You've got quite enough on your hands with the ward tour."

Matilda puts her cards facedown and rises with a sigh. "I'm sorry, gentlemen. I have things I must attend to."

"Be a sport, Dr. Harrison, and finish up Nurse Willoughby's hand," Cuthbert ventures.

About to reach for an automatic excuse, I realize I have a few minutes to spare. Cuthbert looks so eager.

Matilda steps aside and hands me her cards. "Now don't mess things up for me." Her eyes twinkle. "It's the best I've ever done against these cardsharps. I'm counting on you."

"I'm a bit rusty, I'm afraid," I reply. The seat is warm, even the cards carry a trace of Matilda's heat.

"No such thing," Cuthbert says crisply. "It's like riding a bike. Spinning wheels are the name of the game; Psyche on this ship is the dame of great fame." He sweeps us with his gaze, bewildered but pleased by his clever, clanging rhyme.

"Isn't there a separate ward for alcoholics?" Bertram asks, laying down a sequence of cards.

"They're an exotic breed," the Professor chimes in. "Not like your garden-variety melancholic, or your delusional type. There just aren't that many of them, so they're thrown in with the rest of us. But I'm with Cuthbert; in my experience, they're crazy as loons. I've a great friend who was a lush—er, alcoholic—here. He's back out, now. Sends me chocolate cherries, from time to time."

"They do very well on Hall Four," I say. My eyes drift to the doorway just as Matilda passes by; she pauses before the tall window to talk to an orderly. I find myself transfixed; she is framed by the burnt reds and oranges of dogwood and oak, and for a moment, in the crisp autumn light, time freezes. Something distracts her, and Matilda cocks her head. Then, she turns and catches my eye; I am taken aback by the warmth of her smile.

"The drunks are fun to watch, the first few weeks," Cuthbert continues. "They shake like jitterbugs. If we can get this one to keep it up until Christmas, we can plug him in to light the tree."

Bertram and the Professor laugh. I'm struck by how personable and at ease Bertram is here, on the ward, in contrast to his somber, often bristling mood in our sessions.

"Come on, Dr. Harrison," Cuthbert urges. "Make your move.

You have the reputation of one of Shadowbrook's finest nurses to defend!"

In session today, Bertram gloomily raises the subject of a relationship he had with a woman just before entering the hospital; he refers to her gallantly as "my lady friend."

"When I was with her," he says, "I would sometimes feel like I had a chance at a new life. Lately, it's been feeling impossible."

"What has been feeling impossible?"

"The idea that I will have a new life. I don't know how to tell her— if I go back to seeing her after I leave here—that maybe it's not meant to be."

"She's clearly important to you."

Bertram nods, his face etched with pain. "I don't want to disappoint her."

"Do you feel that you will?"

"I'm a psychiatric patient," he says thinly.

"You're a soldier with a reactive disorder," I rejoin.

"Same thing."

I cannot help thinking that the woman is not an old lover, as Bertram maintains, but someone with whom he is involved in the present. Could it be that Bertram is carrying on an affair with a fellow patient? Now that I think about it, on our last mixed outing, I noticed him deep in conversation with Mrs. Seabrook, a young widow from Connecticut. I also noticed Marianne Freeman, a homely girl not yet twenty, staring at Bertram adoringly at Tuesday night canasta.

"Real connections can withstand a good deal more than a temporary hospitalization," I say.

"It's just that she's . . . well, she's fragile," Bertram says. "You wouldn't think it upon meeting her. But I don't think she'd be up to a real knock."

"And being with you is likely to end up being a real knock for her," I say.

He nods. "But when I'm with her . . . the problems melt away. It's as though I'm the man I was before I went off to fight."

There it is: the slippage into the present tense. My heart sinks at the

thought that it might, after all, be Marianne Freeman: a vulnerable soul, and so young.

An image of Delilah flaps into my mind like a delicate, exotic bird; I am crossing the room, sitting beside her, my hand is on her warm shoulder, and her face transforms with the heat of an uncharacteristic smile.

After Bertram leaves, I call Ursula.

"We've had an incident on Hall Eight," I say. "You'd better go ahead and eat without me."

"I made duck," she says, her voice pinched with disappointment. "In red wine sauce," as if the sauce might make me reconsider.

"I'm sorry, Ursula, really I am."

"Should I keep a plate in the warming drawer?"

"I don't know how long it will take . . ."

"Don't forget to order something up from the dining hall, then." I can hear she has resigned herself to another evening alone, but I feel I simply cannot go home.

I drink a half bottle of wine with my meal and then work steadily through a mound of paperwork. Around me, the hospital slumbers: the sane and the insane united in sleep.

When the church bells strike midnight, I lock up my papers and head out. In the dark, everything is transformed: the familiar expanse of grass has turned into the black, unmoving surface of a lake; the trees are animate, silhouettes lurching toward me each time I look away.

At the bottom of the hill, where the path forks, I see movement: a man in evening dress, walking back and forth before the bench. He pulls something from his pocket, strikes a match, cups his hand to light a cigarette. By the time I reach him, he is seated, and I can see that it is Mr. Thomas, Bertram Reiner's servant.

"Good evening," I say.

Thomas regards me without surprise. "Dr. Harrison," he says, rising.

"Please, don't get up."

Thomas offers me a cigarette, which I decline.

"A lovely night," I say, sitting beside him on the bench.

"I was just thinking that myself, sir."

We sit in comfortable silence, Thomas drawing quietly on his cigarette.

"Might I ask you something, Dr. Harrison?"

"By all means."

"I understand you were a medic. In the First War."

"Yes, I was."

He flips the cigarette butt to the ground and steps it out.

"That's something we have in common." His voice is uncertain, as if he wants to say something further.

"You were a medic as well?"

"Once a medic, always a medic. I served in France, and then after VE Day, I was on cleanup duty in Germany. Only it wasn't really over, as you know."

"What do you mean?"

"The casualties didn't stop—on either side. At least, not for some time."

"Did you serve with Mr. Reiner, then?"

"Not exactly." Thomas shifts uncomfortably on the bench. Something unexpected occurs to me.

"You didn't treat him, did you?"

His eyes waver and he turns away. "In a fashion," he says oddly. "We met on the ship, coming home." He glances at his wristwatch and gives a little sigh. "Well, I'd best be getting back. Good evening, Dr. Harrison. I enjoyed talking with you."

The pathway leading toward my home is dimly lit by streetlamps; as I step in and out of the puddles of light, I have the sensation that I am wading into the past. At the fork, Ursula's forced nonchalance on the telephone this afternoon comes back to me. All her fine energy poured into closing herself down. How different from when we first met.

That day, at Dover, we were both twenty years old. The War was over; I had been away for a year—though not the kind of time that can be measured in days. When I had left England on the boat out, it was my final year of secondary school and my parents had been standing at that very dock, wearing threadbare coats and unsteady smiles, waving bravely. I returned an orphan: no one to greet me, no one to celebrate my surviving the madness, no one to take me home.

They died within six months of each other—first my father, of a heart attack, and later my mother, in a freakish accident. She'd been walking along the high street of our town when without warning a

building collapsed onto her. The friend who had been standing beside her was unhurt.

I remembered running as we carried stretchers through mud so cold it stung, the thick ground frothing red, in places, from dripping torsos and limbs. Even when it was too late, and it was mostly too late—when a boy poisoned by gas spewed yellow and blood, or another, ripped open at the middle, tried, wild-eyed, to stuff his entrails back in—even then we ran through the smoky hell, the guns rat-tatting all around us, as if what we were doing were not insane, as if there really were someone, *this one, this boy*, left to save. I wrote it all down in dozens of letters I sent home to my mother and father; I don't know how they felt when they read my words. Later, I found those letters in my mother's desk and felt her presence again, as if she had sprung back to life.

The news of my father's death, and then my mother's, reached me by telegram; twice I sat in a trench, breathing dank air and holding crinkly yellow paper, only to rise again to carry the silent or screaming wounded, the dying or already dead.

Disembarking at Dover, we trudged down a long gangway, safe now but stunned as sheep going to the slaughter. And then there I was, at the end of the ramp, looking into the face of an American Red Cross girl who was offering me a cup of tea. I took the cup, then a biscuit from the chipped plate beside the tea urn. She seemed to see something in me, and I, desperate, bewildered, longed to be seen. I couldn't take my eyes from the healthy plumpness of her cheeks, the smooth pink curve of skin visible just above the uniform, which sloped down snugly over her breasts. Then, she smiled.

What I had seen in France made me old, and yet I was a virgin. I had watched my friends go to brothels and return doleful and drunk; it was not something I could bring myself to do. And had an opportunity arisen to romance a local girl, as some soldiers did, I'd not have known what to do. The terrible rumbling that had plagued me for more than a year—that fanned out from my groin and set my whole body on edge—rose in me again, though differently: no longer an illness but an urge for life.

As I lingered by the Red Cross table that day, Ursula gave a husky laugh and shot me darting glances. Finally, I asked if I might meet her again, and in her warm, American accent, she said yes, that was some-

thing she'd like. In that instant, everything changed; vitality poured through me, and only then did I fully realize that, for the past year, I'd been suspended in a disturbing netherworld—alive, yes, but dormant.

Three days later, having secured lodgings, I came for her. We sat in a teahouse with sagging lace curtains in the window, sipping tea made from overused leaves and whitened with a clump of powdered milk. My eyes clung to her—to her shyly smiling lips, to the shapely hands nursing the warm cup. There, in that tarnished little place, I imagined so vividly Ursula's hands traveling the length of me, my own unbuttoning her clothing, smoothing her round hips, discovering the secrets of her sex.

After two long weeks of agonizing frustration, the landlady, Mrs. Hopkins, took pity on us; she turned a blind eye to the fact that one of her good Red Cross girls was taking a soldier into her room. I climbed the stairs behind Ursula; I'd never seen anything so beautiful as the swivel of her hips in her floral print dress.

In her room, she lit the gas lamp, and then turned and let out a little gasp. "Oh!" she said, as if encountering me for the first time. Her eyes strayed from my face and came to rest on the buckle of my belt. She stood there waiting. The moment elongated, and when finally I raised my hand, it moved as if through water—slowly, thickly, silently. I touched Ursula's chin, lifted her head. Her eyes were bright, the heat pouring from her; it pulled something from me—a bitter hunger, alive as a fox. I made my actions tender, though all of me snapped; I nuzzled my prey without baring my teeth. It was cold in that spare room; as I undressed her, I warmed her all over, kneading her rounded flesh, coaxing the rise from her. And then we were on the worn sheets, beneath the heavy blanket, the world split to ripeness. My gentleness turned determined; I gripped her roughly, felt her stiffen for a moment in fright and then take pleasure in it.

Three weeks later, Mrs. Hopkins hosted our modest wedding in the parlor she'd managed to keep looking elegant, despite the privations of the war. Six of us that day; two bottles of wine, a plateful of hard scones. I held Ursula's hand. I was startled and happy, and for a few fleeting moments, felt my desolation might never return.

The leaking away of our marriage happened slowly: a soft, brutal dripping in the background of our lives. The heat had already begun to evaporate when we discovered Ursula could not have a child, but the

doctor's verdict was the coup de grâce; after that, she seemed to lose all desire. By the time I met Delilah, Ursula and I were living a life of tepid routine.

I come to a halt before my house, which is almost purple in the moonlight. Something tugs at me, weighs me down—and then, with almost hallucinogenic force, I see Delilah smiling once again.

Chapter Two

*I*t is a curious package, carefully, even obsessively, wrapped. Several layers of brown paper, heavily glued, and tied with knotted twine. The postmark reads "Copenhagen, Denmark."

It takes me some time to open. What I find inside is a large, sealed envelope and, within this, a sheaf of papers. On top, a letter, written in English in an attractive, fluid hand. And beneath, a handwritten manuscript of some kind, written on unlined paper in a spidery, cramped hand, every inch of the paper covered. Peering more closely at the first of these pages, I see that it is written in German. Slowly, I read the letter.

> *Dear Dr. Harrison,*
>
> · *I am writing to you because I believe that the well-being of one of your patients may be at risk.*
>
> *My name is Gitte, and I am the wife of Emanuel Reiner. A month ago, my husband disappeared. I now have some insight into the mystery.*
>
> *I met my husband three and a half years ago under extraordinary circumstances. He was working for Herr Duckwitz in the office of the Nazi Occupying Command. I was not in a position to like him—or to have anything to do with him. I am Danish; we were living under German occupation. Emanuel wore the uniform of the German Order Police.*
>
> *I had come to the office with my father, who was a Danish official.*

Involved in many dangerous activities, he placed his own life at risk and also those of his entire family (including me). I was twenty-five years old and had already served for some years as my father's secretary. Fluent in many languages, he taught me English when I was a child.

Our visit to the office of Herr Duckwitz had an urgent purpose: to plead for the lives of Denmark's Jews. We were rebuffed, but we left with a piece of critical information. The Jews were to be rounded up in a surprise operation on the holy day of Rosh Hashanah. Herr Duckwitz was very uneasy when he told us this, and I noticed that his assistant looked at me intently.

That night, as we were making plans to use every boat for miles around to ferry the Jews to Sweden, we heard a knock on our door. We were accustomed to late night knocks, but they were always codes, arranged ahead of time. This was just a short rap—no code that we recognized. I had a feeling it was the assistant I'd noticed looking at me when we were in Herr Duckwitz's office. We'd learned to operate on our instincts, so I opened the door, and surely enough it was him. He said he'd defected from the Order Police and wanted to help.

He proved to be a strong and tireless rower. I spent many nights with him, ferrying women and children, and later the men, across the water. We had countless successes, and also some terrible losses; through it all, I was with Emanuel, and when the War ended, he stayed in Denmark. At the time, he insisted he had no desire to return to Germany. But as time passed, he became morose and sank into a dark place. I now see that his feelings were more complicated than I knew.

A month ago, Emanuel disappeared. I have been extremely worried, needless to say. A few days ago, I found these pages. My German is fairly good, but I cannot bear to reread them, which is why I have not translated them for you. Besides, I wanted to get them to you as soon as I could. I imagine you will find someone to translate them there, if you do not read German yourself.

I was devastated by what I read. I should have known my husband's past was not unblemished. How could it have been? And yet, the mind has a way of twisting things. I point you to the section on page twenty-two, where Emanuel outlines his plan. It pains me to say, but what he writes here suggests that he intends to harm his brother—your patient, Bertram. You will see how I located you; in the margin, on that same page, he wrote that he had found Bertram, and then scribbled down the address of your hospital, as well as your name.

I never knew Emanuel had a brother. I knew only of his father, whom I believe lives in Bonn and is in failing health. I know nothing about psychiatric illness. Perhaps you will determine that Emanuel's words are only an expression of his terrible conflict and pain and not in fact a statement of intention. I can only hope that this is the case. But I fear that he is no longer himself.

As for the rest of my husband's account, I apologize for inflicting this on you. I include it because otherwise none of this would make any sense.

In haste,
Gitte Reiner

I find a translator in the yellow pages. I have no idea what to expect—I only know that I don't want to delay, that I feel some urgency about the matter of the strange pages, sent by Emanuel's wife.

Cruising along the main street of New Rochelle, I follow the numbers until I reach the address. The office of Mr. Hoffstadt is above a boot maker; the creaking stairway smells of fresh leather and tanning stain, and the air is filled with hammerings and a mechanical whir.

Though I made an appointment, and arrive exactly on time, Hoffstadt seems surprised to see me.

"Oh yes—the man with the letter," he says in a heavy German accent, ushering me into his cramped office and nodding toward a rickety chair.

I hand him the pages and tell him briefly what I know. He puts on an ancient pair of eyeglasses and fiddles with the earpieces, his face creased with consternation. Then, he scans the first few pages, his expression changing to one of unreadable blankness.

"It's an unusual request," he says finally, removing his glasses with finicky care. "I've never done anything like this before."

"What I need is the overall gist. I'm not after anything literary."

"I don't know," he says dubiously. "Private communications—well, they can be controversial."

Only now do I notice that Hoffstadt is nervously tapping his foot; I see, also, that his fingernails are bitten to the quick.

"I imagine you've had a good deal of experience."

He flinches; perhaps reassurance is not, after all, what he was looking for.

"I've been here a very long time, if that's what you mean." There is something defensive about the way his mouth twitches.

Suddenly, I feel a fool. Very likely, Hoffstadt was interred during the War: distrusted, made to feel like the enemy in his own adopted homeland. And here I am, asking him to translate a disturbing memoir of a man who very likely participated in barbaric Nazi acts.

"I'm sorry," I say, rising and reaching for the pages. "Perhaps, after all—"

"I'll do it," he says curtly, covering the pages with both hands and drawing them toward him. "But I'm going to need a week."

Approaching the nurses' station, seeing Matilda through the glass, I feel a little rise of excitement. When I enter, she looks up from a stack of prescriptions and gives a relaxed smile.

"I was hoping you'd stop by before rounds," she says.

"Were you?"

She reddens slightly and gives a little laugh. "It's your right hand I'm after," she says, her eyes twinkling with humor.

I feel an odd flurry of confusion.

"I'm sorry . . . ?"

"Your signature!" She raises the stack of prescriptions and waves them in the air. "These should have been signed last night, at change of shift!"

"Oh dear, in trouble again, then."

"I'm afraid so, Doctor. And the second time this month . . ."

"Keeping tabs?"

"Yes. But that's part of my job."

"Well, then. I don't want to get into more trouble than I'm already in."

I reach for the prescriptions; our hands brush. I have the feeling that the air is speeding up around me. Then, a sudden click, the creak of the door. I am startled; I see that Matilda is startled, too.

"Oh—Vanessa," she says. "You've no idea what's been going on!"

I am momentarily stunned, thinking, *surely Matilda isn't going to say anything about what just happened between us.* But as soon as she speaks, I realize how absurd I am.

"I'm hoping there won't be a mutiny," Matilda is saying. She smiles.

"Oh?" Vanessa says.

"The pastry chef has the flu. Nothing but rice pudding for dessert in over a week."

"I should think the patients could rustle something up in cooking class," Vanessa says.

"That's just it. Several patients swear that they got a whiff of brownies baking on their way back from occupational therapy."

"What does the cooking detail have to say about that?" I ask.

"They've denied it. But one patient was accused of having a suspicious looking chocolaty streak on his jacket."

Vanessa laughs. "Have they turned up any evidence?"

"Well yes, if you count the missing jacket. The cooking detail has been formally charged with baking and failing to share." Matilda is now smiling broadly.

From behind me, a voice: "Pilfering, actually." It is Janice, a trainee nurse; I didn't hear her enter. "They want to set up a patient tribunal."

"We'll have to sidestep that one," Matilda says good-naturedly.

"The Professor was adamant—" Janice insists.

"We'll help them work it out," Matilda says firmly. "We can start in afternoon meeting. Why don't you go and muster the forces?"

Matilda waits for Janice to leave. "Once she graduates, I'm thinking of putting her on staff," she says. "I have one or two concerns, but overall, she's done well."

"She's a bit too serious for her own good," Vanessa says. "But she does have that special *something* that makes a good nurse."

"How many do we need to make a full roster?" I ask.

Matilda reaches for her staffing ledger and flips to the back page.

"In total—six. We'll take the top five girls in the class. Janice ranks eighth, but what Vanessa says is true; she has the makings of a good nurse. Totally committed, and a hard worker. What's more, she has a knack with the more seriously disturbed patients."

"I trust your judgment," I say.

"Now, don't forget these." Matilda taps the prescription orders with her forefinger. I allow my gaze to linger.

The week slips by. First thing in the morning, I return to Mr. Hoffstadt's office. He makes himself busy moving the objects about his desk, giving one-syllable responses to my attempts at small talk.

Last night, as I lay in bed while Ursula slept, my mind turned to the bundle of pages in the translator's hands. I pictured him, his face weirdly compelling, in the cramped room with its tainted, exotic odors and the ringing sounds from below of the boot maker's industry. I drifted off, and in my dream saw Hoffstadt hunched over something: an unwieldy box, hammering away, trying to break the lock. The box burst open with a terrible, shattering peal that pulled me from sleep; it was only the church bells, which completed their measure, leaving a haunting echo.

Now, back in Hoffstadt's office, I hand him his fee, which he takes with forefinger and thumb, craning away from the money, and from me. Finally, he looks me in the face for a brief moment; his eyes are not soft, as I remember them, but embarrassed and pained.

All afternoon, I find myself thinking about the papers in my desk drawer, buzzing with desire to discover what they contain. After dinner I head back to my office; the long hallway rings with emptiness. I glance into Cynthia's office; she left hours ago, and without her, the little room seems forlorn. Beside my office door is a portrait of Dr. Harlow Montgomery Fitzgibbon, the hospital's first director. The painting seems odd. Usually, Fitzgibbon strikes me as severe, a true Victorian asylum director, but tonight I see compassion in his eyes and a pinprick of yearning. In the brow, around the lips, shades of bewilderment, as if he were secretly struggling to come to terms with an aching and irremediable loss. It's as if he's reaching across the decades from beyond the grave to warn me, to offer a steadying hand.

In my office, I pour a few fingers of bourbon and take the parcel from my drawer.

The translation was typed on an old typewriter with a faulty lowercase *o;* the *o*'s drooped all down the page like little emptied-out eyes. For two days, I have been haunted by those pages; as I read, their terrible images burned into me. More than once, I had to turn away.

I don't know how Bertram knows that his brother is a monster—a monster, it turns out, who is seeking absolution. Perhaps Emanuel feels he is going down, and intends to take his brother along with him. Could that be the meaning of his final, cryptic lines?

There is no fixing any of it. I can only hope to put it to rest. Perhaps the only solution is to combat violence—with violence. We were the best of Germans, both of us. I must find my brother and set things straight. A double negative—might I discover that two wrongs make a right?

The night is closing in on me now. I see Emanuel, sitting in the truck, a long way from home, his rifle across his knees. He'd joined the Order Police to avoid combat, and now here he is, speeding through the cold, Polish night. The van comes to a halt; their commander, whom the members of the battalion call Papa Trappe, opens the door, and they all file out. They are in the square of a small town; the church steeple cuts into the sky, where the early morning light is just beginning to glow.

"I tell you of our mission with a heavy heart," Papa Trappe begins. "We've been ordered by our beloved Führer to cleanse the town of Jews. It is not a pleasant task, I know. We may spare no one."

Papa Trappe reaches up to wipe away a tear.

"You have my word for it—*my word*—that you will not have to participate in this operation if you feel it is too much for you. You will be transferred, without question, to desk work without penalty—as important a contribution to the Reich as any. Now, my dear brothers and sons, is your opportunity to step forward."

Emanuel feels a twitching in his feet: he longs to step forward. How can he, who has never killed a living thing, round up children and women and elderly people and shoot them into pits? From the corner of his eye, he monitors his fellow policemen for signs of movement. Who will come forward? Are they all standing there, also with itching feet, waiting to see who will move first?

And then, just as he sucks in the breath that will give him the courage to move, Papa Trappe's voice, again trembling, in the cold, morning air.

"Very well, then, men. We will work together as one."

The grisly images snatch at me. Emanuel gently pushing a youth toward his mother and grandfather, noting that the boy is about the age his brother Bertram was when he last saw him. The boy, the woman, the old man, look at him with puzzlement. He encourages them to remain still, as a photographer might: that's it, perfect, yes, hold it, just

like that. He raises his rifle and takes aim; they fall, one after the other, into the pit.

"I've always been troubled by Velázquez's paintings," Bertram says. "You could lose yourself in them."

"What draws you?" I ask.

"The darkness, I guess. Anything could be going on in there. If you stare into a Velázquez long enough, there's an unnerving effect."

"Are you thinking of a particular painting?"

"Why yes," he says—and now, the shadowy, sly glance. "*Las Meninas*. It's a great success, I'm sure you'll agree."

I struggle to recall the painting and manage to conjure up vague images: a looking glass, darkness, small groups of people here and there, curiously separated, looking one direction or another, a painter peering out from the shadows.

"In what way?"

"In conveying the power of a mirror, when cleverly wielded."

"The wielding of a mirror," I echo.

"Reflecting, deflecting: creating images that multiply. Stealing."

When he speaks again, his voice is surprisingly gentle. "It's a sad trick, when you think about it."

"How so?"

"He sets the viewer up brilliantly—there is the lure of something potent."

"Like?"

"Were you ever in a carnival fun house? As a child?"

"I suppose I was."

"Around every corner, you think you're going to chance upon something exciting—either wonderful or terrible. What you end up finding is multiple versions of yourself—distorted reflections in zany mirrors. You're fuzzy one minute, stretched out the next, suddenly larger or impossibly small. You find yourself as you might wish yourself to be, or fear yourself to be, or perhaps as you could never have imagined yourself. And then, just as magically, you might find that you disappear altogether."

"You were speaking about the Velázquez," I remind him.

"Don't you see? There's the promise of all that—of finding yourself. Of losing yourself. Of being stolen away. You discover that, in any case, it's all just mirrors."

He sits back, a mixed look of weariness and triumph on his face, and continues. "But that even so, there's a secret at bottom. The mirror provides a fabulous illusion. But there is a frightening secret behind it all. Which makes the game itself a game."

Bertram closes his eyes and squeezes their inner corners with forefinger and thumb.

"What is it for a game to be a game?" I ask, aware of an unpleasant dizziness, which I must be picking up directly from Bertram.

He removes his hand from his face and opens his eyes.

"But, Doctor, you know the answer to that question. It's your trade, after all."

"I'm not a painter." My attempt at levity comes out sounding leaden.

"The applying of a mirror to the soul," he says. "Surely there is some skill involved."

His words are like hard little tongs on a raw nerve.

Bertram grows tall in his chair—as if raising himself, while sitting, to full height.

"I've thought all these things many times before," he says. "Sitting here, in your office, with you. Surely, Dr. Harrison, you have, too."

I can feel my own eyes wavering. I try to hold his gaze but find I cannot; I attempt to disguise my looking away as a casual glance toward the window.

"But today," he continues, "I feel it more strongly than ever: the secret behind the mirror."

I can feel his steely eyes.

"Perhaps a whole box load of secrets."

It is late, again, and I cannot go home. Unbearably restless, I cross to the window and see a strong wind at play; the branches of the willow tree gesture madly. A twig scrapes at the glass, setting my teeth on edge. I squint into the shadows; something is moving beneath the willow tree.

A man: dressed in dark clothing and crouched among the low-hanging branches. Instinctively, I draw back from the window.

One drink too many—or perhaps I dozed, the vision only a remnant of dream. I peer sidelong out the window, then draw back in alarm; the man has moved closer, he is crouched right outside the window. Still, I feel his eyes on me, clammy and unpleasant. He is wearing an unusual hat, the kind a hiker in snow might wear, with earflaps and a visor at the forehead.

How could the man have gotten past the guard at the bottom of the hill, or through the front gate, which is kept locked? I sidle back along the wall to my desk—I must call security. But I suddenly see myself from the outside, as if I am someone else, standing across the room and looking calmly, clinically, at the me who is sitting here, about to notify security about a frightening intruder with a clammy and unsettling gaze. Pouring bourbon into a tumbler, I take in a few deep breaths.

A sudden pounding at the door. I jump up from my seat, aware of an outbreak of sweat on my forehead and neck.

It is Bertram, bareheaded, shivering, and pale.

"I'm so sorry, Dr. Harrison." He is mumbling, his voice frantic.

"What are you doing off the hall?" I ask.

"Forgive me, Doctor. I've had the most terrible scare."

He sinks down in his usual chair.

"I've seen my brother," he says. "He's here. I saw him, out there on the grounds."

My own skin feels suddenly splashed with fear.

"Why don't you tell me how you happen to be walking the grounds at one in the morning?"

"I couldn't sleep," he says. "I got up to go to the dayroom and noticed that Nurse Goodrich was dozing in the nurses' station. The other night nurse must have been in the bathroom or coffee room—I didn't think it out. I just found myself walking past the station, and the next thing I knew, I'd left the ward and was heading down the stairs and out through the front door."

"What about the guard at the security desk?"

"I don't mean to get anyone in trouble. But he was also asleep—slumped over in his chair."

"Oh?" I say, though I feel as if Bertram is making the whole thing up.

"I had this hankering to be outside. It can get claustrophobic, being cooped up all the time. Always under somebody's gaze."

Resentment glimmers in Bertram's eyes.

"Might I remind you, Bertram, you are here voluntarily."

"I'm sorry, Doctor, but I find myself feeling very confused. It's not always easy to know what one wants. And when you're not in control of your life—" He breaks off.

"Yes?"

"Well, I find myself looking for someone to blame."

The veneer of deceit has gone from his voice.

"You were saying," I prompt.

"It felt good to be out there—the wind in my face. Good to be alone. But then the wind picked up—it took me unawares. I lost my footing—spun around awkwardly and fell. Landed on my arm—it's actually hurting pretty badly."

Only now do I notice that Bertram is nursing his left arm.

"We should get that looked at," I say.

"Tomorrow morning will be fine," Bertram says.

Unlocking the cabinet behind my desk, I retrieve a bottle of aspirin and pour a glass of water from the carafe on the credenza.

"Here," I say, handing him the water and pills. "This should help."

Bertram swallows the aspirin and then continues. "It's true, I hurt my arm, but I was quite alert. I suddenly realized that I wasn't alone. It was as if something was thrown at me, and that this was what knocked me down."

"Thrown at you?"

Bertram's face creases with distress.

"*The past,* Dr. Harrison. It came back at me like it was happening all over again. Only worse, because I knew what was going to happen."

He scans my face, as if searching for a way to proceed.

"The past," I say gently.

"Then I was running. Holding my twisted arm. Like I was trying to run right out of the past. For one second, I thought that maybe I'd succeeded. But then I saw him. Some distance away—standing under a tree, almost blocked out by the shadows of the branches and leaves."

"Bertram," I say. "You were distressed. You're injured. It's windy and dark. Perhaps it was just a shadow?"

"How could I not know my own brother? Though he was changed—very changed. It's been eighteen years since my mother and I left Germany. There was something disturbing about his eyes."

Bertram is looking at me with urgency. "He seemed like a dead man, come back to life."

It would be nearly impossible for anybody to break onto the grounds—to pass the sentry in the guardhouse down by the road, to enter through gates that are kept locked. The fence encircles the entire hospital property, including the large patch of woods, the deserted area on the far side made more forbidding by the steep drop beyond—what the patients refer to as "the gorge." Although I suppose the fence could be scaled. Or could Bertram just be imagining things? But then, I saw the man myself. Perhaps Bertram is himself the intruder—all of this an elaborate playing out of his internal, psychological drama.

"He's not the same person," Bertram says. "He wants me gone, I am certain of it."

"Why would he want you gone?"

"My brother did terrible things during the War."

"What does that have to do with you?"

"He knows that I could turn him in."

"Why would you turn him in?"

Bertram's face transforms.

"Because he's a war criminal. And war criminals must be punished."

"What did your brother do?" I ask.

"Unspeakable things."

"How do you know?"

I feel as though I am no longer looking at Bertram; I am sitting with a stranger.

"You ask a lot of questions," he snaps.

"I've made you angry," I say mildly.

"How I feel is not exactly the point," he says.

"No?"

"Doctor, you are failing to grasp the situation."

"What is the situation?"

"Can I put it more plainly?" Bertram jumps up from his seat. "My life is in danger. My brother—he wants to kill me."

"Bertram, please sit down."

He suddenly looks bewildered. "You don't believe me, do you?" he says, falling back into his seat. "You don't believe my brother was here. You don't believe I'm in danger."

"I'm not sure what I believe," I say.

"I don't know what I'll do if you stop believing me," Bertram whispers.

"Why?" I ask. "Why is that so important?"

"Do you know what it's like to wonder if everything you believe is nothing but madness?"

"No," I say softly. "I can't say that I do."

Bertram's gaze is uncanny: as if he's reaching into me and dredging up the memory of Delilah, bringing her back from the dead. Her face: not as I last saw her but as she was when we first met on the admitting hall. We were young—almost the same age, in fact.

"Doctor?" Bertram asks. His voice is barbed with anxiety.

"Yes?"

"What are you thinking?"

I feel myself reddening, look down at the glass-covered desk between us and place my hands on the cool surface, as if the unscratchable strength of the glass might pour up into my fingers and reclaim me.

I saw him, I want to say. *Bertram, I saw your brother, too.*

"What was he wearing?" I ask.

"Who do you mean?"

"You said you saw your brother. What was he wearing?"

For a moment, Bertram's face goes blank. Then, he lifts his good hand and gestures toward his head.

"He had on an unusual hat. Something with earflaps. And a black coat—I think it was a raincoat. It made his body disappear against the trunk of the tree."

"I see," I say.

"There's something you're not saying," Bertram says, a suspicious glint in his eyes. "Whatever your failings as a doctor, I never thought you would actually lie."

"You feel that I'm turning on you, too. As if perhaps I also intend to do you harm." I loathe myself the instant the words are out of my mouth. The cheapest of all psychiatric ploys: blame it back on the patient, plant the seed that he can be certain of nothing, that he must question all of

his perceptions. My mouth feels rubbery and controlled by some external force; I am aware of its awful, patronizing expression.

"You're looking at me oddly," Bertram whispers.

"How do you feel I'm looking at you?"

"Like I'm—"

"Yes?"

"Like I'm some sort of a specimen."

In the dining hall, I join Matilda, who is seated alone at a table by the window.

"I've been meaning to ask you," she begins. "When Dr. Fairbairn visits, could we hold the case conference in the auditorium so that we have more space? The student nurses were very disappointed when told there wouldn't be room for them to attend. It's not often we have such an important person visiting Shadowbrook."

"I'm afraid it might be a bit much for the patient," I say.

"They do complain of feeling ogled, don't they, even when it's held in the conference room." She looks thoughtful. "Weren't you at Craiglockheart Hospital yourself at one time?"

"Yes, after the First War. It's where I did my training."

"Was Dr. Fairbairn a teacher of yours, then?"

"He's a few years older than I am; we trained together—and he supervised me for a time after he qualified. He's been a great influence on my thinking."

"Perhaps you've also been an influence on his." She gives a shy smile. "His article in the latest issue of *The British Journal* owes a lot to one of yours."

"Oh?" I am taken aback by Matilda's familiarity with my work. "Which article do you mean?"

"The one on the role of trauma in the development of as-if personality. When you comb through what he is saying, Fairbairn's premise is really the same one you put forward. I know he references you, but without that key element, he wouldn't have an article at all." Matilda is holding her fork in midair; she seems to have forgotten her food.

"I see it more as teamwork," I say. "We build on each other's ideas.

I'm sure I've had ideas that are more indebted to Fairbairn—and others—than I realize when I'm writing. In any case, it's kind of you to say."

"Not kind . . . truthful." Her eyes shine with admiration. "Your section on the ways in which different kinds of patients experience *time* has stayed with me. I find myself thinking about it, when I'm on the ward."

"I owe that to the phenomenologists."

"You're being modest."

"No, Matilda. Not modest—just truthful."

Again, that shy smile; how very different she seems here, away from the ward: so open and relaxed.

"Have you decided who you'll do at the case conference?"

"I was thinking of presenting Bertram Reiner."

"Oh?" Matilda reaches for her napkin and wipes her mouth.

"You seem surprised."

"No, not really. But don't we usually present our most challenging patients to outside consultants? I suppose I think of Mr. Reiner's case as rather straightforward."

"I'm afraid his illness is a bit more complicated than I'd initially thought. As a matter of fact, I wanted to discuss something with you that concerns Mr. Reiner's treatment."

Nurse O'Halahan and Percy Fenton are taking their seats at a nearby table; I nod in greeting and then turn back to Matilda.

"It's a rather delicate matter. Perhaps we'd best discuss it in my office."

"By all means," she says.

A sunbeam strikes the crystal jug of water on the table between us, releasing a shard of light.

"I could come when I get off the afternoon shift." Something wavers in her eyes—as if she's involved in some inner, private calculation.

As the afternoon drifts by, I find myself frequently checking the clock and realize I'm counting down the time until change of shift. When the knock finally comes, I suppress a flutter of excitement.

Opening the door, I see anxiety unmasked in Matilda's face.

"I don't mean to be mysterious," I say, ushering her in. "It's just that I had a visit, very late last night, from Bertram Reiner. At one o'clock in the morning, in fact; he said he'd been out walking, which you'll agree is extremely out of the ordinary."

Matilda reddens.

"I can't imagine how that happened." She looks away. "Let me think who was on night duty . . . Mr. Reiner does have grounds privileges, but the middle of the night! Heavens, he knows better than that."

"He said one nurse was sleeping, and the other was out of sight. The security guard at the main entrance—sleeping as well, according to the patient. Snoring, in fact."

Matilda starts—apparently at the word *patient.* "I can assure you, Dr. Harrison, I will take the matter up immediately with my staff."

"We should also go over night security procedures at the general staff meeting. It's not the first time Mr. Reiner's gone walking about at night. We've been lucky with him. But even on an open ward, we can't be too careful."

Matilda is biting her lower lip, such a sweet gesture.

"Yes, Dr. Harrison, of course."

"Please," I say. "Call me Henry."

The sleeplessness has returned. At home, afraid to get into bed, I remain in my study in the grip of a feverish exhaustion. As the hours leach away, I become powerless against the images from Emanuel's manuscript that during the day I manage to push away.

They are banging on doors, which open to reveal pale faces. The policemen call out: *Run Jews! As fast as you can! That way! Yes, over there, up there! As fast as you can!* Emanuel notices that Wilhelm's eyes are lit with the fun of sport. Now, a small boy, maybe four years old; his mother pushes him ahead. *Yankele, run!* she shouts. He is wearing a bib to protect his shirt. He starts to run—pulls at the bib, trying to take it off. *Run, Yankele!* The boy stumbles. Wilhelm raises his gun and *crack,* a perfect shot to his back, right between the shoulder blades. *Yankele!* The mother is running to her boy—she is carrying something. Wilhelm calls out, in Polish: *You can run faster! Let's see you run! That way!* He gestures in the direction away from the boy. Emanuel thinks Wilhelm will give the woman a chance to escape, to live—if she can run away from her dead boy. But she comes right at them, her hair flying behind her. Wilhelm lowers his gun. *He's going to let her go,* Emanuel thinks.

Wilhelm moves quickly. He grabs the thing from the woman's arms as she flies by, throws it into the air—he is tossing a clay pigeon. Up, a perfect arc. Gun swings up, another perfect arc; bullet hits its mark at the height of the object's flight. It freezes for a second in the air and then dives and lands at the feet of its mother. The woman, looking back and forth between the two lifeless forms: her young son up ahead, crumpled, the bib clutched in his hand, and the baby at her feet, face up in a spreading pool of blood. Emanuel sees that the baby is wearing a hand-knit cardigan; he notices the intricate pattern of cables.

I drift off, stretched out on the couch. But sleep offers little relief; I tumble from Emanuel's horrors into the old, haunting dreams of Delilah. I awaken with a start at three in the morning, stiff from my awkward position, dream fragments swirling, filled with the longing that pained and enthralled me back then. A memory I'd forgotten; the time, after a meeting with Delilah and her parents, that I'd walked the family down to the hospital lobby and was saying good-bye. It had been a difficult session; Delilah's mother's eyes were red from weeping. *I only want my baby to come home,* she kept saying. Delilah stood stone-still; I could feel her mortification. I fumbled for words of reassurance, still raw in the role of *doctor,* and a little ashamed to be offering advice to people twice my age. *We will take good care of your daughter,* I heard myself say, and *She couldn't be in better hands.* Inwardly, I cringed at my words; I sounded like a novice priest. But Delilah's mother was nodding gratefully; her father patted his wife's shoulder and looked at a loss. *We can't thank you enough, Doctor.*

Just then, I realized there was someone else in the lobby, seated on the banquette closest to the door. Ursula, so young, looking lovely in her yellow spring coat, hands tidily folded in her lap, a proud, patient smile on her lips. I had the terrible impulse to run: to bound out through the imposing doors and on down the stairs, all the way to the front gate. Ursula must have seen something in my face; her eyes grew wide with confusion. I was still mumbling platitudes, Delilah's father was pumping my hand. I could feel Delilah's alarm; her eyes moved slowly, tentatively, from my face across the distance of the grand lobby to Ursula's, back and forth. I watched as Delilah's parents made their way down the front stairs and across the gravel. They turned in the direction of the visitors' parking and disappeared from view. I felt horribly stranded, there on the

parquet floor, caught between my wife, sitting on the banquette in her yellow coat, and the patient beside me, Delilah, whom I secretly adored.

When Bertram enters my office this afternoon, dressed with his usual care, his eyes are rheumy, as if he is suffering from a cold. His arm is in a sling—nothing more, it turned out, than a sprain.

"You seem distressed."

His face flashes with irritation.

"I've irritated you," I say.

"You're quite the observer." His voice is clipped.

I feel the rise of exasperation. "What have I done to annoy you?" I ask.

"Everything's changed, and you're still acting like the perfectly controlled psychiatrist."

"I'm not sure I know what else I can do but carry on with the treatment."

"Are you aware of how ridiculous that sounds?" Bertram's voice is restrained. "*I saw him.* Here, on the grounds. I saw my brother. I have no doubt that he's determined to harm me."

I sit silently.

"Well?" he insists, peering at me closely. "Don't you have any response?"

"We don't have all the answers, Bertram," I calmly remark.

"Well, then, *what's the point?* Why go through the charade?"

"I don't see it as a charade."

"How *do* you see it, then?"

"The same as any human endeavor, I suppose. Stumbling about in the dark. The occasional moment of discovery." This sounds mealymouthed, even to me.

Bertram springs up from his seat; the muscles of his neck are pulled tight.

"It's not a game," he says. "We're not here for your edification."

"Sit down, Bertram."

"I don't stand or sit at your pleasure, Doctor. I'm not an entertainment, and I'm also not a pet."

"Okay, Bertram," I say. "Perhaps you'd like to enlighten me as to how you see yourself." The irritation in my own voice surprises me.

Bertram takes a step backward and sits down. "I'm sorry," he says.

He is silent for a moment.

"Who can blame you? A lot of what I say sounds more than half-crazy. Cloaks and daggers: long-lost German brother lying in wait to stab me in the heart."

"I don't see this as a game," I say. "I truly believe I can help you gain a certain perspective on things."

"There are some things for which there is no gaining of perspective."

"Like what?"

"Like what the Nazis did to their own countrymen."

"You've taken that on, haven't you?"

"What do you mean?"

"You feel responsible."

"I *am* responsible."

"You're responsible for the Nazis' crimes?"

"Yes."

"Why is that?"

"You forget, Doctor. My father fought for the Kaiser. And my brother, as you know, is a Nazi. He did unspeakable things."

Again that sideways glance.

"How do you know what your brother did?"

"I read the papers, like everyone else. What they did is no longer a secret. Though, if you want my opinion, it was never quite the secret everybody now claims that it was."

He leans forward, the suspiciousness in his face blooming unpleasantly.

"There was a conspiracy of silence—people knew what was going on, long before Pearl Harbor. Let me ask you this. Why is it that the Allies bombed the hell out of every second German city but left the railway tracks to Auschwitz intact? I mean, why would *America* have wanted to risk anything for the *Jews*?"

"What is it—specifically—that you think your brother did?"

"The same things they all did."

"Like what, exactly?"

He squints at me. "What are you, Doctor? A voyeur? Why would you

have me rehearse the filthy secrets that haunt me? For me, there is no distance, no getting away to somewhere else. Only the awful, sickening truth."

"A truth for which you are culpable."

Bertram's nod is almost imperceptible.

"I've been thinking," I continue. "Perhaps another course of hydro-therapy might be helpful."

Bertram addresses his response to the window. "Have you ever had one of those treatments?" he asks.

"No, I haven't."

"How do you imagine them to be?" he continues. "Sitting for hours in a canvas straitjacket, submerged in water. Bored beyond reckoning. As if someone had played a dreadful trick with time and made it stop. They say the oil helps the puckering, but I can assure you it doesn't. It feels like you've been sucked all over by leeches."

"It's not a straitjacket," I say. "It's a canvas hammock. And I recall that you found it soothing. I remember you saying it calmed you down."

"I did? I said that?"

"Yes, Bertram, you did."

He is silent for several long minutes.

"Very well, if you think it might help."

"I'll write an order for a five-day course," I say, reaching for my order pad. "I think it will do you some good."

The patients hoot good-naturedly, and Mr. Rutherford, head orderly of Hall Eight and easily the tallest staff member at Shadowbrook, waves a hand high in the air, then returns to fiddling with the projector, which is famous for its rickety starting mechanism.

"Patience, ladies and gentlemen. Patience," Rutherford booms.

"No shortage of *patients* here!" someone calls from the back of the room. Laughter erupts.

"You'll see just how many if you don't get that thing going!" calls another. "You're big, but there's strength in numbers!" Gaiety ripples through the audience: smiling faces, friendly arm punches, a contagious echo of laughter.

"Hold your horses!" Rutherford, usually serious to a fault, gives a quick grin, revealing large, white teeth.

I haven't been to movie night in a long time; almost every seat in the auditorium is filled, the patients freshly showered and neatly dressed. Some puff on cigarettes or pipes; faces are expectant and bright. Scattered among the patients are orderlies, nurses, and doctors in white uniforms or coats. The projector goes *put-put-put* like a car that won't start. Rutherford repositions the reel of film, and this time the machine gives off an encouraging purr. A cheer goes up.

"It's a go!" he calls out, and the crowd settles. Someone turns off the light, and the room flickers with ghostly light.

I'd planned to stay only a few minutes but find myself absorbed in the picture. The room is silent now; collective attention pulses toward the screen. They are an uninhibited audience—sighing and laughing and letting out *aah*s of surprise or fear when the moment calls for it. *Everybody's troubles at bay*, I think, *including my own.*

The screen goes white, the film's tail flaps as the reel turns. Someone turns on the overhead light, and Rutherford jumps up to attend to the projector. The chatter starts up—excited reactions to the film, people calling across the room to their friends; some rise to stretch their legs or take a bathroom break, and orderlies weave among the patients, lighting cigarettes clamped between teeth. I remain at the back of the room.

Matilda approaches me.

"Haven't seen you at movie night for a while," she says pleasantly.

"I'm an Anne Wendon fan," I say. "And I've always loved horses. Did you know that, after Lassie, the stallion who plays Black Beauty—I believe his real name is Fury—is the highest paid animal in Hollywood?"

"That's a useful bit of information," she says, then smiles, turning to look fondly at the audience. "I thought they'd balk at yet another movie with an animal lead, but they seem to love it."

The patients mill about in small groups, joined here and there by a staff member. I glimpse little dramas of coyness and flirtation, feel the heightened emotion that typically marks mixed gatherings. Cuthbert strolls by, arm in arm with the new patient, Mr. Featherstone, who believes the hospital is a concentration camp and is emaciated from months of self-imposed starvation. I'm told he whimpers pitifully through his daily ordeals of forced feeding.

"Are you enjoying the picture, gentlemen?" I ask.

"Mr. Featherstone's finding it a trial," Cuthbert says. "I've been attempting to put it in a different light for him. I've seen the movie before, but I noticed something this time: Black Beauty is no dumb beast. The signs are unmistakable. He's every bit the intuitive thinker. Watch his eyes—there's nothing mechanical about his mind when he races; it's all just pure intuition."

Featherstone scans the room, his hollow eyes startled. Cuthbert leans toward me and whispers, conspiratorially, "It's taking his mind off things. Distraction *from* distraction *by* distraction—that's my aim. It never fails." He turns to Matilda and gives a glowing smile; for a moment, he looks somehow holy.

Matilda pats Mr. Cuthbert's arm affectionately, and the two men head off.

"I understand Mr. Reiner is to receive some more hydrotherapy," Matilda says casually.

"Yes. I thought we'd start him up tomorrow."

"But he's been doing so well."

"He has been doing well on the hall, but in our sessions, he's becoming increasingly agitated. I suspect he's slipping into paranoia; some hydrotherapy may settle things down."

"I reread that article you wrote. About war neurosis." Matilda gives me a sidelong glance, and I sense she is trying to hide something. "The first time around, I missed quite a few of the ideas."

I laugh. "Funny you should say that. I felt the same way when I recently reread it myself."

Matilda gives one of her rare, radiant smiles. "Perhaps that attests to the brilliance of it."

"I'd say it has more to do with the diagnosis itself. And with the fact that we've both by now had quite a lot of experience treating these kinds of patients. I often think that the more I know about treating a disorder, the greater the mystery—and the more there is to discover."

Matilda shakes her head. "I'll stick to my explanation." There is tenderness in her voice. "I wonder if it will ever really make sense to me."

"If what will make sense?"

Her hand strays to her breastbone and forms a gentle fist. "What we're trying to do here."

There is a fragile little flame in the back of her eyes. "I wish I knew as much as you do, Dr. Harrison. You always seem so wise."

I have the feeling she wants to say more.

"Perhaps I'm just good at seeming wise."

"No," she says slowly. "I'm a bit of a divining rod when it comes to such things. And I've seldom been proven wrong."

Rutherford has the second reel on; this time, the projector starts up first try. Everyone hurries back to their seats; the lights go down.

Matilda remains standing beside me; too aware of her proximity to lose myself in the picture, I find myself longing for the decanters in my study, desperate to steal away and slake my thirst. But I am held by this room, which brims with hidden troubles and illicit urges, and most of all with the disconcertingly compelling presence of Matilda beside me. I feel suspended, mesmerized by the silvery images and the unearthly, shadowy light.

A loud collective gasp goes up when Black Beauty takes a fall. Anne Wendon hovers over him; the camera pans across her anxious face. Someone jumps up from his seat; a low, shrill squeal skims above the sea of heads, accompanied by the rhythmic sound of a single pair of clapping hands. The black-and-white light flickers over Mr. Featherstone, emaciated, tricked out in his Sunday best, standing and applauding, his gaunt face lit from within by ecstatic distress.

It is the third day of Bertram's hydrotherapy treatment; I take the long way to Nichols Cottage to visit him. I pass the men's occupational therapy building and glance in through the windows at the print shop. Light falls through the leaded panes, throwing bright yellow squares over the enormous metal wheels and their sturdy wood and iron bases; they seem like dormant life-forms, awaiting their moment.

The November air promises early snow. I take the path winding toward the edge of the main lawn; down on the lower playing field, a game of badminton is in progress, patients and orderlies wearing winter coats, their movements awkward. The players hold the flimsy racquets aloft, their breath coming in frosty, white puffs.

I reach Nichols; beyond the wooden doors, the warm air is filled with

the continuous hiss of steam pipes. I pass the curved stairway, with its ornate polished banister, and take the service stairs leading down to the treatment rooms. Below, the lights are kept dim. I pass by the cold pack room and glimpse, through the open door, two patients stretched out on metal cots, bound, like mummies, in wet sheets, each watched over by an attendant. The two attendants are engaged in conversation; both are smiling roundly. The patients' teeth chatter loudly. I continue on past the insulin coma therapy room. Through the glass panel in the door, I see a nurse drifting alongside a row of beds in which patients lie, some immobile, like corpses prepared for a viewing, others twitching or thrashing. Another nurse attends to a patient in the grip of violent spasms.

In the hydrotherapy room, my footsteps echo loudly: floor, walls, ceiling, all covered in white tile. The air hums steadily with the swishing sound of circulating water, pumped in and out by the metal contraption fitted at one end of the bath and attached to a shiny collection of pipes that snake to the wall. Bertram is the only patient in the room; I tell the nurse to take a break and, after he leaves, sit beside the bath. With his body suspended in the oversize tub within the canvas sling, and covered by a tightly drawn waterproof sheet, Bertram's head is the only part of him that is visible. He strains his neck in my direction.

"Day three," Bertram says. His voice sounds surprisingly normal.

"How is it going?"

"I'm a giant prune," he says without humor. "But it hasn't been unpleasant this time. I've been feeling floaty and calm, like my body has disappeared. It's given me time to think—and also time *not* to think. I like that best."

Bertram's voice does, indeed, sound calm, though I see angst in his eyes.

"Would you like to talk about any of it?"

"Which part? The thinking or the not thinking?"

"Either one."

Bertram looks at the wall in front of him, with its impressive colony of metal pipes. "There's something I've been meaning to tell you," he says. "I've almost brought it up several times, but it never seems like the right time. I've not been entirely straightforward with you."

I stifle a laugh; after all the cat-and-mouse we've played over the last few months, it strikes me as a comical thing to say.

"Something happened a week or so ago," he says. "Something alarming. I woke up in the middle of the night to find myself in another patient's room."

"Have you been known to sleepwalk in the past?"

"I did, on occasion. When I was a child."

"Not since then?"

"Perhaps every now and then," he says.

"You were saying . . . a week or so ago . . ."

"When I came to, I was confused. I was in Mr. Featherstone's room, by his bed, with no idea how I got there."

It would be near impossible for a patient to walk about in the middle of the night without the night staff being aware of it.

"I had a terrible feeling inside," he continues. "I don't know how to describe it. I was looking at Featherstone, he was asleep, but he didn't seem like a person. He seemed—I don't know, like an object."

Bertram has swiveled his head and is looking directly at me, his gray eyes dilated in the dim light.

"What was going through your mind?"

"It's going to sound a little crazy," he says quietly.

"Go on."

"I heard her voice."

"Whose voice?" I ask.

"Rosamund's."

"What was she saying?"

"She was begging me to stop the pain. She was lying naked on a table in an awful, cold room. A scientist was doing some awful experiment on her, and she was begging *me* to stop the pain." His voice sinks until it is almost inaudible. "I couldn't bear to see her suffering."

"But then, you woke up."

"That's just it, Dr. Harrison! I was so confused! Even though I could see plainly that it was Featherstone there, in his bed, I also really *believed* it was Rosamund on a table, begging me to release her from pain."

Bertram says nothing for a while. Then, his face darkens. "I would kill him, if I had the chance," he says.

"Who would you kill if you had the chance?"

"My brother," he says thickly. "He may as well have sent Rosamund to her death himself. Rounded her up, shot her in the head."

"Bertram," I say. "You came to the hospital because you feared your brother intended to do *you* harm."

"Yes, that's what I told you."

"Just now you said you would kill him if given the chance."

"When I saw my brother here, on the grounds, I realized I had known all along he would come after me."

"There's something I must ask you," I say.

"Yes?" he replies mildly.

"Did you come here because you feared for your own life? Or because you feared you would commit a murder?"

Bertram stares at the tiled wall.

"Both are true," he says flatly.

The nurse appears at the door, and I rise.

"I'll come again tomorrow," I say. "We can talk more about this then."

Bertram doesn't reply.

Matilda seemed surprised, but not displeased, when I suggested at change of shift that she join me in my office for a nightcap.

Now, pouring a brandy, I swirl it gently for a minute, then hand it to her.

"Do you mind?" she asks and draws a slim silver case from her pocket.

"I didn't know you smoked."

"Bad habit I picked up in the Philippines," she says. "I try to keep it to a minimum."

Before I can reach for a match, Matilda has struck one herself and is holding it to the tip of her cigarette. She draws in deeply, leaning back in the upholstered armchair.

"What made you choose psychiatry, after you got back?" I ask.

"You might recall I had the dubious honor of a publicity tour to help sell war bonds. It left me desperate to return to work that felt important."

"But you might have returned to any branch of nursing. Why psychiatry?"

I see that Matilda is weighing something—which version, perhaps, of the truth to tell.

"I saw a lot of people die in Bataan and Corregidor. I suppose I learned that dying is not only a physical business." She pauses, as if remembering something. "I daresay the physical part of it is secondary."

She gently taps ash into the glass ashtray on the coffee table.

"I get the feeling there was more to it," I say.

Matilda lets out a little sigh. "It's a complicated business."

I'm about to say "I see," or "Go on," but I catch myself. "Yes it is, isn't it."

"I wouldn't be sitting here now," she says, "if it weren't for the fact that the closest friend I ever had fell apart. People don't talk about battle fatigue among military nurses, but I can assure you, it was not uncommon."

"What was her name?"

"Shirley."

"What happened to her in the end?"

"She's never been able to return to work."

Matilda tells me how she and Shirley had labored together for months in a hospital rigged up in the open jungle, where wild monkeys stole their food and snakes dropped from the trees into patients' cots. They were overworked and hungry, and suffered constant strafing; she describes the way that sometimes, after a raid, you would see dripping, blown-off limbs hanging in the trees, still in pajama legs and sleeves.

"Shirley fell in love with a young soldier. Nurses weren't allowed to marry, but by that time the chaplain rode roughshod over the regulations. I made her a wedding gown out of a torn parachute; she looked beautiful in it. We had a clear day—no rain, no raids, just sunshine. The chaplain married them on the banks of the river. Someone brought in a box of mangoes, and we moved a tent by the river and chipped in extra hours to give Shirley the day off for her honeymoon. Three weeks later, her new husband was killed in a raid. Shirley was devastated, of course, but for a while we thought she would be okay."

Matilda draws on her cigarette and then carefully taps off the ash.

"When it became clear that Bataan was going to fall, they told us we were being moved to Corregidor. It was impossible to move the patients—we had more than two thousand at that point; the cots stretched out into the jungle as far as the eye could see."

I don't normally notice the sound of the gold clock on my desk; now, its slow ticking seems to fill the room.

"It was the hardest thing I've ever done." Her voice sinks to a whisper. "Abandoning all those patients. We knew what the Japanese would do to them—terrible, *terrible*. They knew it, too, we could see it in their eyes. It was more than I could bear, but there was nothing we could do. Shirley was still holding it together, working her shifts, though she wasn't really there, not the Shirley I'd known. It was only after we got to Corregidor that she snapped."

"What made her snap?" I ask.

"The Japanese were bombing us seven, eight times a day. Even in the tunnels, under seventy feet of rock, the pounding was sometimes unbearable. During operations, we'd have to watch for bits of falling plaster. Shirley developed a kind of phobia about that; she'd shake all over whenever plaster shook loose.

"We were cleaning out a soldier's leg one day—he had gas gangrene, the leg was the size of a hog. Close to the bone, we found maggots; we were scooping them out when the pounding began. That's when Shirley fell apart; she started screaming, just stood there staring at the maggots in her hand and making the most awful sound.

"The next day, she didn't get up. In the evening, I dragged her to the mess; it took endless coaxing just to get her to choke down a few bites of weasly oatmeal. I made her walk up and down the main tunnel for exercise; she clung to my arm like a drowning person."

"Sounds like she really was drowning," I say gently.

"We were all drowning."

I feel an urge to reach across: to touch her arm or take her hand.

"I don't know how we survived, any of us," she continues. "At the time, I felt sure none of us would make it. There was a lot of talk about what was going to happen when the island fell to the Japanese. Not *if*, but *when*. Nanking was on everybody's mind. We were terrified, but we kept up our duties, as if the future would just be more of the same. And of course, Corregidor fell; everyone was captured and sent to prisoner of war camps. I was one of the lucky few who got away—because of Shirley."

Matilda rises and crosses to the window. "I don't know how you get any work done in this office; the grounds are so captivating from here."

"It is a challenge sometimes."

With her back toward me, I am able to gaze at her openly; I trace the lines of her form—the slim ankles, shapely calves, the slightly yielding curve of her spine.

"How do you manage it?" Her voice sounds different: husky, unguarded. "All the responsibility."

"The same way we all do, I suppose." Why is Matilda speaking to me this way?

"It can't always be easy."

"No, it isn't always easy."

She turns, holds my gaze, her eyes unwavering. I feel again that heat-edness between us. Only here, alone with her in my office, the feeling has a dangerous edge.

"You were telling me about Corregidor," I prompt.

"Yes, I was." She walks slowly back to her seat.

"How did you escape?"

"We were on tenterhooks, waiting for the invasion. And then one morning, early, my commanding nurse came to get me. She'd had news from General Wainwright that a submarine was coming in. At that point, we were about seventy nurses. If the submarine got through, there was only room onboard for eleven. It was clear Shirley would never survive capture; and in the condition she was in, she posed a risk to everyone else. We knew what the Japanese were capable of; having a loose cannon would only make things worse. So Shirley was on the list, but someone had to care for her, so my name was on the list, too."

Matilda has let down her guard; I find myself riveted.

"I'll never forget the sight of the *Spearhead*, rising from the water," she says. "The sky was full of bombers; we didn't think we'd make it. A couple of corpsmen rowed us out. And then, we were up on deck and down the hatch. Shirley went ahead of me, and when I got to the bottom of the ladder, I found her in a heap. I told her it was all behind us. But I was wrong. It wasn't behind Shirley. She never left, not really. She probably never will."

"But you did," I say. "You were one of the lucky ones."

"Yes," Matilda says uncertainly, her eyes glistening with anguish. "I suppose I was."

"Being a survivor poses its own difficulties," I say.

"You say that as if you know from personal experience."

"I served in the First War. The finest men I ever knew—"

"Yes?"

"My Army buddies were the best friends I ever had."

"How have they fared?"

I hesitate. "I'm the only one who made it back."

She looks at me boldly, telling me something without words, crossing some boundary, changing things between us. I am taken aback by her fearlessness.

"How awful," she says. "You were surely very young."

"Yes, I was."

"Your family must have been tremendously relieved—that you survived, against such terrible odds."

An unexpected lump of emotion rises in my throat; I find I'm unable to speak.

"I'm sorry." Her voice is tender. "It's really none of my business."

I clear my throat. "Don't be sorry. It's just not something I'm accustomed to talking about. Both of my parents died while I was fighting at the front. But then, there was so much death; it was almost the normal state of affairs."

Matilda is not fooled by the attempt to deflect my grief.

"It's terrible, isn't it," she says. "When tragedy becomes the norm."

Outside, the sky is dimming; shadows hang in the room. I do not move to switch on the lamps.

"Survival is a funny thing," Matilda continues. "The body goes on, but the spirit sort of leaks away." Her voice breaks slightly on the words.

"I've always thought the spirit more enduring than the body."

"Yes," Matilda says.

"The body can be beyond saving—I can't tell you how many soldiers I saw during the First War staring death in the face whose spirits shone, right up until the very last. We might be helpless when it comes to saving the body." The lush stillness of the room pours between us, bringing us closer. "But the spirit is another matter entirely."

"Perhaps you're right."

An unexpected fantasy intrudes, something from a movie I once saw—a nurse, pulling off her cap, releasing her hairpins, shaking loose a halo of shiny hair.

"Sometimes, I feel as if it's all still happening." Matilda exhales a long stream of smoke. "Do you ever feel that way?"

"You mean, as if the war's not over?"

She gives a quick nod.

"I think I know what you mean."

"Do you?" She gives me a searching look. "Sometimes a memory will pop up—only it's not like a memory. It's more like there's another reality happening at the same time as this one, and I'm peeking through an invisible window and watching it happen all over again."

"It's not always so easy to leave the past behind," I say carefully.

"I feel as if they're with me all the time—as if they'll be with me every day for the rest of my life."

"Who?"

"My boys," she replies, not taking her eyes off me. "There's one in particular who haunts me. His name was Charlie. He could not have known that I would carry him with me forever. Not that it's any consolation, I suppose. Death is death. Gone is gone . . ."

"Can you tell me about Charlie?"

Matilda describes the underground hospital set up in the Malinta tunnels of Corregidor. One section was cordoned off for the worst cases.

"There was a boy so damaged his own mother wouldn't have recognized him. He'd lost both legs and an arm. Even after everything I'd seen, the shape his body made in the bed came as a shock—the perfect flatness of the sheet beyond the buttocks. His remaining arm was almost completely paralyzed, half his face was burned away; he had only one eye and half a jaw. Feeding him was almost impossible; the mush kept sliding out.

"I was sitting with him when I realized he was trying to signal me— darting his eye and pointing his tongue toward the end of the bed and then back at me. He seemed to be indicating the chart, so I went to get it and looked at his name. 'Charlie Sullivan. Gambier, Ohio. Age eighteen.'

"I said his name out loud several times, and the boy seemed to get agitated, as if I was missing something. I closed my eyes, and a memory came back from that magical time after I got to Manila, just before Pearl Harbor. I was off duty, relaxing on the porch with Shirley. We heard someone whistling before we saw him, a young soldier with blond hair

coming around the corner, carrying a parcel of envelopes. He had a wide grin: I recalled his straight, white teeth. I'd never have known his name if Shirley hadn't asked.

"I'd found it—the memory he was willing me to find. I told him what I remembered—that he'd done mail drop that day, when I was sitting with Shirley on the porch. He just kind of melted with relief; he'd wanted me to remember him. He didn't want to die being *no one*." She lets out a tiny, agonized sigh. "I held his hand when he took his last breath."

I allow the silence to swell; it is filled with the steady, gentle sound of her breathing.

"I think about him a lot," she says finally. "Though I barely knew him."

"Perhaps you did know him, after all," I say.

"Yes, perhaps I did."

I eye my empty brandy glass. The moment feels fragile; I'm afraid to move, lest I shatter it.

"You presented some very moving cases in your *American Journal of Psychiatry* article," Matilda says. "Were you also interested in the war neuroses during the First War?"

"I wasn't much more than a boy, then—my medical studies still lay ahead. But yes, I was interested in the psychiatric side of things; of course, they thought about it differently then—for one thing, it was called 'shell shock.' "

The term jangles even now, after all these years. I, too, must endure the torment of an invisible window—and there he is, as ever, on the other side: Fergus, his eyes ablaze.

For six long months we carried stretchers together. The cold, at night, was brutal—in tents, in billets, in trenches; we huddled together, sometimes we slept in each other's arms. Everything about him became second nature to me: the singsong of his Irish brogue, the stealth of his smile. The feel of the stubble on his cheeks and chin, even the smell of his breath after a night without sleep. The odor that comes when mud mixes with sweat, and once, when I cleaned a wound in his thigh, the intimate smell of his blood.

Coming off his watch that time: thrusting his gas mask up close to my face. *We don't need these!* The frightening grin: a glistening slash

across his face. *Don't you see? Enemy tactic. To slow us down.* He hurled the mask into the mud, then leapt up, readying to stomp on it. I snatched it away, just in time. *It's not gas, I tell you! What sort of man fears liquefied honey?* He gave a frightening laugh and then began to shake and jerk. For a moment, I thought it some kind of joke—a parody of an Irish jig. But then, I saw the terror in his eyes. I reached out to hold him, but he threw me off. He jittered and twitched, his eyes staring, suddenly strange and unknown.

"Would you say there's been progress?" Matilda asks.

"That's a hard question to answer. We want to believe in progress, don't we—to suppose that, in science, we're always moving toward ever greater understanding. But if there's one thing we learned in the last war, it's that many directions are mistakes. We're just as often bumbling about in the dark as we are heading toward the light."

"Oh." She looks a little deflated.

"Not the kind of answer you were hoping for."

"No, I suppose not."

"But in a way, we have to believe we're making strides, or else we'd throw up our hands in despair."

"You're talking about hope," Matilda says.

"I believe I am."

"Are we still making mistakes—with patients suffering from war neurosis?"

"Well, what do *you* think?"

Something passes across Matilda's face—an attempt to mask what she is feeling. "I suppose I'm wondering if you feel psychiatry has come up with a cure."

"I can't speak for all of psychiatry. I can only talk about my own efforts."

"Are you developing a new model?" she asks.

"I'm doing the best I can." Now, I rise to fetch the brandy. "I'm toying with a new formulation. It's not ready to parade about, though at times I feel as if I'm inching toward clarity."

I remain standing above her, even after I've refilled her glass.

"Psychiatry has always been such a rational field. That may seem like an obvious thing to say. After all, how could there be progress in a scientific discipline without rigorous thought? But as you know, psychiatric

disturbance is all about the fracturing of the rational. Perhaps the cure might be found in the same kinds of processes."

Matilda's face is alive with interest.

"If you think about it," I continue, "so much of daily life is constructed on things that aren't the least bit rational. Marriage, having children—built on love. Or religious practice. Even the concrete things of this world—great buildings, for example—are born in the imagination. In a way, everything is built on mirages: nothing but ripples of heat."

"I'm not sure I follow," Matilda says.

I'm feeling the effects of the brandy. "If you'll forgive the familiarity," I say, "the best analogy I've come up with is that of sexual intimacy. What else in life is so unshakably real and yet at the same time so ephemeral? The ultimate example of the incomprehensible—and yet at the same time, perhaps the most grounding experience any of us will ever experience."

Matilda gives a knowing nod.

"For the shell-shocked soldier," I continue, "the disruption is at the mystical level. The illusory foundations are sucked to nothingness, and everything collapses. Why should the cure not therefore—by necessity—come from the same domain?"

"What would that mean concretely, as far as treating such patients is concerned?"

"This is where it becomes fuzzy. My hunch is that one has to try somehow to enter the patient's realm with him, to stand beside him, as it were, and make out the contours of the mirage."

Matilda's eyes waver.

"To join him," she says. "To really feel what he feels."

We sip our brandy. In the hazy warmth of the room, languid from the liquor, I have the sudden unpleasant image of myself as a giant mosquito hovering above Matilda, approaching a vital vein and preparing to lunge.

Chapter Three

*T*he cars lined up in the driveway remind me that Ursula is hosting her book club.

Inside, I hear animated voices coming from the living room. The women are seated around the coffee table, which holds finger sandwiches and strawberry shortcake; Ursula is pouring tea, her face lit with a smile. "Heaven knows, she was taking a risk," she is saying. "I can't imagine *what* she was thinking!"

They turn as one, seven pairs of eyes directed my way, the lively conversation cut off. On the coffee table, seven copies of *The Idiot,* each showing a painting of a crazed man, his hair a thicket of straw. I'm surprised by their choice; none of them seems very intellectual—I can't quite imagine this group discussing Dostoyevsky.

Ursula rises. "Hello, dear," she says stiffly, the relaxed smile gone.

The other women greet me, addressing me as Dr. Harrison.

"I'm sorry to disturb you, ladies. I left something here that I need, but I won't be a minute."

In my study, I gather my papers and then tidy my desk, aware that I am dallying. Finally, I head back into the hallway. The sounds from the living room are more sober; when I pass through, the women have their books open on their laps.

"I do hope you enjoy the rest of your discussion," I say.

Ursula sees me to the door. "Have a good afternoon, dear." She avoids my eye.

"And you." I pat her arm, regretting how perfunctory it feels, not knowing how to change that, wishing I could make things right.

Outside, a cold wind ruffles the tops of the trees. I should have attempted the kind of veiled, intimate farewell that husbands and wives exchange in front of an observing group. I imagine the sting for Ursula at having been treated little differently from the rest, women who exist for me as an interchangeable gaggle of faces and names.

When Bertram arrives for his session, he is wearing a smart gabardine jacket.

"You were right, Dr. Harrison," he says. "It's a trial, but those baths do help. Still, I'm happy the treatment's over."

Despite his careful appearance, there is something dark in his face. "We spend a lot of time blaming the Germans," he says, as if this were not an abrupt change of topic.

I raise my pen above a clean sheet of paper. "Should we not?"

"I was there, remember? I saw things. But the point is, I've discovered the root of it."

He looks at me expectantly. "Why aren't you writing down what I am saying?"

"I don't write down every word."

"So you decide what's important."

"That's not how I think of it."

"How do you think of it, Dr. Harrison?"

"As a map of our progress. Sometimes my memory lets me down."

This seems to satisfy him.

"The root of it," I prompt. "You were saying you think you've discovered what that is."

"There was a conspiracy of silence. Perhaps it's infectious, or perhaps mankind is just a disgusting breed. This willful silence went on from the beginning, right up until the end. It's going on still, I'm certain of it. Young people being raised in silence. *Let's just forget it all happened.*"

He pauses, lost in thought, and then continues. "As for our own blemish-free democracy, we knew what was going on long before any-

one cares to admit. We kept our mouths shut—it suited us. And now we keep talk of what we saw to a minimum. *Move on.* Build alliances. Why bring the perpetrators to justice when they're running the new order?"

"You said something earlier about being there, having seen things. I was wondering what you were thinking about specifically."

"I was thinking about the day we found the American soldiers."

He has spoken of this before—how after VE Day, he and his tank division came across the skeletally thin American soldiers, many of them of Jewish origin, who had survived a death march from their slave-labor camp.

"The truth is, Dr. Harrison, that as horrendous as their condition was, they were the most cheerful sight we saw in those weeks."

Bertram places his elbows on his knees and rests his head in his hands. "They won't leave me be," he says.

"Who?"

"Thousands of them. The ones who didn't make it."

I wait. When he speaks again, he keeps his eyes on his lap.

"Some were curled up in a fetal position. Others were on their knees, in a posture of prayer. Women, children, men, young and old. The Germans knew we were coming. They didn't want us to find these people in the camps. But they were Jews; the Germans couldn't stand for them to go on living. How is one supposed to understand that?"

He looks up. "Well, Doctor? You're a psychiatrist. You're supposed to have the answers."

"Am I?" I ask quietly.

"*I* certainly don't have any. I only know that they shot them at the side of the road. Days from liberation—days from the possibility of reclaiming some sort of life. The ones that couldn't make it up the hill were shot as they fell, a single bullet to the head. That's what we did to them. Shot them on the spot."

I catch Bertram's slip of the tongue. *That's what* we *did to them.*

"How am I supposed to live with this?" he pleads. "You're supposed to help me live with this."

"I'm wondering about something."

Bertram's eyes flash with anger. "I do wish you'd stop wondering things. If you want to ask a question, just ask it."

"You seem to feel responsible for their deaths. For the Jews who were killed at the side of the road."

Bertram sits up straight in his chair.

"Where would you draw the line?" he asks. "Where does responsibility begin and end for *you*?"

"There's no getting away from the horrors of the War. I'm not saying there is. But you were among the liberators—you freed concentration camp victims, you took charge of American prisoners of war. And yet you're focusing on the people you couldn't save—the people who were killed before you even got there."

"*Shaddai, Shaddai.*"

"Excuse me?"

Bertram's eyes seem to burrow inward, as if the bones of his face are somehow closing in around them.

"The true name of God—the unspeakable, ineffable truth of Him."

"What makes you think of this now?" I ask.

"It's what they call Him. Sometimes, looking into the pit, waiting for the bullet, they would say it. Sometimes they would recite the *Shema*—as much of it as they could get through. *Shema Yisrael, Adonai Elohenu, Adonai Ehud.* Hear, O Israel, the Lord our God, the Lord is One."

"Help me, Bertram," I say. "I don't know what you're talking about."

"A country can ask too much of a man," he whispers.

I leave the silence—allow it to grow and then subside.

"What are you thinking?" I venture after a time.

"You seem to refuse to talk about the scientists," he says.

"I'm not refusing to talk about them."

His words come more quickly and loudly. "Last time the subject came up . . . it seemed clear that you approve of the fact that our laboratories and universities are crawling with Nazis. That they're using data they collected torturing concentration camp victims to further the scientific aims of the United States government."

He squints, as if peering at me through fog. "Will you applaud when they put a man on the moon? Knowing that the way he got there was through experiments that carefully detailed how much physical pain a person can endure before lapsing into unconsciousness? Or at exactly what temperature a child freezes to death?"

"It troubles you greatly that those German scientists are working here."

"*Nazi* scientists. Does it not trouble you?"

"It is a complicated world," I say carefully. "You know as well as I do that if we hadn't co-opted them, the Russians would have."

"Yes." His eyes look glazed. He falls silent once more.

"What are you thinking?"

"I was just thinking how baffling it is," Bertram replies, the anger gone.

"How baffling what is?"

Bertram looks over to where my diplomas hang on the wall.

"All those years of training, all those degrees. And yet, you really don't seem to know all that much about any of this." His voice is not scornful; it is helpless. He glances about the room, looking forlorn. And then, he puts his head in his hands and I realize that Bertram is crying.

Tonight, in my office late again, the stillness outside is especially thick; I feel the dampness in my sinuses. From my window, I look into the darkness. Everything seems hidden—from itself, as well as from me. And then, a blur of movement; I feel a rise of anxiety at the memory of the intruder, the man Bertram felt certain was his brother. This time, I must call security.

There, again—a ghostly streak of white. Someone hurrying across the lawn. A woman, wearing a light-colored sweater. She turns; her face looks like a slender, moving flower. It is Matilda, heading toward the servants' entrance at the far end of the East Wing. The clock reads ten minutes past one.

The hallway is eerily still, and dim. Along the East Wing, down the stairs; I reach the ground floor, hear the quiet *click* of a latch at the end of the passageway. Gaining the door, I gently turn the handle and find myself on the darkened stairway that leads down to the underground passageways.

Belowground, the windowless mustiness disturbs me.

Footsteps up ahead.

I move as quietly as I can. The walls are stacked, floor to ceiling, with

desks, wooden chairs in a tower of stiff, rickety limbs; in the wan light, they take on the shapes of frozen beasts. Through one section, the hallway narrows where mattresses are piled, kept in place with a webbing of heavy twine. I strain to hear the soft footsteps, then pull up short. The sound of her movement has vanished; she seems to have disappeared.

A creaking. Footsteps again, but coming from the other direction—not Matilda's light step, but a heavier tread. Coming closer. I glimpse him for only a brief moment before he disappears behind a wall of bedside tables, into what appears to be a little alcove. Voices whispering; the creaking again like the groaning of old bedsprings, and then a soft silence that is not silence at all. Overcome by dizziness, I close my eyes and strain to hear what is happening. There are murmurs, then sighs and gentle moans.

Tears well behind my closed lids.

Another dark, closed-in space lurches up from the past. Me a child of twelve, curled on the floor of the closet in my room. The warm, slippery feel of the secret, *my* secret: the exquisite, vacuum-sealed privacy, my eye pressed to the wall. Once, hiding in the closet, away from my parents, I'd found a tiny hole, down by the floor. When I realized that my parents' room lay on the other side, I carefully picked at the plaster with my fingernail, enlarging it slightly to make a peephole. It worked perfectly; squinting in just the right way, I could see into their room. I learned that I had only a few minutes to gather intelligence; soon after entering their room, my parents would turn out the light. Undressing in the dark, they would climb into bed, my father falling asleep almost as soon as his head hit the pillow, my mother tossing and turning. Sometimes, she'd quietly rise and walk about, her slippered feet, barely visible in the darkness, drifting back and forth past the peephole. From time to time, she'd let out a hot, troubled sigh.

I found it exhilarating, being the watcher, hidden, unseen.

That day, on a whim—perhaps I sensed something?—I told my mother I'd be at a friend's after school but instead snuck home. From the end of the street, I saw my mother hunched over in the front garden, weeding. Cutting around to the alley behind our house, I climbed over the back fence and entered through the back door, then crept up to my room. I don't know how long I lay on the floor of the closet, my heart pounding. After what seemed an age, the front door squeaked open: the

sound of footsteps on the stairs—not one set, but two; my mother was not alone.

The door to my parents' room opened; two sets of legs crossed to the bed. My mother's good black shoes with the slim heels—odd that she'd wear those while weeding. And a man's trousers and brown dress shoes. *Not my father!* I craned my neck, but could see only up to the man's waist. Clothes being removed—*this can't be happening*—and then the man lowering my mother onto the bed.

Scarcely breathing, I watched as the two figures rolled onto each other, into each other, emitting baffling sounds: whispers and groans. Then the man on top, writhing strangely; my mother's sounds—muffled, smothered, urgent. His voice rising, my mother: *Sssssh, darling, not too loud.* This stranger, doing unimaginable things to my mother; she called him *darling.* I should have been terrified, outraged, alarmed. But I was only exhilarated, inflamed to the core.

Later, when my father returned from the office, my mother smiled demurely as she set down his bowl of beef stew. I was dumbstruck by the majesty of my discovery: that a person—my *mother*—might carry such a secret, live a secret, *be* a secret. It is breathtaking to me, still.

And now, impossibly, Matilda and Bertram, on the other side of this stacked row of bedside tables. The brief, scratchy sound of a match being lit; a faint, watery light spills out of the hidden space. As I crouch by the wall, my breath rasps in my head. I inch closer to where Matilda and Bertram are moving together. I press my eye to a crack of light between two pieces of furniture and hold my breath.

The candle fills the little space with a liquid, shadowy light; they move on the bed as if underwater. Their garments are open; the tail of a silky blouse curls by Matilda's torso. I see Bertram's mouth on her breast, on her lips. She fumbles at his trousers, he raises her skirt.

I pull away, coiled silently. Stifling a gust of breath, I move carefully: three steps, four, back against the damp concrete wall. Ashamed of the hardness in my groin. I close my eyes, all of me trained on what I can hear; in that red-tinged darkness, I see them again, watch in agony as Bertram peels away the blouse, allowing it to slither to the floor, one hand moving slowly from her throat, tracing her collarbone, lingering first on one breast, then the other, the pink nipple tightening against the flats of his fingers, the other hand reaching beneath her skirt, finding

the warmth. The rhythm of the creaking bedsprings builds; I see them behind my closed eyelids, I see him enter her. He moves slowly, prolonging the moment—I am choking on the gusts within, my own hardness a stifled, unquenchable scream, my mind a blur.

Back in my office, standing against the locked door, I fight for breath; my chest feels tight, like a fist is pressing hard against my breastbone.

The room is filled with uneven moonlight, light spliced by the branches and leaves of the trees outside my window; a thick shaft settles eerily in my desk chair, making it seem inhabited by a ghost. I cannot bring myself to sit there. I move toward the armchair on the other side of the desk. It is not as comfortable as it appears, though the patients never complain. The seat is too firm and seems to tilt forward. In all these years, I've never once sat in this chair.

I close my eyes, and the sounds from the tunnel are again in my ears: the soft rustlings and groans. I struggle against the suffocating lump in my throat, fight the longing that lacerates me still. And then there she is again: Delilah, sprung back to life in the private, sealed space of my memory.

"There's something I never told you," she says, her face doused in misery. We were in my small office, under the eaves, the late afternoon light slanting in through the high window, lighting up Delilah and casting a shadow over me. "I see things I'm not supposed to see. I listen in . . ."

"Listen in?"

"My grandmother used to say I was eavesdropping. But I wasn't! I couldn't help it! I tried not to, but as long as I was around people, it just happened."

"I'm not sure what you mean."

"I can hear what people are feeling," Delilah said. "They only have to look at me; it comes through in their eyes."

Instinctively, I looked away. She couldn't know what I was feeling, I told myself; we were taught to sequester our feelings, trained to be masters of our own souls.

"That must be difficult," I said.

Delilah looked away, then. "People are sad," she said. "No one seems to talk about it. But some people know that I see it. They know that I know how they feel."

"Is that a burden?"

I hardly knew what I was saying; I was watching, mesmerized by the expressiveness of her features.

"Not always," she said tentatively, raising her eyes to meet mine. "It can be . . . well, beautiful."

With all my strength, I slammed my feelings someplace deep and far away. In the filmy afternoon light, Delilah was so still, as if she'd transformed to a sculpture.

My eyes snap open. I am thirsty, and my face feels grimy with dust. My head pounds, I cross to the bathroom; the light buzzes to fluorescent life. I splash water on my face and drink from my hand, catching sight of myself in the mirror.

I know that look: but it is Bertram's, not mine.

I have not been to Firefly Pond in years. When Matilda asks me to come along—*an invitation,* she says, *from the patients*—I feel I cannot say no.

The pond has frozen early this year; the gardeners tested it this morning and declared it safe. It is a mixed outing, men and women together. As we walk, I am aware of the patients' heightened moods. The orderlies take turns carrying two large boxes of skates.

We make our way through the woods along a path that is kept trimmed and neat, a contrast to the wildness of the vegetation that rises around us. The sun is high overhead; the trees sparkle with hoarfrost, and the dusting of snow that remains from last night's flurries is astonishingly white.

Matilda's lips move, but her words scatter before I can gather their meaning. In my mind's eye I see her again, hurrying toward the back entrance, the dim flash in the darkness of her light-colored sweater.

We reach the pond. I glance around, stunned by the vividness: memory forged back to reality, but altered. The mature swamp maple over there was a sapling when I last saw it, almost twenty years ago; and the red sassafras, which was rich with mitten-shaped leaves, is now naked against

the sky. The nurses and orderlies help the patients tug on skates; there is laughing but also distress over the business of getting them on. No one is watching me, so I take my chance and retreat back, toward the woods. It is a relief to be on my own; I duck off the pathway and head into the underbrush. Something thorny snags my ankle; I feel it through my sock but keep on, pushing away at branches and leaves. Cutting across a dense patch, I find myself back on an old trail, off-limits here to patients but used on occasion by staff members who are fond of hiking.

The cold feels foreign; my mind has flown to that long-ago summer. There was birdsong then, like splashes of bright paint in the air. I run now up the incline, stumbling, kicking away stones and forest debris, the blood pounding in my ears, my breath coming in harsh bursts. At the top of the hill, I lean against a large Scotch pine and look down at the clearing and the pond. Patients move about on the ice, some gliding freely, others supported by staff members and awkward, like fresh-born colts.

On that earlier outing, the fireflies were in abundance, fluttering up and down, their tiny, phosphorescent flashes pinching into the diffuse dusk.

Delilah loved the fireflies. I close my eyes; the cold is sucked away, and I feel again the sultry air, see her before me, hear her: *It's hard, Dr. Harrison. Seeing what I see.* It had been very hot all that summer; the women patients left their shoes on the bank, held up their hems, dipped their feet in the water. She turned toward me: the first time I ever saw her smile. Just then, a small cloud of fireflies magically appeared, as if they'd been awaiting their moment—and here it was, Delilah holding her hem, smiling at the feel of her toes in warm mud.

"They asked me to sit in on Wernher von Braun's interrogation," Bertram says.

In talking about *the scientists,* Bertram has never before given a name. I don't know much about von Braun: only that he was a rocket scientist, and a crucial catch for the Allies.

"Although, *interrogation* is probably the wrong word. He spilled everything without coercion—the stenographer had trouble keeping up.

He didn't care that he would be working with the former enemy. All he wanted was to continue his research."

"We've never really discussed your own work," I say. "It was quite a feat, to finish your Ph.D. in biochemistry in less than two years. I wonder, being a scientist yourself—"

"Scientists are a funny breed," Bertram interrupts, giving me a slightly hostile look. "Afflicted with the need to know. They'll stop at nothing . . ."

"I daresay that's not true of them all," I say. "What struck you most about von Braun's testimony?"

There is a suspicious gleam in his eye.

"Everything he said is classified information."

"You seem to want to talk about it."

"Do you think *what I want* is relevant?"

"I would think it has some bearing."

"Some bearing on what?"

"On our discussion," I say. "You're no longer in the military. You're in a psychiatric hospital; I should think you're free to discuss whatever feels important to you."

"I only mention Wernher von Braun as an example," Bertram says. "To indicate that knowledge can't be disposed of to rot harmlessly back into the ground. Human actions are not organic. They're more enduring than that."

Bertram stands and walks to the window. He turns to me just as a beam of sunlight strikes the glass, sending a halo of brightness around his face. He taps his temple several times with his forefinger.

"His story is here. The figures, the facts, the human experiments, the sick Nazi dreams of power. The things he witnessed, the things he acquiesced to, the things he did and planned on doing. It's not in his file—that's a blank page now, white as snow. He might have been born a grown man on August fifteenth, 1945, the day he set foot on American soil. But it's all here"—again, Bertram taps his temple—"preserved. Ready to be recited at the Pearly Gates."

"Why do you say the Pearly Gates?"

"There will come a day of reckoning."

"But not on this earth?"

"I won't betray my country," Bertram says darkly. "Not even you can get me to do that."

"I'm not asking you to betray your country. You're clearly troubled by your encounter with this man; it might help to talk about it."

"We were under orders not to shoot," Bertram responds. "That's why I didn't rush to kill them. He had his hands up—they were planning to surrender. Just before the grenade was released, he called out, *Nein!* He must have seen someone reach for it. I didn't see it—I leapt out of harm's way on instinct—but he must have."

Bertram is staring into the middle distance.

"You said you were under orders not to shoot," I say.

"We suspected there were scientists there; we were expected to take them alive. They were worth a lot to us."

"You weren't to know one of them had a grenade. You just told me they were in the process of surrendering."

"What is it about reassurance that you find so intoxicating?" Bertram pauses, as if to let his words sink in. "Do you see me as that shallow? As if a word from you could make it all go away? I don't need you to pardon me. What would that achieve, in any case? Deeds are deeds. The need to try to undo them is naïve, with all due respect. The fact is that *their* lives were worth more to us than those of our own soldiers. My CO was ecstatic when he learned about our catch. I was decorated for it, for Christ's sake. He didn't say so much as two words about Jared."

Bertram squints at me again in that vaguely accusatory way. "I should have killed the Nazi bastard," he mumbles. "Jared must have known it—that it was their lives or his. Maybe he knew it was coming, too—saw the pin release, or something. But I was his superior; his desire to obey me was stronger than his instinct to survive.

"Do you have any idea what that feels like, Doctor? For someone to trust you, that way, with his life? Do you have any idea what it feels like to betray that kind of trust?"

Bertram's eyes are rimmed in red.

"All five hundred of those Nazi scientists learned the Pledge of Allegiance. They can sing 'The Star-Spangled Banner' like a high school glee club. You've got to laugh."

Bertram is not laughing, however; he is looking at me with hatred.

"You'd call yourself a patriot, wouldn't you, Doctor? A believer in the red, white, and blue?"

Once again, I find myself in that disarming, shimmery space—not

knowing what part of his narrative is delusional, and what based on objective fact.

"I know what you're thinking," Bertram says.

"You do?"

"You think that what I'm saying is madness."

"Actually, no," I say. "That's not what I was thinking."

"What then?"

"I'm trying to wade through the things you've told me and make some sense of it."

"Make it coherent," Bertram says, with a back note of triumph.

"Yes, I suppose you could put it that way."

"Well, good luck," he says flippantly. But then his face clouds. "There's nothing you or I can do to change the truth. No story I can make of it—no story you can make of it—so that everything will be all right. If you want facts, I can give you facts. Those Nazi criminals are working for the United States government, their pasts sanitized. And Jared is in the grave—nothing, now, but bones. And this decorated officer, who has shaken hands with the President of the United States—he told me my country was proud of me—is in a mental hospital spilling his guts to a doctor who wants it all to be packed up neatly in a box and tied with a bow. Those are the facts; that's all we have to go on."

He leans back, spent. Silence hangs heavily for a moment, and then, he speaks again. "You never told me what you think about them."

"You think I endorse the fact that these scientists are now working for our country."

"Please don't tell me what *you* think *I* think about the matter, Dr. Harrison. I'm asking you, directly, what *you* think."

"I suppose I'm a pragmatist," I say awkwardly. "I no longer believe that anything in life is simple or clear-cut. I don't like the idea that former Nazis are working for our government. But if they were not working for us, they'd be working for the Soviets. And that's not a pretty picture either."

"They could be working for no one," Bertram says quietly. "They could have been executed, or put in jail."

"I should think that their cumulative knowledge is extremely valuable."

"Yes, yes," Bertram mutters, looking away.

When he next speaks, he appears to be talking to himself. "I should have made the connection earlier. I'm such a fool—the clues were right under my nose. Maybe I knew it all along—that *he was one of them.* My own brother, Emanuel!"

I pick up my pen. "New delusional elaboration," I note. "Brother is Nazi scientist."

"But if that were the case," I offer, "why would your brother want to track you down? Aren't the German scientists protected by the government? Given freedoms far greater than any they've probably ever known?"

Bertram's eyes glow. "Yes, Doctor. But as you yourself once said, reality—*Truth*—does not always operate according to the principles of logic. Human motivation is complex and can defy rationality. With Emanuel, perhaps there is something else going on."

The cold bites through the wool of my coat, the wind creeps in at the collar. Since I began walking again in the woods, I've been avoiding the clearing where the accident happened, a truck coming from nowhere—Delilah, having seen me, running toward me—the whole thing incredible, perfectly impossible, surreal.

I only now realize the truth: that I've been searching for the place all along, trying to find a way to go back. It all looks so changed; the woods, denser than I remember, have had their own dramas. Blackened stumps, charred trunks, a patch where sphagnum moss hangs like shrouds in the trees.

I knew I would never utter the words to Delilah, so I wrote them down in a notebook—not crazily, over and over, only once: "I love you." I hoped the journal would serve as a kind of self-exorcism. I had consulted my supervisor, Dr. Greely, but he'd been of no help. Dr. Greely with his thick, oiled mustache that belonged to another time, another place: the antebellum South, perhaps. Not only his whiskers but the whole of him seemed dipped in grease, from the up-curling lips to the wildly shined shoes that clicked smartly as he walked the corridors of the wards. Amazing, really, that I ever imagined he could be of help.

In those days, there were a good number of staff dinners and lun-

cheons to which wives were invited; Ursula was always by my side. *A fine woman,* Dr. Greely had said on a dozen occasions. *A man needs a good wife, if he's going to progress in this profession.* His views about the importance of a solid wife made it all the more difficult to raise with him my troubling feelings for Delilah. But I was fresh, then: a believer in psychiatry's liturgy and incantations. He was my supervisor, and one of the first American psychiatrists to embrace the new science of psychoanalysis. Sitting in Dr. Greely's office, I'd recited the details of my despair in a deadened voice, while he smiled mildly and puffed on his pipe.

"A classic case of transference and countertransference," he'd said. "Once you have that straight, there's really not that much to it."

"But don't we also develop transferences to our patients?" I'd replied. "Doesn't the patient have countertransference reactions to the feelings we broadcast out to them?"

"Freud is quite clear about the power relations, Dr. Harrison," Dr. Greely had said. "*You're* the one in charge. Think of it on the model of an electrical generator. The *source* of the power is always the *source*. You're the *trained* one—the one who knows the code. Once you've deciphered your own internal conflicts, it's simply a matter of neutralizing them. Everything then becomes about the patient."

Some weeks after the outing to Firefly Pond, sitting in my attic office, I finally acknowledged the truth—that I was at sea, with no one to help me and no way out. That I'd made a mockery of my life's work: that I'd betrayed not only my profession but also my patient, Delilah, not to mention Ursula, my wife.

"Don't you know, Dr. Harrison," Delilah had said sadly. Being called "Doctor" was still foreign to my ears; it made me feel like a child playing grown-up. "None of it matters."

"What do you mean?"

"We only ever really have the moment." She looked at me with such intensity; I felt as if we were traveling somewhere eternal together, to some true and enduring home. Silently, in my mind, I mouthed the words: *I've loved you from the start, Delilah,* from the moment I saw you sitting so tidily, so distressed, in the interview room, the sun streaming in behind you, lighting you up like an angel. The way you held yourself all bundled together, as if trying not to take up too much space, your

eyes revealing the oldness of your soul, your gaze a beam of knowing: turning from nothing, seeing it all. And seeing, as well—miraculously— fully seeing *me.*

Even back then, I hid behind silence. Nothing happened between us. But I wanted it to. And I lived it in my dreams until it threatened to swallow me up. It was worst when I was with Delilah in session, sitting opposite her, illicit dream images crowding my thoughts. I feared they'd peck a hole in my professional mask and show through.

The woods are confusing now, the pathways unfamiliar. I sense I am heading in the wrong direction and turn back, walking with haste. The brambles and twigs underfoot make the going difficult. I retrace my steps, and it is with some relief that I finally break out from the woods into the open; before me, in the bright afternoon, the main building sits in the middle of the vast lawn, like a bulwark guarding something important and obscure.

"I don't know how my mother met Tony," Bertram says. "It wasn't long after we arrived in America. Tony was a small man; he'd wanted to be a jockey. But that hadn't worked out, so he took care of racehorses."

Bertram fixes me with a querying eye. "Didn't you say you were in the cavalry, in the First War?"

"No, Bertram, I don't believe that I did."

"Damn stupid," Bertram says under his breath. "Taking horses into battle, in that day and age."

"What are you thinking about specifically?"

"How backward America can be. Everyone else seemed to understand there was no place in that war for mounted cavalry."

"Change can be agonizingly slow," I say.

"*Agonizing* would be the right word," Bertram says drily. "They had to shoot hundreds of them—it was the terrain, as much as anything, and the patterns of visibility. The moment the horses were out, they either broke a leg or got hit."

"Why are you thinking about this today?"

"Why does anybody think about anything?" Bertram asks blandly.

He doesn't wait for an answer.

"I remember the first time I saw a horse shot—a chestnut quarter horse. A yearling, who'd taken a bad fall. I was helping Tony at the stables—I'd gone outside for water when I saw the horse lying on the track. So patient, not wriggling or neighing: peaceful, almost. He looked at me as if he were trying to tell me something. There were guys yelling, running around, and I heard Tony calling me—he sounded very far away. I just stood there. I knew what they were going to do. I felt Tony's hand on my arm, but I pulled away. I knew I had to stay.

"Then I heard the crack of the rifle. I watched as the blood flowed from the side of his head. The horse kept his eyes on mine the whole time, no shock or anything, just that patient look, like he was waiting for something: looking right at me. Whatever he was waiting for, I felt it was my duty to wait with him. I knew that if I walked away, I would be letting the horse down."

Bertram looks at me expectantly—as if he is now waiting for something from me. "I'm sorry," he says.

"What are you sorry about?"

"The way I ask things. The way I say things."

"What do you mean?"

"I woke up this morning thinking about that horse—maybe I dreamed about him. I don't remember. Just that, when I walked in here today, he was on my mind."

"You know what we psychiatrists think about that."

"Yes, I do."

"Perhaps it seems artificial, sometimes. But experience tells me that it really can help just to talk: to see where your associations take you."

Bertram nods.

"You must have experienced it, too," he says. "Soldiers torn up. Begging you to put them out of their misery."

"Yes, I did."

"Watching a man die—someone you love . . ."

I see Fergus again: he has died a thousand times.

When the gas attack came, we'd been marching for days, drunk with lack of sleep, almost delirious from starvation rations. How many times had I forcefully strapped the mask to Fergus's face? I had begged him to humor me: there was no talking him out of his fixed belief—that the gas was harmless. I probably should have made sure he was removed to

a place of safety, but I couldn't bear to imagine him there; I'd seen what happened to soldiers who were labeled "shell-shocked"—seen them at the military hospital, bound in straitjackets or tied up to trees, barked at or slapped, treated as a kind of enemy within, despised, reviled, cast off. And I'd seen what they'd done to themselves: a blown-off foot, the bloody socket of a gouged eye, a sliced-open leg. I told myself that Fergus was a mild case, the madness, for him, limited to the business of the gas. Surely something I could help him contain and thus save him from a dreadful, unthinkable fate.

The taste of the gas; I have only to think of it and my throat swells. No warning; it was just suddenly there, and me madly coughing, forgetting, *that one time,* in my own frantic fumbling for the mask, Fergus's recent touch of madness. A horse-drawn wagon appeared, men jumped on, clinging to every part, hanging off the wooden sides. Behind the milky green glass of the mask—unforgettable, like being underwater—I remembered. I scanned for Fergus, my breath loud in my ears, the air thick with yellow gas; men stumbling, hurling themselves on, all from another world, faces of tarnished metal, green glass, outlandish elephant-trunk tubes. Scanning, moving, breathing—and then I saw him, surprisingly close, clutching his throat, stumbling, the mask dangling from his other hand. Running toward him: moving through mud, through yellow fog, dragging, slow motion, like not moving at all. Through the thick, greenish yellow air, guns, *rat-tat-tat* in my ears. Pulling one foot up out of mud, being sucked down, pulling up the other foot, forward, slowly inching forward. Fergus down now—coughing, yellow spume frothing from his mouth turning ghastly orange with blood. His eyes bulging, bewildered. Reaching him: too late. Fergus knew it, too. Heaving him into my arms. Feet sucked down, plowing through mud, regaining the wagon, flinging him in. Up onto the running board, clinging to the side. At every bump, watching new blood burble up from his mouth: never taking my eyes from his choking, sputtering face, furious with the last of his life.

Bertram is speaking: "And you were a medic—so maybe it was harder."

"Harder?"

"You couldn't pull the trigger—you had a code. But we didn't have the same rules."

"How was it for you, Bertram?" I ask.

"I couldn't do it," he says in a small voice. "My buddies knew; they'd seen me in that situation—the way I froze."

"Was that a problem?"

"Yes."

"Are you thinking of a particular time?"

"Perry Stewart. Shrapnel to the gut; he begged me to put him out of his agony. There was blood pouring out of his mouth."

"What did you do?"

"Nothing. I couldn't move. I just stood there and watched him die."

Something changes in Bertram's face. "My CO would shoot anyone who asked him to—even when they weren't injured."

"What do you mean?"

"One time, we'd cleared out a bombed village. The stench was unbearable: rotting flesh. A German boy in uniform came out from a basement. I don't know how he knew I spoke German, but he singled me out, walked right up to me and asked me to shoot him. He said it calmly, like he was asking the time. His eyes weren't calm, though. I told him to give me his shoes and go home. He said he didn't have a home. He pointed to my gun, gestured that he'd do it himself. My CO asked me what he was saying. I translated. The boy then turned to my CO and asked him, in English, if he would shoot him.

"There was something about the place—it was so empty. Rubble everywhere, tremendous heat coming from the buildings. The smell— worse than you can imagine. My CO raised his gun, and the boy nodded. I wanted to scream, to tell him not to do it. But I couldn't—I opened my mouth but nothing came out."

Bertram falls silent.

"What happened?"

"My CO shot him in the chest. He folded up and fell to the ground— neatly, as if he didn't want to make a mess. The boy kept his eyes on me—just like the horse, that day on the track. Patient, waiting for something, and wanting me to wait with him. So I did. My CO walked away, and I stayed there, until whatever he was waiting for arrived and his eyes went blank."

"What happened after that?"

Bertram is looking at me from the past—bewildered, it seems, to find

that I am still here. "I also walked away. Just left him there and walked away."

I say nothing.

"But something else happened." Bertram looks at me sidelong, his eyes glint.

"What?"

"I didn't leave him, not really. When I walked away, he followed me."

"He followed you . . . ?"

"Those moments that happen sometimes—you know it immediately. When your life changes. It was like that."

"How did your life change?"

"I don't know how. I only know that I felt different. And that I had the distinct feeling that he had chosen me. That when he died, he left something unfinished."

"Something that it was up to you to take on?"

"I didn't think of it like that at the time."

"How do you think of it now?"

"I really don't know. I only know that whatever happened that day between us was old—it was already there in me, and maybe in him, too, in the boy. That it was an exchange that had been set up a long time ago."

I don't know what Bertram sees in my face, but he visibly falters.

"I know it sounds extraordinary. But it didn't feel crazy, then. And to be truthful, it doesn't feel crazy now. Believe it or not, I can tell the difference."

At Monday morning meeting, Mr. Cuthbert glares angrily at Matilda.

"Something is troubling you, Mr. Cuthbert," I begin.

"I don't see how a person is supposed to get better with that kind of illegal activity going on," he says heatedly. "Frankly, I'm sick of the lot of you."

"Why don't you tell us what's bothering you?"

"I will do no such thing. Do you think I want to end up in jail?"

Beside me, Mr. Featherstone's hollow eyes burn hungrily.

"Mr. Cuthbert has been upset, ever since Mr. Collins's family came by to collect his belongings," Matilda says gently.

"As if they cared two hoots about him. And, with all due respect, Dr. Harrison, I'd appreciate it if you instructed Nurse Willoughby to refrain from addressing me."

After the meeting, Matilda and I head over to the conference hall for grand rounds.

"What was all that about?" I ask.

"Mr. Cuthbert?" She gives a sympathetic smile. "He's gotten it into his head that I'm running numbers."

"We are rather colorful this week. Prison guards one minute, bookies the next."

"Mr. Featherstone took me aside this morning and told me that Cuthbert could help me—being a mathematician. Apparently, he once made a tidy sum in Las Vegas, counting cards."

"They've become friends, I see."

"Featherstone's in awe of Cuthbert—and a bit afraid of him, I think. They've both signed up for the pageant. It'll do them good."

"What have they chosen this year?"

"*A Midsummer Night's Dream.* Mrs. Brown is going to help them with an abridgment. I went to the read-through, yesterday; it was quite poignant."

"How so?"

"Most of them know what it's like to wake up one day and find the world has undergone a baffling metamorphosis."

A loud clanging splits the air. A thrumming wail and then two short bells, indicating the incident is on Hall Two.

"Oh dear." Matilda gives a quick, apologetic shrug. "If I'm lucky, I'll get to catch the end of grand rounds."

She hurries back in the direction of Hall Two. There is a sudden thundering of boots: orderlies and male nurses, responding to the alert. Calling on an in-house telephone, I discover that our new alcoholic has taken on several staff members.

"We'll be fine," Nurse O'Halahan's calm voice says. "No serious injuries. Dr. Marlowe is on his way over. Wallis has the patient subdued for now, but it's going to take several Wallises to get him into four-points. Funny, he didn't seem the violent type."

"They seldom do."

After grand rounds, I head downstairs to the billing office, which is

tucked away at the far end of the east corridor. Mr. Parker, vigorous and ancient, receives me graciously. I ask who is paying for Bertram's care here, and he leaves to locate the file. A few minutes later, he is shuffling through the folder. The funds to cover Bertram's hospital stay, he says, come directly from the Veterans Administration. All incidentals are covered, including the salary and keep of Bertram's personal valet.

The Veterans Administration sends us patients if they are overcrowded or think a particular case might be best handled elsewhere. To pay for a servant, though; that seems out of the ordinary.

"Are you certain no part of the monies comes from a family trust, or some other account?" I ask.

"No," Parker assures me, peering at his ledger. "Absolutely certain. The entire amount is deposited monthly from the bank account of the Veterans Administration." He removes his spectacles, without which his eyes seem unnaturally large, and gazes at me sharply for a long, uncomfortable moment, as if trying to figure something out.

"Thank you, Mr. Parker," I say, looking away. He replies affably, and when I glance back at him, I see that after all there is nothing awkward about his regard.

After lunch, I draft a letter to the Veterans Administration, asking for any information they might have about Bertram Reiner, beyond the documents they sent upon his admission: Army discharge papers, early history, family or other contacts, any information about a German brother who may currently be residing in the United States. I also insert an inquiry into his financial situation.

When Cynthia comes in to take dictation, I hand her the letter.

In my office, close to midnight, I think of Ursula lying in bed, the gentle snores issuing from her sleep-heavy form. The desire to return in my mind to the tunnels beneath the hospital feels irresistible. I close my eyes and allow myself to sink into the moment. I strain to hear what it is they whisper to each other, Bertram and Matilda: listen, again, to the sounds of their passion, inhale the dusty, close air of the tunnel and feel the rising of my own blood.

In the distance, the church bells chime midnight. Grabbing my coat,

I head outside, leaving the lights on, neglecting to lock the door. Outside, I cut around behind the main building and take the stone path that leads to the highest point on the hospital grounds. It has been years since I've walked this way; when I first came to Shadowbrook I took this walk in the evening whenever my schedule allowed in order to view the sunset. Even now, in the pale moonlight, I know each step in my bones, and yet everything is changed; it's as if I'm walking both toward and away from the past. The bushes and trees have grown considerably; a bench here or there that was once new is now weathered.

By the time I reach the top of the hill, I am breathing heavily; years ago, I was never reduced to breathlessness. Leaning against the trunk of an enormous sugar maple, I wait for my breath to steady. In the distance, the sliver of Long Island Sound glitters black against the horizon. To the east, the darkly twinkling lights of Manhattan, each one flashing an unknown story. Directly beneath me, at the bottom of the hill, the cozy houses of the village. It is flat, all of it: this familiar scene, once so alive, is now wickedly sucked of life.

At the sound of snapping twigs I spin around and scan the line of bushes and trees. Perhaps it is only a squirrel or chipmunk, though surely they are too light and too quick to break a branch like that. Then nothing—no movement, no sound. The cold air slams against me, a harbinger of snow.

That long-ago weekend, the blizzard took us by surprise. We'd had steady snowfall all week—four or five inches already on the ground. But then, it came down in sudden fistfuls; orderlies and nurses rushed about organizing for the inevitable shutdown, ferrying meals and other items between buildings so that each hall would be self-sufficient for the duration of the storm. By the time we realized that three women patients were stranded in the Occupational Therapy Pavilion, the conditions were blinding. Delilah, I was told, was among the three, along with an elderly woman who'd recently taken a fall and was in a cast from ankle to hip. The orderly who'd accompanied them probably realized he couldn't manage to bring them all back on his own and, unwilling to leave anyone unattended, was awaiting assistance.

I volunteered to help bring them back. The hallways were eerily transformed: no sunshine, only a smothering whiteness, the heavy snowflakes beating soundlessly against the windows like a plague of pallid moths.

When I broke from the indoor warmth into the bitter cold, I realized I'd neglected to retrieve my coat. Hail was mixed in with the snow—it whipped at me, stirred to violence by the wind. I pulled my doctor's coat tightly about me and stumbled along, squinting against the snow and hail, the buildings velvety shapes obscured by the turbulent, opaque air. I was unable to control the swelling panic.

I did not know I was veering off the pathway; the wind had made shifting dunes of the snow on the ground. Stopping to catch my breath, I looked about me, shielding my eyes. My white coat was stiff with snow melted by my body's warmth and then refrozen by the frigid wind; my fingers pulsed with pain. Through the whiteout, I could discern the shapes of buildings—though their forms seemed to be shifting. No choice, I realized, but to lumber as best as I could toward each, one at a time. I threw my body against the wind, laboring to move forward. Finally, I found myself up against a door—not of the pavilion, it turned out, but of Brown Villa, the women's residence hall: hopelessly far from where I wanted to be. A terrible confusion took hold; resting my head against the wooden door, I struggled to regain my bearings. I pictured the layout of the hospital buildings, and mustered the mental discipline to locate myself on the imagined map. Slowly, it came clear; I must backtrack now and then head east.

A sudden gust sucked a hole in the whiteness, and I found myself looking across the vast lawn to the main building, revealed, for an instant, before disappearing once more behind the snowy thickness. I ran, stumbling, in the direction of the pavilion, and soon I was rounding the curve in the pathway that suddenly reappeared, blown clear of snow.

And then, I was there: not two feet from the misted-over panes of the back window, which shone dully with light. One square was wiped clean; in that clear patch, itself misting over as the seconds passed, I saw her, Delilah, her face pressed up against the glass, peering out into the blizzard with electric intent. Her face transformed; she had seen me, but she showed no surprise. She looked at me as if she'd been expecting me, her face naked with love. I was delirious with happiness and relief. I had saved her!

In that split second, I was caught unawares; battling the snowstorm had stripped me of my professional disguise. I know it now, though in the dumb shock of the moment, I was able to hide from myself the

truth: that standing there, before the window, I responded to what I saw in Delilah's face and, with my own eyes, silently confessed my love.

How is it possible that Delilah has been gone for almost twenty years? A bloodred bloom opens slowly within me, painful and beautiful and raw.

I am staring down at the view, the finger width of water, the small, sleepy houses, as if through a thickness of muffling glass. No storm now: no hail, no snow. Only the screeching loneliness—

Chapter Four

*A*reply to my letter arrived unusually fast; it's been little more than a week since Cynthia mailed off my inquiry. I suppose I was hoping to learn that there was nothing untoward about Bertram's situation: a heroic soldier had cracked under the duress of his long tour of duty; it was the government's duty to fund his care to the fullest degree.

The first thing that struck me was the look of the red stamp at the bottom of the page; it seemed phony and childlike—block letters, surrounded by a rectangle of red ink and positioned at an angle above the official seal. CLASSIFIED. Above this, several typed sentences.

> *Dear Dr. Harrison,*
> *We regret to inform you that we cannot be of help in your inquiry. All files on record pertaining to Lieutenant Bertram Reiner, discharged honorably on November 18, 1945, are sealed, due to their classified nature.*

I think about the way Bertram skirts certain matters when they are raised; the practiced quality of his evasions, as if he has been trained to elude detection.

I arrive at the ward ten minutes before change of shift. I find Janice in the coffee room, waiting for the kettle to boil. In her three years of

apprenticeship at Shadowbrook, Janice has evolved from a fretful novice to a competent nurse, though she is still shy, especially around me.

"May I join you?" I ask.

"Of course, Dr. Harrison. Allow me, please," she says, placing powdered coffee in two cups.

I inquire about her Christmas plans, and she politely answers.

"I'd like to talk with you about something," I say. "One of our patients is here under the auspices of the Veterans Administration."

Janice pours steaming water into the cups and then adds powdered milk.

"I've been asked by the VA to follow up on certain matters they began when he was under their care, just after the War."

"You are speaking about Mr. Reiner, of course," Janice says, glancing nervously around the coffee room.

"I am," I say, a little perplexed to see how flummoxed she has become. Perhaps I overestimated her; perhaps she is a less reliable choice for this task than I had supposed.

"It would help me if you could keep an eye on how Mr. Reiner occupies himself during his free time—whether he writes letters, for example, or keeps a journal."

"Of course, I will do what I can," she says.

We stand by the bench, sipping our coffee.

"It's important that you remain discreet about this," I add.

"Oh yes, I completely understand." Janice gives a prideful little smile.

"Well then," I say, glancing at my watch. "Time to head over for change of shift."

Back in my office, waiting for Bertram to arrive for his session, I eye the liquor cabinet, aware of an unpleasant gnawing in my gut. I wonder if I'll be able to wait until wine at dinner; perhaps I'll allow myself a quick nip, after Bertram's session.

When he enters, Bertram appears to have come to some kind of decision.

"Dr. Harrison, I have reason to believe you have information relevant to my life, something you are refusing to tell me."

"What gives you that idea?"

"You wrote to the Veterans Administration."

I have a sudden, unpleasant feeling that Bertram has snooped in

my office when I am not here—that he has been riffling through my papers.

"We typically seek out relevant information, in the interest of treatment continuity." I immediately regret the smugness I hear in my voice.

"I'm not talking about an exchange of information with doctors," he says slowly.

"Why don't you tell me what you're referring to?"

"It's not so pleasant, is it, when one's interlocutor talks in circles," he continues. "What I'm saying is that it's not your place to make inquiries into my finances, is it?"

"We must consider all aspects of a patient's life," I say steadily. "We're planning for your discharge back into the community. How you will support yourself is an important matter."

"I don't suppose you found out all that much." Bertram's voice is mild, though I see an angry glint in his eyes.

"It depends on how you look at it. I queried the Veterans Administration, as they are paying for your treatment here. They wrote back to say that they could not discuss your case."

"And did they say why?"

"I was told only that the details of your situation are confidential."

"That was the word they used?" Bertram asks, now with obvious interest. "Confidential?"

"Actually, the word they used was *Classified.*"

"I see." Bertram turns to look out the window and seems to lose himself in thought. When he directs his gaze back at me, there is something unreadable in his expression.

"You always do that, then?" he asks slowly. "Control what the patient knows. Reveal some things, keep some things hidden. Is that how it is with others you treat?"

"I don't think it's helpful to talk about other patients."

"You don't? Well *I* think it would help me to know what you do with other patients—sequestered in your hiding place, sitting behind that desk, the emperor of the land. We have a number of those on Hall Two at the moment, but I don't need to tell you that. How am I to know you're any different from those who walk up and down the ward, muttering about mutinies? Perhaps the only real difference is that you have an uncontested kingdom here, in which no one can really question you.

"But that's not what we were talking about, is it," he continues. "You were telling me about a secret you've been keeping from me—so I can only imagine that you must be in the habit of keeping secrets from other patients."

Bertram is regarding me with such unblinking force I find I must look away. I make a show of scribbling a few words into the notebook before me on the desk.

"You can write what you like," he says steadily. "That's not going to change anything."

I finish what I was writing, aware of a rising spike of anger. *Counter-transference,* I tell myself. I am responding to the patient's assault on me. But the anger I am feeling is wild and unfamiliar—perhaps not counter-transference after all, but *projective identification*: Bertram projecting his own primitive emotions directly into me. I feel a rush of exhilaration—a kind of psychological second wind.

"I can see you are furious with me," I venture, laying down my fountain pen.

"No, Doctor, I'm not furious with you."

"What then?"

"I don't know. I suppose I'm wondering whether you turn it all on yourself. That analytic eye of yours. Psychiatrists are supposed to analyze their own psyches, aren't they? They have to know their unconscious twists and turns in order to sort through those of others. Isn't that the theory?"

No sign, now, of challenge or contempt, only frank interest.

"Go on," I say.

"Well, how does that work? How do you probe your own psyche while keeping hold of your secrets? You must have secrets, like the rest of us. How could you not?" I see that Bertram's mind is ticking over. "It's very complicated, I see that now. I wonder how you keep it all straight—dodging around the land mines and bullets of your patients while having to do the same regarding yourself. There's a tricky thought . . ."

"Yes?"

"It must be rather like being on a battlefield and suddenly realizing that the enemy fire is coming at you from your own hands."

"We've gotten away from where we started today," I say.

"Yes, we have, haven't we." Bertram gives me a pointed look. "I believe you were about to tell me some of your own secrets."

Delilah, again: the dreadful sight. Her face oddly unharmed—staring green eyes, lips parted in surprise, but a blue tinge already evident in her pale skin, the rapidly spreading wetness dyeing her blue dress black.

I feel the heat rising to my face.

"Ah," Bertram breathes. "I see that I've hit the mark."

Lying in bed beside Ursula, I find myself in a state of agitated alertness. I know I will be unable to sleep for hours.

In my study, the hissing steam pipes seem shrill, the windows rattle with the wind; every now and then, the house gives off an inanimate groan, as if expressing weariness with its own existence. Almost jumping out of my skin, I try to read, but the words swim on the page. The radio buzzes with static; I spend a good ten minutes trying to find a station, with no success. In the kitchen, I brew a pot of coffee; the smoky odor brings on a wave of nausea, hauling into this brittle midnight the bright associations of morning. I empty the pot down the sink and take my chances with a bottle of port.

So many years since I've been in the clutch of this insistent appetite; it's like a beast, clawing at reason. I pace the living room, then my office, the dining room, and back to the living room, as if I might shake off the dreadful gnawing if only I walk quickly enough, if only I continue changing rooms, if only I hold my breath long enough to push it away. But I do not have enough fight in me; before the night is out, I know I'll climb the stairs to the attic, pull aside boxes and files, slide away clothing and books and whatever else is up there in that no-man's-land until I find what I stashed there all those years ago, until I have it, again, in my hands. It has been waiting for me. I must have known when I packed my pillow box away—not discarding it, as I might have—that one day I would again take up my opium pipe.

Making my way upstairs, I feel something exhilarating, illicit, like I'm an intruder. The final flight of stairs creak; I freeze. Who do I imagine is tracking my movements? The hiss of the pipes is bizarrely encouraging, as if egging me on.

It is dusty in the attic; this, too, somehow excites me. I pull the chain

switch, and the lightbulb comes on swinging, sending a moving circle of light about the space, making it feel as if I am on a seaborne ship whose contents are sliding uneasily from here to there. When I steady the bulb, the room comes to a standstill.

The pillow box is not as easy to find as I'd hoped. I pick my way into corners, move about boxes and bits of furniture; I startle at what I think is a scuttling rodent, pick cobwebs from my hair, conscious of a swelling despair. The shadows bristle; I recall the lost journal I agonized over, after Delilah died. Had it found its way into an old box or desk after all? Perhaps, now, I will open a drawer and, instead of my pillow box, discover the notebook.

It feels unbearably hot; the steam pipe running the length of the attic gives off too much heat for the space. I find a chest full of old towels and use one to wipe the sweat from my face; the towel is dusty and sends me into a fit of coughing. Opening the door onto the stairway to let in some air, I hear footsteps: Ursula moving about. I freeze, aware of a growing terror; she will find me, she will know what I am hunting for, she will look at me with damning eyes. The toilet flushes, I hear Ursula on the landing outside our room.

"Henry?" she calls down toward the kitchen. "Are you going to come up?"

She waits for a response. There is a heaviness in her waiting—something long-suffering and weary that sends a pang of guilt through me. I listen with her, as if also expecting an answer: hold my breath, hear her sigh and turn, and then the *click* of the bedroom door, and a fade back to uneventful silence. Fired, shamed, I return with renewed determination to my task.

I drag everything out of the farthest corner of the attic; my eyes fall on the old, rolltop desk and my memory lazily stirs. Tugging on the pull, I suddenly know it will be locked—*put it away, throw away the key.* Who was I fooling? A bitter laugh rises within; I was fooling myself, of course, and not unsuccessfully. I try each of the drawers—perhaps I'll find the key rattling around in one of them—then tug again on the pull, hoping to break the lock, but no luck; I need some kind of tool. No choice but to go down to the basement to look for one.

It is on my way back up that the bedroom door opens; Ursula appears just as I reach the top stair.

"I've been waiting for you." She gives a tentative smile.

"Darling, you shouldn't have." I'm uncomfortably aware of the wrench and screwdriver dragging down the pocket of my bathrobe. "I couldn't sleep, so I thought I'd make the most of my time."

"The case conference?"

For a moment, I don't know what she's talking about. "Yes—some background reading. It's proving to be a difficult case."

"Mr. Reiner, isn't it?"

I start at hearing Bertram's name on her lips.

"Henry, what's wrong?" Ursula sounds worried. "You've gone white!"

"Nothing, my dear. It just took me by surprise, that's all—you knowing the name of my patient."

"The papers were on your desk. I only took a quick glance." She sounds flustered. What else has she looked at in my study?

"I never usually go in there, you know that." She seems to be reading my mind. "I couldn't find my book; I thought that maybe Samantha put it in there by mistake when she was tidying up."

"Not to worry, truly," I respond. "I'm afraid I'm still not tired, though. I just came up to brush my teeth. I had a piece of your marvelous apple cake."

"I smelled the coffee." Ursula smiles. "Would you like some company?"

The briefest beat, only, but I feel it, as Ursula must: the hesitation—a moment in which to come up with a deflecting response.

"I'm quite deep into it—I may have stumbled upon some important material. I want to incorporate it into the summary while it's still fresh in my mind."

"Yes, dear, of course. Good luck, then."

The door clicks sadly behind her. I continue on to the bathroom, noisily brush my teeth, and then return downstairs, where I sit in my study watching the clock, waiting until I can be sure that Ursula has gone back to sleep. Half an hour passes, and then I gingerly make my way upstairs, pausing outside our bedroom door. Only silence; I continue on to the attic with rekindled excitement.

It doesn't take long to break the lock. Slowly, I slide open the rickety top, and the pillow box reveals itself: the beautiful wood, inlaid with ivory, and in the center, an elaborate, engraved dragon. The box

is smooth in my hands; I stroke the polished surface and feel a sensual tingling, aware of the pounding of my heart—little smashing beats against my ribs. Quietly, I slip down the stairs to my study and stash the box in my duffel bag. By the time I return to bed, it is after three in the morning. I lie beside Ursula, dazzled by the roiling emotions within, and struck by a clanging awareness that my life is about to change.

Over breakfast, I glance up from the newspaper to find Ursula looking at me and watch as the mildly hurt expression on her face gives way to a habitual smile. She fetches the coffeepot, and refills my cup.

On the ward, Janice asks if she can come to see me in my office. I schedule an appointment for the early evening, midshift, when fewer people are likely to be about. I realize I'm thinking like someone who has something to hide.

While waiting for Janice, I am too distracted to work. I fix myself a drink and stand by the window, staring out over the lawn. Dusk hangs in the trees; clumps of shadowy light give shape to things that are not there.

Janice's distinctive knock comes at the door. She enters and looks nervously about.

"Thank you for coming," I say, gesturing to the chair across from my desk. She holds herself carefully, as if afraid she might break something, and seems startled out of the faculty of speech.

"Perhaps you have some news," I gently urge.

She looks uncertain. "I'm not sure I did the right thing, Dr. Harrison. It was when I went in to change the sheets. Mr. Reiner was in the art studio with the other patients. You told me to look around, but he keeps his room very neatly."

Janice reddens, which has the unsettling effect of making her light orange hair appear to be on fire.

"You didn't say as much, but I assumed you meant I should actually look *into* things—the closet, the drawers. That would be the only way to find anything, because of how neat the room is."

"You've done nothing wrong," I say reassuringly.

The girl visibly calms. "I've been fretting since yesterday. I tossed and turned all night."

"Have you brought something to show me?" I prompt.

"Mr. Reiner's servant folds his shirts carefully, but they were all the way in front—and those drawers are deep. I had the feeling there was something in the back. I took the shirts out and felt around—sure enough, I found a long wooden box."

Janice pulls a wad of papers from her apron pocket.

"Filled with papers. Also, some small notebooks. I thought he might miss those, so I just took a few of the papers to show you."

I walk around the desk and take the papers. Janice purses her lips as if to stop herself from speaking, her face alive with the suppression.

"Was there anything else you wanted to say?" I ask.

"It's all terribly important, I suppose." Her voice is hushed.

"What is, Janice?"

"Mr. Reiner's work. It's *top secret,* isn't it?"

"What do you mean by 'his work'?" The papers Janice has given me are tightly written with scientific formulae.

"He's not really a patient, is he," she whispers triumphantly. "That's why he has to work so hard."

"Perhaps," I say ambiguously.

"I'm very careful," she says, conspiratorial now.

"That's good," I say.

"I'm glad you both trust me."

"Both?"

"You and Nurse Willoughby. I'm glad you agreed that *I* was the one to be trusted."

She scans my face anxiously. "You *have* discussed this with Nurse Willoughby, haven't you?"

"Why yes, of course," I say. "Though I think it best you don't tell her about our little talk. Better we keep things, well, separate."

"I'm to continue letting Mr. Reiner leave at night then, Dr. Harrison? So that he can go on with his work? He still has the key."

"Yes. You are to change nothing." I hesitate. "When you say the key, you mean . . . ?" I look down at my desk, pretending to try to locate something.

"The key to the door at the back of the medical supply closet. The one that used to have the heavy glass cabinet in front of it. The janitor moved it."

Janice must see something in my face.

"You needn't worry," she says hastily. "We pulled a linen chest in front of it—no one else knows, I'm sure of it. Just that the linen chest is easy to pull away. It slides quietly."

"Yes. Very good," I say. "The door at the back of the supply closet . . ."

"The one leading down to the underground tunnels. I've never been down there." Her voice is hushed. "I *am* curious to see those tunnels—"

"Well, we don't encourage it," I say a bit sternly.

"Oh no! Of course not. Especially now that Mr. Reiner has his work down there. I'm sorry, I didn't mean to suggest—"

"It's all right, Janice. You have been most helpful, my dear. Truly. I'll give these papers back tomorrow. I know I can count on you to return them to the drawer at the earliest opportunity after that."

"Oh yes, Dr. Harrison. I will!"

I escort Janice to the door. "I don't need to remind you that this matter is of the utmost confidence." I close the door carefully behind her, relieved to be alone.

Back at my desk, I examine the papers Janice brought more closely. Each one is crammed: formulae, mostly, also phrases and short sentences in German. The writing is messy and the pages are worn; I cannot easily make out the words.

I need to know whether the hand matches Bertram's; I call Cynthia and ask her to have Medical Records send up the battery of psychological tests administered to him upon admission.

"Do you think it puzzling," Bertram is asking, "the way Wernher von Braun could go so easily from being a Nazi to being an American?"

"In truth, I don't know anything about it," I say.

"I've given it a lot of thought," Bertram says, giving me an appraising look.

"And have you come to any conclusions?"

"He was perverted by science from an early age. At thirteen, he strapped fireworks to a wagon and launched it into the center of town. The thing caught fire and he was arrested, but the experience only whet-

ted his appetite. Even then, he dreamed of sending a man into space. By the time he graduated from the university, he knew his only chance for living his dream was the military. Where else would there be money for that kind of technology? Don't you see how this would color everything? How it would make a brilliant man like that long for the kind of war Hitler inflicted on the world? I can imagine his excitement when he was assigned to work on the Vengeance weapons. Vast amounts of money, an endless supply of slave labor."

Bertram is looking at me oddly now, as if he's addressing his critique at me. "In his debrief, he mentioned a visit to Buchenwald to lobby for more slaves; he had his pick of living skeletons. It was all part of the dream; what did it matter to him, which side he was on? As long as he had his labs, his workers, his equipment. All in the name of science."

"I can understand why this troubles you," I say carefully.

Bertram's eyes are challenging. "Yes. Scientific inquiry is a troubling matter, wouldn't you say?"

"Like any human endeavor, scientific inquiry can be a great many things," I respond.

"It's like a forest fire," Bertram says steadily. "It can turn everything in its path to ash."

When I return after lunch, Bertram's file from Medical Records is sitting on my desk. The handwriting is different from the scrawl on the pages Janice brought me. But there is some resemblance in the slant of the letters, and in the slightly flattened circles of the *d*'s and *b*'s.

I don't know what I'm looking for. I feel as if clues abound and yet defy me—not unlike the experience that certain patients describe: eyes everywhere that flick away the moment one turns to track them. I glance at the calendar; two weeks until my old colleague from Edinburgh visits—Ronald Fairbairn, who has become a luminary in the field. Only now do I realize how strongly, even desperately, I've been anticipating seeing him. I am no longer in control of Bertram's treatment; guilt overwhelms me, along with an appalling thought: that I am like a lifeguard with the terrible, secret knowledge that he does not himself know how to swim.

Outside, I duck into the woods, deciding on an untended path I don't normally take. It is strewn with forest debris—pine needles, fallen branches, dried leaves. The cold snap has abated; it is still chilly, but the air is softened with a trace of warmer climes.

For once, I do not think, giving myself over to the rhythm of movement and the feel of the sun on my face. Rounding a curve in the pathway, I stop short. Thirty feet away, on a bench half-obscured by overgrown bushes, sits Matilda, deep in thought. She does not seem to have heard me. I hold my breath, aware of a visceral longing pulsing somewhere between my throat and my heart. Matilda is leaning back against the bench, her legs crossed. Her coat is unbuttoned; her uniform traces the slope of her bosom, then nips in at the waist. I allow my eyes to skim the length of her body. At that moment, she turns and sees me. Her face is pooled with sadness; I expect her to exhibit surprise, but she only looks resigned, and a little ashamed.

"I see you're fond of the woods, too." I cross the distance between us.

"Yes, I am." She seems distracted.

"It clears my head, being here." I approach the bench. "May I?"

Matilda slides over. "Funny you should run into me here. I was just thinking how deserted this spot is. I imagined no one had been here in years."

"I've discovered a few places like this on the grounds. You might say I have a habit of chasing them down."

"And here you are, having chased me down, too." I expect her to smile, but she doesn't. I allow her remark to hover for a moment in the silence between us before speaking.

"I've often thought it was deliberate. The way Olmsted left these patches of wilderness. As if he were making a statement."

"And what statement would that be?"

"As if he knew society would expect tailored lawns and formal gardens, which he made sure to provide, but wanted to make his own private comment about the truth of mental illness."

"Is this the truth, then?"

I follow her eyes, which flit from the overgrown bushes to the enormous trees crowding the sky with their tangled branches, then down to the pathway thick with sloughed off leaves that are broken where our feet recently crushed them.

"I was thinking about it more as the unruliness of nature—the stark beauty of the untamed."

"That's an antiquated notion, isn't it?" Matilda's voice is distant. "The madman as wild man, boiling over with instinct. Freed from the constraints of civilization. Forgive me, but I find that view a little romantic and, to be frank, just a bit condescending."

"I didn't mean it that way." I feel a rush of sadness. "That's just sometimes how it strikes me. The truth is, I find tremendous solace here. I prefer it by far to the botanical perfection the gardeners labor over in the formal gardens."

"I daresay the patients see us as rather like those gardeners." Her eyes are suddenly full of feeling.

"Perhaps. More often, I get the sense that they're relieved to let someone else manage things for a time."

"Funny you should say that."

"Oh?"

"What we do here—it's poles apart from regular nursing. Not at all what I imagined." The distress is visible in Matilda's face. "It's a kind of juggling I'm not very good at."

"You're one of the most gifted nurses I've ever known. What you're talking about . . . what I think you're talking about . . . well, that's part of the gift."

"When I think about the work I did during the War, I can hardly bear it, the number of lives that slipped through my fingers. But no matter how bad it was, it made a certain sense. When things go wrong with the body . . . well, it's something you can understand. I was always aware of feeling, *There but for the grace of God go I.* I felt like we were in it together."

"Is it really so dissimilar here?" I am blindsided by the frankness of Matilda's gaze.

"I don't know. Is it?"

On my way back to the office, I stop by the Rogers Gymnasium, where some patients are working on the sets for *A Midsummer Night's Dream.* This year, among our residents, we have a reputed artist; he has turned

the far wall into a beautifully rendered woodland. A delicate backwash of silvers and yellows peeks through the leaves and shows in places among the clouds. The walls are stacked with large canvases in various stages of completion; one is the set for the play within a play, an abstract in primary colors that provides a dramatic contrast to the ethereal realism of the woodland.

"What marvelous sets," I say.

Mr. Frieling shyly smiles. This work seems to have helped him shed the last vestiges of the depression he came in with a year ago; after the pageant, he'll be going home.

Janice hastens toward me from the far side of the room, her face expectant.

"I'm so happy you came," she says a little oddly, as if this were a party she were throwing.

"The sets are coming along nicely," I offer, heading back out of the gym. Janice walks with me.

"Could we have a word?" she asks breathlessly, once we're outside.

"Aren't you on duty?"

"Nurse Jansen just relieved me. I'm on my way to the cafeteria for my coffee break."

"Very well, then. I'll accompany you."

"It's the patient—the one we talked about before. He said something yesterday that may be important."

"Oh? What was that?" On the far side of the great lawn, the Scotch pines cut precise green wedges from the white sky.

"We were on our way back from the print shop. He's very skilled—he seems to do everything well. I asked him how the printing had gone. That's when he said it."

Janice halts and unfolds the piece of paper she's holding.

"I wrote it down afterward, so that I wouldn't forget. These were his exact words: *The printing press can be put to good or to ill use. That's true of all progress, don't you think? Machines are dogs, but they're also cobras.*"

Janice looks up eagerly. "It sounds . . . well, loopy, doesn't it?"

She blushes. "I don't mean that disrespectfully, Doctor. Just that it seemed a bit . . . disordered. But then I thought about it. Dogs are a man's best friend, and cobras can kill. It's rather clever, really, don't you think?"

"Yes, I do. Thank you for taking the trouble to note it down: more food for thought."

We part ways at the fork, and I head back across the lawn toward the main entrance. I pass by Featherstone and Cuthbert, who are bundled up for their walk; Featherstone is tossing crumbs ahead of him to a squirrel, tame as a cat, who hops along picking up the pieces as he goes.

"Quite the *bouleversement,* hey, Doctor?" Cuthbert grins. "Usually it's the squirrel who chases the nuts. But here we are—a couple of nuts chasing a squirrel!"

"I daresay he's not complaining," I reply.

Featherstone cocks his head skyward and anxiously scans. "We should go in before they strafe."

"Oh, don't worry about the enemy," Cuthbert announces cheerfully. "They never strafe when the squirrels are out."

This seems to satisfy Featherstone, who continues intently on behind the squirrel.

I arrive at my office five minutes before Bertram's session to find him seated in the waiting area beside Gilmore, the orderly who accompanied him up. He eyes me with interest; I feel a little caught off guard.

In my office, he picks up where he left off yesterday, as if there had been not twenty-four hours since we last spoke but a gap of only a few minutes.

"Don't you find it distressing? That a scientist would overlook everything in the name of his work? As if science were more important than human suffering—than human life."

"You seem to assume that I don't find such things distressing," I say.

"You've never said or done anything to indicate that you do," Bertram replies.

"What would you expect me to say or do?"

"I don't know."

"You seem determined to see me as lacking in moral conviction."

"Yes, I suppose I do see you that way." Bertram's gaze is not challenging, only probing.

"A bit like Wernher von Braun himself," I offer.

"I hadn't thought of the connection, but now that you make it . . ." A suspicious look passes across Bertram's features.

"What makes you most angry about von Braun?" I ask.

"I would think that's pretty obvious," he replies.

"It's not obvious to me."

Bertram appears to lose himself in thought. After a few minutes, he continues. "When he surrendered, he had a broken arm; it was hanging awkwardly in a sling made out of a shirt. There'd been a car accident . . ."

Bertram's voice trails off. There is something rehearsed about the way he's talking.

"Later, they had to rebreak the arm and reset it—it hadn't been done right the first time." He gazes out of the window. "I can't remember whether it was his left or his right arm that was broken."

"Is there a reason this is of significance?" I say, thinking it odd that Bertram didn't mention the broken arm before, when he told me about finding von Braun behind the wall in the concentration camp.

"Well, yes. It has to do with his prowess—pulling off their incredible escape. How much harder it would have been if it were his dominant arm that was broken."

Bertram has a disconcerting, faraway look in his eyes.

"I'm not sure what you're talking about," I say.

"He was in command of five hundred scientists—engineers, mostly: the minds behind the V-Ones and V-Twos. He stole a train, forged a mass of papers. Can you imagine what that journey across Germany was like? Complete chaos, everything in ruins, playing cat-and-mouse with their own army—under orders from Hitler to execute them on sight. Hitler didn't want their knowledge falling into the Allies' hands. It was von Braun who managed to get them safely across Germany in order to surrender to the Americans."

Bertram speaks rapidly in a pressured, almost manic tone, tripping over his words to get the story out. This account of von Braun's surrender to the Americans shares nothing with his earlier telling: the capture in the concentration camp, in which the American soldier was killed.

"What happened after the surrender?" The sound of my voice seems to startle him.

"Oh," he says. "Well, the engineers had hidden their papers in a mountain. The U.S. Army made efforts to recover the paperwork, and also whatever they could of the V-Two rockets in development at Peenemünde. They took what they could and destroyed the rest. The scientists—von Braun was the jewel in the crown—went through a short

debriefing in Germany. Then, they were transferred to the United States to undergo more questioning."

This is not the first time I've heard more than one version of a war tale from Bertram. "I'm wondering how this fits in with what you told me some time ago: about how you found von Braun hiding behind a freshly built wall."

"But, Doctor, you are mistaken. That wasn't von Braun. That capture was straight SS—nothing to do with the rocket scientists. I should have killed that bastard when I had the chance. He walked, you know; he's free as a bird. Probably running some government agency in the *New Germany*."

At change-of-shift meeting, Matilda seems preoccupied. I find myself studying her, wondering if anyone else notices the inward gaze, the way she fiddles with her handkerchief, the rote quality of her replies.

After the meeting, I accompany Matilda back to the Nurses' Residence. It is a clear night; above us, the sky is bright with stars.

"I'm sorry about what I said earlier today," I say.

Her face sags with strain. "You have nothing to apologize for. I was being testy. And ungracious."

"I don't mean to intrude, but something seems to be troubling you."

Matilda nods, her lips drawn tight.

"If there's any way I can be helpful—"

She searches my face.

"I don't mean—in a professional capacity." There is uncertainty in my voice. "If there's anything you'd like to talk over—"

Matilda's control slides away; she averts her eyes. "Actually . . ." she begins, then pauses. "My mother has not been well . . ." Her voice trails off.

"Well, if there's anything I can do—"

"I appreciate that, Dr. Harrison. Really, I do."

We come to a halt outside the Nurses' Residence. Matilda looks down at her feet. She seems so helpless, so lost; I do not wish to leave. I find myself wanting to take her in my arms, to draw her to me, to remove the starchy white cap and press my face into her hair. I want to hold Matilda and make things right.

"See you tomorrow, then," I say. My arms hang heavily at my sides.

"Yes," she replies. "Thank you for seeing me home."

I watch as she disappears through the front door. The lighted-up windows make a checkerboard of the façade; I wait to see if a new bright square will appear—Matilda entering her room—but the pattern remains unchanged.

My toes are painfully cold; I realize I must have been standing here for a very long time. Aware of an aching emptiness, I turn and head toward home.

I slept badly last night, plagued by a disquieting dream; I was clinging to the top of the Williamsburgh Bank Building—I saw it once when we visited an aunt of Ursula's who lives in Brooklyn on Lefferts Boulevard. I'm quite afraid of heights, and in the dream, teetering wildly as the sky threw up an unbalancing wind, I castigated myself for getting into such a dangerous and impossible situation.

At breakfast, Ursula suggests we take a drive this weekend to Old Black Point to visit some friends. The thought of the weekend I can expect brings on a headache: holed up in a drafty mansion with endless rooms and lugubrious furnishings, being waited on by elderly servants in the vast dining room, hours of canasta and dreary conversation.

"I'm knee-deep in work," I falter.

"Why not bring it with you?" She attempts to sound breezy, though the anxiety in her eyes gives her away. "You could spend the day in their library; we wouldn't bother you until dinner."

"I think it will have to wait until after Fairbairn's visit."

"Very well, dear," she says flatly, clearing the table while I finish my coffee and try to read the newspaper; I am thrown by the monitoring glances she throws my way like silent, invisible darts.

In my office, I struggle through my morning sessions, jangled by restlessness. By lunchtime, my chest feels tight and my office is uncomfortably close. I decide to skip the cafeteria and get some fresh air.

Outside, I head directly to the woods, which have begun to feel familiar again, though altered—as if I'm seeing everything both as it was many years ago and as it is now at the same time. The cold sun sparkles through the leaves; I walk through little pools of light.

Once, I held a session with Delilah in the Women's Occupational Therapy Pavilion; she was the only one signed up for weaving that day, so I walked her over. I would do that sometimes—meet with patients while they were busy working with their hands. I see her now, leaning into the loom, her lips pursed in concentration, the window behind her a square of waning afternoon light. My eye catches on the arrow of Canadian geese that appears, like a constellation, in the sky. Delilah has seen them, too; she turns to watch their movement.

"Is it preposterous," she says lightly, watching the geese as they wheel and then disappear from sight, "to think that a doctor might fall in love with a patient?"

I am struck speechless. I cannot take my eyes from the nape of her neck, where her hair is piled softly in a loose bun. She waits for me to say something. It is silent in the weaving room, Delilah is preternaturally still; the air seems brittle.

"No, Delilah," I say. "It is not preposterous."

"Does it happen here, do you think?"

Everything goes muffled and milky.

"I imagine it might," I say, my voice unfamiliar and far away.

"Has it ever happened to you?"

Now, she looks at me—slowly, allowing her eyes to settle on my face with deliberateness and care. I hesitate.

"No, Delilah," I say softly.

My words wound the air between us.

"And if it did happen? What would you do?"

"There are rules in our profession. We have ways of dealing with such situations."

"Oh?" With her eyes, she is beseeching me to tell the truth. "What kinds of ways?"

"It's part of our training." I have no idea what I am saying.

"What sort of training would do that to a person?" she almost whispers. Her eyes: I feel their intoxicating pull.

"I am trained to keep the patient's best interests foremost in my mind."

I see it now, in the dizzying depth of her gaze: Delilah is drowning. And pleading with me to save her. To tell her the truth so that she might survive. Her hands fall lifelessly into her lap.

I snap back to the present—and walk, only walk, trying to numb my mind. I have lost my way, but I no longer care. The raw air pulses with white sunlight. And then, the faint sound of water: the brook for which this hospital is named. It plunges me back again, the sound a trip wire, and my feet seem suddenly possessed of knowledge beyond my awareness. I veer off the narrow pathway into tangled vegetation, pulling aside branches and vines, stepping over logs; lizards dart out of my way, and a hardy bird gives a few shrill peeps. The brook is more distinct now: I train my ears on the gentle warbling.

I was out walking that day, almost twenty years ago, battling with myself. The conversation with Delilah in the weaving room had rent something in me; I couldn't put the moment from my mind. Around Ursula I had become tongue-tied and ashamed, certain she could see I was at war with myself. I was afraid of looking at her—afraid that I would inadvertently say Delilah's name and that the terrible, blinding passion I felt for Delilah would spill out through my eyes and give me away.

The sound of the brook becomes louder.

Here—the place that was cordoned off, after the accident. I have never come back to this spot. Now, I move past giant tree trunks the workers dragged around the area and piled with logs; they are covered in brambles and lichen.

That day, taken aback by the deserted beauty of the place, I came to a sudden halt. It was hard to believe that so close to the hospital there existed this lush wilderness, alive with birdsong and bright with glimpses of woodland berries. Then I was startled from my reverie by the approach of a group of patients, out on a walk with a nurse and two orderlies, who had ventured beyond the customary pathways, perhaps because of the unseasonably warm day. They were picking their way across the ground cover of sword ferns, dragon's blood, and creeping flox; I watched them, aware of an unusual shift in my perception, all of us being out of context. Not patients walking there, avoiding the snares underfoot, but people: people with whom I felt a greater affinity than anyone else in my life.

And then, I heard the distant crashing, through low vegetation and branches; at first, it sounded like a wild beast. The truck that had lost its way. Later, the grounds staff found the section of ruined fencing, not far

from where the "gorge" began, by the wildest section of woods, where no one typically went. I saw Delilah before she saw me: saw the abandon in her face, the pleasure at being in the fresh air. The jarring, out-of-place shriek of failing brakes, the crashing, growing louder: the truck cutting through trees, crushing flowers and vines, tearing off branches, inciting the unseen wildlife to panic.

The patients turned their heads in the direction of the sound, turned almost as one person to identify the source of the unexpected commotion, but I kept my eyes on Delilah.

Now, I climb up over the barricade and walk toward the clearing.

How unlikely, that a truck would lose its way and end up on that unused length of road running through the woods. That the patients would cross paths with the truck at just that moment—and that I, out on my daily walk, would find myself at this exact spot, *all at the very same time.* How impossible, and yet it happened: a dreadful aligning of planets.

Delilah saw me, just as the truck broke through the trees, moving faster than anyone could have expected. The driver must have been gunning his engine, afraid he would get caught in the soft dirt of the abandoned road. The crunching of twigs and leaves, the harsh revving of a low gear being ridden fast: Delilah turned her head; I looked into her face to see a blossoming of pure joy—sensual and alive and directed toward me. In that instant, she seemed to forget herself, to forget the strictures of our situation; she walked toward me, dipping her head and smiling with touching coyness, closing the gap between us. And then she stopped short; she was studying my face—looking into me, beyond the surface, in that unsettling way she had. It was only an instant, and then I watched as her face clouded, the joy snuffed. I parted my lips to say something—and then bit down on my words, grinding myself, the man, beneath the heel of my doctor persona.

She stared right into me, an expression of disbelief growing on her face, her eyes frantic, and then hopeless. Still the grating of the gears, growing louder: the crashing through leaves, branches being ripped from their trunks. Delilah snapped her head in the direction of the sound, then back to me, and again toward the trees. We all saw it then, the old, heavy pickup truck with its peeling red paint and rusted fenders, barreling around the curve and breaking out into the open. The male

nurse and two orderlies sprang to action, like giant sheep dogs instinctively roused: the patients drawn back quickly, deftly, one after the other, by the powerful arms of the attendants, both accomplished wrestlers, a condition of their hire. Had they not seen that Delilah had pulled away—that she'd strayed from the group and was hastening toward me? Did they assume I would see to her safety?

It was an instant, less than an instant: in her eyes, the quick calculation, a sharp beam, all of her intelligence put to the matter. For several crucial seconds, she held herself tightly back, in preparation, part of the calculation, like a runner awaiting the *crack* of the starting pistol. Our eyes locked—I was unable to move. And then she flung herself toward me, deliberately throwing herself into the path of the truck; I felt it—the query in her face—as if she had screamed it above the crashing of the truck for all to hear. *Dr. Harrison, do you love me, too?* And then, she gritted her jaw: her own answer to the question she'd asked me in that final moment, wordlessly, with her eyes.

No sound but the screeching of brakes.

It is after midnight when I realize I forgot to order up dinner from the dining hall. My stomach contracts. The ice in the ice bucket has melted; I don't like neat whiskey on an empty stomach, so I switch to vodka.

Out in the woods this afternoon, I knew that tonight I would open my pillow box and take out the instruments I've not seen for so many years: the long needles with their thickened tips, the cloisonné stem and saddle, the pipe bowl, carved from lapis and engraved with two tiny, dancing phoenixes. The exquisite little paktong lamp, the slender bottle of oil; the oval box made of layered Peking glass, which contains a large chunk of purified opium, perfumed with ginseng. I give in to the anticipation with an overpowering sense of relief.

After closing the curtains, I retrieve the pillow box from the back of the closet. The flying dragon, etched in gold on the polished wood, is full of magical promise. My ears are trained on the quiet ticking of the clock; I wait for the sound of the church bells.

A single chime. No chance, at this hour, of being surprised. I snap open the brass latch—there on the tray, all those beautiful objects, just

as I remembered them. The night enhances my concentration; I can breathe more freely in the unencumbered darkness.

For a moment, I hesitate, thinking back to how it was almost twenty years ago. I see Ursula again, urging me to stop, me insisting there was nothing to worry about, that smoking was no different from taking a sherry or two after dinner, that it had no impact on my work. *It's not your work I'm worried about,* she'd said. *What then?* She'd given no answer, though I saw in her face that Ursula believed—wanted to believe—that our marital distance was due to my habit. Not knowing how to respond, I'd said what I shouldn't have: *Dr. Greely, whom you so admire, makes a practice of it, says it sharpens his mind.* In fact, I'd never discussed any such thing with Dr. Greely, but I was certain he was a habitual smoker, now that I, too, was a devotee and could therefore recognize the signs. And it was true he was as sharp as ever; everyone thought him at the height of his powers.

Putting these thoughts from my mind, I light the oil in the lamp, assemble the pipe, and then scoop a pellet of opium onto the tip of one needle. I hold the pellet carefully above the heat, transferring it back and forth from one needle to the other, watching it soften and swell. When it is ready, I place the sticky lump over the little opening in the pipe bowl and carefully pierce it before inhaling. I inhale once, and then again, holding it in until I am dizzy. The room is thick with the distinctive sweetness, which is touched with a bitter spice. It courses through my being, clarifying, dissolving, slaking a desperate ache I hadn't fully realized has been throbbing angrily at the back of things.

I can breathe, again; my muscles relax and I melt into the bliss.

Delilah is smiling, only smiling. We are at the pond; together, we watch the fireflies. As they dart, their colors change: not white light, now, but orange and magenta, a streak of blue. *How lovely you are,* I say.

<div align="center">≺≺⋅⊱≻</div>

Part II

Chapter Five

I'm in trouble," Bertram says simply, after he has taken his seat.
"I'm listening," I reply.

"I won't offer apologies or mea culpas. I've been involved with some-one. Here, at the hospital."

Bertram is scanning me to gauge my response.

"Matilda," he says. "Nurse Willoughby. We meet at night, in the tun-nels. We've made a place there for ourselves."

His eyes stray to the window. I am aware of how much Bertram has changed in the months he has been here; he seems physically altered, wilder, somehow, and deeply shaken. His admission hangs turbulently in the air, startling me so that I, too, feel shaken. Until now, my knowledge of their affair has been private for me, wholly inner; having him declare it like this has the peculiar effect of making me feel exposed.

The truth slams into me; I am failing my patient, Bertram.

"It has happened once or twice before, but never like last night . . ." Bertram's voice fades. He stares out the window, lost in thought.

"What has happened before?" I quietly ask.

He turns to me, his eyes filled with pain. "I get terribly confused."

"That's one of the reasons you're here."

"With all due respect, Doctor, that's not why I came here."

"Maybe so, but if that's what you're experiencing now, perhaps it's something I can help you with."

"It's the closest thing to love I have experienced, since . . ."

I wait.

"Since losing Rosamund. I feel very grateful that we've found each other. It might not have happened. Especially given the circumstances."

He moves his gaze around my office.

"The way I feel about Matilda is so like the way I felt about Rosamund. It's hard to make it separate. It's inside *me,* and it's the same as how I felt before. Sometimes it feels like Rosamund and Matilda must—well, must somehow be the same person."

The agitation grows in Bertram's face and spills out into the room.

"Rosamund and I never even kissed," he whispers. "That tortures me. Sometimes, when I'm with Matilda, I lose myself. I don't know where I go: somewhere that contains all three of us. I know this must sound odd; Rosamund is dead. But *feelings* don't die, do they?"

I don't answer the question.

"It happened once, at the beginning, with Matilda; I opened my eyes while we were kissing and realized that I expected to see Rosamund's face, not hers. It startled me. But I quickly shook it. I'm not an expert on love. I figured that these things happen—that it's just the way it can be.

"But then, it happened again, and this time, it wasn't fleeting. I was with Matilda, but I felt as if I was with Rosamund. It's not how it sounds—I wasn't thinking of Rosamund or trying to fantasize Matilda away, nothing like that. It was just as if Rosamund's spirit was there with us, in the room."

I can hardly believe Bertram is talking so openly, taking me to the place he goes with Matilda—to the very place I stood, that night, and spied. I feel jittery, unmasked, though he cannot know what I have done. The longing leaps back to life, the longing to be part of it—to be the one who moves silently around the jerry-rigged wall of bedside tables and lowers her onto the bed.

Bertram is gazing out the window.

"But last night . . ." I prompt.

"Yes. Last night." Feelings pass across Bertram's face like tumbling clouds. "I was with Matilda, and I found myself feeling Rosamund's presence more and more strongly, and I—well, I wasn't even there. Not really. I was in that place where I disappear. We were moving together, no longer Matilda, no longer me: just two bodies, and feelings—and then, I suddenly felt a terrible pain. It was like someone had hit me on the head with a sharp object.

"I must have dozed off, I must have been dreaming. But it didn't feel like a dream. I was looking at Matilda and I knew it was her, but I also knew that it was Rosamund! I could hear Rosamund's voice—telling me about her brother, her parents, all of them dead. She'd been selected by a doctor. She was saying that they'd heard terrible rumors—that they'd heard the screams of women taken away, some with their newborn babies.

"I didn't know what to do. Someone was going to do unspeakable things to Rosamund and I *had* to do something! Then suddenly, Matilda was looking at me—her eyes were sleepy, and a little afraid. When she said my name, I came to my senses."

"Do you remember what you were feeling in that moment—when Matilda opened her eyes?"

"That I'd do anything to save Rosamund from what she was being put through."

Bertram makes a strangled noise through clamped teeth.

"Isn't there something you can do? Some treatment that will stop this kind of thing?"

"Are you thinking of any treatment in particular?" I ask.

"ECT. Insulin coma therapy. I don't know—surgery," he says quietly. "There has to be something that can make all of this go away."

A chill comes over me.

Bertram looks at me uneasily. "I'd never harm her, Dr. Harrison. I know I wouldn't."

"You don't sound convinced."

"I know myself," he whispers.

"That may be true. But it seems to me that, lately, your behavior has not been entirely under your control. You're going to have to stop seeing her."

"I'm not sure I can." I hear a shadow of fear in Bertram's voice.

"I'm afraid you have no choice."

"*Music Under the Stars* is broadcasting Duke Ellington," Ursula says brightly at dinner. "I wrote down the program." She checks a slip of paper beside her plate. "*New World A-Comin',* and something I've never heard: *Three Black Kings.*"

"I might have time for the first part."

Ursula rises to clear the plates. "Still a lot to do for Fairbairn's visit?"

I nod.

"Well, then. I'll get dessert and we can listen to the first part together."

We sit side by side on the couch. The music is wonderful; halfway through the piece, I take Ursula's hand. Her face shines gently with happiness. The music floods the room, and for a moment I forget about the hospital. But then the audience erupts into applause and I become aware of a sudden pounding in my head. Delicately, I remove my hand from Ursula's and stand.

"Off you go, then," she says without reproach. "I won't wait up."

On a whim, instead of going directly to my office, I take the back staircase up to the servants' quarters on the third floor. Approaching the lounge, I hear lively sounds: talking and laughing, and the continuation of the Duke Ellington broadcast, the music brimming with the promise of pleasure.

Seeing Mr. Thomas in his shirtsleeves and slippers, settled over a game of cards, I realize it was a mistake to come up here at this hour. But he has already noticed me. A discreet look passes between the two players, and then Thomas excuses himself and crosses to the doorway where I stand against the jamb, trying to look at ease.

"Good evening, Dr. Harrison," he says, as if there were nothing unexpected about my visit. Even in his shirtsleeves, Thomas is in full command of his professional demeanor.

"I wonder if we might have a word," I say. "Would you care for an evening stroll?"

He gives a quarter bow and pops back into the lounge. "I'll hold the game then, Reggie," I hear his friend say, and then Thomas disappears

down the hallway, reappearing some minutes later wearing jacket, tie, and shoes.

Outside, we slacken our pace to an amble.

"I hope you'll forgive me," I begin. "I only came because of what you mentioned—the last time we spoke."

"I beg your pardon, sir, but I'm not sure what you're referring to."

"When you told me you were a medic—well, it changed things. The situation is complicated, but you see, we are in a sense colleagues. Didn't you yourself say: once a medic, always a medic? Between you and me, Mr. Thomas, I'm a believer in the idea that rules are sometimes best handled by judicious bending."

Thomas's expression is studiously patient.

"I was thinking you might have some useful information about Mr. Reiner from when you were, like me, in the position of administering care."

Thomas gives a slow nod. "I see your point, sir. Before I entered his employ, I did in fact tend to him in a medical capacity."

"I was puzzled by what you implied—that you treated Mr. Reiner for some injury. But you also said that you only met him on the ship home—the ship that sailed from Germany. Surely by then whatever injury he'd sustained would have healed? By that point, the War had been over for months. Unless it was some repercussion from an earlier wound?"

We round the corner and walk along the edge of the formal gardens, which seem vaguely menacing in the thin moonlight glow.

"There were many injuries after the fighting stopped," he says. "Why, there were all kinds of dangerous situations, not to mention accidents."

There is something too smooth in the sound of his voice. "Is that what happened to Bertram? Some kind of accident?"

Thomas allows a long silence.

"I don't feel comfortable discussing the details of his situation, sir." He says this in his distinctive, unruffled tone. "I agree with you about rules, and how they sometimes serve us best when set aside. But the fact that Mr. Reiner and I met under different circumstances than those in which we now find ourselves puts me in a difficult situation. Friendship has its own code."

He gives me a meaningful look, as if something were now under-stood between us.

"I wouldn't dream of asking you to betray a confidence. It would just be helpful for me to know how Bertram sustained his injury. He's been reluctant to talk about it, and I thought—well, from one medic to another—"

"I must respectfully redirect you to Mr. Reiner. If he's reluctant to talk about it, why then I imagine he must have his reasons."

"We often rely on information from external sources. The patient does not always know best in these matters."

Thomas allows another lengthy pause.

"In truth, I do not think of Mr. Reiner as a patient. Perhaps this is a failing on my part; he is, after all, a resident here at Shadowbrook. But I can only reiterate that I suggest you direct your questions to him."

Thomas's gaze lingers on me; he seems to be puzzling over some-thing, though he says nothing further.

Back in my office, I pull out Fairbairn's article on the schizoid per-sonality. Scanning the opening sentences, I feel a flush of hope: perhaps my distinguished colleague will be able to help me turn the corner in treating Bertram.

Close to midnight, I head over to Hall Two for change of shift. Through the window of the nurses' station, I see Matilda and two senior nurses, sharing a laugh.

"Good evening, Dr. Harrison," Nurse O'Halahan says as I enter. "Did you know that Mr. Cuthbert has put together a compendium of jokes about psychiatry? A farewell gift to the hall, if you please. He's typed them up and mimeographed copies to hand around. Some of them are priceless."

"How about a sample?" I ask.

"Go on, Vanessa," Matilda says. "Tell him the one you just told us. I can't tell a joke to save my life."

"Heavens, putting me on the spot—and it's hardly a flattering joke."

"I'm up for it," I say, curious now, and wanting to prolong the plea-sure of seeing Matilda smile.

Vanessa tells a joke I've heard before that never fails to amuse—about a patient who believes himself to be General MacArthur. She tells it well,

and when she's finished, I smile, and Matilda lets out a husky laugh. I realize I've never heard Matilda laugh before.

"Mr. Cuthbert is threatening to do a reading at his farewell lunch," Matilda says.

"I think it will do the patients good," I say. "We could use a little more levity around here."

"It was beautiful, perfect, whole," Cuthbert says, his eyes glistening with tears.

It is our second lap of the formal gardens; two gardeners are busy placing burlap bags over the plantings, cozying them up for the long winter ahead.

"In the entire history of human thought, there has never been anything like *this*. Everything captured, explained—the mind-body problem merely one of the quandaries finally put to rest. I had it all, right here." Cuthbert points to his temple. "Exploding in my head like Fourth of July fireworks; I didn't think it through so much as witness the brilliant eruptions. It was breathtaking, Dr. Harrison, truly breathtaking."

He has spoken of this often: the best moment of his life, but also the worst. Cuthbert was a graduate student in mathematics when he had his first psychotic break, which included an ecstatic experience in which he felt as if all of human experience was revealed to him in the form of a dazzling, and original, scientific theorem: what he calls a "psychomathematical proof of the meaning of life." So entranced was he, so convinced it was burned into his consciousness forever, that he failed to write any of it down. And then, the revelation evaporated.

He was found in his student lodgings dazed, unwashed, muttering under his breath, and inflamed with rage; he'd had his hands around *Truth* and all that was left was an echo of a memory.

"Do you remember," he asks thoughtfully, "how last year, at Christmas, Leo Grimaldi hid behind the tree, eating the silver balls? I was sick with worry about him for days. It's a miracle he didn't lacerate his innards. I'm afraid that Featherstone might do something like that this year."

"What brings this to mind now?"

"There's an example of how useful my lost theorem would have been. Just think how much easier it would be if you could predict such things before they happen. As it stands, you're shooting in the dark."

"The tree trimming is still some weeks away. I assure you, we'll keep a close watch on Featherstone."

We pass the pedestrian crossing sign, which reads PED XING, and Cuthbert pauses, his intelligent eyes twinkling.

"We are now entering the Chinese Village!" he declares with self-mocking pomp.

"You were saying," I prompt.

"Featherstone's not the only one I'm worrying about. I've had a message—it came through the metal grille in the elevator. Did you see how changed it was this morning? The pattern was entirely different."

"It looked unchanged to me."

"We're not all given the privilege of second sight, Dr. Harrison. But you have other gifts."

"Who are you worried about?"

"The Professor. The rooster thing was charming—and harmless. But he's given that up. I think he really has succumbed to *hatch* illness. Nothing's been spared—it's the 'so-called hospital,' and 'my so-called wife,' and the 'so-called patients.' At morning meeting, he referred to you as the 'so-called hospital director.' He won't take his medicine—phony nurses, he says, giving him phony pills. He said that when we put up the 'so-called Christmas tree,' he's going to set it on fire. Featherstone said he'd help: a pagan act for a pagan festival. I suggest you help us with the trimming this year; we need you to keep things in order."

"We have able staff on the hall. I'm sure they can take care of things."

"How I wish that were so. But everything's run amok. It's a far cry from how it used to be."

"Are you talking about anyone in particular?"

"I'm not at liberty to give names," he says. "But 'a certain head nurse' is toying with me—changing the terms of the communication system. I can feel my mind disintegrating; it's collapsing as we speak. I'm not thinking, so much as rummaging through the filing system in my brain and removing pieces of data. It's a retrieval system, not intuitive thought. Intuitive thinkers create; I just regurgitate."

Cuthbert falls silent. We pass more flower beds covered in burlap.

"I miss the daffodils," he says sadly. " *'For oft, when on my couch I lie, in vacant or in pensive mood,'*" he recites. " *'They flash upon that inward eye, which is the bliss of solitude.'* Daffodils are the antidote to knowledge. That's what Wordsworth meant; remember, he'd been *'wandering lonely as a cloud.'* Clouds are nothing but gas—he's saying he'd been vaporized, destroyed by his own mind. It was the daffodils that revivified him, brought him back from the final, gaseous disintegration brought about by *too much thinking.*"

"Why would thinking have made him disintegrate?"

"Because knowledge is a dangerous thing. Do you know what *analyze* means? *To break apart.* To destroy, in effect. Freud set matters on a very destructive path, with his invention of psychoanalysis—accurately defined, *destruction of the psyche.* We're in a very difficult situation, having to protect ourselves from the efforts of the staff who are well-meaning but, with all due respect, deluded: thinking that treatment is somehow predicated on *knowing*—on always *knowing more.* The truth is, we're being killed by the cure."

"I agree with you that knowledge can be misused," I interject. "But I find myself more often focusing on the ways in which it is put to good use."

"Do they sugarcoat those psychiatry diplomas they hand out?" Cuthbert asks. "Or is it enough just to have you believe all of that?"

"All of what?"

"The *rosecoloredglasses* crap. Try pulling that with Featherstone. He'll tell you stories that even a saint couldn't cast in a rosy light. Speaking of whitewashing—I never see you in Sunday chapel. Is there a reason for that? Do you consider yourself a godly man?"

"I suppose I do, in a way. Why?"

Cuthbert gives a hearty laugh. "It's a treat, listening to Preacher Snow. That's what we call him—he's *Snow White,* and we're his *dwarves*: hundreds of us. I'm a *Happy,* and I needn't tell you that Featherstone's a *Grumpy.* It's all a fairy tale to him. His sermons are *the triumph of pablum.* It does provide entertainment, I suppose, and there's something to be said for that."

"You were talking about the dangers of knowledge."

Cuthbert looks thoughtful.

"I suppose you have a point there."

"A point?"

"Perhaps Preacher Snow is only trying to protect us from the dangers of *knowing*: you can be sure there's not a single intelligent word in anything he says. Maybe I should take my hat off to him, but they don't let me wear my hat in the chapel."

"You asked if I was a godly man."

"I made a study of Hebrew—for biblical purposes. Do you know that in Hebrew—and this is true of Aramaic as well, from which it derives—there is no actual present tense? You take the abstract root and construct the tense using dispensable vowel symbols: little dots and lines that tell you how to understand what you're reading. In all of the Hebrew language, there's only one word in the present tense; to pronounce that word is forbidden—*Y-A-H-W-E-H*: that's how it's written. It holds two meanings that are one and the same: God's name, and *Being*. So, what do you take from that?"

"What do *you* take from it?"

"Ha! Exactly!"

"I'm sorry?"

"Yes, you have it! Turning it back to me is precisely the right—the *only*—answer. It means that in order to truly *be*, to live in the divine *presence*, you must not *know* anything *in* the *present*. Memories are safe, if you can erase their original livinginthemoment source—like forgetting a sound but remembering its echo. That is permitted, that is safe. You may *remember*, but you may not *know*."

Cuthbert is looking at me with urgency.

"You seem to be trying to tell me something."

"*Of course*, I'm trying to tell you something!" he says, exasperated.

"I don't think I'm getting the meaning you intend."

"You have to look and listen *beyond* what is audible, what is visible," he says intently. "Otherwise, you'll incur God's wrath—and then you'll be made to know nothing at all."

We round the corner to see the Hall Two occupational therapy contingent returning for lunch: fourteen men carefully bundled in heavy coats, scarves, hats, and gloves, walking single file behind Matilda. They walk obediently, men with a destination they've not chosen. All of them but Bertram wear similar expressions—world-weary faces, relaxed to a

kind of relieved emptiness. Matilda greets me in the sanitized, cheerful tone staff adopt with one another in the presence of patients. As Bertram passes, he gives me a probing look.

Cuthbert eyes Bertram and then waits until they are gone before speaking. "There's a dark horse," he says grimly, shaking his head.

"Who's a dark horse?"

"You know very well who. There's trouble in paradise, surely as I'm standing here. I've set it all down in my new theorem. Psychiatry could benefit from a set of psychomathematical proofs."

"Tell me about your new theorem."

Cuthbert steps up his pace; his speech, too, accelerates, and his face becomes animated. "About what's going wrong at the hospital. The downward spiral. The beginning of the end. All ends start at the beginning—down is up and up is ending. Start the part that stops the heart, chart the start that ends the lark. No more lark means stark depart."

Cuthbert suddenly looks fearful. He steps off the pathway and hastens down the sloping lawn.

"We need to be getting back," I call out, veering off the path behind him.

"There's just a little something . . ." he calls back, coming to a halt by a circle of soil set in the lawn from which a large rosebush rises, barren now, its thorny arms crooked and sad. Cuthbert reaches over and snaps off a thin twig, then hands it to me, smiling broadly.

"For your friend," he announces magnanimously. "I happen to know she's very fond of roses." Cuthbert licks his full lips a few times, scanning my face expectantly.

"It's a nice thought," I say, "but there's no bloom. Perhaps we ought to wait until the spring."

" '*One must have a mind of winter,*' " Cuthbert recites. " '*To regard the frost and the boughs of the pine trees crusted with snow . . .*' "

"We must be getting back," I say gently, taking the twig Cuthbert offers and slipping it into my pocket.

At lunchtime, I arrive in the dining hall to see Matilda rising to leave. I finger the dry twig in my pocket, wondering just how much Cuthbert,

in his preternatural way, knows about my feelings. Matilda's plate looks barely touched; a large piece of fish sits in a pool of congealing butter sauce.

"You wouldn't recommend the haddock, then," I say casually.

"Oh," Matilda says uncomfortably, glancing at her plate. "I'm sure it's very good. I just don't have an appetite today; perhaps I'm coming down with something."

How changeable she is, I think, recalling her lightness and warmth last week in the nurses' station. It strikes me now with force; what a terribly confusing time it must be for her. But then another pang, recalling the sounds they made, Matilda and Bertram, in their secret, underground place.

"You know," I blurt out, "perhaps I should make dinner for you, sometime. I've mastered a few recipes."

I don't know what possessed me to say such a thing; I regret it, the moment the words are out.

"That's very thoughtful," Matilda says uneasily.

"Ursula makes wonderful desserts," I add, attempting to undo the awkwardness. "I'm sure she'd be delighted to have you come round one evening to the house."

"I'd like that, thank you," she says, looking away.

Back in my office, I try to focus on the matter of Bertram's treatment plan, but every time I inch toward clarity, everything tumbles back to murkiness. The alternative protocols cycle through my mind: electroconvulsive therapy, insulin coma therapy. Lobotomy: taking a saw to the skull and inserting a needle to damage the brain. How distressed Matilda looked in the dining hall—and no wonder.

For so many years, this office has been my entire world, and a refuge—the rows of books, dutifully read and underlined and read again; the carved statuettes I brought back years ago, when Ursula and I undertook what was to be our one big adventure in life, a safari in Kenya. Various trinkets given to me by patients or their families, and the botanical miniatures Ursula and I collected in antiques shops during sedate summer weekends in New England. But now, suddenly, I cannot stand to be in this room.

At the end of the main corridor, I take the stairs up to Hall Eight,

what the patients call "the back ward," where we house our most recalcitrant patients.

The atmosphere hits me the moment the door locks behind me; the air is thick with madness—it almost has a smell. It is never silent here, though the sounds are muffled by solid doors with thick glass panels through which one can watch the insane. My knees feel shaky; I reach for the wall to steady myself, listen to the faint but insistent wail, the sickening thud that is probably a head being pounded against a padded wall. The despair of a thousand patients is coming at me all at once, from the past as well as the present.

Heading toward me is Sherman, an orderly I have known for years, wheeling Mrs. Clark, who is strapped to a gurney. She has been in the hospital several times over the past five years. Her jaws are clenched onto the piece of wood placed between patients' teeth just before they're given shock treatments; she must have been resisting for Sherman to have already inserted the block. Her eyes bulge with rage and fear; she has the appearance of the living-departed.

I force myself to look at her, and she grunts. Blood trickles from the corner of her mouth; her eyes strain in my direction. She arches her thin frame and rises off the gurney: an inch, perhaps two, all that the restraints holding her down will allow.

I step aside and nod to Sherman, who fumbles for the key. I touch Mrs. Clark's clenched hand, a clump of knuckle bones wrapped tightly in skin. Her eyes plead; she is asking me for something. She unclenches her fist and grips my hand.

"Shall I accompany you?" I ask. Again, Mrs. Clark grunts and grips my hand so tightly it hurts.

I hold Mrs. Clark's hand all the way to the ECT room and then wait with her outside the door.

"They're ready for her," Sherman says, releasing the brake on the gurney.

I feel a tug on my sleeve.

"I believe she would like me to come in," I say.

The room, brightly lit with fluorescent lights, is dominated by the machinery, a complicated contraption with dials and switches and long snaking wires attached to small metal plates. I stand awkwardly by the

gurney, still clasping Mrs. Clark's hand, and when the technician casts me a querying look, I manage to extricate my hand and take a step back. Mrs. Clark's face quivers with panic, and she lets out a series of loud grunts.

"The patient is distressed," I say unnecessarily. "She seems to want me to stay."

"That's fine," the technician says nonchalantly.

The orderly removes Mrs. Clark from the gurney and places her onto the wooden table, strapping her arms and legs into leather bindings. The technician fiddles with the machinery, and then clips Mrs. Clark's hair away from her temples, exposing two small, shaved patches a few inches above each ear. He applies a clear gel to the shaved skin and sets the electrodes into place.

"Lights," he says, and Sherman flicks off the overhead, leaving only the dim light of a lamp by the ECT machine. Sherman then places his hands firmly on Mrs. Clark's shoulders; from the clenched set of his face, he seems to be pressing down quite forcefully. He nods, and the technician flips a switch. A loud buzz pierces the silence, and Mrs. Clark's body twitches and leaps up from the gurney, as far as the leather restraints will allow. Her back arches, her limbs seize, there's a sickening cracking sound—joints and vertebrae—and then a *thud* as her head falls back down on the table. Sherman relaxes his grip on Mrs. Clark's shoulders and eyes the clock. No one speaks; the air thrums with the mechanical whir of the machine.

"Very good, well done," the technician says briskly, stroking Mrs. Clark's arm.

Mrs. Clark's eyes roll back in her head; she no longer seems fully conscious. Several minutes pass, and then Sherman resumes his position over her, pressing down again on her shoulders. The procedure is repeated. With each shock, the induced seizure seems to increase in force. After the third application of electricity, Mrs. Clark is out cold.

The technician peels off his surgical gloves. "You may take the patient back to the ward," he says.

Sherman heaves Mrs. Clark back onto the gurney; her limbs fall at awkward angles, creating an impression of extreme discomfort. Sherman deftly straightens her arms and legs. Her face is an expressionless mask,

her skin deathly pale but for bright splotches of red on her cheeks and chin.

I part ways with Sherman outside the ECT room. On my way back to the ward, I imagine Sherman wheeling Bertram, picture his body strapped to the wooden table. The feel of Mrs. Clark's hand gripping mine stays with me all the way through the long, elegant hallways to my office, which now I reenter with the same rush of relief I felt earlier, upon leaving.

I have given over to my dreams.

I am in the underground tunnel, but I am no longer listening. I am the one lying on the old bed with the creaking springs. I turn to see Delilah, who is smiling at me as she lowers the straps of her camisole. My body is swept up in a feverish ache; I raise my hand to the curve of Delilah's shoulder.

And then, the first touch. My hand melts into her skin. I am drifting, falling, disappearing; the pounding in my chest is deafening, I pass my hand gently down to her naked breast and feel the quickening beat—the same as my own—and as our lips meet, the pleasure courses through me, like warm liquor in my veins.

I awaken with the feel of Delilah through all of me. I roll over in the bed to find Ursula, amiable and ready to please, her eyes generous and yet dull. Eyes that do not seek darkness, that are never inflamed: no, Ursula looks only onto her garden, which she tends with the same kind of devotion she applies to me.

I place my hand on her hip and close my eyes. I don't stop to think if Ursula is surprised by my sudden onset of passion. I am even blind as to whether or not she is finding in herself a rebirth of passion; the ghastly truth is that I do not care.

When it is over, I turn from Ursula and cup my face in my hands. Tears come; I am as silent as I can be—not because I care if Ursula knows but because I wish to be alone.

At breakfast, I drink five cups of black coffee, one after the other. I push away the plate of eggs and toast that Ursula offers.

"Stomach bug," I say weakly.

Ursula eyes the coffeepot dubiously but says nothing.

"I've decided to go to Maine early this year," she says, after I have drained my cup. "I was thinking I might go today. This afternoon."

Ursula visits her elderly mother every December—usually in the second week of the month, so that she's back in time for us to have Christmas Day together.

"If that's what you'd like, dear," I say. Three weeks earlier than she usually goes—before Thanksgiving, which we've never had apart—and telling me about it on the morning of her departure. She must already have packed, one more thing I've failed to notice.

"I'm tired, Henry," she says.

"Yes, dear. I know."

"You're tired, too," she adds.

I don't know what to say. I can feel her waiting; the room is filled with the slow sound of her breath.

"I'm sorry, Ursula," I say finally.

"Are you?" she asks softly.

"Our life has been a disappointment to you."

Something catches in her breath.

"The hospital," I continue. "My work—"

"I'd like you to tell me something," she says. "There's something I need to know. Whose fault is it, when a patient suicides?"

The question blindsides me. "Excuse me?"

"Really, I want to know." Her voice is tinged with bitterness.

"I couldn't say that it's anybody's fault," I reply.

"Then why does the doctor take it on as if he's the one to blame? Why does he let it eat away at him?"

Ursula's eyes brim with blame.

"What is it you want to say?" I ask quietly.

"Nothing," she says flatly. "It's just that I thought—"

She leaves her sentence dangling. I look away. From the corner of my eye, I see her raise her arm—see, for a moment, the shadow of her hand, hovering in the air. I look out the window in the direction of the hospital, beyond the white wooden gate and out across the lawn.

"Will you be home in time for Christmas?" I ask, swinging my gaze back to her but focusing, when I speak, on her chin.

"I don't know," she says. Her chin is delicately trembling. "Why don't we see how things go?"

"Yes, of course," I say.

At the door, we are awkward. Ursula leans forward, I turn to offer my cheek; her lips brush my ear.

It is Thanksgiving: the day of the pageant. Such excitement—and no upsets, today, on the halls, the patients holding tight to their most functional selves.

I stop by the gymnasium in the afternoon and find it alive with activity. Even the nurses and orderlies are touched by theater fever; they move about under the direction of various residents—not patients today, but stage manager, props director, lighting man.

By seven o'clock the chairs are in place, and at seven-thirty the audience files in: patients, staff, family members. It is an abridged performance, and so we meet Bottom only after he awakens as a donkey. They have procured a marvelous costume with a fine, lifelike donkey head. Although I cannot see his face, I know, when he speaks, that it is Bertram. He delivers his lines with both conviction and irony. The mood of the audience, at first indulgent, alters as they are drawn in; there is something tender about the collective effort that weaves an unexpected spell.

At the end of the performance, Bertram stands stiffly along with the rest of the cast to receive the enthusiastic applause, cradling the donkey head in the crook of his arm. His gaze drifts across to mine; he nods very slightly, then nods again, as though giving a signal. The clapping subsides. Bertram places the donkey head on a table that is part of the set and walks from the stage. The donkey head tilts and then gently falls onto its side; it appears to be looking at me with animal intensity.

I head over to the trestle table where the servants have set down three large punch bowls and are laying out rhubarb and cherry pies, baked by patients in the Occupational Therapy Pavilion. I mill for a time chatting with hospital residents and their families.

The crowd thins; I find myself standing beside Matilda.

"They did a marvelous job, didn't they," she says warmly. "Who would have thought—Mrs. Long, a comic!"

"She did distinguish herself," I say. "I see now what you meant when you told me how poignant the read-through was. The way the patients played it: dreams and reality, impossible longings. Madness and love—"

I only realize what I'm saying once the words are out of my mouth.

"Yes. It was remarkable," Matilda says quietly.

She glances over to the clock hanging above the basketball hoop. "Goodness," she says. "It's late."

"Let me accompany you home."

The moment the cold air hits us, I can feel something change, as if our familiar roles are snatched away along with the comfortable warmth. We skirt the great lawn without speaking and head toward the Nurses' Residence. I find myself thinking of those peculiar head nods Bertram directed my way when he was taking his bow. I wonder if Matilda noticed it, too.

"Why do you think they chose *A Midsummer Night's Dream*?" I ask.

"It seems rather plain to me," Matilda replies. "As if they were making a point—to the rest of us."

"Oh?"

"That craziness is not the sole territory of the insane."

We come to a halt outside the Nurses' Residence. I see it then—something different about Matilda, something shining from her: a light.

"It really is beautiful here, isn't it," she says, her voice sad and alive at the same time. I look where she is gazing—off at the woods, which slope away and down toward the town. The treetops make dark shapes against the night sky. I shiver. The stone façade and glinting panes seem to be sending out a twinkling cold. For a brief, irrational moment, I fancy that Matilda might ask me in for a drink.

"Well, then," I say.

Matilda meets my gaze. "Yes," she replies. "Good night." But she lingers, a puzzled distraction in her face, as if she'd heard a perturbing sound in the distance, something she can't quite place that demands her complete attention.

During morning dictation, Cynthia seems uneasy.

"Am I speaking too quickly? I could slow down," I say.

"I'm sorry, Dr. Harrison." She sets down her pen. "Perhaps it's not my place, but I'm concerned about you. Since Mrs. Harrison went to Maine—I just wonder if you're taking care of yourself."

"You needn't worry, I'm fine."

"I can't help worrying. You're looking tired. And every now and then—well, you just don't seem quite yourself."

Cynthia is usually guarded; I find her urgency touching. She has missed her métier, I think sadly: devoting herself to a family. I wonder for the hundredth time why Cynthia never married; some deep-lurking fault line, no doubt, such as we all have, her variant having kept her solitary.

"Of course, you're right," I say. "With Ursula away, I have been staying up very late working. That may not be such a good idea." I smile; Cynthia's face softens.

"I'm a believer in fresh juices," she says brightly.

"I'll have the chef squeeze me some grapefruit at lunch."

At eight o'clock, I lock away my papers and head home. Walking up the path to my front door, I look away from the flower beds, ruined, now, by the cold, the debris gathering. One of the gardeners asked me recently if he might remove the dead leaves and weeds, but I put him off. I don't relish the idea of him pottering in the flower beds around the house.

In the living room, I close the drapes, aware of the childish thought that I am in a submarine, readying to be submerged. I take my time pouring the bourbon, listening with pleasure to the crackling sound as the liquor makes contact with the ice. I nurse the second, the glass wet in my hand. The room is listing pleasantly by the time I unpack the contents of the pillow box, laying out the oil lamp, pipe stem, pipe bowl, and needles. I am almost down to the last of the block of opium; I feel a little rise of excitement at the thought that soon I will have to make a trip into Manhattan to procure some more.

Finally, when the globule is swollen and sticky, I place it over the opening in the pipe bowl, pierce it with the tip of the needle, and draw in the smoke, which billows prettily for a moment and is then sucked, like a disappearing genie, into the pipe.

How comfortable it is on the couch, how vivid the colors of the Chagall reproduction on the wall—a painting with a peacock that Ursula

picked up at an estate sale. Through the smoke, the deep blues become touched with purple, the peacock loses its look of innocence, and the figures arrayed around it appear to be swimming.

Drifting, dozing, time frozen: stopped in the free fall.

The figures have sprung from the painting; they are dancing around the room. Threatening at first, but after that charming, handmaidens to my floating pleasure.

"Machines, oh, machines!" the peacock sings, preening. "Dogs are man's best friend—and cobras his foe!"

I know it is a disguise—it is not a peacock singing, but someone dressed up for the pageant. I wonder how they made such a precise and life-sized costume. And those iridescent blue-green feathers! But where is the donkey?

The peacock is removing his head. Not a patient after all. I've never seen this man before, and yet I know him; he smiles obscurely.

"Machines," he says, deliberately, the fun of it gone. "The scientists cannot get along without them."

It is Emanuel. I am dozing—I am awake. I rise to my feet, wait for a moment until I feel steady.

Now I know where I came across that peculiar thought before, and why it nagged after Janice told me what Bertram said that time on the way back from the print shop.

Outside, the air is bracing, and the dark sky is cloudy and without stars. I feel a spring in my step. I pass the night watchman; if he is surprised to see me about at this hour, he disguises it, issuing his usual greeting.

The hallways on this side of the building, away from the wards, are empty.

In my office, I retrieve the large manila envelope from my locked filing cabinet and sit at my desk. Slowly, I leaf through Mr. Hoffstadt's translation, scanning each page from top to bottom. Emanuel's recollections leap up at me, cycling quickly as I skim along. I am caught off guard, thrust back into a world I have no wish to revisit.

Here it is, the line I recall. As I read, there's a bitter taste in my mouth, like bile.

"We've become so efficient. The gas vans have made a difference to the workload. Machines: they're both cobras and dogs."

I remember thinking the expression unusual when I first read it, but I glossed over it then; the pages are filled with cryptic, inscrutable remarks.

Could Bertram have actually snuck into my office—found these pages and read them himself? How else would he come to use the same idiosyncratic expression? I look about the room; it seems suddenly altered. I return to the closet and examine the filing cabinet. The lock does not appear to have been tampered with; the key hangs on the ring I carry with me at all times. Could Bertram have picked the lock? He has already shown himself to be skilled in clandestine activities.

We're the same. Spies, both of us. Bertram said that once, in a session. *Masters of Disguise.*

Perhaps Matilda roped in the janitor—had him open up my office—and then allowed Bertram to slip in. Perhaps they were in here together, Matilda and Bertram. Perhaps they even lay over there, on my couch. I cross the room and stroke the velvet. I chose this fabric myself when I took over the directorship six years ago: a navy blue so deep it is almost black.

There have been occasions when I've rushed out for my walk and neglected to lock the door. Could it be that Bertram was aware of my movements—was, in fact, watching me? A faint shudder passes through me. Falling onto the couch, I look around my office; everything seems so still—too still. All these familiar objects suddenly feel frighteningly pent up, as if waiting to spring to life. *Get ahold of yourself,* a faint voice says inside my head. My throat is parched. I go to the bathroom and drink water from my hand, then find myself looking in the mirror; behind me, the chain hanging down from the ceiling light swings slowly, steadily, eerily, with no sign of slowing, as if in the grip of a ghostly, invisible hand. In the bright, ugly glare of the bare bulb, my face is a study of dark shadows and colorless skin, my lips whitish and my eyes dull. I can see why Cynthia expressed concern, and wonder how long I have looked this poorly. My knees feel weak; when I close my eyes, colors shoot unpleasantly behind my lids. Usually I give myself willingly to the effects of the opium, but now, the giddiness is a form of terror. Suddenly I wish I could throw it off, breathe the druggedness out as easily as I'd breathed it in, claw the fragmented images away from my inner eye and break free from the suffocation.

I return to my desk and again take up the pages. I flip through to the end.

My eye stops on a date—the place where Emanuel mentions, in passing, the last time he saw his brother Bertram. I remember thinking at the time that it must be a typo: that Mr. Hoffstadt, in his haste, mistyped the date.

"I will find him. It has been so many years—I have not seen my brother since 1943."

I recall how I thought that Emanuel must have written "1933"; this date would be consistent with Bertram's report of when he left Germany. I take out the original manuscript. The tiny, insectlike German handwriting makes me uneasy; I find myself wanting to look away.

Yes, here it is. "1943." Not Hoffstadt's mistake, but the date Emanuel intended.

For the first time, I feel as if I can really picture him: a version of Bertram, only taller, thinner, less handsome—wearing the uniform of the Order Police. Now I see him slipping away, unnoticed. A dark alleyway—a clandestine meeting: spy meeting spy, representatives from enemy nations and yet, impossibly, brothers. Four years into Hitler's war—in Germany, or perhaps in Poland—Bertram and Emanuel meeting again, and dangerously, after years of estrangement.

At Monday morning meeting, Cuthbert is indignant. "I don't see why he's so upset," he says.

The Professor is up in arms about the wartime cartoons that Cuthbert has been circulating; the patients seem to be enjoying the drama of the spat.

"You know as well as I do," the Professor says. "We have veterans here. It's disrespectful."

"Go ahead—ask them yourself," Cuthbert challenges. "Mr. Reiner, do you find them offensive?"

Bertram looks unfazed. "I remember a fair number—I read them on the battlefield. I found them funny then, and I still do."

"I should think you'd see the relevance," Cuthbert mumbles. "Humor serves well, under siege."

"We're *not* under siege here, if that's what you're driving at," the Professor retorts, his face reddening. "And I'm tired of your insinuations that we are."

"We're in for another lecture, I suppose," Cuthbert says wearily.

"People have different sensitivities," I intervene. "A joke can be like a valve—helping to let off steam. Others may experience it as a painful reminder, like pressing down on a bruise. I think it's important to recognize both ways of seeing it."

Matilda sits opposite me, listening intently; my eyes stray to the cup of her throat, then along her collarbone to the place where the skin faintly pulses. Seeming to sense my gaze, she reaches up and touches the top button of her uniform, strokes it with her thumb, and then lets her hand fall away.

Back in my office, I am startled when the knock comes at the door; time has speeded up, I was not yet expecting Bertram, but a glance at the clock tells me he is right on time. He crosses to his seat, and I sense that today he is feeling very sure of himself. And then, for an instant, I have the peculiar sensation that I'm seeing him through a kaleidoscope—as if his face is broken into little pieces. I shake my head, and the disorienting effect subsides.

Something flickers in his eyes: things being said between us without words. His face changes again, and what I see comes as a shock: Bertram is looking at me with pity. I hear his voice, but the effect is garbled, as if I have the vocabulary of an unfamiliar language but no way of putting the words together to make meaning. The kindness in his eyes alarms me. He speaks, and I hear myself responding: psychiatrist noises, *aaah, mmm, mmhn,* and clipped statements: *I see. Go on.*

My hand is trembling; the nib of my fountain pen stabs at the paper, spitting up splotches of black ink. Beads of sweat leak from my brow into my eyes. I reach up and wipe the sweat away, hoping also to dislodge the image of Delilah that has taken hold—Delilah splattered, the blood spreading across her dress.

Bertram is looking at me, penetrating me with his gaze.

"You must be thinking how unlikely it was," he says.

"I beg your pardon?"

"That a truck would lose its way. That it would end up on that path. That you, too, would be walking there at just that moment."

For a moment I just sit there, stunned, unable to believe what I am hearing is coming from Bertram and not from my own brain. After a moment, I manage something: "I haven't the slightest idea what you're talking about."

"I'm sorry," he says. "I should explain myself. I've sat in on one or two of their meetings—the Suicide Club, that is. Surely you know about it; after what happened to Collins, I decided to attend—to see what was really going on. Incidentally, I don't think the club had much to do with what Collins did; some people make a pact early on with death."

I wait for Bertram to come to his point.

"The club has a lore—they call it their 'history.' They aim to honor their predecessors—and to try to live up to them."

I steel myself, trying to look calm.

"Did you not know," he says, "that you figure in their prize anecdote?"

I shake my head.

"I'm sorry," he says quietly, his eyes burning.

Bertram says nothing further, just sits there looking into me. And then, he gives a series of quick, curt nods. The same odd, codelike gesture he directed my way the night of the pageant. What does he think he is communicating? I register a distant feeling of alarm, but it seems to be coming from outside of me; I am enclosed in a glassy, two-dimensional space, away from everything.

I lay down my pen. My hands, on the desktop, are fists.

He is reaching forward. Dear God, Bertram is placing his hand on mine.

I leave my hand there beneath his; it is a greater comfort than I'd have dared to imagine.

Chapter Six

I can't remember the last time I went to a Saturday night dance; they'd worn thin, after the first couple of years. But with Ursula gone, the weekends seem long and surprisingly desolate; on a whim, I make my way over.

The auditorium looks festive; cut flowers are placed about the room, and yellow and purple garlands decorate the trestle table, which holds the coffee things and several large, white-frosted cakes. A jazz band is in full swing: four middle-aged men, one singing silkily into the microphone, and an older woman on the piano, all dressed in slightly shabby evening wear and wearing bland, mechanical smiles. The dancers, happily transported by the music, wear more snappy attire, the women in evening gowns or smart day dresses, and the men in dinner jackets or sport coats and ties. Not a uniform or white coat in sight. I stop to watch the couples gliding about the floor and catch sight of several sharp dancers who probably team up regularly. There is little to distinguish this scene from a club or hotel dance—only the knowledge that here, the choice of dance partner is strictly legislated; patients may dance only with staff or the spouses of staff. It is not immediately obvious which of each pair is the patient; a stranger venturing a guess would likely be wrong as often as he is right.

I wander across to the musicians. The pianist, flipping her delicate

wrists, gazes flatly at the lead singer, a corpulent man who sways ostentatiously to the rhythm. A handsome couple, moving deftly, hovers close to the band, clearly comfortable together, though they keep a respectable distance. I notice how well they are dancing, and only then do I realize with a jolt that it is Bertram and Matilda. I stand in the corner, in the shadows: all around me, inmates and their keepers, swept away by the music, their faces misty with pleasure. Matilda and Bertram are breaking no rules; in fact, they are dutifully abiding by them. As the song comes to a close, I leave the auditorium, the sound of the dancers' applause in my ears.

The hallways are deserted, and though I can see there is no one behind me, I have the unpleasant feeling that I'm being followed. The session with Bertram—that moment he blindsided me with his knowledge of Delilah's death. Some clue seems to be eluding me, torturing me, remaining insistently hidden. I find myself not fully believing his explanation—that he learned of the incident through the patients' Suicide Club, Delilah's death one of their celebrated historical successes.

It's a long way to Hall Two; I walk briskly, and the panic eases. By the time I take the final turn, glancing up as I habitually do at the steel engravings of William Tell and King Lear's daughters on the wall, I feel somewhat restored.

Featherstone and Gilmore, the orderly, are playing contract rummy in the smoking room, each with a cigarette and mug of cocoa. Rimsky-Korsakov wafts over from the radio.

"Who's winning?" I ask.

"Who do you think?" Gilmore replies good-naturedly.

"So he's killing you again."

"This round's double or nothing," Featherstone offers.

"What are the terms?"

"A fat zero, of course." Featherstone grins. "Everybody wins, everybody loses. I like an even playing field. Care to join us?"

I glance around, suddenly bewildered; it is so peaceful here. The music on the radio, a gust from another, entrancing reality, only heightens the delicate feeling of being, somehow, untouchable. I reach for a stock response—paperwork to attend to, a meeting, a session, a case conference to prepare. My eyes fall on the wall clock, and I see that it is almost ten o'clock: a full half-hour before the dancers will return.

"Why not," I say, pulling up a chair. "I'll take on the winner."

"That's not how we play," Featherstone says formally. "Loser takes all and then plays the newcomer. It's in the Hall Two Handbook, page sixteen, item four."

"I told her we should stop seeing each other," Bertram says. "I let her believe it was because of our situation—the rules, the regulations."

"You didn't feel you could tell her the truth?"

"The truth?" His voice is low.

"Yes," I say, my own voice loud compared with his.

"And what is the truth?"

"That you're afraid you might inadvertently harm her."

"I didn't think that the most charming thing to say."

"How did she take it?" I ask.

"How would you take it?" Bertram snaps.

"I'm not sure what you mean."

Bertram studies me for a long moment. "Have you ever been in love, Dr. Harrison?"

"I don't see how that's relevant," I say.

"What I see as relevant doesn't count, does it."

Bertram's directness is wearing me down.

"She accepted it," he continues. "But I felt as if something terrible happened to her."

"Can you describe it?"

"Like I had stabbed her and the life was draining out of her."

Bertram is studying my face with alarming intentness. "You're going to have to help me." His tone is suddenly hard. "I need to find a way to escape. I came here in search of safety, but everything has gone awry."

"You don't feel as if you're being helped, here," I offer.

His face flashes with irritation.

"And now I've irritated you." I note a matching rise of irritation in myself. "I sometimes think that you disdain me."

"No more than you disdain me," he shoots back.

"I don't disdain you, Bertram."

"I'm a patient. Ultimately, that's what defines this situation, isn't

it? *You're* the doctor. The one with the answers. I'm only one of your cases—a sample of a particular species of mental illness."

"That's not how I think of you."

"I don't really care how you think of me. I'm asking for your help."

A shudder passes through me; Bertram's eyes are piercing, at the same time vacant and fierce.

"I have to get away from here—from her. I came in here voluntarily, after all; you have to let me out."

"Voluntary commitment is still commitment. We are under obligation to keep you here until we deem you well enough to leave."

"Until you deem—" Now, his voice sounds strangled.

"All of us, the entire team."

"Do you enjoy playing with people's lives? Is that it?"

"I can't imagine how you see me," I say carefully.

Bertram looks at me unfazed. "I imagine I see you the way you see yourself."

"That's an interesting remark." I attempt to sound unfazed myself.

"Perhaps."

I am stunned to realize he is waiting—in an expectant, assessing way I intimately recognize: waiting as the psychiatrist waits, for an interpretive remark to take hold. I open my mouth to speak and find to my horror that I am just sitting there, gaping.

"Dr. Harrison, you seem to have something to say."

I see a storm in Bertram's face, but then he surprises me once more. Not the outburst I expect, not a thunderclap of rage; instead, the unnerving stranger he has been these past minutes lifts away, and here we are again, Dr. Harrison and Bertram Reiner, each of us tethered to his side of the mahogany desk. Outside my window, the bare branches of the blackjack glitter with ice.

"Sometimes, when things start seeming hopeless, it can help to write down your thoughts," I say. "Feeling hopeless is often a sign—that we're finally getting to the bottom of things. Wanting to escape; I know it might be hard to fathom, but this could mean you're turning a corner."

Bertram looks at me with mild amazement. "Actually," he says slowly, "I don't believe in journals."

"Why is that?"

"Things like that can end up in the wrong hands."

Again, that discomforting feeling that Bertram is seeing into me, only this time there's more.

"That shouldn't be a problem here," I say.

"No?"

More than reading my thoughts; he knows something about me, about the past. I feel the set of my jaw—the way I am smoothing the emotion from my features.

"What if someone were to take it?" Bertram continues.

"What do you mean?"

"On the open ward, people are free to come and go," Bertram says. "Who's to say some stranger wouldn't break in and go through my things?"

His eyes hold a perplexing look; he is signaling me again, but in a way that is also a test. Is he telling me he knows about Janice? That he knows she has searched his drawers?

"Are you concerned about someone breaking into the hospital?" I ask.

"My brother got onto the grounds. Why not others?"

Something is swimming up from far away, something troubling. The disturbing burglary, a few years back, toward the end of the War. An unheard-of occurrence here, where life is built upon everyone always being watched and accounted for. I was greatly distressed by the incident, though I took pains to hide this from Ursula. So far as she knew, the only things taken were trinkets, all from my study: a paperweight, a letter opener, a botanical miniature of lavender sprigs. Ursula couldn't understand why anyone would bother with those things, and leave the box of jewelry on her dresser untouched. For weeks afterward, she was beside herself: jumpy and unable to sleep, afraid the intruder would reappear and perhaps harm us.

"I have no intention of committing my thoughts to paper," he says in a tone of finality.

"Perhaps a journal's not for you, then," I reply, my tongue suddenly heavy.

"Perhaps not." Bertram studies me more closely. I feel like he's taken two steps forward, as if he's encroaching upon me.

We never did identify the thief. I assumed the intruder was a patient who either was smitten or else held a grudge. Someone who wanted to

penetrate my private world—in the way, perhaps, that he felt I had pen-
etrated his. Ursula did not, of course, know that I'd kept a journal years
earlier, and I did not tell her that it had gone missing.

I'd taken the advice I often gave patients—to put my feelings down
on paper—and in some small way, it had helped. I inscribed those
moments that tormented me: Delilah at Firefly Pond, Delilah in the
weaving room, Delilah seated on the chaise longue in my office under
the eaves. And once, I wrote the words I could never say: *Delilah, I love
you.* The last entry was the most devastating; I will never forget how it
felt, my eyes tearless, parched, my heart a burning rock in my chest, as I
wrote about her death.

I made a show to Ursula of being unperturbed by the burglary. I
told her the incident of petty thievery was unimportant; we had more
weighty things to worry about, with the War on, and the possibility of
its ending still vague. But that night, after Ursula finally went to sleep, I
turned my study upside down, hoping that I'd hidden the journal some-
place other than in my locked desk drawer, the one that had been care-
fully, expertly, picked open. But no such luck; it was gone. I felt sick
about it, but there was nothing I could do. I tried to convince myself
that the thief would perhaps gloat briefly at my tortured musings but
then throw the pages away.

I brooded about the incident for a long time, tying myself into knots
of anxiety, terrified that those pages would turn up in the wrong hands,
that they would damage or destroy my career. But the weeks passed,
and then the months, and nothing happened. I found myself feeling
enormously relieved—as if I'd dodged a bullet. But now, the terrible
anguish again rears up; I cast back, trying to recall who I'd suspected
at the time. Something about the look in Bertram's face; could it be
that, against all rational possibility, the journal has made its way into
Bertram's hands?

No—impossible! Surely only a peculiar paranoid thought.

"Coincidences are not what people think," Bertram says slowly. "A
chance coming together of events, perhaps; but the fact of the chance
is anything but arbitrary. Here's proof; I don't know anyone without a
handful of completely implausible—and yet verifiable—stories to tell."

"I daresay you're right," I reply.

Bertram pauses; he seems to be thinking something through.

"I know what you did during the War," he says finally, his tone matter-of-fact.

"And what is that?"

"Patched people up. Sent them right on back."

"I have no reason to deny that, Bertram. It was my job."

"*Wastage,* they called it. Right? Your job was to *staunch the wastage.*"

"That's what they called it," I say. "But you were talking about coincidences."

"Yes," he says. "I was."

Bertram crosses his legs and folds his hands rather deliberately in his lap.

"It must have rung a bell, when I told you about my commanding officer. Did I mention that, before taking charge of us, he'd lost two tank squadrons? All of his men killed, both times—all but him. I didn't tell you his name, but you must have known—"

Hammersmith—my God! Who came to Shadowbrook after the loss of his second tank, after simply refusing to return to the front. The Army could not afford to have him become a psychiatric casualty; I had one of the highest send-back ratios in the country, so they sent him to me.

"Captain Hammersmith," I say slowly.

"Yes," Bertram says, watching me closely. A pause. "He was with us for two months before he was moved. One hell of a good CO."

"Why the secrecy?" I try my best to leach the anger from my voice.

"I wasn't being secretive."

"Was it some kind of test?"

"I didn't think it was relevant," Bertram says.

"He told you about me, then." I return his unwavering gaze.

"He more than told me about you," Bertram says. "You were an obsession for him; he talked of little else."

Another long pause.

"So it wasn't a coincidence—that you ended up here, at Shadowbrook."

"I've already told you, I don't believe in coincidences," he replies.

Bertram shifts in his chair and then looks at me appraisingly. "I suppose it's not often that you get to hear about the fruits of your labor."

"Meaning?"

"Meaning that, in the case of my CO, he *did* end up as a psychiatric

casualty after all—despite your efforts. He had quite a career, after being sent back. The German boy wasn't the only one he shot at close range. And I can assure you, the rest of them didn't ask him to do it."

"What became of him?" My voice sounds like an echo, as if it is bouncing at me from the walls, rather than issuing from my own throat.

"He told me that if his tank got hit again," Bertram says, "he'd go down with his men."

I see him once more—Harland Hammersmith, whose mixture of guilt and grief I was able to dissolve sufficiently so he could return to the European Theater. I cannot believe he had, as Bertram put it, an obsession with me. He was such a rational man: bereaved, to be sure, but well clear of a battle neurosis, and he'd never shown signs of an unhealthy transference reaction. Perhaps it is Bertram who had some fixation on him; perhaps this is a case of displacement—more to do with Bertram Reiner than with Harland Hammersmith.

The hospital is abuzz; we do not often have a visitor of such international renown as Ronald Fairbairn. Every staff member I pass in the hallways looks expectant, and morning greetings are offered with particular enthusiasm.

When I first met Fairbairn, more than twenty years ago, I'd been amused, hearing him talk about psychoanalysis in his Scottish burr. He was brilliant on every subject, and though he was only a few years older than I, he always felt like a mentor. It is a relief, now, to have him here.

The conference room is filled to capacity; a few extra chairs have been snuck in. Several junior trainees sit in the back, looking slightly abashed. I do not see Matilda. Fairbairn is beside me, fit and trim as ever, though his hair and bottlebrush mustache are a little more gray than I remember. He exudes his characteristic air of good manners and self-control. After introducing Fairbairn, I give a brief account of Bertram Reiner's history before entering the hospital, and then signal to the orderly by the door. He disappears and returns a few minutes later with Bertram, who is dressed in flannel pants and a sports jacket, and looks serious and composed. He sits in the empty seat across from me and calmly surveys the room.

After introducing Dr. Fairbairn to Bertram, who regards him with polite interest, I begin by asking Bertram about his Army experience. I find myself feeling acutely aware of just how intrusive these case conferences are: conducting an interview before a crowded room of onlookers, while pretending to be in the private bubble of the doctor-patient relationship.

Bertram's manner is fluid, though I see something flinty in his eyes. I run through the usual general questions, establishing the symptoms that brought him into the hospital and the broad outlines of his background.

Things get interesting when I ask him to talk about the War.

"It was the strangest thing, returning home, after it was over. There was something so unreal about being back."

"Can you tell us more?"

"I don't know . . . When I was there, it was just moment to moment. Dealing with one crisis after the next. Hanging on. Then, when I came back—"

"When you came back?"

"While it was happening, I don't remember having nightmares."

Bertram has not talked before about nightmares. "But when you got back?"

"That's when they started. At first, I just shook them off. But then, they would hang around me all day long. It was like everything came rushing at me in my dreams—things I wasn't even aware of when I was fighting. The meaning of it all: what was *really* going on."

I can feel the tension rising in the room: an acute, collective, atmospheric charge.

"If you think back to the actual fighting, what were the things that were most difficult?"

Bertram looks at me calmly, something vaguely indulgent in his regard. He glances quickly around the room and then leans back in his chair.

"We all got jumpy about the strafings," he begins. "Only it affected some more than others. I had a buddy who was so afraid, he stopped sleeping. Ten days of that—well, they took him away in a straitjacket."

"How was it for you?"

His mouth twitches impatiently. "The strafings weren't what got me in the end."

"Was there something in particular—?" I break off.

"That sent me over the edge?" The shade of a smile. "It isn't always clear-cut, is it? You've seen more cases than I have, though I've seen my fair share."

"Of course, you're right. But you seemed to be implying that you were aware of some kind of—"

"Trigger." Bertram cuts in. "Yes, I suppose I was. I didn't realize it at the time, but I've had a lot of time to think, since coming to Shadowbrook. We've got all sorts of time in here; you might say it's our greatest luxury." Bertram smiles wryly at the audience; he has them in the palm of his hand.

"You were saying," I prompt.

"Yes, well sometimes, it's the most unlikely thing—some small or seemingly unimportant event. I suppose you would say that, whatever the *trigger* is, it connects with something deeper."

I feel a nagging discomfort; Bertram is wresting away control of the interview. Leaning back in his chair, his legs crossed, talking about the symbolic meaning of *triggers,* he seems the picture of the impressive, eager young doctor.

"In my case—well, it was the death of a soldier under my command. It wasn't the first time it happened, and it wasn't the last. It was the circumstances. You see, I could have prevented it."

"Can you tell us about the incident?"

"The soldier—Jared—was standing beside me when a hand grenade was thrown. He was killed instantly. As impossible as this might sound, I was completely unharmed."

Bertram is no longer playing to the audience but looking only at me. "I wonder, sometimes, if mental problems happen because of the more abstract side of things, rather than because of the concrete realities."

"I'm not sure I know what you mean."

Bertram is looking at me as if through a fog. "Do you remember the Professor's problem with the toast? Oh—is it all right to talk about another patient in here?"

He's serious, now, no longer playing games.

"I don't see the harm in it. And no, I don't remember a problem with toast."

"He'd get very upset at breakfast when they put the toast rack on

the table. We all thought it was a weird phobia or something, but then he explained that it wasn't the toast itself, but the *meaning* of the toast. He told us that the significance of the toast changed from day to day; perhaps today he was supposed to eat it, but tomorrow not, or one day use butter and another day jam. At any given time, he had no way of knowing the right way of behaving. If he did the wrong thing—well, he was certain he'd bring on a catastrophe. The rules were always shifting, and that's what panicked him."

"You were talking about Jared," I gently remind.

"Yes," Bertram replies quietly. "It pains me to say this—I don't mean to belittle Jared's death. It was horrible, *horrible*. I helped scrape his remains off the walls. But the fact is, I'd lost many men by that point. I felt badly about his loss, but it was *the meaning* of his death for me that was so hard to bear."

"The meaning?"

"We've discussed this before—in our sessions."

"It might be helpful if we discuss it again, here." Without breaking eye contact, I give a slight nod to indicate the audience.

"His death was a kind of exchange." Bertram's voice is low. "A young American soldier sacrificed to save an important Nazi scientist."

Something elusive in Bertram's eyes—and a flare of anger.

"A gift to the government of the United States. What's a death, here and there—this soldier or that who doesn't get to live his life. They were replaceable."

"When you talk about the abstract side of things, do you mean the moral dimension?"

"What difference does it make—what it's called?" He is suddenly surly.

"Clarity is often a good starting point."

"For what, Doctor? For an interesting intellectual discussion?"

"For making peace with oneself."

He sighs impatiently. "Oh, that again."

"That—what?"

"It's kind of a Holy Grail around here. You can waste a lifetime in search of things like inner peace—and we all know they don't exist. Fairy tales should be kept for children."

"I'm not sure I follow."

"What would you call trading one of your own men for a Nazi, so you can give the Nazi as a gift to your country?"

"What would *you* call it?"

"I'd call it *collaboration*."

Bertram's eyes dart around, as if he's just remembered we're not alone but talking before a small crowd. His gaze comes to rest on the far side of the room, and only after an instant do I realize he's looking at Matilda, who is sitting very still at the back. I had not noticed her entering.

He sees that I have seen Matilda and continues, his features marred by a scowl. "I should have thought the word would spring to your lips."

"And why is that?"

"You did your fair share of sending young men back to the front, where they could become target practice for the enemy. You must have had feelings about what you were doing. I wonder—what name do you give to *that*?"

I immediately note a shift in the audience's focus; all eyes, now, are on me. At the fringes of my vision, a blur of faces: my staff, deeply familiar, and yet suddenly strange. Bertram is waiting, the audience is waiting: the tables are turned. The moment prolongs. I sit there with growing horror, waiting for some response to come to mind.

"If I may be permitted to say something—" Fairbairn's gentle, authoritative voice breaks the silence. I can feel the swing of attention away from me, now, over to him.

"Of course, Dr. Fairbairn," I respond, trying not to sound relieved. "Please, go ahead."

"Mr. Reiner, you're saying something important about the complications that arise from doing one's job. The moral quandaries—especially during wartime."

He pauses, as if to allow everyone in the room the chance to adjust to the subtle realignment of power.

"We have tribunals to deal with matters of collaboration. What you're talking about is something altogether different. You were a soldier: a brave and talented one, I'm told. Doing your duty. Anyone who has fought in a war—and I did my time in the previous one—knows the chaos and ambiguity. The need to act instinctively. But you're making a mistake, using the word *collaboration;* you were doing your job—*against*

the enemy. That one of your young soldiers died is the tragedy of war-
fare."

Bertram is looking at Fairbairn with intensity, as if struggling to grasp
his meaning. "But at the level of the symbolic—?"

Fairbairn looks back at Bertram with a mirroring intensity. I can see
him deliberating. And then, a flicker of irony in his face. "Sometimes
toast is just *toast*."

Something also flickers across Bertram's face, but it is not irony; he is
staring into the middle distance, no longer here with the rest of us, but
off in some other world.

After the case conference, Fairbairn and I retreat to my office for a quiet
moment before the formal dinner.

"How is Mary?" I ask. "You will send her my warmest wishes."

"She's in fine health, thank you," Fairbairn says perfunctorily. "And
Ursula? I trust I'll see her this evening?"

"I'm afraid not."

"Is she away?"

"Actually, Ronald, our marriage has become rather strained. She's
staying with her mother in Maine; it's not clear when she's coming
back." My voice sounds tense.

"I'm sorry," he says. "Since marrying, I've often thought our line of
work lends itself more to the bachelor. Such a demanding business, and
so very private. One thing I've learned about wives—certainly my wife;
there's a tremendous desire to share in the husband's life."

"Yes," I say. "I've found it very hard to please her."

"I'd venture to say that sometimes it's simply not possible to please
one's wife."

"Then what is one to do?"

"Humor them, I suppose."

I give a dry laugh. "I have a patient who believes that humor is
the only antidote to madness. He collects jokes about psychiatry and
mental patients, as a matter of fact. Perhaps I'll treat you to a couple
later on."

Fairbairn smiles. "I suppose marriage is itself a form of madness. By

rights, we should be experts on it. I can't say I've made such a success of my own."

I fetch the bottle of port. The smile fades from Fairbairn's face. "Mary complains that we don't lead a more active social life. She's furious at my work for taking up so much of my time."

I nod. "Ursula has felt the same way, though it's not her way to complain. I also suspect she feels that the work has changed me in troubling ways."

"I think I know what you mean," Fairbairn says quietly.

"It may be all of a piece—my strained marriage and the problems I'm having with the case I wanted to talk over with you."

"The patient you presented today at the conference," he says.

"Was it that obvious?"

"I shouldn't think it was to the rest of the staff. But I know you."

"And—?"

"I had the feeling you were in deep waters. We both know that it's inevitable, from time to time. But it doesn't make it any easier."

"There's no question in my mind that Bertram Reiner has pockets of psychosis, but I can't seem to make the usual sense of it. Whenever I feel that *frisson*—the feeling you get when a patient's slipping into psychotic experience—well, those tend to be the moments Bertram seems at his most sane. Sometimes it feels like I'm the one losing my grip."

"He does sound unusual," Fairbairn says thoughtfully. "Tell me more."

"Well, we all know that the will can dissolve under the sway of emotions—acting on impulse, without the detachment that allows for rational thought. With madness an extreme case of this: the wild man, all impulse, no ego, the complete exclusion of rationality. But what of a madness that comes from extreme detachment? An out-of-control reason that strangles feeling? The case of the person who cannot, thereby, ever really just *feel* because he is always at the same time also *thinking*?"

Fairbairn has gone quiet; the gentleness has gone, leaving a severity that frightens me a little.

"Are you talking about the patient, my friend, or about yourself?"

"Perhaps I am talking about us both."

"Of you and the patient—or of you and me?"

"I'm not sure. Perhaps *you* could answer that."

Fairbairn laughs drily. "There is a certain *deformation professional* that comes with years of practicing as a psychiatrist. We don't talk about it much, I know. I'm starting to with my students, as a matter of fact. It helps to have some warning, though I suspect it doesn't make all that much difference in the end; it's not something someone can really understand until it happens to them—and by then, it's too late."

"Perhaps it's not the profession that deforms us," I venture. "Perhaps whatever you become as a professional is really only the expression of your own nature—that same nature that made you choose the profession in the first place."

"Ah yes, chicken or egg."

"It's not a theoretical matter for me, Ronald." I can hear the strain in my voice. "I feel like I'm failing the patient. I don't know how to proceed."

"Do you feel like you're also failing yourself?" he asks quietly.

"Of course," I say without hesitation.

"You need to understand that first. You'll not see your way clear to helping the patient until you do."

"There's something I've not told you."

Fairbairn waits.

"The patient—Bertram Reiner; he's in love with one of my nurses."

"That's not so uncommon, is it?"

"This is different."

"Oh?"

"It's not the usual thing—unrealistic fantasy, or even delusion. It seems to be a true meeting of minds—and hearts."

Fairbairn's curiosity is piqued.

"That's not unheard of—patients who recover and end up marrying a doctor or nurse who'd cared for them at one time," he says. "I know of a number of such instances; most of them have worked out quite well."

I am taken aback by Fairbairn's open-mindedness. "We don't encourage it," I say.

"It's sometimes easy to forget," he says evenly, "that the patients are not children; it's not our place to tell patients what to do or how to live. Ultimately, our role is no more than that of a guide."

"But we do need to enforce the rules." I sound ridiculous, I know. I notice that the quality of Fairbairn's attention has shifted into a clinical mode—as distinct as a change of temperature.

"The rules," he says vaguely. Something shifts in me, too, at the altered tone of his voice; I feel an unexpected clutching of grief.

"They've been conducting an affair—here, at the hospital. I know I should have put a stop to it immediately, but I kept finding reasons not to; in fact, it has crossed my mind more than once that the affair might be the one thing keeping Bertram sane. The trouble is, I can't get clear on the case. The diagnosis keeps slipping through my fingers; it's like trying to grab hold of dry sand. At times, the treatment plan seems sound—and he does go through periods of improvement. But then it comes undone again and I find we're back where we started."

"I can understand why you're feeling at a loss. Mr. Reiner is a complicated man: intriguing, to be sure, but changeable. Like trying to treat a mirage. During the case conference interview, I found myself being reminded of someone." Fairbairn pauses to reflect. "Yes, yes of course, I remember now. A patient I treated many years ago. Perhaps equally challenging."

He pauses again, apparently deep in thought. After a time, he speaks.

"I admire you, Henry," he says slowly. "I always have. There aren't many like you in our profession."

I brace myself for a blow.

"This is where the true challenge lies," he continues. "The real test. Discovering one's own demons in someone else; having to battle oneself in order to help another—and with no choice in the matter. There's no escaping it—not if you're honorable, not if you take your responsibilities seriously. I've been there, my friend; I remember how trapped I felt. How hopeless and alone."

I feel nauseated and giddy; an agonizing exhaustion suddenly overtakes me, making my eyes heavy. I must summon enormous effort to keep them from closing. The desire for sleep pulls at me with the force of a sedative.

"It's all right," Fairbairn says, reading me. "It might help if you let yourself close your eyes. I can try to help you. I can't promise anything, but I can try."

I allow my eyes to close; it's a glorious relief. Fairbairn keeps talking, his voice melodious and profoundly comforting.

"Tell me a little more about this patient—and about his feelings for the nurse."

"She's one of my finest," I say, floating on a new feeling of calm.

"You sound proud when you say that."

"I am very proud of my staff."

"And particularly of this nurse."

"She's been through a great deal. She was in the Philippines, on the island of Corregidor. One of the few to get out, just before it fell. I admire her spirit; she's not allowed the world to beat her down."

"And the patient?"

"I think they're truly in love."

"Now, you sound sad," Fairbairn says gently.

"I am sad," I say, a gulp rising in my throat. "I envy them."

"What do you envy?"

"Their intensity. Their soul-mateship. Being in the grip of love; it's everything to them."

"And you? Where are you?"

"Outside. Excluded."

"You said earlier that you should have put an end to it—that there are rules you should be enforcing. You said you thought you were failing the patient."

I only nod, aware of an engulfing sense of hopelessness.

"I see it differently," he says.

My eyes glide open; Fairbairn's face radiates kindness.

"How do you see it?"

"The rules help keep us feeling safe—the patients don't know we struggle with the same kind of double bookkeeping that they do. The Napoleons and Caesars go off uncomplainingly to woodworking without worrying who will command the troops in their absence. And we—well, we have to be the experts all the time, always steady and sure. Knowing at the same time that we're afflicted with the human condition, just as they are. We come up with all kinds of strategies to put this out of mind—and mysteriously, for the most part, it works. But every so often, a patient comes along who denatures our devices, and we find ourselves stripped bare. Forced to confront them—and ourselves—in the nakedness of our shared humanity."

The drugged fatigue has fled; now, I feel uncannily alert.

"To allow yourself this—rather than box yourself and your patient in with rules and regulations; perhaps this is an act of generosity, rather than an instance of failure. I'm not saying there aren't risks; you have after all thrown away the compass. But I know you, Henry, and I suspect that the potential gains are tremendous."

"There's something I'm not telling you," I say.

"There's always something," Fairbairn says. "And whatever it is, you must look there, directly into it."

I have spied on them; I have listened to them in the throes of passion, I have glimpsed their bodies, unclothed, entwined. And I have wanted, desperately wanted . . .

"It's too terrible," I whisper, aware of a ferocious pain, starting in my throat and clawing its way into my innards.

"I know," Fairbairn says softly. "But don't turn away. Feel it, acknowledge it, stare it down. If there's an answer, you'll find it. But you know as well as I do that there isn't always an answer. Perhaps that's the greatest risk in all of this. And instead of an answer, you might find some other, possibly awful truth."

<div style="text-align:center">◄◄◄‥►►</div>

The mood in Sturgiss Hall is almost giddy. At the Christmas Eve cocktail party, the hospital staff congregates en masse, minus the skeleton staff on duty. Afterward, we break into caroling teams and head back to the wards; typically, I manage to join about half the teams each year, so that every two years I cover the lot. But tonight, as the evening progresses, I find myself dreading the singing.

Vanessa O'Halahan snags me by the hors d'oeuvres table, then gestures to Matilda, who joins us.

"I dug this up for you," she says brightly, offering me a gaudy, oversize tiepin: Santa Claus surrounded by elves. "No symbolism intended, chief. Only a bit of fun for the patients. We're all wearing pins this year." She indicates a large brooch fixed to her collar: Rudolph, with a shiny red nose.

"I'm afraid I've got a rather sore throat," I say. "I gargled with hot water, but it hasn't done any good."

Both women look disappointed. "We promised the patients," Vanessa says.

"I can be the advance guard and switch off the lights." I make my voice sound gravelly. "If I try to sing, I'll only break into a coughing fit."

"It *is* a shame," Matilda says. "You have a lovely voice."

On the ward, I go ahead of the carolers, turning off switches, leaving only the fairy lights in the hallways, and in the dayroom, the blazing tree. This year, I skipped buying a tree for the house; it is something Ursula and I always did together. The holidays were difficult for Ursula, though she made an effort to be cheerful; it was lonely, just the two of us, the house echoing even more than usual with absence. Now, the thought of returning home this evening to an empty house leaves me feeling hollow.

The patients are assembled before the tree, plucked from the shadows by the tiny lights strung in the branches. Gilmore gives the signal, and the carolers begin. *Silent night, holy night.* Instead of the usual lyrics, the singers simply repeat the same words, over and over—*Silent night, holy night*: another act of hospital censorship, born of the fear of setting anyone off.

I train my ears on one voice: Matilda's soprano, which is soft and true. I steal around to the tree and stand with the patients so that I might watch the singers. My trusted staff; I know them all well, but now, in full throat, they are transformed. I see them as they might have been when children: back in the places of their beginnings. Matilda closes her eyes; to my ears, the rich sound of more than a dozen voices thins to her voice alone: clear, haunting, reaching for something unknown. What might Matilda have dreamed of as a child, singing before her own tree? Having a family, one day, of her own: choosing a juniper or spruce to carry home, to the delighted squeals of her children? Not severed limbs blown into branches, or a thousand wounded soldiers, abandoned to their deaths in an open-air jungle hospital.

Her eyes snap open to meet mine; not happy childhood memories reflected back, only pain—and surprise to find that I am over by the tree with the patients, scrutinizing her while she sings. I expect her to look away: to be embarrassed or put out. But she holds my gaze and her pain melts away. When the song comes to an end, the repeated

words—*Silent night, holy night*—conveying the full, poignant meaning of the carol, despite the hospital censorship, Matilda offers a smile: not to the group, not to Bertram, only to me. I am left startled, ecstatic, lost.

Between Christmas and New Year's Day, the normal hospital routine is suspended as family members come and go. The patients, dressed in their finest, walk the hallways and grounds with the air of liberated coeds at the end of term.

Bertram received no visitors, but, throughout the holiday week, he appeared in good spirits. Some of the other families seemed to take him under their wings. At Christmas dinner, he sat with Cuthbert and his parents; at other festivities, I observed him chatting, listening, as if in the role of host.

After the New Year, the Christmas trees on the halls are undressed and carted away to be chopped for firewood. With the decorations boxed and the last of the spruce needles swept away, we return to our normal schedule of meetings and activities.

In our first session back, Bertram doesn't mention the holidays; there is no evidence of the spiritedness I observed with others, only the somber, scrutinizing manner that had marked our sessions before the holidays. In that idiosyncratic way Bertram has of making intervening time vanish, he picks up the discussion where we left off.

"Once a tank was hit, the commander was really the only one who had any chance of surviving."

"Why is this on your mind, now?" I ask.

"I don't know—it keeps coming back." The church bells chime; in the heavy pause, they sound unnaturally loud. Bertram waits until they have completed their measure. "What must that be like?" he continues. "You hear the hit, you feel the unbearable heat: you have one split second to make the decision. You're the only one up in the neck of the tank—you could fling the hatch off and jump. Or else stay where you are and burn to death with your men."

"You're thinking of Captain Hammersmith," I offer.

"It's not really a decision, is it—how could it be? There's no time to

think. More like pure instinct, whether you jump or stay. And whatever the commander does: *that's* the truth about who he is. Not thinking, only *acting*. The hidden secret of the soul—not even known to the man himself."

Again, that sidelong glance: the distinctive shadow of suspicion.

"And yes—I am thinking of Hammersmith. In the end, whatever secrets Hammersmith had, he took with him to the grave. If you can call the burned metal carcass of a tank a grave."

"Are there any secrets in particular you're thinking about?"

"I was thinking that perhaps this was a question you could answer." Bertram looks at me challengingly.

"I don't read minds."

Bertram leans forward. "Hammersmith knew more about—*your situation*—than you know."

I feel overcome by a swoon, as if somebody had slipped something into my drink. My thoughts turn to sludge. I struggle to lay claim to an interpretation, but each formulation balloons in my mind, then fades before I can settle on a course.

"What are you getting at?" I am battling to stay alert.

Bertram leans back and looks at me, his lips pursed.

"You're not going to say, then," I continue.

"You've said it often enough yourself," Bertram says. "That the most meaningful insights are the ones one has to fight for."

"So—whatever it is you're hinting at is something I'm supposed to fight for," I say, incredulous.

"You could put it that way."

"Might I remind you that this is your treatment, not mine?"

"Is it?"

I feel a sudden spear of rage. "Why not just come out with it, if you have something to say?"

"Very well then," he says briskly. "That incident with the truck, all those years ago—I didn't hear about that from the Suicide Club."

"You heard about it from Captain Hammersmith," I say, as if in a trance.

"Precisely," Bertram says.

"What did he tell you?"

"He didn't exactly *tell* me anything."

I can feel that Bertram is not lying, not dissimulating: only telling the truth.

"What, then?" I ask, though I suddenly know the answer.

"He showed me," Bertram whispers. "I read it for myself."

Silence fills the room; I almost dare not breathe—sense dimly that something dreadful is about to come crashing about my ears. My heart beats heavily against my ribs and I feel sick with dread. I do not want to believe it: Hammersmith stealing my journal, keeping it with him, showing it long ago to a soldier who is now sitting here in this room with me. It cannot be that, all this time, *I* have been the specimen: watched from the other side of a wall.

"The fact that he showed me—that he gave me the journal—only a week before he was transferred back, before his tank was hit—" Bertram takes in a short, sharp breath and then slowly exhales. "I didn't know you, of course. You were nothing to me at that time but a name."

He searches my face. It's as if he's trying to see me again in that light—trying to go back, reclaim himself as he was, reclaim the nothingness I was to him then, nothing but a name.

"No." He shakes his head slightly. "Not nothing. Hammersmith had a way with words—maybe you remember that about him. He put me right here, at Shadowbrook, alongside him. We were camping out in a house in Cherbourg that must have been very grand at one time. A lot of the roof was gone, but the stairs were pretty much intact; in the evenings, we'd climb to the top to watch the sunset. We ate in the dining room, under the stars. They had some marvelous wine in the cellar—and a huge round of Gruyère. One night, Hammersmith and I sat up drinking and eating cheese."

"I can't believe he had an obsession with me," I say slowly. "He wasn't that kind of a man."

Bertram studies me for a moment.

"Perhaps I misspoke," he says. "Perhaps it would be more accurate to say he found you of great interest."

"In what way?"

"He was intrigued that psychiatrists were called upon to fix people up mentally so they could be given another chance at getting killed—that a man had to be right in the head to be sent back into all that craziness."

"Was he angry about being sent back?" I ask.

"It wasn't as simple as that. Of course he was angry, but he also wanted to avenge the deaths of his men. I would say that his interest in you was—well, sort of philosophical."

"What on earth do you mean?"

"To be perfectly frank, Dr. Harrison, he wanted to understand how someone in your position made sense of what he was doing. We talked about it that night, in Cherbourg. About the fact that, as a doctor, you'd taken the Hippocratic oath: a commitment to put the patient's well-being first, to do everything in your power to ease suffering and save lives. And yet there you were—"

I move to speak.

"I know what you're going to say," Bertram says quietly. "That things were complicated. That nothing is black and white."

I was, in fact, going to say something like that.

"I think that's what Hammersmith found interesting. The kinds of things someone like you would have to say to himself to make it all palatable."

"Where did he get the notebook he showed you?"

"He didn't say anything about that," Bertram says.

"Didn't you wonder?"

"We'd just fought a battle—lost dozens of men. My mind was on other things."

"How did you know the notebook was what he said it was? Perhaps he made the whole thing up?" I hear the tinge of desperation in my voice and feel further sickened with shame.

"Why would he do that? What reason could he have had to go to so much trouble?"

"Why are you bringing this up now?"

"I really don't know. Perhaps you have some insight into that."

I think back on the past four months—Bertram sitting here, in my office; harboring this knowledge of my darkest truths.

"How did you feel?" I am unable to mask the tremble in my voice. "When you read the pages Captain Hammersmith gave you?"

"They meant nothing, then. You weren't a real person to me. You were just a character, someone that Hammersmith had talked about."

"When did that change?"

"It didn't."

"But you ended up coming here."

Bertram looks surprised, as if this thought had never occurred to him.

"You're not going to tell me you came here—by chance. That you just happened to end up in the care of the same doctor your commanding officer told you about."

He says nothing. Just sits, looking at me.

"Did you come here to Shadowbrook to find me?" I persist.

"No."

"What, then?"

"I came here to find myself."

Chapter Seven

When I call Cynthia and ask her to reschedule my last two afternoon appointments, supervision sessions with residents, I hear a heavy silence on the other end of the line.

"Very well, Dr. Harrison," she says. "But I'll have to take your lunch hour tomorrow. I don't see any other way."

"That will be fine, Cynthia. Thank you."

Passing Cynthia's office on the way out, I glimpse her sitting idle at her desk, staring glumly at the door.

"Have a good evening." I smile politely.

"You, too, Dr. Harrison."

I arrive at the station with three minutes to spare. On the train, I try to read a journal article, but my attention strays. I give up and gaze out the window: houses and trees and yards, hovering beyond my own transparent reflection, oddly static and yet whisking away to ever fresh versions. Stately homes give way to simple row houses and then factories and long, low warehouses. Soon, we are gliding through the Bronx. As the train clangs into the 125th Street station, the blunt reality of what I am doing hits me. No shame, no fear: only excitement and an old, familiar yearning that is curiously comforting.

A woman and her three young children take the seats across the aisle. They have scrubbed faces and neatly combed hair; their clothing is thread-

bare, their shoes shabby. The woman looks harried and responds distract-
edly when one or another of her children speaks. I don't realize I'm studying
the little group until I find myself looking directly into the woman's eyes.

"They're a bit rambunctious," she says apologetically in a thick Bronx
accent. "Don't mean to disturb you, sir."

"Not at all, madam." My heart fills unexpectedly with sadness. "I was
only thinking what charming children you have."

Her face blossoms with pride. "Little monkeys, really." The smallest boy
takes his mother's hand; she looks down at him, flushed with happiness.

At Grand Central, I join the throng hurrying toward the subway. I
ride the eight stops to Chinatown in a rush-hour crush, retreating to
the same private, dazed space I see in the faces around me. I get out at
Canal Street and head briskly along the old route, ducking into the non-
descript side street I walked so many times, long ago. A world war has
intervened, and still these streets look plucked from old Shanghai: the
same stinking fish stalls I remember, vegetable stands with exotic greens,
Chinese women haggling, elderly men shuffling, and here and there a
rickshaw rambling along the cobblestones. I am aware of one change:
the sight of young Chinese women and men in Western dress.

I turn onto a narrow alleyway lined with tenements marked by
neglect. Each doorway releases tantalizing smells: frying onions, pun-
gent broth, glazed meats. My stomach contracts hungrily, sharpening
my anticipation, setting me further on edge. And then, abruptly, I find
myself before the red-painted door; I marvel at how the faded strips and
peeling paint form the identical pattern I recall. Uncannily, without my
knocking, the door creaks open to reveal a girl, no more than ten years
old, looking boldly through the crack. A different child, of course, than
the one that opened the door long ago, though, in the dreamlike repeti-
tion of the moment, I have the unreasonable feeling that it must be the
same girl, bewitched into agelessness by my own solipsism. She nods, as
if she's been expecting me, and then closes the door. I wait, and a few
minutes later, the door opens once more, this time swiftly and fully, and
a young man, tall for a Chinese and strikingly thin, ushers me in. I fol-
low him down the long hallway, my leather-heeled shoes clicking loudly
behind his silent, slippered feet. We arrive at the elaborately carved door
I remember and the man leaves me, without having uttered a single
word. I pause to collect myself before knocking.

If Hong Weng's face is more lined than before, I cannot judge; he looked wizened then, and looks wizened now. He shows no surprise to see me.

"Come in, come in." He returns with mincing steps to a red and gold armchair set before a small, blazing fireplace. "I've been expecting you."

Hong Weng's remark should strike me as preposterous, but I find myself accepting each moment as peculiarly preordained.

"I confess, I didn't think it would take you so many years." He smiles his distinctive smile—smug and yet generous, as if delighting in some secret wisdom he intends at any moment to share.

"I won't ask what brings you back now." The smile broadens to reveal teeth that are crowded and stained. "I'll simply say *Bienvenue.* If I remember correctly, the perfume you favor is ginseng. Only yesterday, I received a shipment of the very finest."

He tugs on a long silk cord that ends in a fist-sized tassel. The bookshelf to the right of the fireplace slowly turns, as in spy movies, and the young man who deposited me at the door not five minutes ago appears from a gaping interior darkness. In his hands is a bundle, enclosed in a bright, embroidered cloth. Carefully, he sets the bundle down on a table inlaid with ivory and unfolds the cloth. I recognize at once the cloisonné dish, with its dozen or more compartments holding chunks of opium of different textures and shades.

"You must sample one or two," Hong Weng says, his smile now a grin that seems fixed and reminds me unnervingly of the Cheshire cat of *Alice in Wonderland.*

I shake my head. "I don't have the luxury of time, right at the moment." I sound stiff, but no matter; Hong Weng is not a man who troubles himself with social nuances.

"Who among us has the luxury of time?" The sigh he gives is at odds with the grin that continues to dominate his face. "I can almost hear the grains of sand slipping through the hourglass." Hong Weng prides himself on his command of English colloquialisms; his eyes glint with self-satisfaction. "Let us conclude our transaction then, my friend, so that you can be on your way."

I choose a sizable chunk of the ginseng-perfumed sample, and the young man wraps it in a square of blue silk.

"It's always nice to see an old friend," Hong Weng says, not rising to

see me out, not asking when he might see me again; I imagine he feels this is something he can predict.

In the short time I spent inside, the late afternoon has become night. The streetlights flash dimly, the alleyways glimmer, the smells no longer seem appetizing. The pleasant edginess I felt earlier has given way to agitation; I dodge among the people on the street, who seem to have appeared from nowhere and now form a small crowd. I wind back past the fishmongers, whose raucous cries compete with other confusing sounds that rise all around me: squawking, scratching, a continuous, grating clang. A strange, electric feeling taunts; I swivel to look behind me, certain I'm being followed. Panic thumps in my chest, sweat breaks out on my forehead. Perhaps it is the law, perhaps Hong Weng is being watched—or worse, collaborating to save his own neck. Maybe behind his fixed grin was the knowledge that I was being set up as a stooge. I glance from side to side as unobtrusively as I can, cast another quick backward glance. Everywhere people, spilling around me, closing in. At Canal Street, I break into a run.

I gain the subway at last, and then I am on the train, hurtling beneath the streets of Manhattan toward Grand Central. My hair and neck are damp; I relax, feeling anonymous once more, free to sink into the privacy of my own thoughts. The lump in my pocket feels like a prize; inwardly I smile and allow my shaken heart to give a little leap of joy.

But at Grand Central, the terrible, dogged feeling returns; every step I take seems echoed by a step somewhere behind me, malevolently matched to my own. Who could it be? And what do they want? The main concourse is alive with people crisscrossing the floor, moving around the information booth with its ornate gold clock. Something seizes my attention, and I stop short; I hear more than one mutter of disapproval at my having interrupted the moving stream. My eyes drift upward, scan the curved ceiling with its celestial constellations. My gaze comes to rest on the sheer face of glass against the back wall, which is interlaced with wrought-iron arches and reaches from the ground all the way up to the ceiling. Now I see what caught my attention: movement along one of the walkways behind the glass. A man in a light-colored trench coat and fedora hat, looking like the cliché of a spy. The figure stops in the middle of the walkway, about halfway up the metal and glass

structure. He looks down at the concourse—looking directly, I believe, at me. I cannot see his eyes, but I feel the terrible force of his gaze; I am being watched, but I am also being judged and condemned.

Plunging back into the crowd, I hasten downstairs. I reach the platform just in time to hurl myself onto the train before the doors snap shut. Panting, I double over from a sudden, painful stitch. When I straighten up, I find myself the object of bland interest: from businessmen, already settled with newspapers folded into manageable columns, and a group of women in smart clothing, likely returning from a day outing to the city.

"Getting a bit old to make a run for the train," I say, still breathing heavily. My smile feels affected, but the other passengers nod and smile back with perfect acceptance and ease. As the train pulls out of the station and my breath finally steadies, I feel an overwhelming relief.

Back at the hospital, I head to my office, where I stand for a long time looking out of the window. The sky is dark, a strong wind rises— branches waving, everything stirred up. Matilda emerges from the side door of the East Wing; she walks briskly, with precision and fluidity, her uniform hugging her form, her head at an angle, as if she's listening for sounds she knows others can't hear. There's a fiery intentness in her face.

She disappears back into the building through the entrance that is almost directly beneath my office. I return to my desk and reach for the charts I've neglected these past few weeks. There's a gnawing in my gut, an unpleasant clutching in my head, a painful scratchiness in my limbs, as if someone were taking tiny, sharp combs to the underside of my skin. I open a fresh bottle of vodka. By midnight, I notice that a third of the bottle is gone.

I pack up my things and head out, intending to return home to my pipe. The lawn is black under a starless sky; there are small pools of green at its edges where the lamps blindly stare. A frightening stillness hangs in the air; I find myself heading not home but over to the East Wing, back into the hospital through the side door. These back hallways hold paintings of lesser interest and worth; my eyes roll heavily over a large oil displaying oversize calla lilies in a gaudy vase, then pass to a New England landscape with a poorly proportioned red barn. The silence crackles.

I gain the door leading down, and then, I am below. The buzz of the fluorescent lights, the dust, the odor of damp cement; the linoleum instantly absorbs my footfalls, as if it were not a man walking here, but a ghost. On the wall, my shadow is curiously truncated. A mountain of mattresses is dimly familiar. A little farther on, tables and chairs rise up to the ceiling. I think I hear footsteps and come to a halt beside a bank of night tables; they look like squat wooden animals, hopeless and dignified, awaiting slaughter. The footsteps, steady and light, are coming my way. I train my ears on the darkness—hear, with dismay, the loudness of my own breath and hold it in. Nothing but the silence of the tunnels, a hundred years echoing between heavy brick walls.

Desperate now, I close my eyes; in the back of my throat I can almost taste the spicy-sweet, smoky taste I crave. In a flash, Hammersmith's face comes back to me: strong jaw, slightly crooked nose, something premeditated about the mouth. A man in the habit of judging others, and accustomed to getting his way. *I'm going back,* he'd said. *But not because of anything you've done.* His insistence that I'd been of no help had shaken me. I picture him stealing into my house, rummaging silently in my desk. The dust in these tunnels—it is rising; it has turned to smoke. My throat closes; I struggle for breath.

I wait for the intruder to creep toward me—a stealth attack, trumping me, calculating, cold, intent on hunting me down.

I listen. There is only silence.

And now, the dark encroachment of dread: and memories . . . my eyes wide . . . running through mud, the old thunder of gunfire, my throat squeezed with panic. Where is Fergus? He was there a moment ago, on the other side of the stretcher. I squint in the darkness to see someone I don't know gripping the poles across from me: between us, a wounded soldier, thrashing. With each wild flail, drops of blood fly upward then disappear. A whiz by my ear, a brief, scorching heat. Sliding down into the trench, the mud thicker, here, and frigid. I hear the loud *thwack* of gunshot; the man holding the other end of the stretcher crumples. I try to whip around but feel I am moving through sludge, the air itself like the mud sucking at my feet. I see not a man, only two bulging eyes: the eyes of a boy, a boy like me. Not angry, not afraid, but surprised, apologetic. A glint of metal: in his shaking hand, a gun. The

stretcher is heavy, the other end fallen; from the corner of my eye, I see the injured soldier rolling off the canvas and into the mud. The stretcher is suddenly weightless.

I swing back around, my movements suddenly crisp, hand tight on my gun—and then aim and shoot. His whole face comes clear, popped from the darkness in a sudden halo of light, like a clever trick of theatrical lighting. Did a sudden movement of the soldier's foot trigger his flashlight?

Now, I see his helmet, the enemy uniform; his arms dart toward me, his own gun thuds into the mud. His face is lit queerly with a smile; another horrible, unnatural smile gapes wide in his neck, dripping red. And now, a torrent of blood. I stare stupidly, realize the obvious: that my bullet met its mark in his throat.

I am dragging myself through the mud, the wounded man I'd been carrying on the stretcher now a deadweight over my shoulder. I see again the face of the enemy, surprised by death—surprised by me. Did he recognize himself in me, too, in that final moment, before I pulled the trigger? Did he also think, *Here is a boy, just like me, whom I must either be killed by or kill?*

Next thing I know, I am running across the lawn; I am cold, very cold, and realize I have taken off my coat, which is draped across my arm. My breath is coming in short, hard bursts; my head splits with the sound. And again, the feeling—that I am being followed. Of course! I tell myself, the want of the pipe, nothing more—a tinge of paranoia that will soon melt away. *My cocoon,* I think: *my dim study, my pipe.*

At the door, I battle the usual thicket of feelings that await me on entering the empty house: relief mingled with despair. No unspoken accusations to delicately sidestep, no need for dissimulation: freed, now, from the tug of guilt, from the pain in Ursula's eyes. But also a black desolation that punches me in the gut.

I head directly to my study and—fingers trembling from the cold, my breath not yet steady, the unbearable hunger clawing within—I prepare the opium and then suck at the pipe. Ecstatic calm washes through me, cleansing away the distress. My breath steadies; I sink

onto the couch, close my eyes, await that inner blossoming, expansive and sweet.

For days I have toyed with that glimpse, in Monday morning staff meeting, of Matilda raising her hand to her top button, passing her thumb across its surface. Now, I summon back the moment and allow it, finally, to play over, slowly, deliciously. My gaze moves down to her bosom, her nipples visible beneath the starchy uniform. Only now do I see that her hips are more rounded than one would suppose from the slimness of her form.

Bertram opens those buttons; they slip through his fingers like pearls. In the dark, her uniform peels away. Her neck arcs—she strains away from him, he sweeps her toward him, her hair in his fist. She stands naked against the cold wall. The sounds, only, of their breathing, the dampness closing in around them, shutting me out. I clutch at my groin; it flares angrily at my touch. My eyes are turned inward, feeding on images of their own making: the whiteness of full breasts where Bertram touches them, where he finds their diamond tips. I move with them— I track Bertram's hands with my own. Heat seeking heat; I hear them again, those illicit, fugitive, throaty sounds, along with the rhythm of the old bed frame. I can hardly breathe—

When it is over, I feel consumed with shame. I pack away my pillow box, open the curtains, and sit in the darkness, looking out onto Ursula's ruined garden. The house is silent, but for the occasional rumble and sigh of the steam pipes. Listening to the sound of my own breath, I feel, wrenchingly, that my vitality is ebbing away. Something rises in my chest, something bitter and brutal, and before I can calm myself, an ugly, wet sob bursts from me.

I feel as if I am the only man alive.

I touch my face and startle at the stubble that covers my cheeks, my chin, my neck.

On the landing, I hear the creaking of the door. *How astonishing,* I think; *Ursula has come back, without warning!*

"Ursula?" I call out.

The memory of how she looked that first day on the dock at Dover overwhelms me. I see again her lively face: recall that hopeful pulsing toward a glorious, unknown future. The way she smelled as a young woman, the give of her flesh, her eyes half-closed, unseeing, as she

yielded to me. I want to cry for the loss, for the waste. I want to weep for Ursula; I have failed her as surely as I have failed myself.

How unexpected that she has come home, that she aims to surprise me this way. Perhaps—stranger things have happened—perhaps, after all—

The door to our room is closed; surely I'd left it open this morning. Living alone, I have no reason to close doors. I take hold of the smooth glass handle and turn.

"Ursula?" I say tenderly, already anticipating the sight: my wife in her lilac robe, the velvet worn in places, propped up in bed, a book open on her belly. I register vaguely that the light is off—not reading, then, but waiting for me nevertheless, waiting for me in the dark.

I flick on the light switch only to find the bed empty, the coverlet stretched tightly across in the fashion Ursula insisted upon.

"Ursula?" I repeat, casting about the room. But there is no one, no one but me.

I undress, wash my face, brush my teeth, and retire.

When it comes, the dream has a different light; nighttime, not day—the woods filled with frightening sounds. Animals with claws or fangs, smelling like vermin, bad omens. I'm at a clearing—the stunned faces of patients; I know, before I look, that the victim is not Delilah. An older woman with a crushed chest, the intact face, the blue dress slowly turning black—not Delilah, who said she loved me (I loved her, too, though I never said it)—but Ursula, my wife, as she looks now: weary, defeated, her love for me squeezed away.

I cannot bear to see her like this; there is nothing I can do. But I don't go to her, I only turn and walk away.

<div align="center">⤙•➤</div>

The alarm clangs, and in the corridor, the sound of running feet—orderlies, attendants, male nurses, all headed toward Hall Two. I hasten in the same direction. On the ward, the air is not hung with the panic-tinged, theatrical charge that typically accompanies an alarm-worthy incident; the staff seem

jittery, but nobody is galvanized, there is no rush to action, no spontaneous thrust toward trying to set things right.

"What happened?" I ask.

Before anyone can answer, Matilda appears, looking grim. "Good. You're here," she says.

The patients are assembled in the dayroom, showered and neatly dressed, their shoes polished, awaiting the attendant who comes for them at exactly half past eight to take them to occupational therapy. They are sitting together in little groups, some talking quietly, all of them somber. Even Harlan, our habitual cackler, given to eccentric fits of laughter and eruptive guffaws, sits silently, his jaw working nervously. I note that Cuthbert and Featherstone are not among the group; I clench against the sinking feeling in my stomach and chest.

Matilda says nothing. We walk down the spotless, buffed linoleum floor, past the patient rooms on either side, past the medical supply room. Outside the bathroom, she pauses.

"They won't come out," she says.

"Cuthbert and Featherstone?"

"Yes. They're unhurt—I'm sorry, I should have said that at once. Featherstone's in a state. He's made a mess in there. The head janitor is coming to clean it up. Says his staff shouldn't have to contend with something like that."

Swinging open the door, I see the two patients sitting on the floor by the farthest of the four stalls, streaked with blood. The floor and walls are splattered; bright red drops fall down from on high. I crane to locate the source and am overcome by revulsion. Strung up on the tops of the stall doors are two dozen or more enormous rats, their throats slit and still dripping blood. A sign—it looks as if it is written in blood—is taped to a stall door: UNKOSHER RATS.

"I did it, Dr. Harrison," Featherstone says. "I paid them back."

I battle a wave of nausea—the same nausea I felt when Featherstone told me, several weeks ago, the terrible story recounted to him by a skeletal concentration camp survivor he liberated. Nazi soldiers had rounded up more than a hundred inhabitants in the man's Polish village and taken them to the kosher abattoir, where they strung them up on meat hooks and slit their throats, while the rest of the village was made to watch. To the wall, they tacked a sign: KOSHER BEEF.

Cuthbert's arm is draped around Featherstone's shoulder. "I didn't know he'd been collecting rats," Cuthbert says. "Keeping them in a box somewhere—he won't tell me where—and sneaking them food."

He sounds surprisingly unperturbed.

"I know," he continues. "It looks absolutely terrifying; the entire ward's scared stiff. But the truth is, Dr. Harrison, it's a symbolic act—a powerful one. I believe it's done Featherstone a world of good."

Cuthbert's complacent, optimistic tone is a pitch-perfect emulation of the psychiatrist's stance.

"We need to wash you down," I say. "Stevens is coming to clean this up. Come along, we're going to the showers."

Together, they rise. I point to the sinks, and Cuthbert and Featherstone wash their faces and hands. It's true, Featherstone seems different; his eyes have lost that crazed, hollow look.

All day long, I have been watching myself, as if standing in the wings of my own life. Still in my office, I look out at the bright half-moon hanging in the black sky. I feel the myriad hauntings of this place—the aching cries and laments. Snowflakes waft down, larger than any I've ever seen, flung this way and that by the wind. They're coming from nowhere; the sky is clear, no clouds, no mist, only blind eternity.

A single chime: one o'clock. It fragments, like light spliced by a prism, reaching me across the roofs of the sleeping town, across roads and woods and grassy inclines. I sense it; tonight is a night they will meet. I don't believe what Bertram told me—that they were planning to stop seeing each other. I cross to Cynthia's office to check the staffing list; sure enough, Janice is on night duty.

Outside, the snowflakes are an onslaught; they settle in my hair and on my clothing, brush at my face with their shrill velvetiness, stinging and soft. My muscles tense as I move through the cold. The hospital is a ghost land, filled with the eternally stricken; and I am the ghost-chief, in charge of the unburied.

I pull open the heavy wooden door and am enveloped in warmth. Moving swiftly now down the deserted hallway. The plain door ahead of me leads to the tunnels. I do not feel my hand on the handle; it

seems to open of its own accord, as if it had been waiting for me. Below-ground, it is dimmer, and once again cold. The gooseflesh rising on my skin fires me.

The hallways are charged, as if I were returning to a childhood home: the mattresses piled high, the carcasses of furniture, from which the stale mutterings of a thousand patients rise in a single, silent exhalation.

My instincts have not failed me; I press up against the wall, feel the unyielding brick against my spine. A rustle, the echo of a whisper. I hold my breath; the scrape of a match being struck, then a whiff of sulfur. A flickering light springs from the space into the hall where I stand unnoticed.

The sounds build—different from last time, but also the same. The creaking of bedsprings, every now and then a whisper, and finally, a sweet sound that cuts me like a knife, the trace of which I have played over and over in my mind since that first night: a slow, quiet moan. I still taste the tart, tarry residue of opium; my body swells with it, clarity and colors everywhere—in my veins, my heart ripening, opening within me like a frosty bloom touched with heat.

I dare to creep forward—fearless, now, I find again the crack in the wall of bedside tables and press my face up against it, as before. My eyes skim the hidden space, with its wavery, liquid light. They are no longer in this world but somewhere else, unlikely to mark my presence in any way; Bertram's torso is pulled away from her, Matilda's lips are swollen and parted. For an instant, her eyelids close and her neck arcs. Bertram is moving slowly, but with brutal force.

Matilda's eyes snap open, and then Bertram bucks—the thrust so violent I see Matilda rise a little from the bed. Bertram releases one hand from where it supports him on the bed; I see Matilda's breast, full and white, with a large dark nipple, pulled tight. Bertram's hand meets her breast—he squeezes, making a fist, and Matilda lets out a little cry as Bertram slams her body into the sagging bed.

When Bertram enters my office today, I am blindsided by the recognition that everything is awry. As I watch him cross the room, my pulse quickens with subtle, defensive fear.

"Featherstone has stopped referring to the hospital as *the Camp*," Bertram says. "And he's eating real food—no more hideous forced feedings. Perhaps we've had one of our unexpected miracles. Dramatic, I'll grant you; Lacroix's got nightmares from the sight, but his screams are worth it if it's given Featherstone the cure."

I sense with relief that Bertram seems completely unaware of my internal struggle.

"It was very upsetting to everyone," I say. I marvel at the way Bertram is looking at me, after everything that has happened: with a kind of trusting admiration.

"Is that how it always goes? Some kind of catharsis, and then the madness just disappears?"

And now, astonishingly, that terrible feeling—that Bertram and I are adversaries, that I am apart in a glass cage—simply vanishes.

"It's not usually quite as simple as that."

"Seems like it might be for Featherstone. It's like all he needed was prolonged rest and exercise, and kindly people taking care of him—just watching and waiting for something to happen. Well, that something *has* happened, and now, maybe, he'll be able to get on with his life."

It is true: Featherstone's curative crisis is mysterious, wonderful, but it could not have been predicted. I feel a pang of pleasure at the thought that Featherstone might, after all, be released from his suffering. While the transformation may not have arisen directly from our efforts, I've learned that the psyche works in inscrutable ways, and that life here, at the hospital, in all its complex rhythms, can lead to extraordinary change.

"It's early days yet," I say. "We'll have to see how things pan out."

"More watching and waiting, then."

"I suppose you could put it that way."

"I know it beats the old methods hands down, but I find modern psychiatry baffling. A rest cure with a twist."

"A twist?"

"Something unexpected that turns everything around. Nothing the doctors could plan." Bertram pauses, then adds wryly: "Or are there studies on the rat-massacre treatment?"

"Featherstone faced his fears," I say carefully. "I concede it was awful, but it took courage for him to do what he did. His war experiences left

him in a state of constant terror—and last week, he stared that terror down. Perhaps this is what has freed him, at least for now."

The expansive connection between us, the feeling of really working together, has returned. I feel a tiny, precious surge of joy.

"You think I'm running away from something," Bertram says quietly. "You think I'm a coward."

"No, Bertram. I don't think you're a coward. But there may be things you've shunted underground, things that are too painful to confront. The psyche can be devious—and unjust; it has a way of turning trauma into punishment, very often directed at one's own self."

"That's a pretty theory," he says blandly.

"Not one that rings true to you?"

Bertram stares out the window. "I'm going to miss Cuthbert. Hall Two won't be the same without him."

I smile. "We'll all miss Cuthbert."

"He's one of those people everyone likes; I imagine he was always like that. Funny how going off the deep end doesn't seem to change a person's nature. Take Johnson—he's surely been nasty as a rattlesnake from the moment he was born. Not even a mother could love him. But Cuthbert—charming as the day is long."

Bertram loses himself in thought. "I envy him. Getting to go back out."

"You'd like to leave, too."

Bertram's face darkens. "Lovable as he is, Cuthbert is still crazy as a loon. You know that as well as I do."

"He'll continue in day treatment, while living in the care of his parents."

"I've made real friends here."

"Yes, you have."

"I don't think I'd be much good anymore—out there. I wouldn't know how to relate to civilians."

I smile. "It is a bit that way, isn't it. When you've been on the front lines, it's hard to know what to do with white picket fences."

"Who'd have thought a madman could be so jolly? So loving and harmless? I swear, Cuthbert seems to have no dark side. It's odd, we all have this deep commonality, despite our differences—like a species, I suppose, as different from one another as a Doberman is from a poodle, but we share the fundamentals."

"It's called *Homo sapiens*."

"You agree, then—that in the end, we're all the same. Patients"—he pauses heavily—"but also staff."

I nod and, for a time, say nothing. Something settles between us, wordless, a pool of feeling. When I speak again, I'm aware of one of those subtle shifts, a silent little Morse code flash.

"There's wisdom in what you say about one's nature. One has to acknowledge the cracks and then work around them."

"I take it you say this from personal experience." Bertram's voice is quiet, though his eyes are bold.

"When you said you'd stop seeing Matilda," I persist, "you were doing the right thing."

"I see. This is about right and wrong."

"It's about taking responsibility."

"For being a nut job."

"For being aware that certain things are not wholly within one's control—at least for a time."

"That sounds very tidy."

"I'm not sure that sparring is the most helpful approach."

"I can't do anything right, can I." Bertram says this as a challenge.

"I'm not only thinking about you, Bertram."

"You don't believe me, do you."

"Have you continued to meet with her?"

"No, I haven't."

My heart sinks. I didn't imagine that Bertram would out-and-out lie.

After he leaves, I buzz through to Cynthia. "I'll need the staffing roster for Hall Two," I say.

There is one, simple solution; I'll switch Janice's hours. Since we're considering her for a full-time position, she should in any case clock up sufficient experience on the more demanding day shift before she completes her apprenticeship.

Floating, floating. I can see nothing around me, but somehow sense that I am in a dark basement. The air stinks, but in my state of excitement, I don't mind—in fact, I welcome it. Now there is candlelight. Wearing

a medieval costume, I hunch over a table on which lies a fresh corpse, sliced open from pelvis to neck. Assistants attend me as I labor over the dissection. We work in secret; something illicit hangs in the air. Body fluids still warm, my ungloved hands moving about in the interior slime. A mounting thrill, almost erotic in its intensity—the feel of being 'on a new frontier. And then the organ is in my hand—a heart; it begins, faintly, to beat. The corpse is not a corpse but a living person, and now this person begins to writhe in pain. I do not jump backward, only fix my hand more tightly on the pulsing heart, the better to palpate it and feel its slippery form. The table is whisked away. I am in the basement, still, but now my assistant is handing me a filthy cloth, which I rub on an open wound in my chest, infecting myself with some dreadful disease in order to study the results.

When I awaken, I have a pounding migraine; it feels like an ice pick is lodged behind my left eye, just the way Ursula used to describe it.

I get to my office early and sit for a long time at my desk.

My morning sessions begin; fortunately, I can just sit in my chair, taking comfort in the psychiatrist's right to remain quiet. Then, at last, Bertram's knock. He sits silently across from me, his eyes rheumy with distress.

"It happened again," he says simply, his voice flat.

"What happened?"

Bertram seems to be choking back tears. I feel a jolt of alarm.

"I heard Rosamund's voice, clear as day."

"Where were you?"

"In the print shop. I couldn't go on with it—the machinery was—"

"The machinery?"

"Not printing—it was a place of torture. Terrible things are being done with those machines." Bertram's eyes fill with tears. "You have to do something," he hisses. "You have to stop what they're doing."

"No one's doing anything, Bertram."

He looks about wildly, then cocks his head, alert. "She's here." He scans the molding on the ceiling. "Ssssh—listen." He listens intently, his face trembling.

"Bertram," I ask. "Have you been cheeking your medication?"

Bertram jerks his head my way, looks at me with dark, wavering eyes.

"Are you on our side?" he whispers. "I no longer know who I can trust."

"You have, haven't you. But you'd been doing so well."

There is a shifting in Bertram's eyes. "From one standpoint, perhaps."

"Which standpoint is that?"

"Yours—the staff's. Not from the standpoint of the soul."

"How long have you been doing it?"

"Two weeks. Maybe more. I couldn't say exactly. The medicine blocks some of the storms. But it's also a kind of death. The storms—they're who I am."

After the late night change-of-shift meeting, I remain in the nurses' station to complete my chart notes. I look up to see Matilda, who has just come off a twelve-hour stint, walk through the door.

"You do burn the midnight oil, don't you," she says. Her face is strained.

"The pot calling the kettle black," I manage.

"Just a thing or two to finish up." She opens the logbook.

Bertram's face floats into my mind—I see the agony in his eyes.

"Matilda, I've been meaning to talk to you about Mr. Reiner."

Her eyes flash a secret pain, but she quickly suppresses it.

"He's been cheeking his medications," I continue. "I believe he's slipping into real psychosis—and might possibly become dangerous."

Her hand flies up to toy with a lock of hair peeking out from her white cap. "I had no idea."

"Mr. Reiner is practiced in the art of deception," I say.

Her steady gaze gives nothing away. "We'll make sure he swallows his meds."

"I'm going to talk about him tomorrow at morning rounds. We might need to move to another form of treatment. I've not yet discussed this with the patient—"

Matilda reddens slightly. "ECT?" she asks.

"That's one possibility."

"I certainly don't see him as a candidate for surgery," she says with quiet ferocity.

"We'd only consider that as a last resort."

"We both know how destructive it can be," Matilda persists. She

seems to be struggling to maintain her composure. "You say he might be dangerous. What do you mean?"

"He's been wandering around at night—sleepwalking I think." I wait for her reaction. "Somehow, this has eluded the nursing staff. Once he found himself in another patient's room—holding a pillow, with the idea of lowering it over the patient's face."

I wonder if she realizes it is she who has been in danger, not one of the other patients.

"That can't possibly be true." Matilda's voice is thick with disbelief. "I know him—there's not a violent bone in his body."

"Mr. Reiner is a compelling man; in some ways, he's the picture of rationality. But you and I both know how stealthy mental illness can be. It's a tricky and seductive business."

"Was it a particular patient—whose room he found himself in? Is there someone he's been having problems with?"

I shake my head. "It's nothing like that. He seems to slip into a delusional state, perhaps while he's dreaming; he believes that a childhood friend is being tortured, and is begging him to put an end to her suffering."

"Oh! I had no idea!" she repeats.

"I'm afraid Mr. Reiner defies our usual formulae." I can feel the tightness of my mouth, the pained expression in my own eyes. I try to shake the disconcerting feeling that I am watching myself from a distance. "Even more reason to proceed with caution."

Matilda is changing before my eyes; I'm watching the dawning of some kind of critical understanding.

"What are you saying, Henry?"

I remember the moment I told Matilda to call me Henry; how long ago it seems. But this is the first time she has actually uttered my name.

"That you should be careful."

"*I* should be careful?" Her voice is a whisper. She seems, of a sudden, fragile.

"Yes," I whisper back. "Your safety is of the utmost importance"—she raises an eyebrow, waits for me to finish my sentence—"to me."

"Is it?" A tiny wisp of sound through parted lips.

I nod. And then I see in her face a delicate, slow flush. Matilda raises her hand; for a moment I think she's going to reach over and take mine, but she only touches her cheek.

"I'm glad to know it," she says. We sit there for a time in silence; her words ring in my ears.

"Oh happy day!" Cuthbert announces, bursting into the dayroom, holding a stack of papers to his chest. "Gifts for all!"

The cooking detail has baked a towering seven-layer cake for Cuthbert's farewell luncheon; he eyes it approvingly, setting down his armload and sweeping a finger through the frosting.

"Egad, but it's lovely!" he exclaims. "Orange buttercream!"

Cuthbert's expansive mood is contagious; I can feel it spreading among the patients, touching the staff, myself included. Featherstone appears from somewhere and hurries to Cuthbert's side. Cuthbert slaps his arm around his friend, who smiles proudly, though I see tears in his eyes.

"I'll come on visiting days," I overhear Cuthbert whisper to Featherstone. "You'll be out before you know it. I'll host you at my residence—now *that's* something to look forward to."

He turns to the assembled group. "And now, let them eat cake! With apologies, should there be a Marie Antoinette amongst us."

"No Marie Antoinettes," Lacroix calls out. "Two Napoleons and one Caesar at last count—oh, and maybe one Mary Mary Quite Contrary, eh, Professor?"

A laugh goes up; several patients cheer.

"I am in many ways sad to be leaving the Hospital Cosmology. Each of us here carries a prime piece of the emotional universe—expresses it, I suppose, would be a more accurate way of putting it."

Cuthbert glances meaningfully about the crowd. "Living specimen jars. You have only to look around the room to see we have everything pretty much covered. Fatal romanticism; seething rage; ruthless cunning; feverish hope. Patients, staff; we all do our bit on that score."

I flinch a little at Cuthbert's metaphor—*specimen jars*. Aware of the feel of eyes, I turn to see that Bertram is studying me from across the room. Thoughts cycle slowly through my mind: *I know nothing . . . He knows too much.*

"I beg your indulgence," Cuthbert continues. "A few words of wis-

dom, if I may. Whatever your calling, maintain the faith. We are the collective color of things; imagine a world in black and white—endurable, perhaps, but what would be the point? If you are purple, scream it out loud! If your color is the palest blue—well, that is not only your sky it is everybody's: do not relinquish what you have to give."

Cuthbert squints around the room; he seems to be looking for somebody. His eyes settle on Bertram, standing at the edge of the crowd.

"Eureka!" Cuthbert continues. "That's the point; it's all about the discovery. There's not a lot more to it than that. And remember, it's gone before you know it, so find a way to have a good time."

He beams at the assembled crowd, passing his eyes slowly from person to person. When his gaze comes to rest on me, I feel the power of his charisma: that way he has of making a person feel special, loved, at peace.

"And now," he continues, "the giving of the gift."

Cuthbert passes among the group, handing out his booklet. "I give you my magnum opus," he says grandly. "I've called it 'Down the Hatch.' Catchy title, no? A compilation of the finest nuthouse jokes in America. Brought to you by one truly qualified to judge."

Bertram is no longer looking at me. Something else has caught his attention: Matilda, busy at the refreshment table, laying out napkins and spoons. His face is suddenly gripped by torment.

"There's something you've been missing all along," Cuthbert continues cheerfully. "The cure for a metaphysical illness of the kind with which I am afflicted must be found in its opposite case. And what is diametrically opposed to the abyss? To the great void at all of our feet—which starts, of course, in the Mind, and then trickles down to form a dangerous vacuum? The answer is *humor*."

Matilda has seen Bertram looking at her; her shoulders sag, she curls into herself, as if absorbing a blow.

"After conducting hours of private thought experiments"—Cuthbert is in full stride—"I have compiled the data. The result is rigorous and scientifically sound."

I cannot take my eyes from Matilda. I have the crazy feeling that, if I do, some harm will befall her. Perhaps she senses my gaze, as her movements become self-conscious. *Look at me,* I think with fervor as she heads discreetly toward the door. *Give me a sign—*

I hear Cuthbert's voice, tripping along in the background, though I pay little attention to his words.

"All traces of metaphysical illness disappear when one is telling, listening to, or responding to a joke. A person cannot question his existence while laughing."

Matilda halts, and now, she turns. Her gaze scans but settles on no one—not Bertram, not me—and then, she disappears through the door.

"As a token of my goodwill toward everyone here—patients, doctors, the rest of the staff, the institution itself in its benevolent modern incarnation—I have prepared a treatment manual which will save you a lot of time, money, and woe. The definitive compendium of psychiatric jokes. They needn't be jokes about psychiatry and hospitals to have a curative effect, but I have circumscribed the content to tip my hat to the wheres and whyfores of our present existence."

Cuthbert tips his fedora, which he's being specially permitted, today, to wear indoors.

"It is, after all, a *present* I am giving you, and for those of you who care to look deeper, there are other resonances concerning the *present* as it pertains to *God*—"

The booklet dangles from Cuthbert's hand; he seems to have forgotten it. Bewilderment grows in his face.

Bertram appears at Cuthbert's side. "I, for one, am eager to see the joke book," he says kindly, placing an arm around Cuthbert's shoulder and then shooting me a glance.

Am I imagining it? Or are Bertram's eyes, above the genial smile, ringed with despair?

From the back of the room, Featherstone gives an uncharacteristic yell. "The *jokes,* Cuthbert. Hand out the jokes!"

"Yes, good, of course."

"Orange buttercream cake!" someone else yells. Another patient takes up the cry, and then a third and a fourth. Soon, the room echoes with spirited cries for cake. For a moment, Cuthbert looks stunned, but then he reclaims his manic good cheer.

"All in good time, my good fellows. Cake will ensue, but first, a quick reading. A single joke to show us all that, no matter the delusion, no matter the hallucinations, in the end, it's all a lark, not unlike civilian life

out there: you know, those sorry folk pressing their noses up against the window *truly envying* all the nut jobs inside."

Now, a round of hisses and hoots and fists in the air, everybody smiling. None of the staff intervenes with the usual insistence on respectful language—not *hatch,* people, but *mental hospital.* Not *nut jobs* but *psychiatric patients.*

"Settle down," Cuthbert says, enjoying the performance. "A little patience, please, patients; the dessert will not desert."

Cuthbert flips through the mimeographed pages, finds the joke he wants, and gives a fine delivery. Laughter erupts, and Cuthbert smiles with satisfaction. Some patients look gleeful, others uncomprehending or confused.

"Speaking of chicken and egg, which animal can you eat before they're born and after they're dead? Oh dear, I've given it away—"

Cuthbert's smile fades. "It's easy to forget, sometimes." His voice is suddenly tender.

"Forget what?" Featherstone asks.

"Well, that we're all just a little cracked. But there's hope—in something you can *hold* without *touching* it."

None of the patients venture a guess; there is something melancholy about the silence that fills the room.

"That's right, folks," he almost whispers. "A *conversation.* Though at Shadowbrook, I daresay, it touches us all, and deeply. You might say transformatively."

He lets out a deep sigh. "We really are riddles, in the end, aren't we."

Now, he sweeps his gaze over us all—patients, nurses, orderlies, doctors, the handful of servants standing at the back of the room.

"Rather like pins. Pointed in one direction and headed in the other. But you see, I've done it again! Answering the question before it's rightly been posed. And there's the rub; turning the riddle upside down—inside out, outside in. And that's where *I'm* headed, if truth be told—going from *inside* to *outside.* Which is where the confusion begins all over again . . . An *outsider* now *really out there,* in the *insider* world, where he *can* never, *will* never, belong . . ."

Cuthbert's eyes fill with tears, but then he suddenly lays down his booklet and hurries across the dayroom.

"No, no, no, *no!*" he calls to Featherstone, who has crept, unnoticed,

over to the trestle table; his face is covered in orange buttercream. Featherstone grabs again at the cake and crams a fistful into his mouth.

Cuthbert reaches his friend and pulls his hand away from his face. "You're going to be sick as a dog, I tell you. Stop!"

Two orderlies materialize beside Featherstone, who is frantically chewing, his enormous Adam's apple bobbing up and down his thin neck. They take him by the arms and gently lead him away. Cuthbert follows behind, visibly fretting, reaching every now and again to pat his friend's bony face.

"Won't take a minute to clean you up," I hear the orderly say. "And then you can rejoin the festivities."

Featherstone turns; he looks at Cuthbert with sadness and love.

"I know what you've done," Bertram says.

"What do you mean?" I ask.

"You've put a stop to it, haven't you." Bertram says this without anger. "You didn't believe I could do it on my own, so you took care of things yourself."

I wait.

"Matilda is distraught," he continues.

"How do you know that?"

"I know her, I can tell." The calm in his voice is unsettling; he is watching me with an animal kind of intensity—tracking me, is how it feels. "I'm not enjoying the mouth checks. I sometimes wonder, Dr. Harrison. Have you ever tried to put yourself in our shoes?"

"That's a fair question."

"Then it deserves an answer."

"Yes, Bertram, I try very hard to see things from your point of view."

"But you don't really believe the tables could be turned, do you. I forget that I have a Ph.D.: that in some circumstances, it would be me who would be referred to as *Doctor*. There's an unexpected thought."

"It's important to you—to think that, in some sense, we're the same."

Bertram's face falls. "Can't we just talk, for once—person to person?"

I feel myself coloring. "I'll do my best."

"It's mortifying." Bertram's voice has dropped to a whisper. "I'm a grown man, locked up in a nursery."

"You're here of your own free will."

"I'm helpless as a babe. They look into my mouth to see if I've swallowed my pills. And now, you've taken away the few shreds of manhood I had left."

"Something you said the other day—about Featherstone."

"Yes?"

"I was thinking: perhaps we might try a session of sodium amytal therapy. Traumatic events often bury themselves deeply; it can be extremely difficult to get to them. An injection of sodium amytal can have the effect of freeing up the psyche—of taking the person back to the moment or place of the trauma. I know it's hard to believe, but patients have told me it's like gently gliding down a stream to a hidden spot. I've seen some dramatic results—you've seen them yourself among your hall mates."

"The truth serum," Bertram says; there's a spark of hope in his eyes.

"That's actually a misnomer. It seems to have the effect of dissolving the defenses: easily, safely, and often with dramatic effect."

"It got thousands of broken soldiers back into battle, didn't it," Bertram remarks.

"Another way to put it would be to say that sodium amytal helped to cure a whole range of terrible symptoms: paralyses, blindness, deafness, depression."

Who am I trying to convince? That crushing feeling, again, in my chest: the thought of all those traumatized soldiers who passed through Shadowbrook. And my work, day in, day out, coaxing, encouraging, galvanizing. Lots of talk about bootstraps, about courage and duty, endurance and will. And I—did I notice their eyes? Did I see the pleading, the agony, the strife? Was I *really* aware that I was holding the fate of these young men in my hands?

I continue, almost insistent: "It gave these men back their lives—"

"Not if they didn't get to come back," Bertram cuts in.

"The point isn't what happened to other soldiers. The point is what's happening to you now."

There is no anger in Bertram's face: only suffering, and a silent plea.

The following morning, the orderly escorts Bertram to the treatment room—a narrow, spotless space with whitewashed walls and tile floor, furnished sparsely with a cot and wooden chair. The sunlight, strained by a gauzy curtain, hangs in the room like a gleaming fog.

"What am I to expect?" Bertram asks as he rolls up his sleeve.

"You'll feel drowsy, and then you'll have the sensation of falling asleep, though in fact you will remain conscious and able to communicate. After the interview, you will very likely forget most of what we discussed. Sometimes, there are lingering images, fragments of the conversation, like snatches of a dream."

"What's the point of it if you don't remember?" he asks.

I plunge the needle into the vial and withdraw the liquid.

"We might be able to establish some connection in your unconscious mind," I say, squinting to look at the dosage. "Between things that are happening in the present and painful experiences from the past."

"You mean Rosamund," he says quietly. He does not say, *And Matilda*.

"I can't promise any miracles, but I can say that I have seen some wonderful results. Once certain experiences come to light—well, it can restore a person to his old self. Particularly for soldiers who have suffered trauma."

"What combat soldier didn't suffer trauma?" Bertram asks quietly. "In any case, I'm not sure anymore what my old self is."

Tentatively, I stroke Bertram's forearm in search of a good vein. As my hand makes contact with his skin, I feel a little flare of intimacy. And the sudden burn of tears behind my eyelids, which I quickly blink away.

I find a good blue vein on Bertram's forearm and slowly inject the sodium amytal, eyeing the clock on the wall to titrate the dosage over the course of a full minute.

"We'll do another injection or two in the next ten minutes," I say. "Just lie back, try to relax."

"I can't imagine . . ." Bertram says drowsily; his eyes cloud, and then close.

After a few minutes, I give the second injection, then wait a little longer before administering the third.

Bertram's breath slows, his face relaxes; he looks more at peace than I've ever seen him.

"Very well, then," I say. "Why don't you go ahead and tell me your thoughts."

Bertram winces; his hand flies to his abdomen, and his face contorts with pain.

"What is it, Bertram? What's happening?"

"He was a Jew."

"Who was?"

"Heine. The poet."

"What about Heine?"

"The Hitler Youth sang his 'Die Lorelei.' Grown soldiers, too. We all sang it—he was a poet of the *Volk*. It was easy enough to eradicate his name—*Anonymous,* they said. He predicted it all, a hundred years before it happened. *If Germany ever forgoes Christianity,* he said, *their martial ardor and savagery will rise again.* He warned his German readers that they were their own worst enemy. And warned the French: *The German thunder will roar as it has never roared before in the history of the world.* The French Revolution would seem harmless by comparison, he said. Nobody listened; even his friends thought he was a crackpot."

"You're rubbing your abdomen," I say gently.

Bertram draws in a sharp breath. "He took me by surprise."

"Who did?"

"Emanuel. I don't know how he found me. I'd been very careful. All my training . . ." His voice trails off.

"What do you mean 'all your training'?"

"Three months, fourteen hours a day. That's how they do it."

"That's how who does it?"

He clenches his jaw.

"Bertram Reiner. Rank: Lieutenant. Service Serial Number: 37337566."

"I'm not interrogating you, Bertram."

He looks surprised—and then, fearful.

"You were talking about your training," I prompt.

"I didn't want to do it," he whimpers. "I was coerced." He looks through me, his eyes are blank. I wonder who he thinks I am.

"What were you coerced into doing?"

"*Remarkably suited.* That's what they said. I was still recuperating from shrapnel wounds. You might say they made me an offer I couldn't refuse."

I wait to see if Bertram will say more; it can be a mistake to push too hard when the patient is in this chemically induced, highly suggestible hypnotic state. He moves his mouth as if speaking, his face mobile with expression, but no words come out, not even a whisper.

"Bertram," I say, "I can't hear what you're saying."

"I've told you; I eluded detection—right up until the very end. Someone must have slipped up; that's how it happens. It must have been an ungodly coincidence—it couldn't have been otherwise. I mean, what were the odds?"

"You once said you don't believe in coincidences," I say.

"You don't know what the hell you're talking about," he says. Then he raises his hand to salute and adds, "Sir."

"You said it must have been a coincidence," I say firmly.

"It was the thing I was most afraid of," he says, still saluting. "But it's also why I agreed to do it."

"To do what?" I am in the dark, but it feels as if I'm pushing up against the heart of the matter.

"To spy," he says simply. The whole of his body slumps.

"If you don't mind, sir," he says, and he lowers his hand back down to his side.

"The thing you were most afraid of," I prompt.

"Every day, I wrote down the numbers. 2463. 1992. 3287. We brought some Poles onboard—upped our ratios considerably; greater numbers, fewer bullets. The Poles had their techniques. One bullet, two people; smash the heads of children, no cost to an extra swing of a club. Our best day ever—more than eight thousand."

"What has this to do with your brother?"

"He didn't know I was there, I tell you," Bertram hisses. "I watched him—the way he raised the rifle to his shoulder. He was an expert marksman. Who'd have thought he'd become an expert marksman?"

"You saw your brother, then," I say.

"I *worked with* my brother," he says. "That was the mission. But he wasn't supposed to know I was there. They assured me of this—*promised* me."

Bertram gulps back a cry.

"I shouldn't have been surprised. It was probably a setup. They do that kind of thing. Not a coincidence, after all. I didn't understand it, though—why they would bring us together like that and then spill the beans. Although maybe—"

"Maybe what?"

Bertram's eyes dart about the room, then settle again blankly onto my face.

"I don't know," he says, looking startled. "I suppose I'll never know."

I remind myself that it can go on like this for some time—this scudding around the edge of the traumatic memory.

"You were rubbing your abdomen," I say carefully.

Bertram's hand flies back to the spot, and again, he winces.

"It was such a surprise; I didn't have time to defend myself. I'd left my weapon in the mess—there was no reason I'd have brought it with me. *The War was over!* We were headed home. So, when he attacked, all I had was my bare hands."

"You fought him off, then—" I say, hoping to learn more.

"Yes." Bertram says it as a quiet sob. "He had a knife. I don't know how I managed to fend him off with only my bare hands—"

He bows his head.

"It was self-defense." His voice is broken. "The blood was gushing out of me. I thought we were both going to die—I was sure the wound was fatal: I could feel my guts spilling out into my hands. I don't know why I survived."

"Who knifed you?" I ask quietly. "Who did you have to fight off?"

"I pleaded with him," he whimpered. "You have to believe me."

His face transforms again; now he is galvanized with rage.

"But the facts were the facts. I knew what my brother had done. *I was there.* I saw it with my own eyes."

An oddly familiar ring in those words: *I knew what my brother had done.* Yes, only yesterday, Bertram said something like that about me. *I know what you've done.* And with the same weighted resignation.

"Are you talking about Rosamund?"

"Rosamund?" Bertram says with surprise. "I'm not talking about

Rosamund. I'm talking about all the others: the pits, the rifle shots, the convoy of vans filled with gas. I'm talking about thousands of Rosamunds—and their parents and grandparents and sisters and brothers."

"Your brother knifed you," I say quietly.

Bertram clutches his abdomen, his face fierce. "After he dropped the knife, I grabbed it. But it was slippery with blood, it fell out of my hand."

"And Emanuel?"

"He got away," he says in a strangled voice. "He's out there, waiting to finish off the job."

I leave Bertram to sleep it off in the interview room under the watchful eye of the orderly. An hour later, when I return, he is sitting up in the chair, drinking a cup of coffee.

"How are you feeling?" I ask.

"Like someone slipped me a mickey," he says, averting his eyes. "Learn anything helpful?"

"You talked about your injury," I say.

"Oh?" Still, Bertram looks away. He sounds weary: not just tired but worn down, worn out.

"Rest, now," I say. "We can take it up in our next session."

He puts down his cup: his eyes glint with a look I've seen before in the eyes of men—feral, uncanny, as if he were at the same time too close and very far away.

"It's in the Bible," he says, his expression turning menacing. *"An eye for an eye—"*

At home, I stay up late to document Bertram's sodium amytal interview, aware of that exhilarating feeling that comes just before a breakthrough. Fairbairn's seminal formulation on the schizoid personality gleams in my mind as I write; the paradoxes suddenly seem a perfect fit. Trusting innocence along with paranoia; the ache to get close sparring with a desperate need for distance; acute sensitivity coupled with alienated coldness. Mystery and allure, and a disconcerting sense that behind the inscrutability is perhaps, well, nothing: not emptiness, but the kind of endless,

atmospheric nothingness of the sky. Incubate such a complex, delicate soul in the battlefield and the balance will tip in a particular way; the veneer of self-sufficiency may harden to steel, which in turn keeps the psychosis in check—or at least carefully hidden from the outside. This is what Fairbairn would argue. Finally, as I write, I feel as if the puzzling pieces of Bertram's case are beginning to form a coherent picture.

By the time I finish, I am so alert I know I will have no rest without a pipe. I smoke one pellet and then head up to bed. I move in a trance, and when I awaken, I am lying under the covers wearing my pajamas, though I have no recollection of anything beyond climbing the stairs with the intention of going to bed.

I lie perfectly still, my nerve endings tingling with dread, and squint through my lashes. I can feel the interloper; his presence is like a blast of cold air. I hear it, now: the slow creak of the floorboards, the sound of someone taking a single step, attempting to remain undetected. A band of moonlight falls from the hall window in through the doorway to my room; I can just make out the elongated shadow in the shape of a man.

An eye for an eye—Bertram's words from earlier today swell in my mind. I do not move a muscle. I stay like that for what seems an age, coiled with fear. Nothing moves, nothing changes.

When I awaken again, the shadow is gone; in its place is streaming sunlight.

Chapter Eight

Early Spring 1948

On Hall Two, the patients are in a flurry. Matilda is not on duty; throughout the long evening, my mind keeps flying to her. Will she have heard, by now, that Bertram has disappeared? At Shadowbrook, such news travels like wildfire.

The police have been notified, but in truth, there's not much they can do. Bertram committed himself voluntarily; though he has left against medical advice, he has done nothing criminal. As long as we do not consider Bertram dangerous, there's no cause for the police to pursue the matter further.

An orderly comes to tell me that Featherstone insists on speaking to me alone. I find him pacing in his room, in a state of great agitation.

"He came to our meetings—you know, the Suicide Club. He pretended he was only there to observe. Like he was studying us, or something. But he was really there to learn. *I knew he was going to do it.* I've known all along. You staff thought you broke up our club after Collins's death, but you didn't. We kept on meeting. We were just more careful."

"What did Bertram say?"

Featherstone's eyes bulge disturbingly. "He told me he'd done ter-

rible things. But it's not true! Cuthbert told me Bertram saved—" He breaks off.

"Yes?"

"Well, people like me."

"What do you mean 'people like you'?"

"He liberated concentration camps, at the very end. He was a hero. Cuthbert says he has medals."

"I'm told Mr. Reiner was a brave soldier."

"Why did he say all those things?" Featherstone's eyes are watery with bewilderment.

"I don't know to what you're referring," I say.

"I want to tell you something," he says, his voice trembling. "This place isn't as bad as I say it is. I told Bertram that—I told him you were all here to help us."

"What did he say?"

"He said it didn't make any difference. That it was all rotten and there was nothing any of us could do about it, so why bother."

Featherstone lets out a little sob. "I told him that's not how heroes talk."

"Did he reply?"

Featherstone struggles to speak.

"He said he wasn't a hero. He told me he was a bad man, a very bad man. And very tired."

"Was that the last time you saw him?"

He nods.

"I wish Cuthbert were here." His eyes droop with grief. "Cuthbert would make things right. It's true, Bertram didn't free *me*, but he freed many of my fellow prisoners. Maybe we didn't show enough gratitude. Maybe we didn't let him know that we'd all be dead if it weren't for him. Maybe . . ." Tears drip down Featherstone's face.

"I can assure you, Mr. Featherstone, that Mr. Reiner's leaving had nothing to do with you."

"I wish I could believe you, truly I do."

"You will, in time. But for now, why don't you have the orderly put a call through to Mr. Cuthbert? I know he'll be happy to hear from you."

Back at the nurses' station, the head nurse informs me that Janice is extremely upset and has rushed off to the medical supply room.

I find her there in a flood of tears.

"It wasn't my fault, Dr. Harrison. It wasn't!" she says, trying to regain her composure.

"No one's blaming you, Janice."

"Nurse Willoughby is going to be furious. But I was only doing what she told me to do!"

I reassure Janice and relieve her of her shift, then make my way up the back stairs to the servants' quarters. In the common room, I find someone reading a newspaper and ask him to direct me to Mr. Thomas's room. The narrow hallway turns this way and that; underfoot is a luxurious runner in a Persian design of reds and browns. The walls are covered in delicate, pink-patterned fabric, hung decades ago but still in fine condition. Thomas's room is at the very end; the door is ajar, and Thomas, in his usual formal attire, with a starched white handkerchief peeking out of his jacket pocket, is busy packing a large, black suitcase.

"Thought I'd stop in to say good-bye." It is a breach, my coming to his room, but Thomas now seems unconcerned for the unspoken rules of hospital propriety.

"I appreciate that, Dr. Harrison."

For a moment, neither of us speaks.

I am the one to break the silence. "Did it come as a surprise?"

He pauses, hand on the open lid of the suitcase. "I'm not sure how to answer that."

"I know. These things can be very complicated." My voice sounds oddly fragile, almost lost.

"When I first met Mr. Reiner onboard the ship, I wondered if he'd be one of the men who cracked. But when I saw him again—well, he seemed solid as a rock. I ran into him on the street, if you can believe it. I was living on Morningside Drive—he'd started back at Columbia. I hardly recognized him; he was a new man, excited about his studies. Like all of us, I suppose, he was happy to be getting on with his life. When he asked me to work for him, I said yes, without really thinking it through."

"There's something about wartime friendships, isn't there," I say.

"He was a brother to me." Thomas's voice is thick with emotion.

He searches my face; I have the feeling he wants to say something

further, he purses his mouth and seems about to speak. I wait, but he says nothing.

"Do you have any idea where he might have gone?" I ask.

"He's a very private man," Thomas replies. "We were as close as two men can be, but there's a lot I don't know."

"And probably a fair amount that you do—"

Thomas smooths the clothing at the top of the suitcase.

"I wish I could be of help," he says. He snaps the lid shut, then regards me squarely.

"I've often wondered, sir. Why it hits one man and not another."

"I've often wondered the same thing myself, Thomas."

All the way home—across the lawn, along the pathways, up the hill, and through the white, wooden gate—my mind is a relentless beam of focus on just one action. At the front door, my hand trembles so violently, I have trouble getting the key in the lock. Finally inside, I go directly to my study and retrieve my pillow box, willing my fingers to steadiness.

Scooping out a little pellet, I hold it over the lamp, wait until it is puffy and soft, and then place it on top of the hole in the pipe bowl. Reclining on the couch, I draw in the smoke. The billowing smoke turns to brightness; it feels as if youth is pouring in, effacing the emptiness. I peer into the thick white haze and sink into relief.

—‹‹•›•—

When I awaken, the early morning light seems to be struggling up from the flat, black lawn. My eyes are slits; my parched tongue sticks painfully to the roof of my mouth. All of me screams with a want that is like nothing else and that promises to be slaked by nothing.

Only then do I remember: Bertram is gone.

The day awaits; I must shower and change and prepare for morning rounds. I try to move my arms and legs, but they will not obey me. I

only watch as the light rises and fills the room; it is white and thin and uncompromising.

<p style="text-align:center"><<-+-></p>

Since Bertram's disappearance, Matilda has lost weight. Her face is a little haggard, and there's a gray tinge to her skin. She avoids me on the hall; now and then, during meetings, I catch her eyeing me darkly. I find myself wanting to say something—to offer comfort—but she has erected a barrier, making it clear she wants to be left to herself.

Today I am at the nurses' station early, an hour before the end of the graveyard shift. I see Matilda through the glass before she sees me.

"Oh," she says, opening the door. "I didn't expect to see you here at this hour."

"I could say the same," I say, attempting a smile.

She looks at me with confusion, as if trying to decipher a code. I hate myself for forgetting what she must be going through.

"I've been thinking. When was the last time you took leave?"

"I really don't know," Matilda says blankly.

"Why don't you take some time off? We could spare you for a week or two."

"I couldn't possibly do that." Her gaze flutters anxiously about the cramped space.

"The work takes a toll—you know that better than anyone."

"I need to be here. In case—"

"Yes?"

"In case Mr. Reiner comes back."

Matilda reddens; in her face I see a taut mixture of determination and despair.

"The rest of the staff can deal with that."

I let a silence settle between us. Then: "Matilda?"

"Yes?" Her lips and cheeks are touched with heat.

"In the end, this might not have been the best place for Mr. Reiner. Perhaps he intuited it—and didn't know of any other way to leave."

"That can't be true." Matilda distractedly takes up a chart from the

desk. "He was making progress—we were beginning to plan his discharge. There's a junior faculty position open at Columbia, and he was going to apply."

"I suspect Mr. Reiner needed to do things on his own terms. Without our arranging his life for him. He's a strong-willed and independent man."

"I know what kind of a man he is." Matilda's voice is trembling. She sets the chart down and flips through to find the first blank page.

"Sometimes things don't go the way we plan."

Matilda begins her chart note; there's a little tremor in her hand as she writes. "I'm perfectly aware of that, Dr. Harrison."

"I'm sorry, Matilda. It's just that I think you could do with a break."

She sets down the pen. "In truth, I have nowhere to go. This hospital is my life."

"Doesn't your mother live nearby? Perhaps you could stay with her for a few days. Just to get away. It might do you some good."

Matilda's shoulders droop, her eyes empty out, I can almost see her pride evaporating.

"My mother and I don't have an easy relationship. And she's not been well."

"All the more reason, perhaps, to spend some time with her."

She looks helpless, her face is stark with bewilderment. She sits there, hardly moving, for several minutes, saying nothing. Finally, she speaks. "Maybe for just a few days . . ."

The next morning, I instruct Cynthia to alert me of any calls to the switchboard for a taxicab. At noon, she buzzes through to say Admissions has called for a taxi in Matilda's name, due to arrive at one o'clock.

I reach the main foyer at a quarter to one. Matilda is sitting on a brocade banquette, wearing street clothes, her head bare. Her eyes are frighteningly vacant; for a moment, I have the unreasonable thought that this is a new patient, awaiting admission. But of course it is Matilda—still beautiful, despite her pallor and exhaustion, like a consumptive patient aflame with waning life.

"I've come to see you off."

"Thank you, that's very kind." She glances absently around the foyer.

"I hope you'll have a good rest," I continue, feeling desperate to say something more.

The sound of tires on gravel; through the window I see the taxicab pulling up.

Matilda rises.

"Let me help you with that." I reach for her case.

We step out onto the wide steps. I follow her as she descends; her hair glimmers in the sunlight. I hand her case to the driver and hold open the back door, then lean to assist her; she dips to get into the car, her arm briefly brushing against mine, her scent wafting close.

As the driver starts up the engine, Matilda glances at me through the window, and then looks away.

"The mail boy just brought this up." Cynthia is here for dictation, her stenography notebook in one hand and, in the other, an envelope.

"You know I don't like to disrupt my mornings with such things."

"I'm sorry, Dr. Harrison. It looked important."

"Very well."

She hands me the envelope, and I set it down on my desk.

I keep Cynthia for over an hour, pacing as I dictate; I've fallen behind on my correspondence, so there's a lot to cover. I'm eager to see who the letter is from but don't want Cynthia to know this. Her pen flies across the page. Her face is tight; every now and then, she presses her lips together, as if gritting back her unhappiness. I have upset her with my curtness; I don't know why her meekness is irritating me. I must try to make it up to her.

"Well, then, that will be all," I conclude, and Cynthia rises, still averting her gaze.

"Will you be needing me through the lunch hour?" she asks in a small voice. Cynthia typically brings a sandwich and eats it at her desk while reading. When I'm particularly snowed under, she offers to keep working through her break.

"No, that won't be necessary."

"I only thought—"

"Really, no need."

"Very well, Dr. Harrison. If there's nothing further."

"No. As I've already said, that will be all."

Seeing the distress in Cynthia's face, I think of apologizing, but she turns and is gone.

I take up the letter immediately and see that it is from the coroner's office in Phoenix, Arizona. I tear it open, pass my eyes across the official-looking letterhead, scan down to see the coroner's signature above the typescript of his name. The letter is only a few sentences; I sense what is coming, but still my heart skips a beat. The coroner regrets to inform me that a former patient of mine, Bertram Reiner, was found dead in a hotel room on the outskirts of Phoenix, an apparent suicide. A note bearing my name and address was found on the nightstand, with the request that I be notified. Nothing more.

I stare down at the page in disbelief; it doesn't feel real, something about the letter makes me think it must all be a mistake. And yet I feel a dizzying turbulence—as if my own being were somehow threatened, as if I myself were coming to strange new life; as if I were someplace else, as if I were here more than ever. A numbing fatigue shuts everything down; I feel I could almost sleep, but then a knock comes at the door. I am not expecting my first patient for more than an hour.

"What is it?" I call out.

Cynthia opens the door and stands there without entering, looking nervous.

"Yes, Cynthia?"

"I'm sorry, Dr. Harrison. I just wanted to remind you of your wife's upcoming birthday. Two weeks from today. But if you're going to send something to Maine—"

"Thank you, I'll keep that in mind. Now please, I have some important things to attend to."

Cynthia looks as if she's been slapped. I recall fuzzily that, in past years, she has taken a trip into town to choose some trinket or scarf for Ursula's birthday, though I never recall her prompting me about the date. Her eyes flit to the desk, taking in the hastily torn envelope, and the single sheet of letterhead before me.

"Of course. I'm sorry," she mutters, but then the veiled hurt on her face seems oddly to transform to uncharacteristic surliness. Impossible, surely; how could devoted, kind Cynthia be looking at me that way?

"I really must insist that you don't interrupt me again," I say, alarmed by what I am seeing—Cynthia plumping up disturbingly with what I can only interpret as spite. Something foreign quivers within: confusion and fear.

"Of course, Dr. Harrison," she says, seeming for a moment to challenge me directly with her gaze. But then she turns and leaves, clicking the door shut with care.

All day, the letter haunts me; it failed to describe the details of Bertram's death, though I picture it a suicide by hanging, which is not to say that I grasp the news as a reality. In fact, I find myself feeling convinced that the letter is some kind of hoax.

It is only following afternoon rounds that it occurs to me to call the coroner's office directly; it would surely be an easy matter to verify whether or not the letter is a fraud. I buzz through to Cynthia; her voice sounds guarded. I ask her to find the telephone number; in her response—"Yes, Dr. Harrison, right away"—I detect an unfamiliar, somehow ominous undertone.

Bertram's voice comes back to me: *An eye for an eye.*

I remember Dr. Greely once saying that behind every suicide is a homicide. I picture him now, the oily smile to go with his greased mustache, the way he puffed his pipe, peering complacently through the smoke. Am I the one upon whom Bertram has wreaked revenge? The fury that has been quietly seething within all day erupts; I leap to my feet, sweep the papers from my desk onto the floor. *"Damn him,"* I say aloud. *"Damn him and me both."* I stand there—aware of how ludicrous I am—and watch the last of the papers flutter theatrically down.

When I'm halfway across the lawn, aroused almost to feverishness with longing for my pipe, it hits me; the smoking has become a sickness. I feel a fresh bridling of anger at the thought that I must give it up—my one solace, my one true joy. I will prove I am in control—that I am not an addict. I hasten along, passing a number of staff members, slowing momentarily to utter a greeting—*yes, it's a mild evening; no, I don't think we'll have rain*—biting down on the growing perception that there's something awry about everything: the words people

are choosing, or the way they say them to me. Even the sky looks
anomalous; wispy clouds gather and disperse with unnatural speed, as
if something were being secretly communicated. Perhaps I should skip
my evening pipe after all; perhaps I should take a sleeping pill and go
straight to bed.

But I find myself in my study, handling the needles, manipulating
a pellet of opium. I'm down to the last; I must take a trip this weekend
into the city. But no—perhaps now is the time to put an end to it. Just
this small, crumbly cube—a particularly potent sample, scented with
jasmine. Perhaps this will be my swan song: one last evening of pleasure
to prove that I am, after all, still my own master.

I suck down the acid-sweetness: pleasure and release. Sinking onto
the cushions—perfect comfort. Silky visions, glorious, vibrant. Cyn-
thia—wearing a hundred veils, a smile on her face. Swirling, dancing,
shedding the sheer, delicately colored swatches that wrap around her,
clinging to her shape. I reach for her, delighting in the vision, blink into
the half-light; new evening fills the room. The colors change, Cynthia
disappears: now, a shimmering desert, tents and buttery sand, a blood-
orange sunset. Heat on my skin; I peel off my jacket. But my temples
start throbbing; has someone turned up the steam? Hissing: the pipes—
or a snake? I jump up in fright, see again the severed head of a green
snake Mac grips; his grin widens, blood spurts. He lifts the headless
body to his mouth—I call out, then turn and run.

I am outside—when did I pack up my pillow box? Why am I holding
it now? Running down the pathway, away from the hospital, into the
woods. Sweat drips from my brow. I am in the woods, running deeper in
among the shady trees, desperate to escape the heat. A terrible sound—
screeching, a grinding of brakes.

"Who's there?" I call out.

Something is shaking, rustling; I scan the trees—a huge sugar maple
is shuddering violently, as if possessed.

"Who's there?" I call out again. This time, a voice—coming from
directly beside my ears.

"How did he die?" demands the voice—deep, male, gently accented.

"I have no idea—the letter didn't say."

"You know very well; it was hanging. You see him, don't you, dan-
gling down from the light fixture. Have you ever seen a strangled man?"

"I tell you, it didn't say!" I call out. "And in any case, it's not true!"

I see Bertram's face before my eyes; if I were to lift my hand, I could touch it. Bertram's lips ballooning, ready to split and spray blue blood. I jump back.

"Why don't you touch it? Go ahead—I did!"

"Emanuel?" I ask in disbelief. "What do you want from me! Why are you here?"

"I don't want anything! That's the best joke of all!"

"Joke? What do you mean joke?"

Twigs snap behind me; I spin around. Is that Cuthbert? Galloping toward me? On a donkey—the same donkey head Bertram wore in the Thanksgiving pageant? Waving his compilation of jokes above his head, as though it were a flag. In his other hand, a spear.

No, I have the spear in my own hand; it is heavy, and I look with wonder at the handle. Smooth wood, heavy like an ax—no, it *is* an ax, I have found an ax in the woods. Why would the gardeners leave one about? But no, I am not in the woods; where am I? The gardener's shed perhaps? I put down the ax and see my keys splayed on the concrete floor. I reach to retrieve them; the touch of the cool metal reassures me. I didn't realize I had the key to this shed; it must be the medium-sized one here.

The object at my feet—my pillow box, carelessly thrown down. The polished wood is scraped from falling onto the concrete. The air is moldy, gritty with dirt. I raise the ax: *Crack*. The pillow box splits, fragments fly, the ax comes down again and again. The shattering of glass, metal on metal. Everything broken, smashed, and still I go at the pulp.

Who is banging like that?

I hear a voice; something different now, breaking sharply into my world. "What's going on in there? Open up, I say, open up!"

With an efficiency that surprises me, I kick the ruined box and its contents into the corner, drag several rakes and brooms to cover the mess, then open the door to see it is George, the night watchman. When he recognizes me, his face arranges itself into its usual respectful expression.

"I was just passing by," he says.

"Yes," I say, marveling at the blandness of his regard.

"Checking to see that everything is all right," he adds.

"Yes, quite all right." I step outside, suddenly unsteady, and trip into his arms.

"There we go, sir." George props me onto his arm. "Allow me to escort you home."

Stumbling along, the world dim, trees and bushes, the sweep of black lawn. We reach my house in a flash.

"I can see myself in," I say, having miraculously found a semblance of my professional voice.

"Are you certain, sir? I'd be happy to accompany you." George allows a conspiratorial smile to break through. "I've been on a bender or two in my time. Does one good, every now and then."

"Truly, I'll be fine." I hold on to the fence for support.

George tips his hat and continues on his way. I wonder what I'll do once I manage to climb the stairs, wonder if I'll find myself suddenly tucked up in bed in my flannel pajamas—if perhaps I'll roll over and discover that Ursula has returned, that nothing has changed after all.

The staff on Hall Two receive the news of Bertram's suicide with strained but resigned acceptance. We decide to inform the patients at Monday morning meeting, to be followed by small-group discussions and the usual extra precautions and support.

I'm suffering from want of the pipe; it's as much as I can do to get through each day. In the evening, I collapse into fitful sleep and awaken covered in sweat, my mind clanging from putrid dreams. I am to be paid back in nightmares, it appears—equal in number to all the ecstatic visions of these past months.

My head still aching, I ask Cynthia into my office. I apologize for my recent unkindnesses and tell her I've been under tremendous pressure. Her face fills with compassion. I want to do something—shake her hand, kiss her cheek, put an arm around her slender, unappreciated shoulders—but only apologize again.

She lingers. For a long moment, neither of us speaks.

"I wanted to mention," she says finally, her voice hesitant.

"Yes?"

"I'm planning to take a couple of vacation days. Next Thursday and Friday. I've cleared it with the administration; they'll send a girl up from typing to cover for me."

"That's fine, Cynthia. Thank you for letting me know."

Still she lingers. I wait.

"You see, I'm going away. It's too far to do in only a weekend." Something flutters in her eyes. "To Maine."

"I see," I say. It is my turn to hesitate. A minute or more, and then I find a few words.

"You will send her"—the words catch in my throat—"my very warmest regards."

Cynthia nods. "I miss her terribly," she says quietly, looking away.

"Yes," I say. "I miss her, too."

Every day I intend to call the coroner's office; I keep finding reasons to put it off.

Another week passes, and then I know; I will not, after all, make the call.

<div align="center">⤙⤚⤚⤜</div>

Outside the door of Matilda's mother's house, I hesitate. It is almost a month since Matilda went on leave. The morning sun is hot on the crown of my head, though it is a cool spring day and the air is crisp. I ring the doorbell.

Matilda looks even thinner than when she left the hospital; her hair is unwashed, her expression blank, gouged of the Matilda I know.

"Hello, Matilda," I say.

She takes a few steps back, and I enter the foyer. In the living room, the furniture is draped with white sheets. She sits on the couch, and I sit opposite her on a shrouded easy chair.

"I assume you have news."

I glance around the room, wondering if Matilda's mother is about.

"She's not here," Matilda says. "She's been in the hospital for two weeks."

"I'm sorry."

"Things have not gone well," she says, looking at me steadily.

"Between my mother and me. The truth is it's been better since she left. Coming here was probably a mistake, but then . . ." Her voice trails off.

"I'm afraid I do have news. You should brace yourself."

Matilda visibly stiffens.

"I received a letter from the coroner's office in Phoenix saying that Bertram was found in a hotel; it looks like suicide."

Matilda continues to look at me. Something shifts in her eyes; they take on the cast of stone.

"Phoenix," she repeats, her voice a fragile sound from another place. She is staring at me, hardly breathing, as if she's afraid to move.

"How did he die?" she asks finally.

"The letter didn't say."

"Who found him?" she asks.

"Really, there were no details. I'm sorry, Matilda. Really, I am."

I am startled by a loud clang—the grandfather clock in the corner of the living room, stridently sounding the hour.

"I've been expecting this," Matilda continues. She takes in a short, sharp breath and holds it; something flickers in her eyes.

"You meant a great deal to Bertram," I say uncertainly.

Matilda looks right through me, as if she were suddenly alone. She glances around the room, then reaches up and slides a strand of hair behind her ear.

"I'm selling the house," she says wistfully, as if she is addressing someone other than me. "The doctors have made it clear that my mother won't be coming back."

Her eyes roam, then come back to rest on my face; they burn with a dying light.

"I don't know what I'm going to do," she says.

"Perhaps it's time for you to come back to the hospital," I say.

"How could I ever work as a nurse again?" she says.

"You may feel differently, once you've regained your strength. Meanwhile, you could take a job at the hospital doing something else. There's an opening in the Medical Records Department for a typist. The position comes with a room in the staff residence; many of those rooms overlook the formal gardens. I recall you were fond of the formal gardens."

Matilda looks down at her hands. "Why are you so good to me?" she asks quietly.

I feel a lump in my throat.

"It would also be a good thing for me." My voice sounds desolate. "We've been through a great deal together, Matilda."

"Yes, I suppose we have."

She rises abruptly. "Forgive me, I haven't offered you anything to drink. I'll go and make some coffee—" She hurries from the room.

I cross to the window and move aside the sheer curtain to see an untended garden: overgrown lawn, flower beds choked with weeds.

Matilda has returned, she is standing in the doorway, holding a tray; there is something frantic in her face.

"What is it?" I stand.

She glances down at the tray. "Why, it's just the coffee things. But if you're hungry—"

"I only wanted to—," I continue, crossing to her and reaching for the tray.

"Oh," she says. Her eyes waver.

I set the tray down on the coffee table, the only piece of furniture in the room that is not draped with sheets.

"You knew about us, didn't you," she says quietly.

"Yes, I did."

"Why didn't you say something? You could have stopped it." Her words are an accusation—they sink into me like leaden darts—but her voice is lifeless.

"I'm sorry," I say, helpless. "I should have intervened." Only now does it hit me—the full force of my failure, the betrayal of my post.

A sob bursts from her; Matilda jumps up from the couch and hurries from the room. I look about at the shrouded furniture and wonder if I should go after her. Finally, I rise. I find her leaning against the sink, her head fallen, her thin frame heaving silently. I place my hand on her back; she turns and rests her head on my shoulder. Carefully, I pull her toward me, and she falls into my loose embrace.

<div align="center">◄◄··►►</div>

Part III

Chapter Nine

Summer 1948

Standing at the returns desk, I am surprised to see Matilda on the far side of the room, sitting at a large table, reading the newspaper. I don't think I've ever set foot in the library before; I've come only because I found an old book while cleaning out the hall closet, borrowed years ago by Ursula and forgotten in a handbag tossed into a box of keepsakes.

The librarian returns holding a catalog card. "Just as I remembered. The book was reported lost; your wife paid for a new one, so you're welcome to keep it."

She is looking at me intently. Ursula was a regular borrower, so I imagine the librarian knew her well. It's a small town; no doubt Ursula's departure has been a topic of local gossip.

"Thank you, but I'd just as soon give it back. I'm sure the library could use an extra copy."

Matilda has raised her head. Her back is toward me, so I can't see her face, but she seems to be listening for something; perhaps she has heard my voice.

The librarian thanks me and takes the book. I stand there, not wanting to leave, hoping Matilda will notice me. And then, she turns and

gives a little wave. In a moment she is up, carrying her things and walking toward me.

"I thought I heard your voice," she says. I still startle a little at the sight of Matilda out of uniform; she is wearing a sleeveless dress, her hair swept up off her face. She is no longer gaunt, but the brightness is washed from her, replaced by a sad and slightly unnerving calm. "I've never seen you at the library before."

"Do you come here often?" I ask, and we both immediately laugh at the cliché.

"Let me rephrase; are you a regular visitor to the library?"

"I come almost every Saturday afternoon. And you?"

"Just returning a book." I hesitate. "Something my wife borrowed years ago and misplaced."

Matilda seems unperturbed by my mention of Ursula. "Were you doing some late spring cleaning?"

"Yes, as a matter of fact. I usually run about a season behind when it comes to such things. I've been known to give Halloween candy at Christmas, and valentines at Easter."

"I hope you're not planning to do spring plantings this weekend. The poor seeds will scorch to death."

"I've never been much of a gardener."

"No, nor have I."

I wonder if it's the sleeveless summer dress; Matilda seems so different, and not just physically. Less serious, as if a weight had been lifted from her shoulders. Perhaps the break from nursing has done her good.

I want the banter to continue but find myself momentarily out of words. Matilda is looking at me, similarly at a loss. We both break into smiles.

"I have a solution," she says.

"To my tardiness with conventional matters?"

Again, she laughs. "No—to the heat!" She eyes my suit jacket dubiously. "Although perhaps you haven't noticed; it's ninety degrees today."

"It had come to my attention. I was planning to take care of things as soon as I got clear of this place."

"Well, come on, then. I'll show you the antidote."

The librarian, still holding the book I handed her, has been observing our exchange, a slightly disapproving look on her face.

Outside, the sun is burning; I remove my jacket and then feel self-conscious, being in my shirtsleeves in public. We walk along Main Street in silence.

Matilda comes to a halt before the drugstore. "My treat."

Inside, we sit at the counter and order milk shakes.

"Now," she says, businesslike. "This is the perfect opportunity to thank you."

"For what?"

"For suggesting that I return to the hospital. It's been a real tonic."

"You don't need to thank me."

"But I want to. I'm grateful that you were so, well, thoughtful." She reddens slightly and looks away.

"I was concerned about you. We all were."

"Yes, but people don't always extend themselves. I also wanted to tell you how much it meant to me, your coming to my mother's funeral. I felt very alone . . ."

"I know how painful it is, losing one's mother. One never really gets over that."

"It was different for me." Matilda has lost her air of lightness. "You see, my mother was angry at me from the moment I was born. She'd lost an infant—a son. I always thought that perhaps she'd used up her love on him. By the time I came along, she had no love left."

"What about your father?"

"He died early in the Great War, when I was a baby."

"That must have been devastating for your mother."

Matilda's face hardens. "I suppose it was."

She falls silent.

"What are you thinking?" I ask.

"I was remembering that day you suggested I take a leave from the hospital and go stay with my mother."

"Was that a mistake?"

"No." Her brow ruffles. "In some ways, it was the best thing I could have done."

"I remember your saying that the stay had not been easy."

"I discovered some unpleasant things about myself." She searches my face. "You'd be appalled if I told you."

I'm touched by Matilda's honesty. "I'm sure I wouldn't be anything of the kind."

"The day I got there, I collapsed. I couldn't do much of anything. My mother took care of me. She made soups, brought me breakfast in bed. It couldn't have been easy for her; she wasn't well, as you know."

"Perhaps she was happy to have the chance to put things right," I say, realizing that Matilda has not smoked a single cigarette; I wonder if she's given it up.

"But she didn't, you see." Her voice has sunk to a whisper.

"Didn't what?"

"Put things right. I wouldn't let her."

"What did you do that was so terrible?" I also lower my voice. There's something intimate about our quiet tones, and I feel suddenly child-like, as if we are whispering together late into the night, the grown-ups unaware.

She looks at me boldly. "I punished her."

"In what way?"

"I became the cold one. She was trying so hard to please me, but *I* felt angry, now. It was crazy; I mean, I'm a grown woman—a nurse who's taken care of hundreds, no thousands, of patients. I loved my work; I know I've made a contribution. But no matter how hard I worked to make a life for myself, I was left feeling I'd only ever be the child who was shunned by her mother."

A tear leaks from the corner of Matilda's eye. "I was cruel to her; I'd look at her sometimes and see that she was fearful. Fearful of *me*! I don't think I'll ever forgive myself for that."

"It sounds to me like perhaps you had no choice."

"What do you mean? Of course I had a choice. *I knew what I was doing!*"

"Just as your mother perhaps knew what she was doing, when you were a child."

Matilda's face fills with bewilderment.

"Turning the tables can be a form of protest," I say gently. "And protest is sometimes a legitimate assertion of one's rights—sometimes even the only way."

"Oh," she says simply. And then, again, "Oh."

Our milk shakes sit forgotten before us. Matilda looks so forlorn; I remember the way she fell into my arms, that day at her mother's house. I long to embrace her again.

"You're a generous man, Henry," she says, reaching impulsively for my hand.

I sit very still, not daring to move, acutely aware of the warmth of her hand, not wanting this moment to end.

<center>⊰⊹⊱</center>

Early Fall 1948

Stepping into the dining hall, I feel Matilda's presence; I turn to see her seated, a smile on her lips. Since that day I bumped into her at the town library, we have taken to sitting together at lunch in the alcove close to the kitchen, which affords a little privacy. She has filled out a little, and there's a new glow in her cheeks.

"That was quite a clangor, this morning," she says. "Hall Eight, wasn't it? Absolutely deafening, down in Medical Records. You might talk to Stevens about adjusting the bell; I thought my head was going to split open."

"We've had a problem with that for years," I say.

"Was it a serious incident?"

"Our boxer, again. We're going to have to bring in some professionals to match him."

"Did he do much harm?"

"He knocked an orderly out cold—then called out the countdown. He couldn't understand why everyone wasn't pleased that he'd flattened his opponent. He's on constant observation now, and not too happy about it."

Matilda smiles wistfully.

"I was wondering when that might happen," I say.

"When what might happen?"

"When you would start missing life on the ward."

"Who says I miss life on the ward? It's a lot more peaceful down in Medical Records, except when the clangor goes off."

"I imagine that *peaceful* is not exactly your speed."

"Well, it is a bit on the uneventful side."

I look into Matilda's eyes more deeply than I should, and my pulse quickens.

"Have you been to the woods lately?" I impulsively ask.

She looks a little confused. "Not since we took the patients ice skating . . ."

"Let's, then. Tomorrow. Instead of eating in the dining hall."

The next morning, I ask the hospital cook to pack a picnic. It's a perfect early fall day, bright and refreshingly cool after the heat of summer. In the formal gardens, the last of the coronation gold blaze beside a fresh crop of snowbank. We pass a sweet gum alive with birdsong; Matilda comes to a halt, and a private look passes between us—tentative and vaguely celebratory. I do not want to take her along any of the routes I walked this past winter, so I steer toward a tranquil path the gardeners keep clear, commonly used for constitutionals.

We pass several staff members along the first part of the walk and exchange greetings. Winding more deeply into the woods, we find ourselves alone. We come upon a bench set beneath a towering shagbark hickory; I set out our picnic and pour coffee from the flask. We sit, almost touching, in comfortable silence; a breeze rises, bringing a whiff of lavender. In the sliver of space between us, where our thighs and hips and arms are close, I feel a ripple of heat.

A few days later, at lunch, I sense a return of Matilda's old lightness.

"Am I imagining it, or has the cook improved?" she asks, cutting into her chicken cutlet.

I smile. "Imagining it. But I can let you in on a little secret."

"Oh?"

"There's someone here at the hospital who has made enormous strides on the culinary front."

"And who might that be?"

"The hospital director, if you can believe it. Though you must promise not to breathe a word to anyone."

Matilda gives a little laugh that is both sadder and sweeter than I remember.

"I promise," she says. "Though I may have to insist on the opportunity of judging that for myself."

I am taken aback by Matilda's forwardness. I have the sudden, not entirely unpleasant feeling that we are being watched—as if everyone around is aware of the electricity passing between us.

Matilda, unperturbed, is still smiling. "I've never met a chef who doesn't leap at the chance to show off."

She leans forward. "Henry, I'm angling for an invitation."

"Why of course, it would be my pleasure," I say.

"Shall we say Saturday evening?" Her smile has turned mischievous. "That will give you all day to prepare."

I do, in fact, spend much of the day at it, rising early to visit the butcher, the vegetable market, and the florist, where I buy a simple arrangement of carnations. I spend the afternoon cooking, moving about the sunny kitchen and listening to the radio. Outside, the tips of the trees are beginning to turn yellow and orange.

By the time the church bells chime seven, everything is ready. I mix myself a martini and wait. Finally, the doorbell.

"I came empty-handed," Matilda says with a smile. She's wearing a navy and white dress; her hair is swept up, her cheeks are touched with rouge. Leaning to take her jacket, I breathe in her light perfume.

In the living room, Matilda sits without looking about, like someone visiting a familiar place. "What is that?" she asks, cocking her head.

"The Baltimore Symphony, live broadcast."

"It's so discordant," she says. "I find it unsettling."

"I can change the station."

"No, leave it."

Only now does she cast an eye around the room. "Everything looks new," she remarks.

"Most of it is."

After I sent our dark furnishings to Ursula in Maine, I refurbished the place with modern pieces in blond wood. "Let me get you a drink."

It was Ursula who asked for a divorce; the letter that came was without rancor. Reading it, I felt a plunging guilt and a deep, sliding sadness, but also relief.

I pour us each a glass of Armagnac.

"Nurse Braithwaite is marrying in the summer," I say. "Moving to Canada. Though this is probably not news to you."

"Yes, I'd heard."

"Why don't you fill the position? Hall Four would be a welcome change."

A ripple of anxiety passes across Matilda's features. "Let's not talk about work."

"You're right," I say. "Let's not."

"What shall we talk about, then?"

I walk around the table to where she is sitting. "Perhaps we shouldn't talk at all."

I reach for her hand and she rises; we stand very close saying nothing, touching only where our hands meet.

"I don't suppose it's right for me to kiss you." I can hardly believe this is happening.

"I don't suppose it is." Matilda's eyes are shining and deep.

"Do you mind, then, if I do?" I murmur, drawing toward her.

She says nothing; her lips part slightly, the tip of her tongue touches her white tooth. Her breath is steady, slow, as if she's descending into sleep. I stand motionless; I want to stay in this moment, unmoving, forever. I reach over and stroke the side of her neck with one finger, and Matilda closes her eyes. My hand settles on her exposed arm. Finally, after an eternity, I lower my head and our lips meet.

My feverish fantasies of months ago burn to nothing; this is another country entirely.

<div align="center">◄◄-►►</div>

Late Fall 1948

We take the train into Grand Central Terminal. I arrange with a porter to have our luggage delivered to the hotel, and then we hail a taxi to City Hall. Matilda is wearing a simple green day suit, which brings out the color of her eyes.

Our witnesses—Vanessa O'Halahan, Matilda's old friend and colleague from Hall Two, and Percy Fenton, my chief of medicine—meet

us outside, on the wide steps. Vanessa is holding a posy of white roses; she hands them to Matilda.

"They're lovely, Vanessa. Thank you," Matilda says. She turns to me, her smile shy but radiant.

"Well, Dr. Harrison. Suppose we head on in and get married?"

After the ceremony, we walk to Little Italy for lunch. The women are chatty and, after two glasses of wine, chattier still; Fenton sits stiffly, puffing on his pipe between courses. Every now and then, I steal a look at Matilda, my new wife, and feel a flutter of astonished happiness. I can't shake the feeling that I've done something illicit; I laugh with the others, drink my share of the wine, and order champagne with dessert, hoping to drown out the disconcerting tinge of anxiety that flares now and then to fear: as if at any moment some authority—a policeman or orderly or judge—will materialize and snatch me away from all this.

We draw out the luncheon to accommodate a second bottle of champagne. Heady from the wine, I turn to see Matilda laughing at something Vanessa has said, her head tossed back slightly, the light falling through her hair. My eyes trace the line of her neck, and my hand aches to stroke her there, where the light kisses her throat.

When the heavy grandfather clock in the corner of the restaurant chimes four, Percy and Vanessa rise.

"There's the four-forty-five to catch," Vanessa says, slurring a little. "Honestly, Matilda, Dr. Harrison—er, Henry—I can't think of a nicer way to have spent my day off."

"I second that," says Percy, offering Vanessa a steadying hand. "We'll leave you two newlyweds to get on with the honeymoon."

Percy puts up a fight for the bill, which I rebuff; he gives a good-natured shrug, and one last arm-pumping handshake, then steers Vanessa from the restaurant, and Matilda and I find ourselves alone for the first time as husband and wife.

"Darling, I'm so happy," she says, adding, almost under her breath, "I can hardly believe it."

I feel choked with emotion; I squeeze Matilda's hand, give a lingering kiss to her cheek.

We decide to walk to the hotel; tomorrow we take the train to Poughkeepsie, where we will spend three days at the Mohonk Mountain House. We glide through the city, the tenements of Little Italy giving

way to broad warehouses, which preside over treeless streets. Soon we are passing the stately brownstones and apartment buildings of Greenwich Village, with its tidy little parks and cobblestone streets, the cafés spilling people and the restaurants coming to life for the evening round. The impossible has happened; the past is peeling away, shedding behind me as I walk. Something is also happening to Matilda, lifting from her like a scent: freedom, newness, another chance.

That night I cooked for Matilda at the house, when I led her to the sofa and kissed her for the first time, I felt startled by a new sense of clarity. Until that moment, I'd never been with any woman other than Ursula; I only discovered in that moment, kissing Matilda, how limited my connection had been with my wife, and how terribly lonely I've been these many years.

I pulled away from Matilda then and looked into her face for a long time. "Let's get married," I said. I wasn't thinking, but I didn't need to. I had never before been truly in love. It only seemed perfect and right that here I was, finally, holding my love: right that I propose, right that she would, within the next moment or two, agree to be my wife.

"Yes," she said, a slow smile dawning. "Let's."

And then we kissed again and again as we sat on the sofa, the room crackling with intensity.

Now, the light dampens as the elegance of the streets fades, and we find ourselves flanked by the stark façades of sweatshops, and tenements again, these with crumbling stoops and paint hanging in dried tongues from the brick. Laundry is strung from windows: underclothes, tatty night things, heavily darned sheets. Doorways give up rancid whiffs of old urine, and an underfed stray dog slinks by, looking to avoid a kick. Matilda doesn't seem to mind the tawdriness; she is sparkling with life. I have the odd thought that we are being anointed by the city, with its distinctive mix of opulence and want, and the garish extremes of its accomplishments and failures. We are a part of it all and at the same time floating above it, together, Matilda and I, at last.

In Hell's Kitchen, the buildings turn grim, though everything still holds an unexpected and intimate allure. A man lurches from a doorway, bringing us to a sudden halt.

"Cigarette?" he says hotly, squinting at me with feral eyes. He is filthy and gives off a terrible stench. His hand flies out; he grips my forearm with unnatural strength. With his free hand, he flicks his fingers together.

My stomach turns.

Matilda smiles with compassion and reaches into her purse.

"Here," she says, offering a coin, which the man snatches. He withdraws back into the doorway, and we continue on, but something has changed; the leaching light now seems ominous.

By the time we reach the hotel, the champagne giddiness from lunch is gone and my head aches. In the room, we order up wine and cheese, then sit by the window. I toy lightly with Matilda's fingers, aware of the thrill rising from her, wishing to go slowly, not wanting to rush. Finally, Matilda rises and goes into the bathroom. I allow the wine to take me over. When the bathroom door opens, Matilda emerges wearing a cream silk negligee, her hair billowing around her face.

"A bride should wear white at some point on her wedding day," she says, crossing the room. I am surprised by her slimness: such a slip of a thing. She comes up behind me, touches the back of my neck.

"You're rather formally dressed," she says quietly.

I ease off my jacket, and Matilda begins to unbutton my shirt.

"Henry," she says softly, concentrating on the buttons. "Did you know? We're married."

"Yes," I say, sinking away to some new place. "We are."

The sheets are cool and smell of jasmine. My hands weave through Matilda's hair, glide across her smooth cheek, down to the small of her back, across the curve of her waist. Soon we are moving slowly on the scented sheets, the length of her familiar to my hand, as if I'd been touching Matilda this way for years; the tiny beats of her rousing do not come as a surprise, the way she fires gently to just this touch at just this spot. *I know you,* I think, watching the flutter of her eyelids, the almost imperceptible ripple of the muscle in her forehead.

We get an early start. The world seems different: more alive and bristling with promise. As the train pulls out of Grand Central Terminal, I feel as if I'm traveling out of my old life to someplace entirely new.

At Poughkeepsie station, we're given a honeymooners' welcome; a beautiful old Buick tourer convertible awaits us, sent down by the Mohonk Mountain House. The air is static and cold; everything glitters in the late

morning light. We drive through the township with the roof down, a blanket over our laps; the world looks simple and sweet—well-tended houses, the streets swept clean, little shops with proud window displays.

Beyond the town, we climb a steady incline, the sky cloudless and ocean-deep all around us. The craggy countryside seems endless, with its woodland and rocky fields. Everything is fixed with a disconcerting vividness, making me want to shield my eyes from the effect. The *purr* of the engine is hypnotizing; I focus on the sound, my breath slowing. We are suspended; I feel as if we will sit here forever, warm beneath the throw, inching up the mountain and into the uncanny blue.

We round the final bend to behold the massive sprawl of the Mohonk Mountain House, balanced on an edifice of outcroppings and reflected perfectly in the glassy surface of the lake. Something about the exaggerated grandness is akin to Shadowbrook; I chide myself for the association—for not leaving my workplace where it belongs.

In our room, Matilda flings open the double windows.

"Oh, Henry," she says. "Isn't this just beautiful?"

Our room overlooks the lake; we lean together on the window sash and look out.

"It really is a lake in the sky, isn't it?" Such simple happiness in Matilda's voice; this is entirely new.

We head out for a hike on one of the less demanding trails. The woodland smells are potent: pine and sage and the reedy dampness of bark. We slip through the mottled light, above us the branches of ancient trees, some naked, others aflame with dying leaves. The thin mountain air leaves me light-headed; I feel giddy with freedom. No duties await, no meetings or difficult decisions and, perhaps most freeing of all, no murky emotional undertows relentlessly tugging, needing to be managed and fought. Matilda turns to me, and there is something startling in her face, something filtering up from the distant past—the way she looked, I imagine, as a child.

I grab for her hand. "Darling," I say, peering into her face, as if we have traveled back together in time—I am not Dr. Harrison, Matilda is not Nurse Willoughby; we are young, very young, I am a boy, electrified, looking into the fresh face of a girl. Matilda's eyes hover with wonder; I draw her to me, feel her resist, as if she knows I want to take her somewhere new, as if she is hesitant and afraid. When we kiss, she tastes

different; it is a first kiss, tentative, tender, fearful, thrilled. We draw apart, my arms loose about her, and Matilda looks at me for a long time, saying nothing. Something unsettling pulses in the air between us. The moment passes; a gossamer sadness settles over me.

After showering and changing, we make our way to the dining room, which is abuzz; almost every table is filled. A waiter brings us soup. The room is enormous and seats hundreds; a fireplace in the corner, larger than I've ever seen, is piled with flaming logs, which release an aroma of pine and sweet sap. The wooden ceiling angles up to a soaring height; the voices of the diners echo roundly, as if the vaulted space were filled with waterfalls and a hundred chattering species, cheerful in theory but pressing in on me and giving rise to a dull throbbing behind my eyes. As the meal progresses, the room becomes closer; the talking and laughter amplify, ricocheting off the high beams and bouncing from wall to wall, a cacophony of sound. I look down at the slab of beef on my plate and my stomach sours.

"I can't imagine how they do it," Matilda says, thinly slicing her meat and bringing a piece to her lips. "It's so tender—and cooking for such a huge crowd."

She chews slowly and glances around the room, quiet excitement in her face. "I can't remember the last time I had a real vacation," she says warmly. "It feels wonderful to be away." She smiles and sips from her wineglass.

"Yes, darling," I say stiffly, wondering if I thought to throw in some aspirin with my toiletries. "It is wonderful."

I choke down what I can of the meal and wave away the dessert—a sticky-looking concoction of pudding and fruit—though Matilda eagerly accepts it.

"I know they were frozen, but it's been years since I've had raspberries," she says. "They're absolutely delicious. And real whipped cream!"

I can't remember ever seeing Matilda so enjoy her food. I sip my coffee, which is too bitter and too strong. All around me, a crush of people—talking, laughing, spooning up globs of pudding. Happy people, *normal* people: none of the ticks and grimaces that have become commonplace to me. Beads of sweat trickle to my eyebrows; I wipe them away with my napkin, unpleasantly aware of the ghastly smile fixed to my face.

Matilda's brow furrows with concern. "Henry, you look peaked," she says. "Are you feeling all right?"

"The room's a bit close."

"Let's get some air," she says decidedly. "I'm ready to leave, in any case."

Outside, the cold brings a little relief, but my head continues to throb. We walk arm in arm around the lake, the glossy surface holding up a glittering portrait of the mountain house, bright with the lights reflected from every window.

"That was quite a crowd in there," she says pleasantly, squeezing my arm. "I was thinking. We should get away more. Living at Shadowbrook—well, it gives one a skewed view of the world, don't you think?"

"Perhaps so."

"We could take some weekend trips to New England. If you can believe it, I've never been to Vermont. And did you know I have a cousin in Massachusetts? Near Alford; I haven't seen her in ages, not since before the War."

I don't know exactly what Matilda is imagining: weekend strolls, perhaps, along quaint little main streets, dipping in and out of antiques stores, eating ice cream from crisp waffle cones. She can't know that this kind of thing was Ursula's passion.

"You know, Henry," she says, leaning over the barrier, looking out onto the lake. "Something occurred to me over dinner. It really is a new beginning—for us both. Sounds corny, I know, but the truth is, I never thought I'd have a chance . . . at this." She raises our clasped hands a few inches, then looks a little embarrassed.

"I know it's not your way to talk about such things, but I just want to say that back there, in the dining room, I felt . . . well, grateful."

Matilda is looking at me brightly.

"We *are* lucky," I whisper, squashing down a childish rise of sadness, as when something promised is unexpectedly taken away.

"Oh, darling," she says, drawing closer, leaning her head against my shoulder. "I'm just so terribly happy."

The three days pass in a whirl: long, satisfying hikes, voluptuous hours in bed. Only the dining room continues to be oppressive; all those vaca-

tioners intent on having a good time, though Matilda seems to enjoy the chatting and is indulgent with my awkwardness. As if to say, *We're a couple now, darling, I'll take care of this end of things.*

On the morning of our departure, Matilda smooths her things into her suitcase and snaps it shut. "There," she says. "Ready to go."

Outside, I draw the door shut; she looks at the room number, *237,* and gives a wistful smile. "Did you know? Seven is my lucky number. We're *two* of us, and the honeymoon was *three* days. Two three seven. Perfect."

On the train back, I watch the landscape roll by, the afternoon light waning, the trees moving awkwardly in a strong wind. The train clangs mournfully as we draw into White Plains station, and we stay seated as the other passengers disembark. I can feel Shadowbrook drawing us back, pocketing these past few days, turning them into something small and artificial—a scene in a snow globe, the two of us plastic figures before a miniature model of the Mohonk Mountain House, the lake in the sky a swatch of silver foil glittering in watery air.

"We're home," Matilda says softly.

I smooth her cheek with my palm; something wavers in her eyes— strange, cold flecks—sending a little dart of fear through me. She bites her lower lip and looks away, gazing out of the window at the station platform.

We are the last to leave the train—the only ones walking the length of the platform, the other passengers already down below, being greeted or climbing into taxis. It's chillier here than it was at the lake; the sun seems to have been sucked away. A leaden feeling tugs at me; glancing at Matilda, I see that heaviness is also claiming her. I have the sudden urge to grab her arm, swing her around, and run back down the platform, call out to the porter to return our bags to the carriage, and clamber up onto the train. I want to relive it all—to lean over the window looking onto the lake, to smile into Matilda's shining eyes and tell her how terribly happy I am.

But we continue down the platform, our footsteps a slow, hollow thudding. I try to catch Matilda's eye, but as she takes the steps down, she is scanning for a taxi.

"We may be in for a bit of a wait," she says, tipping her head sky-ward, passing her eyes over the thin spread of cumulus that is edging out the day's last light.

"It's a bit gloomy, isn't it," I say, meaning the sky.

She snaps her head back and gives me a veiled look. "I can't imagine what you mean," she says. "We're back home. How could it be gloomy?"

"I meant the cloud cover—after the brightness at the lake."

She hesitates; I have the sense that Matilda doesn't quite know which mood to reach for—whether to be disappointed and glum or to make an attempt at ebullience. I feel snagged by anguish, and then she laughs.

"Henry—so serious! You're not going to let the honeymoon slip away so quickly. Emily Post insists that it extend for a full year. You wouldn't disobey Emily Post!"

"Heaven forbid," I say. My voice sounds forced; Matilda pretends not to notice, but I feel her turning in on herself, a shudder of self-containment that stings.

Waiting for a taxi, I feel stiff and old. A black bubbling of self-loathing effaces everything; I'm afraid to look at Matilda, afraid to have her see me this way.

"Ah, at last," she breathes as a taxi glides toward us. Looking at me, her face weary but vivid, she arches an eyebrow and then decides, I think, on a charitable interpretation.

"You're tired, darling," she says, smiling. "Goodness, Henry. You must be the only man on earth who finds three days of relaxation a strain! Never mind, you'll be back in the thick of work before you know it—and happy as a clam!"

Now, a childish burst of joy; the blackness washes away, the pasted-on smile dissolves. Matilda squeezes my arm; we climb into the taxi.

She sidles up close and whispers in my ear. "Remember. One full year." The taxi pulls out of the station and eases onto the road.

‹‹‹·+·›�›

They know me, now, in the reading room of the New York Public Library; I greet the librarians by name.

There is one, Barry, who tends to hover around me: a stout young fellow with watery eyes. When I ask to see the library's collection of Army magazines, *The Stars and Stripes* and *Yank,* his face lights up. "They're my specialty. I never missed one, not through the entire War."

"Where were you stationed?" I inquire politely.

"You misunderstand me," he says, his face reddening. "I especially like *Yank.* Being written by soldiers and all. Don't get me wrong, *The Stars and Stripes* had excellent journalists. But hearing it in the voice of the boys who were actually doing the fighting—"

He hurries off to the archives, promising to return with some choice samples. I busy myself with a stack of journals; some time later, he is by my side, wheezing loudly, a pile of magazines in his arms. He seems to require a profuse amount of gratitude; I do the best I can, and finally, with some reluctance, it seems, he returns to the information desk, leaving me my solitude.

Some of the magazine covers are of pinup girls, many of them well-known Hollywood actresses; here's a pretty, familiar face, though I can't place the name—Norma Jean Dougherty, a brunette, slightly stiff, nervous, holding a weapon of some kind. Others show military photographs: troops in full dress and at attention on the deck of an aircraft carrier; soldiers in battle garb on the front, handsome, sober-faced, at the ready. Not the fighting men who came to Shadowbrook—who are coming to Shadowbrook still. There are also cartoon covers: Sad Sack up to his usual tricks, or other humorous send-ups of Army life.

But here's something different: an artist's rendering of a soldier in battle, nothing like the stagy photographs of good-looking men striking the warrior pose. Heavy charcoal lines sketch a picture of torment: the headline, in severe block letters, reads MENTAL BREAKDOWNS IN THE ARMY. Highlighted beneath this, in a box: "What causes psychoneurosis at the front lines? Usually it does not develop in men who have a clear idea of the necessity for the war and understand why they had to get into a GI uniform and do the fighting."

The article comes with a list of the factors that, according to the author, conspire to bring about a psychological casualty, including "home troubles, fear of fear, lack of incentive." And though the writer breezily insists that succumbing to war neurosis is not the soldier's fault—that the brutal conditions might make a sniveling mess of the best of us—the

message is nonetheless clear. The man who accepts that he must fight the good cause will hang on to his sanity through force of character and moral strength; the soldier must inoculate himself. The tone is subtly sanctimonious, its agenda unmistakable—and familiar. A range of anecdotal cases are presented, each pinpointing a critical moment in which the soldier shows a failure of nerve. "To understand its dynamics," the writer notes, "it should be realized that fear is the core of neurosis." I can't blame the writer; he is only expressing the standard view. The same belief has fueled our treatment of war neurosis at Shadowbrook from the start.

The charcoal sketch on the cover captures a deeper, more accurate truth, though I can't put my finger on what it is. I have an unpleasant inkling that the magazines hold an important clue, if only I am canny enough to find it.

A wave of discomfort comes over me; I look up to see that Barry is openly staring at me—not his usual illicit half glance. Perhaps this man has in the past been playacting: setting me up to believe him the slightly blubbering misfit who failed to make the grade, who failed therefore to have his moment as a soldier-hero, reducing him to sucking on the secondhand experiences to be had within the pages of *Yank*.

Now, his eye is shrewd.

The magazines spread out before me suddenly look uncannily altered, as if they had been chosen with the same calculating intent I saw just now, unmasked in Barry's face. Rita Hayworth smiles back at me, her eyes liquid and reassuring, a white glint of teeth showing between thick, glossy lips. And here, the very first issue after America's entry into the War, blaring the news of Pearl Harbor. Another shows a vast factory floor displaying a fleet of Mustang fighters. The clues swarm, buzzing like bees: a code, waiting to be cracked. Barry now seems to be sensing each nuance of my thoughts. He gives me a knowing, faintly lurid smile. My heart pounds in my ears.

I know I have been deceived; I just don't know about what.

My eye is drawn to a beautiful photograph of a building near Antwerp in flames, late in the Allies' *Operation Market Garden*. I had a patient who succumbed to hysterical deafness during that very operation; I remember him decrying the cheerful code name. Given to sudden fits of tears, he would stutter apologies, over and over, for being a

coward. His cure had come quickly, though, and without complication: three sodium amytal interviews in which the patient relived the traumatic shelling. As he was coming to, after the third, his hearing was restored, and not long after that, he returned to his battalion. That was the last I heard of him.

I see that Barry is still staring my way. I can feel the clues falling into a taunting pattern that slips from my grasp. Warily, I begin to sort the magazine issues, attempting to unveil the pattern. Pinup girls, photographs of war, artists' paintings and sketches: these categories are as good a start as any.

All of the issues are now in stacks, according to the type of cover. Only one issue remains; its cover is a composite—drawings, photographs, a map fragment, a small, statistical chart, and a tiny diagram showing the stages of the moon. My thoughts are electric: speedy, bright; I am on the verge of discovering something pivotal, the clue within the clues. I look up once more; Barry is still there. Infuriatingly, he catches my eye, nonchalant now, and winks. He is raising the flap of the information desk, moving around it, hastening across the room. For a fat man, he moves deftly. And then, in a trice, he is by my side, peering over my shoulder onto the table.

He taps his watch. "Five o'clock," he whispers. "I'd allow you to stay if I could, but you understand—regulations." He curls his lip up in the way I've come to loathe. It is wrenching to leave my work now, with this sense of teetering on the brink of a discovery.

"You must come back soon," Barry exhorts. "I can only keep the magazines out of the archives for a week—two, tops."

Outside, the streets are frenzied. The hurrying hordes are bewildering, and then I remember that next week is Thanksgiving; I feel a twinge of guilt, having been of no help to Matilda. I pictured our celebration as a tranquil affair—just the two of us, after all—but Matilda appears to be embarked on elaborate preparations. The window of an elegant sweetshop draws me in; I emerge some minutes later with a box of expensive chocolates wrapped in gold foil and tied with an ostentatious bow.

The train is crowded; I sit wedged between a woman surrounded by packages and a youngish man in a cheap tweed suit, who has the irritating habit of flicking his tongue repeatedly across his lips. The car is overheated; I'd been hoping to go over my notes or read an article, but

I find myself too hemmed in. By the end of the ride, I am clammy and on edge.

At the station, I am startled to see our car parked in the pickup area. The window rolls down; Matilda, wearing a purple scarf around her head, offers a cheerful wave.

"I thought I'd surprise you," she says as I slide into the passenger seat. "I was hoping you'd make the six o'clock train."

"Made it by the skin of my teeth, as a matter of fact," I say, attempting to match her casual tone.

"Oh my!" she declares, eyeing the gold foil box with the oversize bow.

"A little Thanksgiving something," I say awkwardly.

Matilda plants a kiss on my cheek. "You know I adore chocolates." She puts the car in gear. "Hope you're hungry. I've got pork chops and macaroni casserole."

"Starved."

I feel stiff from the cramped train ride, and slightly put out, having planned to skip my usual cab; I'd been counting on the brisk half-hour walk in the cold to restore me to a better frame of mind.

"How's the research going?" Matilda asks.

"I'm actually not turning up all that much," I say.

"Oh?"

"You sound surprised."

Matilda concentrates on the road as she takes a sharp turn.

"I know how busy you are at the hospital. I suppose I just assumed the work must be going great guns for you to give it so much time, what with travel in and out of the city."

That shading in her voice—like she's trying to cover over what she's really thinking.

"It's like digging in a mine," I say carefully. "You have to get through a lot of rock before you hit gold."

We pull up in front of the entrance to Shadowbrook and wait for the guard to unlock the wrought-iron gates.

"I was surprised when you told me you'd gone back to that article," Matilda says, pulling onto the driveway.

"You were?"

"I don't know what gave me the idea—but I thought you'd moved on from the topic."

Matilda has dropped the casual tone; I sense that we're edging onto dangerous territory.

"I'm not sure I'll ever move on from it. Why only last week we admitted a new case: the war neurosis has taken such hold of the man's psyche, it amounts to a psychosis."

"Mr. Yardley?"

I nod.

"He seems like a classic case of dementia praecox to me; he'd likely have snapped with or without his war experiences."

"Maybe. But that's exactly the kind of thing I want to illuminate. Our categories are still so fuzzy."

"I didn't know they kept medical journals there," she says, shooting me a curious glance.

"It's not medical journals I'm after, at this point."

"No?"

"I've been going through issues of Army magazines—*Stars and Stripes* mostly. They also have some issues of *Yank.* I'm looking for anecdotal accounts; all the cases I've studied have been either my own patients or else patients written up by other psychiatrists. It's become clear to me that the effect of the treating professional—the participant observer, if you will—is rather more tainting than we'd like to believe. What I need now is fresh kinds of data: self-reports, journalists' accounts. Assessments by Army personnel. Anything that will allow me to make contact with the soldier's direct experience."

"Have you found any such . . . personal accounts?"

"A snippet or two. But I'm beginning to get a sense of what it really felt like out there on the battlefield: the raw truth of things, before the soldier is whisked away to a hospital, or some other warping context."

"Before the soldier is turned into a patient," she says.

"Yes, I suppose that's what I mean."

Matilda nods. Her eyes flash, but she doesn't speak again until we pull into our driveway.

"Why don't you wash up and I'll get dinner on the table," she says. I try to catch her eye, hoping for a smile, for some sign that she's decided after all to be cheerful, but she busies herself with stowing the car keys in her purse, her mouth grim.

Later, lying in bed with Matilda, who is already sleeping, I feel

uneasy. There's an unevenness to her breathing; a furrow appears in her brow. Taut, alert, I am uncomfortable on my back, and my arm, which is beneath Matilda, feels achy. Slowly, I tug my arm out from beneath her; she rolls very slightly, and then suddenly lurches upright, her eyes open but unseeing.

"Matilda, what is it?"

She says nothing, stares through me. Her eyes flick rapidly from side to side; she seems to be inwardly seeing, and she raises her hand, as if reaching for something. I hold my breath, afraid to disturb her troubled dreaming, and she lets out a little gasp.

"No, I don't want you to," she says. "You mustn't!"

"I mustn't what?" I ask quietly. She doesn't hear me but grips my hand so fiercely, it hurts. She mumbles something I can't make sense of, rapid word fragments running together. She releases my hand and throws herself back down on the bed and then goes still. I listen as her breathing steadies. She rolls onto her side, her back toward me, and gingerly, I place my arm around her; she nestles up against me and sighs.

I slip into an agitated half sleep and awaken to an awareness that Matilda is not in the bed. I expect to find her downstairs in the kitchen, drinking a cup of hot tea. But the house is silent and dark; it sucks up my creaking footsteps, blots the sound of my breath. I take a tumbler of ice into the living room and pour myself a bourbon. Outside, the hospital grounds look peaceful: spreading out endlessly, tame and controlled— no different from an ordinary park, offering up the promise of lingering walks amid a pleasing abundance of flora. I picture Matilda hurrying along a deserted path, jacket pulled tight, battling some inner turbulence, oblivious to the cold, her eyes inward and dark. A vision of her in a green evening dress comes back to me: she is holding a champagne flute and giving an unself-conscious laugh, unaware that I am noticing her. A different Matilda: happy and free.

The new furniture still feels unfamiliar, as does the fresh color of the walls. But the place itself seems surprisingly unaltered—steeped in two decades of my life, of my coming and going from the hospital buildings, of my waking to Ursula and returning to her in the evening. I glance around, more slowly this time, squinting to detect some evidence of Matilda's presence. The clock on the mantelpiece strikes hollowly: four

o'clock and still Matilda has not returned. The chimes hang in the air for too long, stretching out eerily, as if trying to make a point.

Outside, I see Matilda at the bend in the path, lost in thought, just as I imagined her—jacket pulled tight, taking long, quick strides, her face tight and unhappy. I am on my feet, hurrying up the stairs, two at a time; I get back into bed and roll onto my side. I wait for her, expect any moment to hear her careful tread, and rustlings as she slowly undresses, tiptoeing to the bathroom for a sip of water, then tiptoeing back, sliding into the bed and nuzzling up beside me, shedding her distress, settling back down, sinking into grateful relief—thinking, *Dear, wonderful Henry: my rock, whatever his shortcomings, my future, my love.* Curling a cool hand around my waist—perhaps even feeling a twinge of remorse for having been short with me earlier. I wait, allowing myself to sink into this reassuring fantasy, almost convincing myself that it is happening, that Matilda is in fact beside me and having these exact thoughts. The clock's ticking swells, filling the room, filling my consciousness, dragging me down. Still Matilda does not come. I will myself to stay awake, to wait for her, to wait until I feel her reassuring arm around my waist, but lurch, vaguely panicked, into sleep.

I am up at eight o'clock; Matilda sleeps past eleven. I am plowing my way through a tedious journal when I look up to see Matilda in the doorway of my study, a tentative smile on her lips.

"I've been sleeping the sleep of the dead." She is freshly showered and groomed, wearing a beige dress I particularly like. "Why didn't you wake me?"

"It looked like you needed the sleep," I say, closing the journal and setting it down on my desk.

"I'm going to rustle up some lunch," she says.

"I'll join you."

In the kitchen, I wait for her to say something about last night, hoping for a mild and satisfying explanation, but she is quiet as she busies herself making sandwiches and squeezing juice. As the minutes tick by, I find myself bled of hope, as if something dire and irrevocable has happened, which I am helpless to undo.

"I heard back from Beatrice," Matilda says as she slices tomatoes, her voice airy, though her expression is veiled. "She insists we come up to Great Barrington for a visit. I didn't know she'd moved—not far from

where she used to live, and in a much larger house. She won't hear of us staying at an inn."

"We can go, if you'd like," I say.

She looks up. "You don't sound very enthusiastic."

"I'm not so good at family visits," I say.

"What do you mean?" Her voice has an accusatory edge.

"Small talk has never been my forte."

"Why do you think it will all be small talk? Beatrice is no slouch—she's a high school principal after all. Surely you don't look down on that—"

"It has nothing to do with looking down on anyone," I say. "I just don't do so well on weekend visits."

Matilda sets down the paring knife and folds her arms over her chest.

"What *do* you do well on?" Her voice is low and controlled. "Really, Henry. I want to know. Besides being with patients—besides being the Chief of Shadowbrook."

"I've made you angry," I say, a foggy confusion washing over me.

"I'm your wife, for Christ's sake," she says, her voice even lower. "Don't talk to me as if I'm a patient. I won't have it, do you hear?"

"I only mean that family visits aren't easy for me."

"You seem to have no trouble socializing with hospital people; you're the life of this place—I don't think I've ever seen anybody more in his element. Why is it only once we leave the grounds of Shadowbrook that you clam up?"

I hardly recognize Matilda this way. "What have I done to upset you? I don't understand, really . . ."

"That's the problem, isn't it," she says, wiping her hands on a dish towel. "You'll have to excuse me, Henry, I need to get some air."

I hear her in the hallway—opening the closet, sliding her jacket from the hanger; my senses are heightened, I'm tracking her actions as if I were a bat. Then, the click of the front door, and desolateness pours through the house. I feel foolish sitting here in the breakfast nook in the cool sunlight, my body arranged in the casual pose of a husband sitting and chatting while his wife prepares lunch. I make my way to my study, hoping to shed that unpleasant feeling of being watched: stop myself from glancing back over my shoulder as I exit the kitchen.

Chapter Ten

Matilda has transferred to Hall Eight—the "back ward"—and has returned to the night shift. I've been waiting up for her, watching by the kitchen window for her return. Finally, she rounds the corner, a startling vision in the crisp dawn light.

I greet her at the door. "How did it go?"

"Quite smoothly, I'm happy to say. It's funny, though—I feel terribly tired. It's not like me."

"I have some hot cocoa ready," I say.

"Perfect! Let me get out of this uniform; I must have filled out—it feels awfully tight."

Matilda returns, and we sit together on the couch.

"It's another world on Hall Eight, isn't it," she says. "I kept having the feeling I was in a preschool."

"I had a patient once who called it 'the nursery.' He used to say he liked being taken care of as if he were a very small child."

"I've been thinking . . ." She hesitates.

Matilda looks beautiful sitting on the couch, her legs tucked up beneath her, the filmy night robe hugging her form.

"Yes?" My thoughts become wordless. I caress her shoulder, but she places a gentle, halting hand on my forearm; it feels like a slap.

"I miss general nursing. Perhaps, after a few months on Hall Eight, I might look into a position at White Plains General."

"If that's what you'd like, you should go ahead."

"It might be good for us to work in different hospitals. Now that we're married . . ." Her smile seems a little forced. "It could be a fresh beginning."

"Are we in need of a fresh beginning?" I ask.

"I mean professionally. You're always talking about how difficult the work is here. Lately, I've been feeling like I need some fresh air—like I want to be around people who are n——"

"Yes?"

"Well, not suffering mentally the way our patients suffer. One forgets there's a whole world out there in which people don't go around feeling persecuted, or taking bites out of other people's shoulders, or thinking they're the Queen of England. Or insisting that you're a bookie, for that matter." Matilda has dropped the light tone; her voice is tinged with resentment.

"I had no idea you felt this way," I say.

"I don't think I quite realized it myself," she says slowly. "Tonight, I found myself longing to . . . I don't know, *not* think about heavy, contorted things all the time. To not have to go down such dark tunnels—"

She catches herself. "I'm being childish. You probably think I'm ridiculous."

"I don't think that at all."

In the bedroom, I feel the distance between us; it comes as a sharpness in my chest.

"You must be very tired," I say tentatively.

She nods. "It always takes a week or so, adjusting to the night shift."

I lie down beside her; I have an hour still before I have to get ready for work myself. Beside me, I feel Matilda's thoughts gathering like dark clouds.

"Darling?" I whisper.

"Yes, Henry?" she murmurs, already tipping into sleep.

I feel the warmth of her belly through the warm silk. I slide my hand up to her breast and cup it in my hand; her nipple remains soft beneath my fingers. My own sex swells.

"Nothing," I say. "Go to sleep."

She adjusts her shoulders and hips in little rippling motions, then sighs. I am tensely alert, distracted by a fierce arousal that is angry and animal, that doesn't belong here, with Matilda. I tense up against the brutality curdling within. And then—that snarling ache for opium I've been mercifully free from these past few months.

I can hear from Matilda's breathing that she is only half-asleep. I caress her back, lower the straps of her nightdress, and gently work the smooth skin of her shoulders. She murmurs appreciatively, and I smooth my hands down the length of her spine, massaging the little ridges in the small of her back, and then lightly brushing her panties, feeling tentatively around the lacy edges, finding the tender little creases that I know will make her moan. I feel her response, the heightening, as she waits, expectantly, and then rolls over, her eyes closed, her lips open, seeking my mouth, reaching an arm up, finding my head, and slowly pulling me toward her. Her lips glisten. I look down at her, longing to know what she is feeling, what she is thinking, where she is going behind her closed eyelids: who she is seeing, who she is reaching for. A sudden swirl of panic tells me she is not thinking of me: that her eyes are closed because she wants to block me out. I touch beneath the lace of her panties, my fingers soft in their furtive stroking, and she moans, but I am now out of the moment, seized in a dreadful way back in time—her moan a sound in the fugitive darkness, both of us beneath the hospital, in the underground tunnels, and I not her husband but a prurient listener, an interloper, a spy. I see again the brutal motion—the way Bertram slammed into her: nothing like our gentle, liquid rhythms. Could she have liked such roughness? Could she have in fact wanted it—urgent with a passion more intense than the sensuality she displays with me? I feel a surge of anger. My own blood rises hotly, rageful, now.

We are moving together; Matilda is arcing with slow pleasure, letting out quiet little grunts. Her eyelids are squeezed tight—squeezed against me, shutting me out. What is she seeing? *Who* is she seeing? The rising dawn hangs in the room; Matilda grits her teeth, her fingers clutch my shoulders, my back, with a kind of mounting desperation. Panic swells in my throat: a choking lump, I struggle to breathe. My own desire also swells—cruelly, apart, as if it were a beast I had flung from me that continues to rout with unseemly appetite.

It happens too fast—we climax together; when I cry out, I feel a terrible, grinding loneliness.

<p style="text-align:center">❮❘❙❘❯</p>

The clangor indicates Hall Two; after placing a quick call, I hurry over to find that everything is under control, the eruptive patient sedated and sleeping it off. On the ward, everyone is tending to their tasks with that familiar air of satisfaction and hard-won release.

Walking down the hallway to the nurses' station, I see through the glass that Vanessa and Janice are involved in a heated exchange. Janice's face is red—she looks cowed—and Vanessa appears to be uncharacteristically severe. They see me; body postures change, careful words are muttered, and they get busy with something that needs to be done.

I open the door and enter. "Good work, everyone," I say.

"I'd had my eye on Mr. Racuglia since breakfast," Vanessa says. "He was gearing up for a fight, I could feel it. In the end, though, he wasn't all that serious about it. The only damage was a broken chair leg—nothing a bit of glue won't fix."

Janice is biting her lip, her face still flushed.

Vanessa turns to her. "I'd like you to check on the sheets; I can't imagine what's keeping Laundry. It's not like them to be so late." Janice nods and leaves the nurses' station.

"What was all that about?" I ask.

"We were just talking about Mr. Racuglia's visit with his parents. It appears as if the outing set him off."

"Oh?"

"He didn't say anything about it last night—or this morning, at community meeting. He was stewing, apparently, and only mentioned it once he was already hurling furniture around."

"What happened?"

"He'd been waiting months for a pass, as you know. Poor dear; we always warn them about building up unrealistic expectations. Sometimes I think the first pass assumes magical proportions, don't you? As if they expect that the minute they get off the grounds, the mental dis-

turbance will vanish into thin air and they'll be able to reclaim a normal life." Vanessa shakes her head sympathetically.

"Where did his parents take him?"

"To a diner near where they live in New Rochelle. Everything was going fine, and then Mr. Racuglia started thinking that a man in the corner was looking at him oddly. He was particularly upset that the man was wearing a hat indoors. He kept apologizing to the waiter for the man's rudeness."

"Not so surprising," I say, "that his paranoia would be set off, his first time out. But Janice seemed upset about something."

"Racuglia was convinced he knew the man. When he lost control this morning, he kept asking, 'Why is he haunting me?' 'What did I ever do to him?' At first he wouldn't say who it was. Janice got it out of him. He's always trusted Janice."

Vanessa furrows her brow. "Anyway, the point is, Racuglia maintains that the man in the diner was wearing the hat as part of a disguise, deliberately trying to obscure himself. He insists it was Bertram Reiner—or his ghost. Back from the grave to follow him around and cause him grief."

"Oh dear," I say, affecting a compassionate smile, aware of a sudden, prickling fear.

Vanessa cocks her head and gives me an inscrutable look. "Well, here's the thing. After Racuglia was sedated and everything settled down, Janice was distressed—said she had to talk with me privately. I told her she could talk to me here in the nurses' station as well as anywhere. I don't believe in all that private nonsense; Janice *can* be rather childish. And a little unstable, in my view. In fact, I've been meaning to take that up with you—"

"What did she say?"

"She said it wasn't like Racuglia to make up something like that. That he hasn't shown much sign of paranoia in the past, and on the few occasions he did, it had to do with movie stars. Remember how he thought Clark Gable was lurking around the grounds?"

"It's not much of a leap," I say, "from believing a movie star is stalking you to thinking the ghost of a former patient has materialized in the diner on your first day out of the hospital."

"No, I suppose not," Vanessa says slowly. "But Janice said she knows

Racuglia. She thinks that, if he insists he saw Bertram Reiner, then he probably really did."

Vanessa is still eyeing me, a ruminative look on her face, as if she's trying to work something out.

"You seem to have some further thoughts about this," I say carefully.

"Janice said she has a sixth sense about whether or not a patient is suicidal, and that Bertram Reiner had never been. She went so far as to say she'd swear on a stack of Bibles that he didn't kill himself. That either he'd died some other way—or he hadn't died at all."

"Hmmm," I say thoughtfully. "I see what you mean—about her being a bit unstable. I've had the same thought myself."

"She said something else. Something I found puzzling."

"What was that?"

"That it would be just like Mr. Reiner: to set things up so that we'd all believe he was dead, and then just disappear. Go off and start a new life."

Still Vanessa is looking at me quizzically, chewing on her lip.

"And?"

"And what?"

"There seems to be something more," I say. "Something you're not saying."

Vanessa looks away.

"Well it's just plain silly. I'm not sure why she's got it into her head. I do like her—and whatever's going on for her, I think we should give her a chance."

"What else did she say?"

Vanessa swings her gaze back to meet mine—bold, now. "She said it was you, most of all, that Bertram would want to fool. That he knew how to play you like a fiddle."

"Like a fiddle," I repeat.

"Yes. Peculiar, isn't it, but that's what she said. When I asked her to elaborate, she got stammery and upset and began apologizing. Said she didn't mean it at all, that it had just slipped out—that she was tired and didn't know what she was saying. That's when you showed up."

Vanessa is waiting to see how I react. I can feel it, the way she is assessing me, casting that clinical net my way.

"I think I'll have a talk with her myself," I say. "Sounds to me like the signs of overwork. Perhaps she's due for a few days off."

"Yes, perhaps," Vanessa says. "You might give her a little time to collect herself. I know how much she admires you, Dr. Harrison. I think she'll be embarrassed to know I've repeated all this to you."

I can't shake the feeling that Vanessa is looking at me askance, as if she's making a damning calculation.

"I'll have her come to my office; it might be easier for her away from the ward."

I turn back to the chart before me, acutely aware of Vanessa's gaze, which spreads like a black force field of suspicion through the nurses' station. Finally, I hear the click of the door, and through the glass I see Vanessa walking down the hallway toward the dayroom.

Before returning to my office, I stop in to see Cynthia.

"I was going to bring these in," she says, referring to the usual stack of things for me to look at and sign. She, too, seems to be eyeing me abnormally.

"Is everything all right?" I ask, wondering if there's something about the way I look—something worrisome I know nothing about.

"You look a little flushed, is all," Cynthia says. "Are you feeling well?"

"Perfectly well, thank you," I say, irritated. "Could you please call down to Hall Two and ask them to send up Nurse Dempsey at the end of her shift? Be sure to tell them there's nothing wrong. I only have a few questions about the incident today on the hall."

Cynthia reaches for the telephone, continuing to regard me in that disconcerting way.

In my office, I open my pencil drawer and carefully go through its contents; I feel certain that this is where I stashed the telephone number of the coroner's office Cynthia gave me months ago. Next, I check through each of the other desk drawers; I find it in the bottom drawer behind some files. It would be eleven o'clock in Phoenix now. Just as I'm reaching for the receiver, Cynthia buzzes through to tell me the operator just let her know there'd be a call coming in within the hour from Scotland.

"Very well," I say. "Please reschedule my supervision."

It can only be Fairbairn. An hour later, almost to the stroke, Cynthia buzzes again to say she has Scotland on the line.

"Put it through."

The line is crackly; Fairbairn's voice wavers in and out. It takes several minutes of queries and repetitions before I piece together that he's inviting me to Edinburgh to give a talk, and that the invitation extends to Matilda. All expenses paid.

"Thank you for the card," I shout into the phone, aware of the costliness of the call. "I appreciated it."

"Couldn't be happier for you, old boy."

I inquire after Mary and hear a stony silence.

"Ronald?"

"She's well, very well indeed," he says, his voice falsely crisp. The line suddenly snaps to clarity, the fuzziness and perturbing sense of mistiming gone.

"That's much better," I say.

"I beg your pardon?"

"I can hear you just fine, now."

"Oh, yes. Well, we were hoping you'd have your paper on war neurosis wrapped up in time. We're rather hanging about waiting for it. Don't mean to exert undue pressure, but I have high expectations of what you'll come up with. I agree with you that we may have missed the boat. It's been bothering me for years, now."

"I can't promise anything, but I'll do my best."

Fairbairn gives his appealing, surprisingly uninhibited laugh. "You must be crazy yourself if you think I'm going to accept that. We'll settle for whatever draft you have. The Army Board is snapping at our heels—too many requests for long-term disability payments. They can't sustain it, and they're hoping we'll come up with a protocol to weed out applications. I thought we'd finished with all of that sort of thing in the last war, but it hasn't changed all that much. They want us to say the boys were unstable to begin with—that they'd have cracked with or without battle. Seems to me even with that logic, the onus would still be on the Army for accepting them in the first place."

"I'm not sure my article will be of direct relevance in that regard."

"Well, it can't hurt to have a fresh slant on things. How's everything otherwise?"

It's my turn to hesitate.

"Fine, yes, fine. Couldn't be better."

"Henry—I don't know if it's just the long-distance telephone, but I wonder—there's something about the sound of your voice—"

"Yes?"

"You don't sound quite like yourself."

I attempt a laugh. "I can assure you, I'm very much myself—yes, just did a quick check. All the right pieces, in all the right places."

"Well, good. We can discuss dates once you've had a chance to look at your schedule and talk it over with—" He hesitates. I imagine he was about to say Ursula. "With your wife."

We ring off with good cheer all around, and I find myself looking once again at the telephone number in Phoenix. A knock comes at the door—assertive and tentative at the same time. I shove the little square of yellow paper back into the drawer.

"Come in," I call out, and Janice enters, the expression on her face a curious mix of determination and self-doubt.

"You asked to see me, Dr. Harrison?"

"Yes, my dear, thank you for coming up." I usher her to the chair on the other side of my desk. "I wanted to talk with you about Mr. Racuglia. I understand you were the one he told about that incident in New Rochelle."

She nods.

"I know the gist of what happened, but I thought it might be helpful to hear directly from you."

"Yes, Dr. Harrison. Of course. Mr. Racuglia was out to lunch with his family. A man in the restaurant frightened him; he says he's certain it was Mr. Reiner."

"Did he say the man *looked like* Mr. Reiner? Or that he *was* Mr. Reiner?"

"He was very clear on the matter—that it was Mr. Reiner himself."

"Does Mr. Racuglia know that Mr. Reiner passed away?"

Something fierce comes into Janice's eyes. "Mr. Racuglia doesn't believe that Mr. Reiner passed away."

"Oh?"

"He thinks it's a mistake."

"A mistake."

"Yes, a mistake." Janice sits up straight in her chair, her expression coalescing to defiance.

"And what do *you* think?" I ask softly.

"I think that Mr. Racuglia is likely to be correct."

"And how do you understand that?"

"How do I understand that?" Her tone is one of disbelief. "Mr. Reiner is a man who gets people to believe what he wants them to believe."

"I'm not sure I know what you mean."

Janice's face reddens, and she looks away. "I can't forgive myself for spying on him," she says quietly. "It wasn't right."

"You weren't spying on him."

She raises her eyes again to meet mine. "That's *exactly* what I was doing." Her voice is no longer tremulous. "Patients are people, too. They're entitled to their privacy."

"Of course you're right," I say. "But in a psychiatric hospital, there are other considerations."

"That's very handy, isn't it—that line of thinking. It gives us free rein to do whatever we want."

"It's not about what we want," I insist. "It's about what's best for the patient."

"With all due respect, Dr. Harrison, I'm no longer a novice." Janice's steeliness comes as a surprise; I didn't know she had it in her.

"I think I know what you're feeling—I've been there myself. But I've found there are layers of understanding in our line of work; each year brings a deeper wisdom. Right now, you're seeing certain of the flaws in the setup; I'm not saying you don't have a point. What I'm saying is that there is no ideal society—and in the case of the society we have here, at the hospital, certain inequalities are unavoidable."

"I'm sorry, Dr. Harrison. I'm afraid none of that means very much to me anymore."

"What do you mean—anymore?"

"Everything changed for me when Bertram—I mean Mr. Reiner—left."

"Oh? How so?"

Her eyes cloud with pain; her voice drops. "We had a special relationship, Mr. Reiner and I. He trusted me with certain things."

"What kinds of things?"

"Forgive me, Dr. Harrison, but I don't feel at liberty to say."

"And why is that?"

"I swore to him that I wouldn't." Janice's nerve seems to evaporate; now she looks more like the Janice I know—uncertain, though trying very hard to maintain her poise.

"After he found me going through his things—"

"He found you—?"

"One time, I thought he'd gone to occupational therapy, but he decided at the last minute to stay back. I was looking in his closet, reaching up onto the top shelf. I didn't hear him come in; he had a way of creeping about on cat's feet. I turned around, and there he was, standing there, looking at me. He wasn't angry—he was more puzzled than anything."

"What did you tell him?" It's hard for me to speak; I feel like I've been punched in the stomach.

"The truth."

"What do you mean—the truth?"

The defiance is back in her face. "I told him that the hospital wanted more information about him than they could gain through the usual channels—that I'd been asked to look around a little."

"That the hospital wanted more information . . ."

Janice is looking at me now with controlled anger. "That *you* wanted more information. That *you* had asked me to look around."

"I must say I'm surprised—and perturbed—that you would flout my instructions."

"I decided, Dr. Harrison, that your instructions were best flouted," she says steadily.

"Not entirely professional behavior," I continue.

"I could say the same about your instructions. Besides, to be truthful, at that point, I no longer cared all that much about what anyone else at the hospital might think," she says dismissively. "It's only a job, after all."

There is recklessness in Janice's face. "He's a very special—a very *unusual*—man. It was more important to me that I do right by him."

"And what did that involve—doing right by him?"

She presses her lips together, like a child who has vowed not to speak.

"Whatever you might think about the way we conduct things at the

hospital," I say sternly, "you are a nurse here—and obliged to respond to questions regarding hospital security or a patient's well-being."

Janice jumps to her feet. "I'm sick of hearing that—everyone talking about what's best for the patient. Don't you see how hypocritical all of this is?"

"Sit down. Please," I say.

Janice complies, casting about the room, as if expecting someone to come to her rescue.

"What do you know about Mr. Reiner?" I ask.

"I know that a country can ask too much of a man," she says in a thin, strained voice. The color has drained from her face, and she looks as if she is going to cry. "Mr. Reiner was made to do things that no man should be asked to do. He was sensitive—not crazy, I tell you, only sensitive, like an artist or a poet. It was too much for him; he couldn't bear living with what he'd done." Tears spring to her eyes.

"What was it he did?" I ask gently.

"I can't say." She is almost whimpering. "I promised him I wouldn't."

"Janice, it's your duty—," I begin.

"I don't know anymore what my duty is," she says, the tears now flowing freely. "Please, Dr. Harrison. Don't make me break my promise to him. I don't know what I'll do if you make me do that. It's all I have left."

After Janice leaves, I retrieve the box of Bertram's records—countless transcribed sessions, copies of monthly and quarterly reports—from the back of my locked closet. I call Matilda and tell her I need to stay late in my office.

"Oh, but I have a chicken roasting," she says.

"I won't be very late—if you don't mind making me a plate and putting it in the heating drawer. If you feel like waiting on dessert, we can have that together."

I am surprised by the amount of material I amassed; I pull a wad of pages at random from the session notes and sit on the chaise longue to read them. It all leaps back, time snatched away; I am back there—back here in this room, which is alive with turbulence. Page after page. In the distance, I hear the faint sound of the town church bells, chiming ten.

How could the hours have slid by so quickly? I look up to see that the sky outside my window is black, hung with a lopsided sliver moon that casts a gauzy, inadequate light. I'll have to hurry home if I'm to have any time with Matilda before she goes on night shift. As I'm putting away the folder, something flutters to the floor: a square of heavy, brown paper. A piece cut from the wrapping of the package I received from Denmark a year ago, bearing the sender's address. I look again at the neat hand of Emanuel's wife. Without thinking, I reach for a sheet of hospital stationery and fill my pen from the inkwell.

Dear Mrs. Reiner,

I never acknowledged receipt of the package I received already a year ago. Forgive my impoliteness. I was shaken by the material, which I had translated (I do not read German), and did not know at the time exactly how to respond. A series of difficult events followed, culminating in the sad news that Bertram died by his own hand. I am only now finally able to turn to the matter and, again, must apologize for my tardy response.

I am also writing to you in the hope that you might be able to shed some light regarding Mr. Reiner's condition. Despite our unfortunate wealth of experience on the traumatic effects on soldiers of War, in the end, we understand very little about it. Time and again there are V-days, but the war is never truly over—and we know that the next one will always come. I feel it is incumbent on me to work toward a meaningful contribution regarding the lingering effects of war neurosis. It is my hope that delving as deeply as I can into the case of Bertram Reiner might further these aims.

Bertram talked constantly of his brother; he believed Emanuel wanted to harm him. After reading the pages you sent, I was left feeling that this may well have been the case—and that perhaps Emanuel had in mind a joint suicide pact.

The chance to speak or correspond with Emanuel would be of great help to me; if you know his whereabouts, or have any information about your husband's past, or his involvement with his brother, I would be very grateful.

I await your reply, and thank you in advance for your help.

Respectfully yours,
Dr. H. Harrison

It is Saturday night; I look forward to the weekends, when Matilda is off duty. But tonight, over dinner, she seems tense. After the meal, we settle in the living room. I pour her a glass of wine and then move around the couch and begin massaging the back of her neck. She stiffens beneath my touch.

"Have you given Ronald's invitation any thought?" I ask.

"Yes, as a matter of fact I have."

"And?"

"Can you afford so much time away from the hospital?"

"There's no problem with coverage. I think a real break will do us good. And I'm rather keen to show you where I grew up."

"You are?"

"Aren't you just a little bit curious?"

"Of course I am, Henry!" Matilda's voice fills with warmth.

"Perhaps you were right," I say. "About us needing a fresh start."

"I wasn't complaining, Henry. Truly I wasn't."

Matilda swivels around and looks up at me. "I want everything to be perfect," she whispers. "Maybe that's my failing. Maybe the harder I try, the more it slips out of reach."

"But I'm saying that I think you were right. Coming into marriage at our stage of life—well, it's true what you said. We've both been through a lot; we bring our history into everything."

Matilda's eyes waver. "Henry, I must be truthful about something." She bites her lip.

"Anything, darling. What is it?"

"Your research—at the New York Public Library. I know this sounds a little neurotic, but I can't stop thinking about it. I do wish you'd give it up. I know it's a lot to ask."

"I didn't know you felt so strongly about it."

"But I do, Henry. I remember you saying once that sometimes one can't leave the past behind. You're the brilliant psychiatrist, Henry, not me, but maybe you're wrong about that. Maybe one *can* walk away from everything: start over, almost as if none of it ever happened. I want that, Henry—desperately. Can you understand that?"

"Of course I can," I say. Looking at Matilda, I feel bewildered; she seems suddenly unknown to me.

In bed, Matilda cuddles up to me like a child and falls almost imme-

diately into an unsettled sleep. I lie awake, holding her in my arms, listening to the troubled rhythms of her breath. In the muffled moonlight I watch the delicate dream emotions tumble across her features.

I awaken with a start to an unpleasant coldness, and the feeling once again that I am alone. The bedroom window is open; the cold night air rushes in. I reach for the covers, which have been flung aside, and only then fully realize that Matilda is not in the bed. It is after three in the morning.

On the stairs in my slippered feet, I know from the feel of the quietness that Matilda is not in the house. I check anyway—first the kitchen, then the living room, dining room, sitting room, and finally my study. The furnishings and other appointments seem charged with the eerie, almost animate glow of night.

Back in the kitchen, I drink a glass of milk and look out at the garden, no longer anything like the garden Ursula created. It is unfettered now, and a more uniform green, the tidy little flower beds uprooted and replaced by bushes and ferns. The garden, too, seems released by the moonlight into a kind of sentience. There is something gaping about it all that both frightens and thrills; I have no place in this, but feel the pulsing of the moonlight, feel its otherworldly tug.

It is after five o'clock when I return to bed; I count the distant chimes of the church bells. Faint, early daylight cuts into the shadows, gently licking away the mystery; my head touches the pillow and exhaustion whisks me away.

Over breakfast, Matilda is strained. She pours my coffee, pretending not to notice the way the coffeepot trembles slightly, pretending not to know that I've noticed it, too. We talk lightly of the coming day. Reading the newspaper, I see from the corner of my eye that she is anxious and that behind the anxiety is pain.

In the course of the day, I am alarmed to realize that the plate-glass feeling has returned; everything seems once again at a remove, as if I am enclosed in a separate sphere, unable to make contact with the people and things around me. I feel like a textbook case out of one of Fairbairn's famous articles; I know that the only thing to do is to push through it, to carry on with my tasks. I am aware, too, of the terrible return of that animal appetite for the pipe; it's a form of delusion, the conviction that one can give it up forever.

Over dinner, we are silent. Watching Matilda pick at her food, I find myself inflamed with panicky lust; it is all I can do to stop myself from staring at her bosom. I feign normalcy and calm.

"I'm not much in the mood for dessert," I say, rising to clear the plates.

"I made a pie." Matilda's voice is uncertain.

"We can heat it up tomorrow night."

We stand together by the sink, Matilda with her hands in the suds, me with the dish towel, drying. I feel trapped by the monotonous actions, and gripped by an urge to fling aside the towel, pull Matilda away from the soapy sink, and peel off her clothes: to feel her warmth, her softness. She darts me a glance—preoccupied, wary; her regard doesn't snuff my passion as such an expression normally would. Instead, I feel angered—and further fired. A rise of blood blurs my vision; I have the peculiar sensation of seeing red, as if everything were suddenly dipped in the colors of a lurid sunset. Patiently, I wipe the droplets of water from the plates; I use a lint-free cloth for the wineglasses, then replace them carefully in the breakfront.

"Come," I say, when the last dish is put away.

Matilda looks uncertain, but she takes my lead and we climb the stairs, and finally, in the bedroom, my heart pounding, I unbutton Matilda's cardigan and then the cotton blouse. Her brow is slightly tensed; her eyes glisten softly with misery.

On Hall Eight, a routine change-of-shift meeting, nothing more, and yet there is something vaguely ominous in the air; it almost has an odor. I glance around the room. Attempting nonchalance, I allow my gaze to rest upon each person in turn: the attending psychiatrist, the four residents sitting side by side, then the nurses and trainee nurses and, lastly, Matilda. She has a queer look—alert, scanning, touched surreptitiously with alarm.

I squeeze my attention back to what I am saying.

"We can take Mr. Jrogen off CO and put him back on hourly checks. The bridge tournament can go ahead as planned, now that Mr. Binghamton has calmed down, though I suggest an orderly be assigned to sit with him just in case. We'll reassess Mr. Marino's four-point restraints at change of shift."

Am I imagining it? The way everyone seems to be looking at me, as if aware that I've been speaking without attending to my words? Yet I seem to be perfectly lucid. From Matilda, I sense edginess, discomfort, a desire to get away.

The meeting over, everyone hurries off: clicking leather heels, the slapping of the nurses' rubber soles; important destinations, tasks that cannot wait.

Outside, the sun is bright, the air cold, the grounds sharp-edged and troubling. The gardeners have done something to the hedges; they seem suddenly severe, stripped of their typically reassuring ordinariness. At the bottom of the path loom the rhododendron bushes, ugly without their insistent blooms, filling me with a vague foreboding. Something catches my eye—two nurses walking briskly below, deep in conversation: Matilda and Vanessa, arm in arm. Moving swiftly, I narrow the gap between us.

Where the pathway forks, they halt. Vanessa's back is toward me, but Matilda's face is in my line of vision, and I can see that she is distressed. When Vanessa places her arm on her friend's shoulder, Matilda reaches up and wipes her eyes.

I feel seized by a weightless iciness that threatens to wipe me out, and then, something comes clear. Matilda is surely talking about Bertram, unbalanced by Racuglia's report of a sighting. I press into the wall of beheaded rhododendron; what sort of a fool am I, anyway? Racuglia saw Bertram in New Rochelle; Janice, too, is convinced he is still alive: waiting to come back, perhaps? To come back for Matilda?

I turn and hurry back up the pathway, stumbling in my haste, toss a glance over my shoulder to see the two women peering upward in my direction, Matilda squinting into the cold sunlight, shading her eyes with her hand. Bitter tears press at my eyes, blinding me to everything, including caution, and I stumble again, almost running now, my knees aching, my chest clutching, my breath hot in my throat.

I awaken early, shave and dress so that, when Matilda returns from her shift, she and I might spend a couple of hours together before the start of my own workday. She is later than usual, even allowing for the kinds of

last-minute tasks that often pop up. Finally, I hear the front door open-
ing; Matilda appears in the doorway of my study.

"Hello, Henry." She looks drawn.

"Hello there," I say. "Good shift?"

"A bit of commotion, actually—nothing too serious. We had to put
Colby in four-points again."

"Anyone hurt?"

"He was going after himself. But we got to him before he could do
any real harm."

She yawns. "I'm more tired than I realized. It's such a lovely, clear
night—Vanessa and I took a walk. Why don't you come up and talk to
me while I get undressed?"

In the bedroom, Matilda opens the first few buttons of her uniform
and peels it up over her head. She steps out of her slip, unhooks her
brassiere. The curtains are open, and the room is bathed in the silver-soft
dawn. Matilda crosses the room, her breasts swinging voluptuously and
brushing against the insides of her upper arms. I notice something in the
half-light—something on the white skin between her breasts—and then
she disappears into the bathroom and I hear the sound of flowing water
and gargling. Matilda reappears, her freshly brushed hair moving against
her shoulders.

"Weatherman's predicting a sunny weekend," she says sleepily, lifting
the cover and settling beside me. "I think we should go to the Sunken
Forest. You've been threatening to take me for months."

I reach up to cup her breast, brush with my thumb at the skin
between her breasts. I feel Matilda stiffen, and a sudden weight in the
air between us.

"What's this?" I ask gently. It feels like a sticking plaster.

Matilda gives a false little laugh. "That? Oh, nothing."

"Did you hurt yourself?"

"It's so silly—hardly worth mentioning."

"Tell me, I want to know."

"I tripped on the ward. I was carrying sheets, and heaven knows why,
there was nothing to trip on, but I just slipped and fell."

"You cut yourself? Here?"

Again, I touch the place between her breasts.

"It was the edge of a side table. Embarrassing, really, that it would

catch me just there. No one saw, luckily. I dressed it in the medical sup-
ply room."

What she's saying makes no sense; on Hall Eight, the furniture is
specially sanded to have rounded edges.

Matilda yawns again, a little ostentatiously this time, settles in her
catlike way, and then pretends to drift into sleep, but her alertness is
palpable. Curled together, tense beneath our simulated languor, it feels
as if we're in a standoff.

Her breathing quickens before my own—deep breaths that sound
fearful. My hands move up, velvety slow. I take one breast in each hand,
pressing my thumbs down on her nipples; they stiffen immediately. I run
one hand down to her groin and plunge it into her panties, where I find
she is open and hot, and without any gentling, I push two fingers deep
inside. She draws in a sharp breath; she is hiding something, I can feel
it, something I want desperately, fiercely, to know. I turn her to face me;
she looks at me dimly, her lips slightly open, and then closes her eyes,
seeking my mouth, kissing me hungrily. I slide her panties down, grope
her hips into place, enter her frantically, hearing, in the tense silence, the
blunt sound of my own gasp.

"Matilda," I say, staring desperately at her closed eyes. Her face
contorts with pleasure-pain; she is holding herself to herself, giving me
nothing. Her hips heave against me, moving in her own pleasure. A sob
rises within me, I am caught up in it, kneading her buttock, her hip,
thrusting deeper and deeper still until I fear something inside her will
tear. I struggle desperately to get closer, even closer; a sob bursts from
me—and now, finally, Matilda opens her eyes, and at the sight of her
slowly rising lids, I feel the beginnings of an erupting joy.

But no: her eyes glint—not lovingly, not drawing me in, but coldly,
pushing me away as she explodes and I explode with her. We draw apart,
panting, and she rolls over, curling up, her arms and knees drawn into
her body. I lie there starkly, aware of a terrible, bone-dry feeling: spent,
discarded, alone.

By the time I get home, Matilda has already left; it is a relief to be alone
in the house. After a few drinks, I feel calmer than I've felt in some time,

and lose myself in my book. The clock strikes, startling me from an almost trancelike concentration. Again that upsurge of panic that has been dogging me of late, along with a crushing in my chest; the image of Matilda walking with Vanessa returns—that terrible distress on her face. *It is me,* I think. *I am ruining things.* Another drink doesn't help, it only puts a tight squeeze on my heart, which drums painfully against my ribs.

A rapping at the door—at two in the morning? Like the frantic knocking a lifetime ago—Bertram crashing into my office in a state of dread: *I've seen my brother!* Too much drink; I'm hearing things. But no: that rapping again. Is Bertram, after all, alive? Has he come back to confront me? Cracking open the door, peering into the hallway: a thick, colorless beam of moonlight, slanting down through the transom above the front door. I step through the beam, which breaks up and spills around me.

Outside, it is cloudy, the sky an uneven patchwork of shadows, glazed with uncertain light. My own body flings forward a fuzzy shadow, grotesquely huge, somehow edged with fur. It is then that I see it, up against the tree: not a person but the shadow of a person—detached from the human form and set upright, hovering apart, ghostlike.

The shadow moves out from under the tree.

"What do you want?" My voice is breathy, fearful, not my own.

"I have come to take back *my life,*" the shadow says. I know in that moment that the apparition is Bertram, and that he has returned to exact his due.

"You never lost your life!" My voice is tremulousness. "The coroner's letter was a ruse—to put Emanuel off your scent. To protect Matilda."

"You're forgetting something," the ghost says.

"I am?"

"Yes. You're forgetting the *real* reason you went along with it all."

"I didn't go along with anything!" Short of breath, I have trouble speaking. "Whatever you did, you did entirely on your own."

A step backward, two, toward the door.

"Matilda?" I call, intending to shout; it comes out as a hoarse whisper. In any case, Matilda is not home.

"Yes," the apparition says. "Matilda." He lets out a ghastly laugh.

"That's why you went along with it. You knew all along that the letter from Phoenix was a fabrication. But you had every reason to compromise your integrity—to risk your entire career."

"I did no such thing, I tell you." My voice is a strangled whisper, barely audible even to me. "What you're saying is madness!"

"But it isn't madness. You know everything, don't you, Doctor. As far as the hospital was concerned, I was just a voluntary patient who'd had a change of heart. And Matilda—you knew she'd fall apart when she heard the news. After I left, you went in for the kill. But truly, bringing her back to the hospital—wasn't that going a little too far?"

"You're forgetting. You were as afraid as I was that you might hurt Matilda—"

"There was a secret. You know this as well as I do."

"I do?" I ask helplessly.

Something in me clutches. My hand flies to my chest, where I feel a sudden sickening, ballooning pain.

"You planned it," the ghost says. "All of it. So that you would get what you wanted. That's what it's all about, isn't it. The truth about where you sit—the whole point of your comfortable doctor's chair."

No menace in his voice; unexpectedly, it is shaded with compassion.

"What on earth are you talking about?" I hiss. "What you are saying is perfectly insane!"

The apparition laughs. "Well, I can't say there hasn't been speculation on that point."

A furious rage curdles within; I want to lunge at this hateful ghost, but my chest is bursting. I clutch, fall, can't pry my hands from my chest—

"You'd lost Delilah all those years ago—without ever having her. You were in love with Matilda before I left. So you stepped into my shoes and took her away."

"What are you saying?" I try to scream; no words come out. Stone, up against my face, my lips pressing into the cold step. "Not true—not true—"

Hands on my shoulders; he will strangle me—

I deserve this, I think—my chest, I *must* open it—

<·‹·›·>

I awaken in a clean, white hospital room to the sight of Matilda, peering at me with concern.

"Oh, darling!" She strokes the side of my face with her cool hand. "I'm so happy to see you!"

"Heart attack?" It costs me some effort to speak.

"I'd say so. Fortunately, not dire."

"It felt rather bad."

"I should imagine it would. You managed a good scream, thank heavens—and what great fortune the night guard was within earshot. He found you on the back porch. The doctor's orders are rest, rest, and more rest."

"Very funny."

"I'm not joking," she says. "I've already informed the hospital board that you're taking a medical leave."

"You can't be serious."

"I've never been more serious in my life."

"Far be it from me to argue with a nurse."

"I'm sorry about the fight, Henry. Really I am."

"What fight?"

"I don't know . . . all of our fights. I want so much to be a good wife to you." Her voice wavers. "I don't know why so many things seem to get in the way."

"What do you mean?"

"I don't know, exactly."

My chest hurts, I'm finding it difficult to speak; I squeeze Matilda's hand.

"Let's start over," she whispers. "I know it could be so perfect, if only . . ."

"If only what?" I manage to croak.

"Oh, Henry, I've asked you this once before—maybe it's not rational—but promise me you'll give up the research. That you'll stop going into the city and poking around in old magazines. Especially now; it will only tax you. The doctor said you're not to have any undue stress."

I squeeze her hand again and nod.

"Then you'll give it up?" Such a sweet, wavering smile; she wipes away a tear.

"If it will make you happy." My voice is breathy and thin.

"It *will* make me happy," she says, leaning over and kissing me on the forehead. "You'll see, Henry. I'm going to try harder. I'm going to become the model wife."

Chapter Eleven

Winter 1948

"I'm under orders," Cynthia says, smiling warmly. Something is different about her—less makeup, perhaps, and a softer hairdo.

She indicates the mail, sorted into four separate trays. I eye them almost greedily; the past three weeks of enforced recuperation have been excruciating.

"From whom?"

"Your cardiologist. He said he'd hold me personally responsible if he finds out that you put in more time here than you're allowed."

"I can't say I recall what my allotted time is."

"Three hours per day. To be reassessed in two weeks."

"I don't suppose I can expect that you'll cheat."

"I don't suppose you can."

"Tell me, Cynthia. How have you been?"

"Besides sick with worry over you?" I've never seen Cynthia smile coyly before.

"I do believe you have a beau."

Her face colors, but her smile stays bright. "I'm not in the habit of discussing my personal life at work," she says.

"Well, I won't say another word about it. Except that he's one very lucky man."

Only now do I see that Cynthia is holding a thick letter.

"The mail boy just brought this up—something from Denmark."

After she leaves, I examine the letter. In the past few weeks, resting at home, pottering about in my study, I thought fleetingly from time to time about the letter I wrote to Emanuel's wife more than a month ago. I found myself hoping I would not, after all, receive a reply—imagining that perhaps she'd moved, that my letter had been discarded, unread, by some disinterested stranger; hoping that, as Matilda seems so clearly to want, we can at last put the past behind us.

The handwriting on the envelope is unfamiliar: not the spidery, cramped script of Emanuel's wife, or the uneven, troubling hand of Emanuel's original account. Instead, fluid, sweeping letters, both precise and relaxed: the writing of a person who is determined and unfettered. The return address is the one to which I wrote, but the name of the sender is Knut Dikstar.

I slit open the envelope.

To Dr. H. Harrison,

I regret to inform you that I am not who you think I am. My name is Knut Dikstar; I am American, of Danish origin. I served with Bertram Reiner on two tours of duty, which were separated by more than a year. After the War, I returned to Denmark and have lived at the above address since.

I know something of the package you mention, though Bertram asked me to discuss it with no one. Since he is no longer among us, and your cause seems worthy, I've decided to tell you what I know.

Bertram was a courageous soldier; you no doubt know he was decorated three times. But his experiences cost him. After the first tour, we found ourselves together in an Army hospital in the south of England; we arranged to be placed beside each other. Our friendship deepened during those long days; we shared a great many things.

We were both getting morphine, but Bertram often declined his dose. I asked him why, and he said he wanted to keep his wits about him. One evening, an Army general came to Bertram's bedside and stayed, talking quietly, about ten minutes. He came again the next night, an hour after

evening meds. Time enough for the other patients to be drugged up. The following night, I declined my own dose; I don't think Bertram noticed. The general showed up again. This time, I managed to overhear some of what they were saying—enough to know Bertram was to do some spying. It was only later—when I heard him speaking German—that I realized Bertram must have been in a unique position to serve his country.

In the last six months of fighting, we took a lot of prisoners, but we didn't have the capacity to deal with them all. Sometimes, we had to release them—after taking their weapons and shoes. Once, in a small town not far from Cherbourg, a young German soldier came out of a burned-out building and threw down his gun. Bertram trained his gun on him; he was muttering, it sounded like he was speaking German. I didn't know he spoke German. He started barking something to the young soldier, who looked like he was going to cry. I sensed a nasty incident in the making, so I told Bertram to back off. When he turned around, I saw he wasn't angry but pained. He pointed his gun away and embraced the German boy. They stood there, clinging to each other like long-lost brothers. We never talked about this; it was not the sort of thing soldiers discussed.

One, final episode: it took place on the ship back to the United States, after the War was over. Bertram and I shared a bunk on the lower deck. It was a long trip; we all shared whatever news we had from home. By then, the world knew about the Danish efforts to save their Jewish population from the Nazis; I was able to give details: my relatives back home had been involved. Bertram was very interested in this episode. The first night onboard, we lay head to foot in our bunk and talked most of the night. He asked me if I'd heard of any rogue Nazis in occupied Denmark who'd helped to save the Jews. I knew no such case, but he pressed me—seemed to think I was withholding information.

The mood onboard was often jubilant—there was a lot of beer, the men drank heavily. Bertram kept apart. He was somber, almost gloomy, much of the time. On the last night, only hours from docking in New York Harbor, dozens of us were crammed in the mess galley drinking beer. Bertram seemed surly. Every time someone tried to give him a beer, he refused. Some of the fellows were melancholy, thinking about all the boys who weren't coming back. But Bertram's mood was different; he just seemed angry at everyone. When I tried to jolly him out of it, he turned red, got up, and left.

Normally, I'd have let him alone. But there was something disturbing

about the way he looked. I went after him, but by the time I got belowdecks to the bunks, the place was deserted. When I reached the latrines, I heard muffled noises—a stifled grunting. The door was locked. I banged on it. A deep voice I didn't recognize said, "Go away." I told him to open up, that it was me. He called out "I can handle this myself": short of breath, like he was fighting someone off. Then, he started babbling—something about not needing reinforcements, he was going to take the guy out himself.

I didn't like what I was hearing. I pushed against the door, and just as the lock gave way I heard a scream and Bertram fell from the latrine. His eyes were wide and blank. I'd seen eyes like that too many times—the eyes of a soldier who's been hit and doesn't have long to live. Blood was spreading across his midriff. Something clattered to the floor. Bertram's hunting knife, covered in blood. I ripped away his shirt; his abdomen was sliced open, blood was gushing out. I tore off my jacket and pulled the sleeves tightly around his middle. There was no use calling for help; no one was down there. So I picked him up and rushed back to the mess. Two medics managed to stanch the blood. They stitched him up right there, on the floor.

For a while, it looked like he wouldn't make it. But he survived, against the odds. When we got to shore, he was taken to the hospital. I will add this: when Bertram fell from the latrine, he was clearly deranged. I have never seen such a peculiar expression: triumph, but also terror.

I wrote to Bertram at the veterans' hospital, but he never responded. I heard nothing from or about him until I received the parcel, a little over a year ago. When I opened it, I found inside another package wrapped in brown paper, with my own address as the returnee. Also, a letter requesting a favor: that I send the enclosed package back to the United States, without putting my name on the return address. It was important, he said, and apologized for imposing on me. Perhaps you found a letter inside the package from a Mrs. Reiner. I personally know of no such person—and have no idea if she exists.

At the time, I wondered if Bertram's unusual request had something to do with his clandestine activities during his second tour. He must have wanted the package to bear a foreign—perhaps Danish—postmark. As his friend I did what he asked. I did not know Shadowbrook was a psychiatric hospital, or that Bertram was a patient there. I might also add that Bertram did not, to my knowledge, have a brother. At least none he ever spoke of.

I hope this letter is of some help. I am deeply saddened to hear of his death. He was a good man.

<div align="right">

Sincerely yours,
Knut Dikstar

</div>

My mind is buzzing with confusion.

No *Gitte Reiner;* no Emanuel. The writer of the letter an old Army buddy of Bertram's, his address in Denmark the same one from which the original package was sent: the contents first in Bertram's hands, mailed by him to Denmark, only to be forwarded on to me. What could have been the motive behind this cumbersome subterfuge? How did the pages fall into Bertram's hands to begin with? And Knut Dikstar, his Army buddy, saying he knows nothing about a brother!

Could Bertram have made the whole thing up? Written a letter from a *supposed* Mrs. Reiner—wife of a *supposed* brother? Fabricated the entire account, in German, of a fictional member of the German Order Police?

But I saw Emanuel with my own eyes!

An image springs to mind of the wheezing librarian at the New York Public Library—Barry, his face urgent with surreptitious intent. Barry, Bertram—the names are too close for coincidence. What I am thinking is absurd, I know it is. Still, he seemed to know something, that intrusive, stout man, whose gaze over my shoulder felt unpleasantly sticky. Side glances and knowing looks, as if he'd been waiting for me all along, as if everything were unfolding according to insidious plan. Clues: wriggling disturbingly, slimy and elusive, evading my grasp.

I climb the imposing stone steps past the twin lion statues and head directly to the reading room.

From behind the information desk, Barry gives me a wary look. "Dr. Harrison. I thought you'd abandoned us."

"Hello, Barry. How have you been?"

"I kept those things aside for you," he says a little sulkily. "I was expecting you sooner."

"Yes, I'm sorry about that. In fact, I've been unwell." I'm irritated that I feel it necessary to explain.

"Nothing serious, I hope," he says dubiously.

"No, nothing too serious."

"Very well, then." He reaches beneath the counter and withdraws the stack of magazines. "Every day, I'd say to myself, Barry, you really should refile these. But then I thought, No, the doctor will be back, you won't want to keep him waiting. If we're busy, it can take hours to get them from the archives. But you know how the library works."

"I appreciate that you kept them out. Really, I do."

At the far end of the reading room, I sort through the stack as I did more than a month ago, when I was last here. Time ticks slowly by, in that syrupy way of library time. I study the photographs and illustrations: a bevy of pinup beauties, some of them famous; battle-scene photographs—a swarm of bombers against a cloud-quilted sky. A heartbreaking spread of a battle at Eniwetok, in which the photographer lost his own life; I pause to note his name, one Sergeant John A. Bushemi. Cartoons of Sad Sack; Popeye under a blaring headline: LET'S BLAST 'EM JAPANAZIS! Beneath this, the words "A 25c War Stamp Buys 12 Bullets." A haunting painting by Franklin Boggs, *Night Duty,* depicting wounded soldiers strung in hammocks from wooden posts, illuminated by the beam of a nurse's flashlight.

Gingerly, I take up the *Yank* issue that captivated me last time. The frontispiece is a battlefield painting by William Draper: *Inferno,* dominated by a Saipan sugar mill in flames, the foreground a shadowy landscape of rubble, dotted with Marines. Only now do I realize that this is the last issue of the magazine: December 28, 1945.

When I scan the table of contents, the headline jumps out: GERMAN-AMERICAN OFFERS RARE OPPORTUNITY. I turn to page 6 and read.

Time trips to a halt; I feel as if I am barely breathing.

"So, how's it going?" Barry again, as if from nowhere. Jolted, I almost jump from my seat.

"I'm sorry. I didn't mean to startle you." His watery eyes hover unnervingly, fishlike and disgusting.

"Look here," I begin. "I'm trying to get some work done. I really can't be interrupted."

"I'm only trying to be helpful."

"I don't need your help."

"There's no need for rudeness."

I have a feeling that heads are turning my way. The room is enormous, with its carved pillars and vast, ornate desks; the vaulted ceiling is churchlike, the air has a delicate echo. Two dozen or so people, sitting in that reverent way of library dwellers, almost in deference to the books and archival materials arrayed around them. But now, they are looking toward me, their faces curious, self-righteous, disapproving.

"You're going to have to keep your voice down," Barry says.

I pile the magazines together, stuffing my papers into my briefcase.

"Now wait," Barry says. "You can't take those anywhere. They're to remain here."

"Listen, I don't know what this is all about, but I must ask you to stop following me around."

"Following you around?" he echoes incredulously. "You yourself asked me to help you!"

Being angry with the man is pointless; I try to regain my calm.

"Barry, I didn't mean to offend you. It's just that research requires concentration—and solitude. It's impossible to work if someone is looking over your shoulder."

"What is research but looking over shoulders?" The strange man sounds triumphant. "A poor substitute for living, you won't convince me otherwise."

Huffily, he turns and heads back toward the information desk; with some relief, I return to the article.

An American soldier, born and partly raised in Germany, sent on a secret mission to infiltrate the German Order Police. His name withheld, for reasons of privacy and security. He ends up roaming the Polish countryside in a van. I scan the columns of print: Jews being rounded up and shot into pits. Lists of towns and numbers—the daily harvest of murdered Jews—fastidiously kept by the American in disguise as one of his duties.

I can hardly believe what I'm reading. I return to the beginning, my heart pounding in my ears. Read again the terrible anecdote: a policeman making sport of the killings—seizing a baby from its mother's arms and tossing it into the air as a target.

The byline at the top of the page: "By Reginald Thomas." At the bottom, a note: "Reginald Thomas was a medic who served in France and Germany." Certainly a common name—Thomas. I don't recall

knowing the first name of Bertram's valet; I always just called him Mr. Thomas.

Life has thrown up too many coincidences for me to be surprised; perhaps that's what Bertram meant that time when he said he didn't believe in coincidences. How many startling stories have I heard from the war years? Chance encounters that saved lives, people meeting up again on the other side of the world in some unlikely place, against all odds? Seemingly impossible scenarios—and yet true. I look down at the magazine; the letters spin free and scatter like ants across the page.

I hurry back across the room, holding tight to my briefcase; my breath catches in my throat. I care nothing for the disapproval or astonishment of the library dwellers, nothing for Barry. I want only to escape the stifling closeness, to breathe in the cold air on the street.

Outside, it is already dark. The streets are a blur of action and noise, the ranks of the usual late afternoon crowd swollen further by Christmas shoppers, whose air of tinny excitement jangles my nerves. An earsplitting ring assails me; I scan about, expecting to see a stampede of orderlies heading toward a crisis on one of the halls, finding instead an elderly man in a shabby Santa suit, Salvation Army bucket at his feet, staring dully before him and wildly swinging his oversize bell.

Grand Central Terminal is more crowded than I've ever seen it. I push my way through the horde, squinting up at the board to locate my track: 107, belowground, and boarding now. The throng closes around me, sweeping me along in the wrong direction—across the main concourse and toward the stairway leading up, back in the direction from which I've just come. I turn, using my briefcase as a forward guard. A disgruntled grumble comes my way through the clamor: *"Hey, watch it!"* And *"What's the idea?"* Everything closing in on me. But pressing forward, I finally pull free from the crowd and hurry along the corridor—less crowded here, but still a pulsing disorder, everybody clutching parcels and bags, faces too cheerful. Above it all, syrupy music trickling through speakers. I break into a run, the announcer's voice blares: *"Track One—Oooh—Seven. All abo-a-rd!"* Panting, I round the corner to the track to see the train slowly pulling out of the station. I run alongside it, pointlessly; through the window in the last car, the round eyes of a little girl with a huge pink bow on her head; her face crinkles into a smile, the train accelerates and disappears.

Swallowing a childish desperation, I make my way back into the station and find a coffee shop. The forty minutes until the next train pass blankly. And then, I am in the train car, standing room only, pressed up against the window, crushed by the crowd. I pray that Matilda will not be at the station to greet me; I am frantic for some time alone. Fortunately, when we pull into White Plains station, our car is nowhere to be seen. Braced by the cold, I begin the long walk home.

By the time I reach the gates of Shadowbrook, I have calmed down; greeting the guard, I feel an odd sense of reprieve.

"I could call for a car to come get you," he says.

"No, thank you. The walk will do me good."

Along the driveway, the trees form a canopy that cradles the beginnings of dusk. Instead of taking the hill onto the pathway leading home, I veer off halfway up. I hasten up the stairs of the hospital's main entrance with the intention of stopping in on some of the halls. First, I pass by my office to retrieve my white coat, taking a few minutes to sit in my chair and inhale the calm.

On my way downstairs, I notice something unnerving about the paintings on the walls; they seem subtly altered, as if someone had moved them slightly, so that the light now hits them differently. I try to reassure myself that it's nothing but the low lighting, or the fact that my eyes are still calibrated for the darkening outdoors. At the bottom of the stairs, something startling catches my attention: the grille above the elevator. My eyes are drawn there as if by some external force. The metal is embossed with a pattern, like tiny little fish scales, all pointing in the same direction. I recall how Cuthbert used to examine the grille—how, to his eyes, the pattern would change, seeming to flow in the opposite direction, or to alter from a horizontal to a vertical aspect. How many times, on our walks, did he insist we pause here so he might examine the look of the design, convinced that God Himself was communicating to him through the changing pattern? *There—don't you see? Undeniably different today.* When I'd reply that it looked the same to me as it always did, he would shake his head in pity.

"Henry. I say, Henry!"

I turn to see Percy Fenton beside me, his face creased with consternation.

"Fenton, what is it?" I ask.

"You didn't seem to hear me. I've been trying to get your attention! Are you all right?"

"Of course I'm all right," I say, a little irritated by his sudden appearance and by his absurd display of concern.

"You were staring up at that thing like it held the answer to the meaning of life!" His face relaxes. "I thought you might have been having another turn. How's the old ticker, anyway?"

"I was only wondering if the repairmen had been to adjust the fan," I say. "Apparently the air's not circulating properly; it gets musty in that elevator cage if the air's not properly turned."

"Oh," Fenton says absently, no longer interested in the matter of the elevator.

We head together to Hall Six. I have trouble concentrating on what Fenton is saying; back there, for the first time, I saw exactly what Cuthbert had been talking about—the way the pattern seemed not only different but also charged with meaning. And most disconcerting of all: the enigmatic, palpable thrill, not unlike the swoon offered by the pipe. Fenton is chatting away—hospital business, he never seems to tire of it—and then it comes to me as a bolt: Cuthbert might after all have some important information. Perhaps he's the man to help me solve the puzzle. Toward the end of his stay, he and Bertram were thick as thieves. Yes, tomorrow: in the early evening, after Matilda goes on shift, I will pay a visit to Mr. Cuthbert.

The moment I enter our house, I can tell that something is wrong; unhappiness hangs like a stale odor in the air.

I find Matilda in the kitchen.

"Smells marvelous," I say.

Matilda, holding a plate of sliced lamb, smiles tensely. "Can you bring in the mint jelly and potatoes?"

I follow her into the dining room.

"Difficult day?" I ask.

"No, Henry, my day was just fine. There's no point beating about the bush—I'll just come right out with it. You'll probably say it's none of my business. In a sense, of course, that's true. It's *your* work, after all. But you have to understand something; it affects our marriage. And that *is* my business, as far as I can tell."

Matilda absently piles food onto my plate. I pour wine into a glass and pass it to her.

"Darling, I have no idea what you're talking about. Start again, a little more slowly."

"I wasn't snooping, Henry, truly. I just went into your study to collect the dirty glasses and cups you leave about. It was right there, on the desk, in plain view. You wrote the heading in capital letters across the top of the page. How could I *not* have seen it? You *promised* you'd leave the topic alone! While you were still in the hospital, recovering. Surely you can't have forgotten."

"I remember we talked about it, but as for any promises . . ." I say uncertainly.

"Oh, Henry, how can you be so *reckless?*"

Matilda seems so easily moved to tears lately: fragile and emotionally raw.

"I'm sorry if I misled you," I say steadily. "But I'm on the verge of a breakthrough."

"A breakthrough?" Matilda is looking at me with disbelief. "What about *us,* Henry. Don't you care about us?"

"I really don't see how—"

"This isn't about *war neurosis.* Do you think I'm that stupid?"

"But, Matilda," I insist. "I've been working on a new model for years—you know that. Psychiatry has had it all wrong, I'm sure of it now. It's not about fear spinning out of control, or loss of courage or nerve. It's nothing like that. Our treatments have been aimed at fixing the wrong thing."

"What difference does it make?" The plates stand forgotten before her, each piled with too much food. "The War's over! It doesn't matter anymore!"

"It's not over. The patients are still coming in; the War is with them every day. And it's not as if there aren't other wars—wars that are likely to involve us. Why, with events in the Middle East, and Korea—"

"Why do *you* have to do it? Why does it have to be *you?*"

Something in Matilda's face fires me; I must make her see.

"There's a war on the inside," I say. "Dualities, we all have them. Like two combustible gases. We construct lives that will keep the warring dimensions safely apart—to prevent the crisis that will cause the explo-

sion. But in certain situations, this strategy fails. For some, the trigger might be inconsequential. For others, it is a catastrophe that serves as catalyst, such as a long tour of duty on the battlefield.

"And it's often the men with the keenest moral sense who break down. Being *moral* requires sensitivity, which does not serve the soldier well. The man who breaks down is considered weak. What's to be done when morality becomes equated with failure—and mental illness? Where does that leave us?"

Matilda is looking at me oddly, a kind of horror growing in her face.

"What is it?" I ask. "What's wrong?"

"I've been so stupid," she says. "I really believed you had let all of this go."

"I'm not sure I can ever let it go. Matilda, it's my life's work."

"That sounds a little overblown," she says.

"I didn't mean it that way. I just mean that I've staked my career on this topic."

"Is that what this is about? Your career?"

"You make it sound as if I'm doing something wrong."

"How can we create a new life together if you insist on dragging everything into the mud of the past?"

"That's not how I see it," I insist.

"Well, that's how *I* see it. But I suppose that doesn't count all that much around here."

Matilda is on her feet, holding her handkerchief before her mouth. "Oh, Henry—" She swallows hard. "How can you be so oblivious? Don't think I don't know what's going on—I see it in your eyes, when we're making love. You're not *with* me, you're *scrutinizing* me. And thinking about *him*!"

She rushes from the room. I remain seated, my eyes fixed on the plates of food. I hear her moving about upstairs. The clock ticks. Again, her tread on the stairs; she appears in the doorway.

"If you don't mind putting away the food," she says in a dull voice.

"You should eat before your shift," I say.

"I'm sorry, Henry. I don't know what . . ." She pauses and then tries again. "I can't seem to . . ."

She waits, I wait; disappointment gathers in her face, and she turns, leaving her thought hanging. The front door opens and closes; through

the window, I see her walk to the gate. I hope Matilda will about-face, flash me a smile and mouth, "Don't worry, Henry, it's nothing," wave away my awkwardness, my failings, as she did the day we returned from our honeymoon. But she only continues on through the gate and then hurries toward the hospital, her head lowered as if she's walking into a storm.

<div align="center">❖❖❖</div>

Cuthbert's mother opens the door.

"Dr. Harrison, what an unexpected pleasure!" she declares.

"I'm sorry to appear unannounced," I say, affecting a casual smile. "It's such a cliché to say one was in the neighborhood, but the truth is I was—and I've been intending to pop in on your son for some time. I hear he's doing very well, and we do like to keep up with the members of our Shadowbrook community, once they're back home."

"Well, I'm delighted, and I know Billy will be, too."

A voice wafts into the hallway. "*William,* Mother dear. William."

Mrs. Cuthbert smiles. "I don't know why I have such a hard time remembering not to call him Billy."

Cuthbert is sitting in the living room before a blazing fire and doesn't seem the least bit surprised to see me.

"Dr. Harrison, forgive me for not standing. Do make yourself comfortable. Mother will fetch us some coffee. I always have some at this hour."

He waves his hand in his mother's direction and gives a benevolent smile. His mother disappears, and Cuthbert winks.

"I can't tell you how happy she is since I've been back home. She was born to fuss over someone, and Father won't allow it on his account."

"You're looking well," I say.

"It's well-known," Cuthbert says conspiratorially. "My mother is the best baker in Westchester County. She's won awards."

Mrs. Cuthbert reappears balancing a well-stocked tray. Cuthbert hungrily eyes the large slice of cake his mother places before him. He lifts the entire piece in his fingers and takes an enormous bite.

"Apfelkugel," he says, crumbs flying from his lips. "Though we call it apple cake around here—sensitivities, you know."

Mrs. Cuthbert serves me and retreats, leaving us alone.

"I'm intrigued to know the reason for your visit," he says. "It is a little, shall we say, unusual for a hospital director to make a house call to a former psychiatric inmate."

I feel myself reddening but manage to keep a mild, formal expression on my face.

"I have reason to believe you might have some useful information regarding another former patient."

Cuthbert swallows and takes another bite from his cake. "Related to the matter of the *apfelkugel,* I venture," he says knowingly. "I thought you might eventually catch on."

"I'm sorry, I'm not following."

"It came to you through the metal grille above the elevator, I suppose," he says. "That's the way these things are usually communicated— but then, I've told you that a hundred times before."

That uncanniness—I feel it at the back of my neck. "Could you be more explicit?"

Cuthbert gives a regal wave and takes a gulp of coffee. "I can see it's not easy for you. I'm referring to the matter of nationality—it does make a difference after all, to refer to *apfelkugel* as 'apple cake.' This is a matter about which Bertram Reiner felt very strongly. I think it fair to say that he staked his life on it."

"I suppose that *is* what I'm getting at," I say carefully. "You see, I had a letter from a coroner in another state, stating that Mr. Reiner had taken his own life."

Cuthbert puts down his coffee cup and laughs.

"I'm sorry, Dr. Harrison," he says, wiping his eyes with his napkin. "He was always a bit dramatic, wasn't he, in his quiet, leading-man sort of way. Above the kinds of shenanigans the rest of us were up to, I grant you—but not so very different, in the end."

"I'm not sure I know what you mean."

"I'd heard about that business of the letter—clearly a hoax. I assure you that Mr. Reiner did not take his own life; he was not constitutionally capable of it. Don't get me wrong—he was as crazy as the rest of us; he just had a certain style."

"What do you mean?"

"He had the motivation to appear *normal*. It's really not all that hard, if you only know how. You see, the ladies are not so crazy for the nuts. When was the last time you saw a crazy man get the girl?"

He cuts himself another slice of cake. "That was Bertram's genius. He got the normal person's goodies while managing to hang on to his insanity. We all admired him for that. You must believe me when I say I have no idea where he is or what he's doing, but you can count on it: he's very much alive."

Cuthbert sits back and regards me appraisingly. "Come to think of it," he continues. "I do have something that might be of interest to you. He gave it to me for safekeeping—in case things ever got out of hand—at least, that's how he put it. But first—I'm curious about one thing."

"Yes?"

"Why have you come to me now? According to what I've heard, it's been quite some time since Mr. Reiner allegedly went on to greener pastures."

"It's a professional matter," I say awkwardly. "I've been working for some time on a new model of the war neuroses; breakthroughs very often come in understanding, deeply, one particular case; the experience of an individual can be a distillation of the condition."

Cuthbert's intelligent face is alive with interest. "The way a painting might embody the principles of an art movement?"

"Yes, I suppose you could say that."

"I don't know much about the history of psychiatry—not surprising, eh? You wouldn't expect the elephant to be an expert in zoology!" Cuthbert gives an appreciative snort.

"Still, I know enough to know that the theoreticians often get it wrong. Take Freud's famous case of Daniel Paul Schreber."

Cuthbert shakes his head, faint disgust showing in his face.

"I'm not concerned about the terminology—call it dementia praecox, if you like, or schizophrenia, it's all the same to me. But Herr Freud didn't have a clue; his theories on the matter are a lot of stuff and nonsense. If you ask me, his discussion of the venerable judge's case tells us more about his own convoluted psyche than it does about Mr. Schreber's affliction—if you can call it an affliction. I rather prefer to think about it

as an existential predilection—perhaps not one you choose but certainly a way of being one can embrace."

Cuthbert glances around, suddenly perturbed. "Now, where were we? Where *are* we for that matter?"

His eyes alight on the cake. "Oh yes—we were discussing my mother's exquisite concoction."

"You were also telling me about something Mr. Reiner gave you—for safekeeping."

"Yes," he says thoughtfully. "Now that I know your reason for coming . . . yes, it might certainly help in your quest. Kudos to you, Doctor, for trying to put a point on it. The point about points is there's always a point to a point. You can't say that about much of life, I'm sure you'll agree."

"The item of interest?" I prompt.

"Indeed. Won't be a minute."

Cuthbert disappears. I look around the room, which is appointed with great precision: each piece of occasional furniture—several side tables, an imposing buffet, an ornate serving chest—holds a lace doily covering the entire surface but for a border of about an inch, in the center of which sits a small sculpture or dish. Careful arrangements of sketches and prints hang on the walls, each display lit by just the right lamp in just the right place.

Cuthbert reappears with a briefcase, which he sets before me on the coffee table. "Sorry to keep you. Go ahead, take a look. Not for the faint of heart, I understand."

I snap open the briefcase. Inside is a sheaf of papers: I recognize the handwriting at once. I look more closely and see that it is a carbon copy; in places, the print is badly smudged.

"When he gave me this, he was rather agitated. Said that one day, his life might depend on it."

"Did he explain what he meant?"

Cuthbert eyes me intently. "As a matter of fact, no. I do know he was concerned about what you might do."

"What *I* might do?"

"You must hear this sort of thing ten times a day from patients, but the fact is, Mr. Reiner didn't trust you. He thought you had *ulterior motives.*" Cuthbert laughs again. "For such a complicated man, he really was quite the innocent."

"What do you mean?"

"As you know, I have a long and illustrious career as a mental patient," he says good-naturedly. "I've never met a psychiatrist who *doesn't* have an ulterior motive. I told him as much, but he wouldn't have any of it. He was convinced that you were a special case. He was convinced that—"

Something seems to occur to Cuthbert.

"Is it true?" he asks, gazing at me with that same studious intent of a moment ago. "That congratulations are in order?"

"I'm sorry?"

"The grapevine has it that you are recently married—er, remarried."

"I'm not sure that's exactly relevant," I say uncomfortably.

"No, perhaps not," he says slowly. "Per-*haps*. Mis-*haps*. *Col*-lapse. *Col*-lude."

"I don't follow you, Mr. Cuthbert."

His face darkens. "I never trusted her. In the end, I believe Mr. Reiner came to the same point of view. These papers"—Cuthbert reaches over and slaps the stack—"they were to be the proof. Should it ever come to a court of law. His witness, his evidence, his escape."

"What did he tell you about them?"

"Why, nothing. What was there to tell?"

"What are they? Where did they come from?"

Cuthbert narrows his eyes. "He did no more than give them to me, Doctor. You're welcome to take a look, if you like." He settles back in his chair and folds his arms. "No hurry, I have plenty of time."

I pass my eyes across the first few lines. "I'm afraid I don't read German," I say.

"No, of course not. Neither do I."

"Then how do you know—that they're not for the faint of heart?"

"Bertram took the liberty of informing me—more or less, you understand—of their contents."

A look of weariness comes over Cuthbert. I stand.

"Well, I want to thank you, Mr. Cuthbert. I should be getting along."

Cuthbert stays seated. "Would you permit me a remark or two on another subject perhaps a little closer to home? Speaking of liberty—and since *you've* taken the liberty of visiting me at my home—it does change things, doesn't it? And may I inquire—have you ever climbed all the way up? Into the torch?"

"The torch?"

"The Green Lady—you can see for miles around. The Long Island Sound—pound for pound—in the end he did sue—Marlowe gave Shakespeare the idea for the Jew."

Cuthbert looks around the room, bewildered. "Mother?" he calls out in a thin, high voice.

In an instant, Cuthbert's mother appears at the door. She crosses to where we are sitting and leans down to pat her son's plump hand. He lets out a little cry.

"There you are! I was beginning to despair. Dr. Harrison was just saying how much he's enjoying your *apfelkugel*."

He eyes my plate. "But, Doctor, you've not touched it!" He jumps to his feet. "Please, you must!"

"Come now, dear," Cuthbert's mother says calmly. "It seems as if the doctor must be going. He's a very busy man, I'm sure."

Cuthbert sits down, fixes me with an absent stare. "There was one more thing—just the one."

"Of course, Mr. Cuthbert. Please, go ahead."

"I was only wondering if you'd ever figured it out, after I left."

"Figured what out?"

"The truth about the hospital. Mr. Reiner did. He was very mathematical. It's all in the statistical formulation: *the regression to the mean*. The hallways of Shadowbrook: they're *mean* streets. And we're walking them together."

"I'm sorry, Mr. Cuthbert," I say in my kindest doctor's voice. "I'm not sure what you're trying to say."

"No, please, Dr. Harrison. It is I who must give my condolences to you."

<div align="center">◄←•→►</div>

Outside Hall Eight, I pause to catch my breath: a rare moment of peace amid the Christmas season mayhem.

The dayroom is a dazzle of lights; the tree is especially ablaze. Streamers and Christmas drawings bedeck the walls; a trestle is laden with

goodies—finger sandwiches, cookies, cakes. Hot cider fills the air with the scent of nutmeg, cinnamon, clove. The patients in their Sunday best have the scrubbed-clean look of children, and the sullen disgruntledness to go with it; the usual brisk cheerfulness of the nurses and orderlies has a slightly desperate edge. The holidays are always hard for the patients; the incidents of violence, despair, and general acting up seem particularly numerous this year.

"Here he is, our director!" Nurse Albright chimes a little too eagerly. "We're all terribly excited about our gift exchange, aren't we?"

A table in the corner holds brightly wrapped packages; their ribbons, reused year after year, are looking a little the worse for wear. Cups of cider are passed around, with warnings about it being hot, though in truth it is only warm. Orderlies help the more disturbed patients, who mutter or dribble or stare; one man, under the watchful eye of an orderly, sits apart in a loosely tied straitjacket.

Nurse Albright positions herself in front of the tree and claps loudly, setting up a troubling, angry echo; several patients cringe.

"I'm sure Dr. Harrison has some words of Christmas cheer," she says, beaming.

I join her at the tree and begin the little speech I have already delivered to four of the halls. The words fall automatically from my lips; I scan around, aware of Matilda's absence. Just as I am finishing up, she appears at the door with the new patient, Mr. Yardley, who is dressed in hospital pajamas and looks somewhat disheveled. His face is electric—feverish eyes, trembling lips—and he holds a cumbersome package, wrapped in brown paper and tied with string. Matilda, looking very much in her element, quietly ushers him in. Mr. Yardley glances around the room and then catches sight of me; his expression changes exaggeratedly to that of a mortified child.

"But I've missed the remarks!" he calls out. Eyes turn in his direction, the patients unfazed, the staff with that invisible intensifying of alertness that is their stock-in-trade. "Start over! I can't miss the remarks!"

Matilda leans in to speak to him, but he pulls away and hurries toward me. In an instant, two orderlies are beside him, each with a grip on an arm. He strains against them, waving his package as much as their hold will allow; it swings in a constrained arc by his hip.

"I'd be happy to summarize," I say. Mr. Yardley brightens, and the orderlies lead him to an empty chair. It requires some effort to come up with a précis; my mind is a fog, but somehow I manage. I concentrate on sounding cheerful, allow my gaze to fall on Matilda, and find myself wanting to inhale her effortless efficiency and command. She smiles; it feels like a buoy. Beads of sweat form on my forehead; I reach for my handkerchief and mop them away. Every sconce, every lamp is lit; behind me, the heat of hundreds of fairy lights strung around the tree. Bathed in the hot glare, I look out at the patients, fight the feeling that I'm onstage, blinded by footlights, at the mercy of the audience, which is both too near and remote.

"And now, Nurse Albright, shall we begin the exchange of gifts?" I hear myself say. Though my voice feels pinched in my throat, to my ears it sounds warm and relaxed.

More movement, more bustle, orderlies and nurses dialing up their celebratory cheer, more shepherding of patients from here to there, more offering of cider and admonitions to be careful, to be neat, not to spill. Some patients are morose and seem to begrudge the inducement to spiritedness.

Gifts are passed around and opened—to the *ooh*s and *aah*s mostly of the staff: items made at the Art Pavilion or in occupational therapy. I retreat to the edge of things to observe. My eye keeps snagging Matilda as she goes about her work; I recall the time, not so very long ago, when she was not mine.

She meets my glance; anxiety ruffles her composure. I smile, she looks away. The cider tastes bitter and vaguely alcoholic; I realize that my head is beginning to swim. As I squint into the lights of the Christmas tree, the beam of my vision narrows uncomfortably, as if all of the room, except for the Christmas tree, were suddenly plunged in darkness. I try to move my gaze from the tree but find I cannot; my eyes are dry. I blink and feel a painful scraping. My vision blurs, I stare at the tree, the fairy lights haze and dim, then spring back to brightness. Behind the tree, something moves: a shadow, unseemly and large, moving out from behind the tree. The noise of the room swells and falls: voices chattering, laughter, and in the distance, a wail. The shadow—not a shadow but a person, his eyes excited with feeling. My breath stops in my chest: it is Bertram, coming out from behind the tree. Carrying something omi-

nous, large, swinging it triumphantly, a distasteful smile growing on his face. I glance around wildly—is no one alarmed? No staff, in an instant, by his side, whisking away whatever disgusting thing he is holding and swinging about? A stench fills my nostrils; could the thing in his hand be alive? Is that wail the sound of a dying animal? Why is nobody setting off the alarm?

"Here!" A loud voice, booming in my ear. "It's for you, Dr. Harrison. I made it myself!"

I blink hard several times; my vision clears. Before me not Bertram but Mr. Yardley, thrusting his cumbersome package into my face.

"How very well you look today, Mr. Yardley." The rote words fall slackly. "How very well indeed."

"Are you going to open it?"

"Very kind of you, I'm sure." Gently, I push the parcel away. "But didn't the occupational therapy staff inform you? The gift exchange is among patients. It's not customary to make presents for the staff."

"Yes, yes." Yardley gives a wink. "But we can dispense with all that, you and I."

"I'm sorry, Mr. Yardley. Really, I'm touched by your gesture, but it's not customary."

"It's not customary," he echoes, unperturbed, continuing to push the package into my hand. "Look, I'll open it for you, if you want," he says, and he tears at the paper, haphazardly dislodging the string.

"We're very fond of basket weaving here. You know, the *case* of the *basket.*" He pauses dramatically. "The *basket case.*"

From the torn paper, he withdraws an ungainly basket, woven in a drab shade of brown. "I thought it would do for your *office.*"

He says *office* as if uttering an obscenity, the smile still on his face.

"It wasn't my first choice for a gift. I was going to give you an *article.* You know what I did during the War, don't you?"

"I've gone through your records, Mr. Yardley. Besides, we spoke about it last week, in my office."

"Yes, your *office,*" he repeats. "That's what I wanted to give you—an article. You must have patients who smoke. I can't remember how many articles I wrote in my day, but it was a good number. Perhaps *you* have some idea?"

What is he saying? I rifle through my memory; Mr. Yardley was

indeed a journalist before the War, but as far as I recall, he served as a gunner.

"I do not believe you wrote as a journalist during the War," I say, my breath labored.

"And how do you know you can trust what you believe?" Yardley asks, his eyes wavering strangely. "How can *any* of us *really trust* what we believe?"

"I really don't see how—"

"No, I'm certain you don't," Yardley cuts in. "But if you'll allow me—"

He turns abruptly to face Matilda, who has appeared from nowhere.

"Now, what's all this, Mr. Yardley?"

"He says he wrote for *Yank*," I say helplessly.

Yardley's face ignites with confusion. "No, sir, I never did. I was just saying that I'd wanted to make you an ashtray, but it wasn't my turn with the clay. Why would he say that, Nurse Willoughby? And why won't he take my basket? I worked very hard on this basket."

"Come along," Matilda says. "It's time for our afternoon tea! Now, which cake did you bake in cooking?"

Mr. Yardley's face falls; obediently, he goes off with Matilda, his untied bathrobe flapping at his sides. I look down to see I am holding the basket. Before I can decide what to do with it, Matilda reappears beside me. Confused, I look over to the table and see that Mr. Yardley is now under the supervision of an orderly who is placing a cupcake onto his plate. Something strange is happening to time.

"Henry," she says in a low voice. "You're white as a sheet."

Her arm is on mine, she is steering me out of the dayroom and on down the corridor, which is disconcertingly deserted.

"Where is everyone?" I hear myself ask.

"In the dayroom, of course," she replies curtly.

We are through the door; Matilda turns the key in the lock and guides me to a little hallway furniture setting, the kind we all walk by a hundred times each day but never actually use. I sit down, Matilda loosens my tie.

"What do you think he meant by it?" I ask.

Matilda is holding my wrist and counting the seconds on her watch. "Ssssh," she says abruptly. "I need to get a pulse."

She lets go of my wrist and looks me squarely in the face. "Your pulse is fine. Are you having trouble breathing?"

I inhale and exhale a few times; air pours in steadily, easily. I shake my head.

"I was worried it might be your heart," she says, though knowing that it isn't doesn't do much to soften the concern in her face.

"What do you think he meant by it?" I repeat, offering Matilda the basket I am still holding.

She looks at it, baffled. "Henry, I haven't the faintest idea what you're talking about."

"Yardley. He gave me a basket."

"I shouldn't think he meant anything by it, except an expression of holiday spirit."

"The patients are not supposed to make presents for the staff. And certainly not for the hospital director."

"What difference does it make, Henry?" I can hear she is exasperated. "Patients don't read the hospital rules. And in any case, I don't even know that that *is* a hospital rule."

"It is," I insist. "I know it is."

"What has gotten into you, Henry?" Her voice is tinged with alarm.

"Matilda," I say, taking hold of her hand. "He's trying to tell me something. I don't know what, but I sense that it's important."

"What on earth are you talking about?"

"He was a journalist," I whisper. "During the War."

"And what if he was?" Matilda's eyes are trembling; why does she not see what I'm saying?

"Don't you see? He wrote for *Yank*!"

"Now you're frightening me," Matilda says, rising slowly. "Have you been drinking?"

"Not intentionally. Who could have spiked the cider? We can't have that on the halls—certainly not on Hall Eight." I jump up and head to the house phone. "I must tell them to remove the cider. Matilda, find out who's responsible!"

"Henry!"

I turn to see her still standing there, a desperate look on her face.

"Do as I say!" I call out, hurrying down the hall, passing by the phone; there's no time for that now. Let Matilda deal with the spiked cider—I

have something more pressing to attend to. I am running, Matilda again calls my name. I wave an arm up over my head—can't worry now about that—let her manage it on her own. There is something I absolutely must do.

Almost tripping on the main stairway, I catch myself from falling just in time. The hallways are deserted: everyone is on the halls, preparing for the upcoming Christmas invasion of family members. The thick runner underfoot muffles the sound of my feet. Passing the French doors that lead into the dining room, ducking into the narrow service stairway, past Medical Records, the janitor's office, the narrow corridor of supply rooms. The plain door at the end, leading farther down.

I'm on the stairway, now at the bottom: exhilaration, shame, a violent longing for opium. I feel faint, lean against the wall, close my eyes, breathe in the dampness, clamp down on the terrible desire. An echo in my mind: hurried, muffled footsteps—Matilda disappearing up ahead, around a curve. I creep forward, holding on to the wall: how will I ever find my way back to the little alcove? I have passed these graveyards of furniture before, the discardings of a hundred years of troubled lives; I am going in circles. But the air has lost its mustiness, it's as if I'm walking again behind Matilda, following her lead. Everything calming, dimming, slowing: nothing, now, but my movement, stealthy and sure.

Finally, against all hoping: the cul-de-sac. I move quickly, now, around the false wall. Darkness in the confines of the space. My eyes adjust, the contours come clear, like a photographic image taking form in the developer's vat. Not the space I'd expected: orderly and inviting. But a room torn apart, plundered: the mattress pulled from the bed frame, its cover torn, stuffing wrenched out in fistfuls. Two lamps toppled, their shades ruined. A small chest flung onto its side, its drawers slanted out like stiff, dead tongues. The bed frame: the wooden slats surrounding the springs have been damaged. Two broken pieces point awkwardly upward like huge sharpened splinters.

The ruin of this space is deliberate, calculated, complete; I can feel it. One of the tips of the broken, wooden pieces seems blackened, as if perhaps burned: hard to see in the dimness. I slide one of the bedside tables away, and fluorescent light pours in from the hallway. The blackened

spear—I reach over and touch the tip; flakes on my fingers, the look and feel of dried blood.

I remember touching the sticking plaster between Matilda's breasts, and her evasive reply. I wipe my fingers on my trousers, stare at the bed frame.

A terrible confusion: now the ghastly apparition comes back—the vision I had, the night of my heart attack: Bertram, visiting me from the grave.

You're not in the grave! I hiss into the musty space. *You didn't die, that was only a ruse! Your ruse!*

The silence swallows me, then shatters.

What difference does it make?—I hear his voice, coming from deep within me. *Whether I was alive or not! What right did you have to steal my life!*

I leap up with a jolt.

I've stolen nothing! I have only—

Something stuffed between the bedsprings. A handful of papers. And something else—bulky, made of fabric. With some prying and pulling, it comes out: a hat, earflaps, a visor.

The papers are covered in writing. Back in the passageway, I stand directly beneath the fluorescent tube, which buzzes at my ear. German script, a dozen different hands. Page after page, the same jottings, as if someone were trying to develop a style, like a child practicing a signature, hoping to settle on just the right one.

Here, close to the bottom of a page; it is like a punch to the stomach. The writing, deeply familiar. The hand in which Emanuel's account was penned. I try to grasp hold of the fact: not a brother but an alter ego. A hunch I had early on but dismissed: that Bertram had dealt with an unbearable inner conflict by splitting off a piece of himself, his own *bad self,* to create a brother—Emanuel, a Nazi, who'd done and witnessed terrible things. Unspeakable, murderous deeds that an American soldier, working undercover, had documented as a member of the Nazi Order Police.

I'm struggling to make sense of this. Was this fictitious brother, Emanuel, created in a dissociative, fugue state—the product of a kind of hysterical conversion? As real to Bertram as is the deafness or paralysis to the shell-shocked soldier who can, in fact, hear or walk? Or was Ber-

tram consciously scheming and manipulating—deliberately setting out to deceive me? And if so, to what end?

As if there are answers—as if everything is always *knowable*.

I stuff the pages and the hat back between the bedsprings. Drag the mattress up onto the base and push it down hard, trying to press the broken pieces of the wooden frame back into place. Here is a sheet, and a coverlet on the ground; I make the bed as best I can. Fix the toppled chest, set a lamp on the table by the bed.

I don't know why I am trying to restore order to the little space; I only feel that I must.

When I reach the house, it is in darkness. I do not turn on the lights; I go into the kitchen and startle to realize that someone is there, sitting in the dark: Matilda, staring out at the shadowy outlines of trees.

"Matilda, what's wrong?" Something crackles in the air, a menacing calm.

"I've been waiting for you," she says. Her voice is flat. When I flick on the switch, garish light floods the room.

"I needed to walk," I say. "I hope you weren't worried."

Now, she looks at me, something hyperreal in her stillness.

"Back on the ward . . . Henry, what happened?"

"I'm sorry . . . I don't know. Perhaps I'm overworked. Perhaps—"

Nausea hits; she's not going to reach out to me, no buoy of cheer, no indulging this or that excuse—tiredness, overwork, health. Matilda is looking at me squarely, her gaze piercing me to the core, demanding truth.

"I've been waiting for you," she repeats. "Where have you been?" I hear it now: the hollow resignation in her voice.

"I was in the underground tunnels."

Matilda visibly flinches at my words, then rises slowly; she is facing me, her features harsh in the bright overhead light, the window glinting blackly behind her.

"You were *what*?" Emotions scud across her face; everything seems speeded up and slowed down at the same time. The room bristles. Does she feel it, too? Is it coming from me?

"In the tunnels. Your little room—it was all broken up."

She crumples, falls back into the chair like a rag doll.

"What are you saying?" she whispers.

"I followed you there once. No, more than once. It was damp, and cold. I'm sorry, Matilda. I shouldn't have. I want to tell you that I'm sorry."

She only looks at me, as if searching for something. And then, I see it: the love, draining from her face. It's like watching somebody die. There's nothing I can do about it, nothing I can do. I want to stop, but I can't. I can only keep on going, keep on going until the end.

"You're sorry?" she whispers, her face a mask of disbelief.

"I couldn't help it. You see, I loved you so desperately." I hesitate. "And you . . . I just couldn't bear it."

A long, long silence. Matilda looks back at the window, only now, with the light on, the world is obscured; the window offers only an image of her face, aghast, and of me, standing above her. I have the curious sensation that I am myself nothing but a reflection—that if she were to reach over to touch me, her hand would find only the cold, hard surface of a mirror.

"Yes, I loved him," she says finally. "It was a sickness. I hated myself, but I couldn't help it. *I wasn't myself.* I had no will. None. It was as if I'd been drugged. And then . . . when Bertram left the hospital . . ." She takes in a quick, sharp breath but says nothing further.

"That day I came to your mother's house," I say. My voice seems very far away. "You were devastated."

"Yes, I was," she says quietly. "But you came for me. I was drowning, and you saved me. *Oh, Henry*—" She gulps. Tears spring to her eyes. "I wanted to be with *you.* I broke things off with Bertram because I wanted to be with *you!*"

Broke things off with Bertram? What is she saying? I'm hearing the words, but I don't understand a thing.

"Who did that to the room—in the tunnel?" I ask.

"I did, Henry. I did it. *I* couldn't stand it anymore."

"What couldn't you stand?"

"He was coming between us—and there was nothing I could do!"

"What do you mean, he was coming between us?"

"You wouldn't let him go!"

"*I* wouldn't let him go?"

"I know—that's the worst of it—maybe that's why I couldn't let him go either!"

"So you *do* still love him?"

"How can you be so blind? Don't you see? Bertram and I were the *same*! That's what I couldn't stand—the more I loved him, the more I had to get away—"

"How could you possibly say you were the same?"

"It was always there, for both of us. The things we'd seen, the things we were made to do. Who we were. Who we'd become. The War. Eating away at us like maggots. It was too much—and I couldn't stand myself for what I was doing."

Matilda is staring at me now with the blackest misery. And with a certitude that chills.

"And then, one day— God, I remember every single thing about that day. I remember the exact moment it happened."

"The exact moment?" My voice is a shudder.

Matilda's face is lit with the memory. "The day I awoke from the nightmare. It was you, Henry. You may as well have swooped in on a white horse; you broke the spell. You were going to take me away: away from all that madness. To *your* world."

"My world?"

"Yes," she whispers. "I don't know . . . normal, stable. Sane."

"The exact moment." My words come out as a whimper. "What was the moment you knew?"

"That time you walked me home . . . late at night. After I went up to my room; you waited downstairs. You waited a full twenty minutes."

"How do you know how long I waited?"

"When I got upstairs, I left the lights off; I watched you standing there. I felt it then."

"Felt what?"

"That it was over with Bertram. And that you and I might have a chance."

Matilda's eyes fill with pain; she lowers her head, stares at her lap.

"Do we, Matilda?" I ask, not trying to mask the plea. "Do we still have a chance?"

Her eyes are streaming. "We were going to have a wonderful life . . ."

"I can change, Matilda. I'll be different, I promise . . ."

I fly to her side, attempt to embrace her, but she puts up her hand and shakes her head.

"I've felt so alone with you, Henry. So terribly alone." Her voice, now, is dull. "You're always *watching me,* Henry. Looking for signs."

"It's not too late," I say desperately.

Matilda is looking at me. She is holding her breath. Her eyes are wide, brimming with tears.

"Perhaps it was too late from the start," she says. Her mouth trembles, her face sags with defeat. "Perhaps it was always too late . . ."

I open my mouth to speak. But we are frozen, looking at each other from across a great divide.

And then she turns, her hands hanging by her sides. She is moving slowly, but I feel her motion as a slap. At the door, I see her beautiful face gilded in misery. And now, I glimpse what she means, and the knowledge knifes me in the gut; those moments will be forever with us, they cannot be undone. She will always be in the tunnel, moving beneath Bertram, her lips parted, gazing at him, lost with him, in love *with him.* And I will always be apart, listening in the dark.

I hear her going quickly up the stairs. More noises—drawers opening, shutting, clattering, footsteps back and forth—and then tripping on back down the stairs. Still I am frozen, my breath stopped in my chest, a crushing rock. From the corner of my eye I see her, suitcase in hand, passing by the kitchen door. I sense she is making a tremendous effort. For an instant: silence. She is standing in the hallway, hesitating.

"I must go," she says. Her voice is dry of tears. "I'll send for my things."

Still no movement; she is waiting, waiting for me to say something, waiting for me to respond.

I open my mouth. My throat is parched, I try to speak, I hear only a squeak. She's waiting, still, waiting for me to speak. Words crowd my mind, a jumbled frenzy. Crammed, jammed, unable to flow. I hear a croak. I have managed, after all, to say something.

"I'm sorry, Matilda. So very, very sorry." A dead, flat croak—useless, pointless, nothing.

The opening of the front door, the quiet, careful clicking of it shut.

Still in the kitchen, my back toward the window; I do not turn to look out onto the garden, only stare across the room and into the section of hallway visible from here, watching as the deepening shadows seep into the final, heavy emptiness.

≺⟡≻

Epilogue

Was it a vision or a waking dream? Do I wake or sleep?

I am floating upward, gradually upward; and then, from somewhere above, I hear a voice.

"You're awake, now, Dr. Harrison."

The fluorescent light is blinding. I rub my arm inside the elbow where it smarts, then look down to see four tiny red pricks on the thick, blue cord of my vein. The clock reads four o'clock; when I looked up at it before the first injection, it was one o'clock.

"I need to see about rounds." I try to swing my legs off the cot, but they will not respond.

A hand on my chest, pressing firmly. "What you need now is to rest." A nurse looms over me, the light an unpleasantly bright halo obscuring her face, her white uniform brilliant. I don't know her; she must be new.

My eyelids drift shut; the light mutes, my closed lids are luminous pink.

"Sodium amytal?" I ask. What have I said? What have I given away? Sleepiness, delicious, laps away the worry; with relief, I slide back down, into the illuminated shadows.

"You had a good treatment. The doctor told me it went very well."

Scrambled images flood my mind, a jumble of sentences, my own mumbling voice; a crazed gallop through events, a vanishing point on some distant horizon—the beginning of it all, the day I sat with Bertram on the admissions hall, holding fast to my white coat, so sure of myself, so unaware of what was coming.

I am spent, I feel as if I've left nothing out.

I see their faces—Delilah, Bertram, Matilda; Cuthbert makes an appearance, also Featherstone and the Professor. A gallery of eyes, the sound of my own droning voice. As if everything that could be said, has been said. But have I really been speaking? Has anyone been listening?

"The treatment?" My voice is scorched.

"Yes?" The no-nonsense voice of an experienced nurse, the practiced, impersonal kindness.

"Why was it ordered?"

"I'm sure the doctor went over it with you, Dr. Harrison."

"I don't remember."

"You can ask her about it in your next session. Let's rest, now. Dinner in an hour."

A piercing anxiety, but then the drug takes over. A sense of peace ripples through me, enticing and cool. Images fade, echoes of my own voice disperse. It seems I've been talking for an age; so much prancing around, so much distress. I feel a smile growing on my face; my mouth feels slightly numb.

"Yes, I'll do that." My voice sounds weary, but not unhappy.

I can't imagine what the nurse means: *my doctor*. Who might it be? I smile at the knowledge that this is only a dream, and a habitual instinct rises: to analyze the dream, to unpack its meaning. A dream in which I am the patient, having undergone a treatment, having spewed out every excruciating detail for some other doctor to peer at, analyze, dissect. But that, too, drifts away on the soothing tide.

Dimly, I hear the rustling of the nurse's uniform; a sheet is drawn up to cover me, starched and ironed, smooth on my arms. I wonder what she is thinking, this nurse; wonder who hired her, now that Matilda is gone.

I wonder where Matilda is now. I wonder if she ever found Bertram: if he is on his way to a full recovery, if they are together. Matilda, where

are you? A fleeting image of a woman, running into the distance, and of a man still farther away, fading in and out, fading to shadow.

Then, the onrush of sleep; for a moment, I struggle to lay claim to a thought thrusting up at me from the fog. I could fight for Matilda—claw my way back to health: *Doctor, heal thyself.* As in a dream, moving fast but somehow staying in place, galloping off to find her—*You swooped in on a white horse*—to win her back.

Sleep tugs at me, irresistible: *My heart aches*—the thought slithers away—*a drowsy numbness, pain.* I sigh and drift, cling to a vision of a lunging bird, black against the sky, and allow myself to sink downward, away, ever away.

<div align="center">◄‹·›►</div>

Acknowledgments

*D*eepest gratitude to Doreen Nayman, Michele Nayman, Ilana Nayman Chester, and Marc Nayman, for unstinting love; and again, to Michele Nayman, who read more than one draft, offered invaluable suggestions, and was at the ready for ongoing queries, large and small; to Charles Palliser, for generous, decisive input midway through; and to Louis Sass, who read and reread, worried through everything, and helped fine-tune the final draft. Andrea Masters and Ben Moore, fellow artists and soul mates, were with me at every step. Heartfelt appreciation to Dwight C. Jewson, from whom I have learned so much, for professional and personal support beyond any reasonable expectation.

I am indebted to my editor, Alexis Gargagliano, for her acuity and brilliance, and for giving so much on the book's behalf. Working with everyone at Scribner has again been a privilege; special thanks to Roz Lippel and Whitney Frick for excellent suggestions.

Grateful thanks to Aaron Priest, and to everyone at his agency.

The spirit of the incomparable World War I poet Wilfred Owen was with me throughout the writing of this book; two of Dr. Harrison's flashbacks to the trenches were inspired by Owen's lines. I can only hope I have done justice to his wrenching, hard-won images.

I spent several extraordinary years working in psychiatric hospitals. I am grateful for the training I received and also for the pleasure and privi-

lege of working with and getting to know many wonderful inpatients. I have modeled Shadowbrook on some of these settings; the mood, as well as the inspiration for writing this book, I owe to my own experiences from that time. However, all characters in this novel are entirely fictional.

Finally, admiration and gratitude to my family—Juliana, Lucas, and Louis—who have as ever been gracious and understanding in the face of an unbalancing and sometimes disruptive line of work.

Sources

I relied on many nonfiction books in the writing of this novel. The following were special sources of information and inspiration: Ben Shephard's remarkable *A War of Nerves: Soldiers and Psychiatrists in the Twentieth Century* (Harvard University Press, 2001); Christopher Browning's *Ordinary Men: Reserve Police Battalion 101 and the Final Solution in Poland* (HarperPerennial, 1993); Betsy Kuhn's *Angels of Mercy: The Army Nurses of World War II* (Aladdin, 1999); Diane Burke Fessler's *No Time for Fear: Voices of American Military Nurses in World War II* (Michigan State University Press, 1996); Kathi Jackson's *They Called Them Angels: American Military Nurses of World War II* (Bison Books, 2006); and Ellen Levine's *Darkness over Denmark: The Danish Resistance and the Rescue of the Jews* (Holiday House, 2000).

Thanks to Diane Richardson of the Oskar Diethelm Library, Institute for the History of Psychiatry, Weill-Cornell Medical College, for invaluable help in directing me toward superb materials from the library's collection. Thanks also to yankmagazine.blogspot.com for access to certain issues of *Yank* Magazine.

To create the physical world and mood of the hospital, I relied heavily on several excellent personal accounts of experiences in psychiatric hospitals. In a few instances, I have appropriated certain descriptions or events, which I have transformed for fictional purposes. For descriptions of the hospital setting, I am indebted to Hayden Carruth's *The Bloomingdale Papers* (University of Georgia Press, 1975).

For period details and descriptions, I drew on Henry Collins Brown's beautiful *A Mind Mislaid* (E. P. Dutton, 1937); the baseball scene and the patients' "Suicide Club," as well as two descriptions of suicide, are

based on material he presents. William Seabrook's *Asylum* (Harcourt, Brace, 1935), about time spent in the same hospital (for alcoholism), was an invaluable source of inspiration; I hope that some of his generous humor and appreciation of the ironies of psychiatric hospital life have found their way into my book; on one or two occasions, I have borrowed an idea or perception from his pages. (In both these cases, the author of the memoir is long gone; my hope is that they would find my appropriations the homage that they are.)

I have been deeply influenced by Louis A. Sass on matters concerning psychiatry and psychosis, and have drawn liberally from his work, principally *Madness and Modernism: Insanity in the Light of Modern Art, Literature, and Thought* (Basic Books, 1992); and *The Paradoxes of Delusion: Wittgenstein, Schreber, and the Schizophrenic Mind* (Cornell University Press, 1994). I take full responsibility, however, for any untoward errors on issues pertaining to these matters.

In writing a book such as this, one reads a great many things and over a long period of time; I apologize if I have failed to recall and recognize any other important sources here.

About the Author

S hira Nayman grew up in Australia and has lived in Israel, Mexico, and France. She is a clinical psychologist who spent some years working in psychiatric hospitals, and has taught psychology and literature. In recent years, she has worked as a strategic consultant for corporations and political campaigns. The recipient of three grants from the Australia Council for the Arts, she lives in Brooklyn, New York, with her husband and two children.